EDITED BY

LAURA ANTONIOU

NO
SAFEWORDS 2

STORIES OF THE MARKETPLACE

For more information contact:
Riverdale Avenue Books
5676 Riverdale Avenue
Riverdale, NY 10471

www.riverdaleavebooks.com

Design by www.formatting4U.com
Cover photograph © Miriam Doerr | Dreamstime.com
Digital ISBN: 9781626014886
Print ISBN: 9781626014893

First Edition December 2018
Published under the Circlet Press Imprint of Riverdale Avenue Books

Table of Contents

Introduction

When I first met Laura, I was only writing for friends. They were little pieces, designed as special gifts, usually created through me asking, "tell me something you think is sexy, and what role you see yourself in."

When I met Laura, and she mentioned she was looking for a couple of stories for some porn magazines she was editing at the time, I casually told her that I'd write her a few stories to look over. And I did.

I also wrote her a few stories for her eyes only.

In retrospect, this was awfully presumptuous. I mean, Laura was, even 25 years ago, a pretty well-known author in the BDSM community. I should have been intimidated, I suppose. Who was I to write sexy stories for The Author of The Marketplace Series?

But here's the thing about Laura: for all her big-name cache, she's a remarkably approachable person. She loves to engage with her fans, and she enjoys sharing her world with readers who are curious about the mechanics of, and characters in, The Marketplace universe. So when she said, "hey, why don't you send me a story or two?" it felt more like an extended conversation about power dynamics, SM, queer identity, and above all, sex.

Then in 1996, Laura told me that she was thinking of opening up her Marketplace universe to other authors, and publishing a Marketplace novel that had those stories embedded in it—stories that characters would tell each other, in their own voices. I thought that sounded like a lot of fun. So, along with folks like Cecilia Tan, M. Christian, Michael Hernandez and david stein (of blessed memory), I wrote a few stories for what became *The Academy: Tales of the Marketplace.*

Which makes me one of the first authors to write published Marketplace fan fiction.

It's been over 20 years since *The Academy* was published. Since then, a lot has happened, including the explosion of on-line writing forums, fan fiction websites, and increasing awareness of BDSM in the mainstream community. *No Safewords,* the first published anthology of Marketplace fan fiction came out. And The Marketplace universe expanded from its original trilogy to six books, including *The Reunion* and *The Inheritor.*

When she first decided to invite authors to write for *No Safewords,* I remember Laura telling me, "I want to invite my fans to write the stories I would never think to write," and this collection certainly reflects that vision. For those who love combining their erotica with crime and action heroes, there are stories here for you. The authors in this collection will take you from the highest Victorian affections down to the grit and dirt of the streets. There are even touches of fantasy—yes, even vampires and fairies!—in this Marketplace universe. Because these are the types of things that fan fiction writers do best—mixing genres, playing with the boundaries and demonstrating their love for the original source material.

Since 1996, I've written stories for a lot of other collections, but my favorites remain the tales I've written in Laura's Marketplace universe. Like a lot of fan fiction writers, I enjoy creating a story within the rules set down by someone else, both because it's good to know what the expectations are going in—and, of course, to see how far you can stretch them and still make the tale plausible within the universe. It's also true in my personal life. When I first met Laura, those 20+ years ago, she was a dynamic and engaging person, and charmingly and happily single. What's happened since that time?

Reader, I married her.

—Karen Taylor

The Adventure of the Bowing Doctor
By S. Daithi

This manuscript was found in an antique Gladstone bag, which by the markings was owned by a doctor at one point. The initials JW can be found faintly near the clasp.

As per my contract, I herein give a true accounting of my time with Mr. Holmes. I have sent a copy to the appropriate parties so they may have it for their records.

My chronicles of my time with Mr. Holmes are accurate, but certain facts are left out for reasons that will be obvious later.

I was wounded twice during my time in Afghanistan. My leg injury was not that much of a problem, and I still had obligations. It was the wound in the shoulder that left me at loose ends. Since my obligations were also removed, I found myself back in London, recovering both physically and spiritually.

The family of my employer summoned me to the Diogenes Club. I had no idea why, but out of loyalty I agreed to go. I was taken to one of the visitor rooms, where conversation was allowed, but only in low tones, and told to have a seat.

Shortly a tall man of large girth entered and sat across from me. He watched me for a bit. I was unsure if I should return his gaze or look elsewhere. I opted for a little of both.

"Dr. Watson," the man began, "Army Surgeon. Wounded twice in battle."

I nodded.

"You are probably wondering why you are here," he said, picking up a folder from the table next to him. I recognized the symbol on the jacket and shivered.

"Ah, I think you have an inkling now, don't you?"

I nodded again.

"The remainder of your contract has been provisionally sold to me by Lord Barton's widow. This has been tentatively approved by your training house, based on this interview and if we agree upon terms. If we cannot come to agreement, you are to be returned to your trainers and your stipend adjusted appropriately."

I was stunned at this news. I had expected to serve the Barton family through the current contract.

"I'll give you a few moments to process what I have said, and then I will give you my offer for your services. This is your choice, of course, but you may find my offer acceptable."

I found a glass of whiskey at my elbow on the table next to me. I almost didn't see the man who brought it in as he left the room quiet as a mouse.

I looked at the man seated across from me. He nodded, so I picked up the glass and took a sip. It was smooth on my tongue with that lovely back end of smoke and oak to trip over my taste buds.

"Why?" I asked.

"The family does not require your services any more. But I have need of your particular abilities. Not for myself but for my brother."

"Your brother?"

As if on cue the door was shoved open and in strode a tall, thin man with lots of nervous energy around him.

"Mycroft! What is this I hear of you obtaining a contract for me? We have had this conversation more than once. You leave me alone, and I will help you when you ask. You do *not* saddle me with extraneous baggage I do not want or need."

Mycroft looked at me, and the other man followed his gaze.

"Ah!" said the man, and he sat down in the remaining chair in the room.

"Sherlock Holmes, I would like to introduce you to Dr. John Watson, recently returned... "

"From Afghanistan. I have *eyes*, Mycroft," said Sherlock with a snort.

Mycroft held up the folder he had in his hand. Sherlock reached and snatched it. He flipped his way through the pages, occasionally muttering while he did so. I took another pull of the whiskey and tried not to let my hand shake. He finished looking through it, slammed it on the table between Mycroft and him, looked at me and said, "Stand up and strip to the waist."

I was a little startled at the request. I looked to Mycroft, who gave an almost imperceptible nod.

"Don't look at him! Look at me."

I met his gaze and did as he asked. I placed my clothing on the chair, then took two steps toward him while clasping my hands behind my back crossed at the wrist. He walked around me slowly but did not touch me. He came back to the front and looked at me carefully.

I was unsure what to do, so I did as I was trained and lowered my eyes to his feet.

"No," he said.

I met his gaze again.

"Better. Do either of your injuries cause you to be unable to perform your duties?"

"I don't know. I haven't served since... " my voice trailed off as my throat seemed to close. I fought the tears coming to my eyes. That wound was rawer than the one exposed on my shoulder.

His expression seemed to soften for a moment, but that was fleeting. "No matter, I don't think I will have need of you," he said, with a dismissive wave of his hand.

My stomach dropped. If not this, then what? I was damaged goods.

"I am sure with your abilities and proclivities you will soon find employment," said Sherlock. "Good day." He turned to leave.

"No, Sherlock, it will not do," came his brother's voice. "Mrs. Hudson can only do so much, and I promised our mother that I would take care of you."

"I'm a grown man, Mycroft. I don't need... looking after."

"Sherlock, we have already had more than one *incident* this year. Between running around the city chasing diverse criminals and your dreadful habits when bored, I have serious concerns for your health. Having a doctor around might be terribly *convenient* for you."

Sherlock sat down and glowered at Mycroft.

"And you can see by the file and the man's behavior, he's just what you need."

"You mean he might help keep me out of jail and the public limelight, thus keeping you in the shadows. Tell me, Doctor Watson, ever been buggered? Answer honestly because we can tell if you are lying."

I decided to keep myself together. I would go for the formal approach.

"Yes, Sir," I replied.

"Did you like it?"

"Yes, Sir," I said quietly

"What's that, soldier? I don't think I heard you."

"Yes, Sir. I did," I said in my parade voice.

There was a knock at the door, and Mycroft put his head in his hands for a moment. He got to his feet and went to the door. "Thank you, Jenkins. Yes, we know that it is a bit noisy in here, and we will attend to it." He closed the door and turned to Sherlock, giving him a disapproving look.

Sherlock grinned, and I did the same.

"We'll play by your rules, Mycroft. Wouldn't want you to get shoved out of your own club."

He turned back to me. "Ever been sucked off?"

"Yes, Sir."

"Sucked someone off?"

"Yes, Sir."

"Which did you enjoy more?"

I paused, wondering how I could even answer that question. I enjoyed them both equally.

"Never mind. You have already given me your answer."

"Sorry, Sir."

"You do know admitting this could land you in jail?"

I knew all too well.

"Sherlock, don't toy with him." The warning growl came from his brother.

Sherlock dismissed Mycroft with a wave of his hand. He picked up the file and flipped through a couple of the pages.

"It says here you are considered a pretty heavy masochist."

"Yes, Sir."

"May I touch your back?"

I was taken aback a bit by his asking for permission but quickly collected myself and nodded. He walked behind me and ran his hand down my spine. I leaned into the touch. It has been so long since I had been touched for any reason other than medical necessity. His fingers lingered on the scars from the exit wound; they gently mapped out my back. I could feel my member thicken.

He came around the front and explored my chest. Again, he paid close attention to the bullet wound, but he also was interested in my nipples, palpating and pulling on them until they were hard nubs. None of this was helping me with my now rather stiff cock. It felt like it was being strangled by my clothing.

"Strip the rest off."

"Oh, Sherlock," said Mycroft in an exasperated voice. "Please. Some decorum."

"You want me to take him home with me, I get to see what I am getting. Strip."

I did so and stood naked in front of the two brothers. My member was still at attention even with the cold air.

"Impressive," said Sherlock. Mycroft nodded in agreement.

"May I?" Sherlock asked pointing.

"As you wish, Sir." In for a penny, in for a pound.

He took his long fingers and wrapped them around my cock. I shuddered at his touch. He tugged gently on it, and I could feel the warmth building in my belly. It had been too long.

"Sir, I am sorry, Sir, but I don't know how long I can last."

"Then don't," he replied as he continued to manipulate my cock and balls, exploring how I reacted to various touches and pressure. He knelt down—I thought to look closer—but I felt him blow warm air onto my cock while he twisted my balls. Betrayed by my weakness, I came in his face. I was appalled, but he seemed to take it in stride. He pulled a handkerchief out of his pocket and handed it to me. "Clean me up."

I took the piece of cloth and removed my release from his face and hair. I dabbed at a couple of spots that had gotten on his jacket, but I was afraid they were going to stain.

"Sherlock... let the man get dressed and sit down before he falls."

Sherlock smiled at me and nodded. I quickly dressed and resumed my seat.

"I wonder how many other shades of red I can get out of him," said Sherlock to Mycroft.

"Why don't you see?" asked Mycroft. "*If* Dr. Watson is amenable."

What choice did I really have? It was this or back to my training house and a different unknown future.

"Well, Dr. Watson, care to come home with me and see? Have a go to discover if we are compatible?" asked Sherlock with an expression on his face showing he already knew my answer.

"Sherlock, the contract states... "

"I *know* what the contract states, Mycroft! But this is only going to work if both parties are satisfied with the situation. I propose we agree on a week's trial. Pay Lord Barton's family the monies due. If it doesn't work out, then Watson is no worse off than he is now."

"Agreed," said Mycroft. "Dr. Watson?"

Both men looked at me. I felt both frightened and ecstatic at the same time.

"Agreed," I said. "One week trial period. At the end either party can walk away without penalty except those already stated in the existing contract."

"Shall we?" asked Sherlock, gesturing to the door. "I would say it has been a pleasure, Mycroft, but we both know I would be lying."

"Sherlock, make it work. We both know where this is going if you don't."

I never wanted Sherlock to look at me the way he did at his brother for that brief second. There was a phrase, *if looks could kill*. If it had been true, Mycroft would have been a spot on the far wall of the sitting room we were in.

"Come on, Watson."

We left the club to find a cab waiting for us.

"Do you need to get anything this evening?"

I thought of the paltry number of items I had in a large steamer trunk at the end of my bed in the lodgings I had taken.

"It would not take me long to gather my belongings, but if you would rather... "

He shook his head, "No, let's do this correctly."

I gave the address to the cabby, who got us there in good time. I went to my room and packed those few items I had out, including my toiletry kit. I checked to see if my pistol was still in its box.

Sherlock had the cabby help me get the trunk down and secured.

We arrived at 221B Baker Street in good time. Holmes got out of the cab first and gave a loud whistle. Around the corner came a couple of street urchins running with the abandonment only the young have.

"Ah, Wiggins!" he said to the tallest of the lot. "Need your help here. Take the trunk and bring it up to the second bedroom at the top of the stairs."

He pulled a coin purse from his coat and removed a number of coins, which he passed onto Wiggins. "There's for you and for the lads."

Wiggins doffed his filthy cap. "Thank you, Mr. Holmes." He turned to the other boys and said, "Come on, lads."

Holmes unlocked the door and let the gang of youth manhandle my trunk up the stairs.

"Mrs. Hudson is out for the evening. I suggest we clean up and go out to dinner this evening." He gestured that I should enter.

As I started to, the boys ran by me, almost knocking me over.

They started down the street but stopped when Holmes shouted, "Wiggins!"

They returned to the stoop of the flat.

Holmes held out his hand to one of the smaller lads. "Return it."

"But, sir, I... "

Wiggins cuffed the boy across the backside of his head. "Give it, Paulie. You know the rules. Mr. Holmes has been good to us."

Paulie pulled out my wallet from under his shirt and handed it to Sherlock sheepishly.

"That will be all, Wiggins."

"I'm sorry, sir. I will have a talk with him." Wiggins glared at the boy, grabbed him by the scruff of the neck, and marched him off with the other lads.

Holmes handed me my wallet, as though his awareness of the youngster's larcenous intentions were a matter of course. "Sorry about that, Watson. The lads are very clever and sometimes too cheeky for their own good. Come on up."

We walked into a sitting room that was both order and chaos at the same time. Holmes flopped down on one chair. "Your trunk is in the upstairs bedroom. For appearance's sake, that is where you will keep your clothing and personal items. Feel free to use the bed now if you need a short nap before we go out this evening."

He waved his hand in dismissal, and I went upstairs to find my trunk at the foot of the bed. I unlocked it and put my clothing away in the standing wardrobe. I placed my few personal items around the room. I took the box with the pistol and buried it in the wardrobe.

7

I took Holmes' suggestion and tried to take a nap, but sleep was elusive at best. I dozed a bit before hearing Holmes shout up the staircase, "Time to get ready for dinner."

I dressed in my best suit and went back down to the sitting room. Holmes looked me over with a keen eye. "We are going to have to do something about your dress sense if we continue. I thought we would dine at Simpson's tonight."

In the cab, I again fought back tears. Lord Barton and I had dined at Simpson's on a number of occasions through my years of service.

We were greeted by the maître d' warmly. Holmes apparently had a regular table in the place. We sat down and ordered our meals. Holmes requested a bottle of wine.

The sommelier came with the bottle and paused, looking at me.

"Dr. Watson?"

"Laurence, how are you, man?"

"I am well... I... I heard about Lord Barton. My sympathies.."

"Thank you."

"Tragic thing."

"Casualties of war, Laurence, casualties of war," I said, trying not to make a fool of myself.

"Yes, sir."

He served the wine, leaving me with Holmes, who studied me intently. During the meal several other members of the staff came by our table to extend their sympathies for Lord Barton's passing.

I ate, but it was difficult.

We finished up and returned to Baker Street. Holmes pointed to a chair. He went to a sideboard and poured us both a whiskey. He handed me the glass and sat down across from me.

"I apologize," he said, "If I had known about your reaction to returning to Simpson's, we would have dined elsewhere."

"There is no way you could have known, Sir. It was one of Lord Barton's favorites when we were... "

And that was it. I couldn't hold it in anymore. I sobbed at the remembrances that came to my mind. Of Lord Barton. Of what we had. Of the confused look on his face as he bled out. I had tried so hard to save him, but I couldn't. I should have been the one in the ground, not him. *I failed. I failed him, and I failed my family.*

I came back to reality and found myself rather awkwardly in Holmes' arms. He allowed me the release of my grief in comfort and with what dignity I had to spare.

"Come to bed, Watson," he said. "My questions can wait for another day."

He took my hand and led me to his bedroom. He undressed me and put me under the covers, doused the lights and left the room.

I was so exhausted from all the emotional turmoil I had gone through that day, I quickly fell sound asleep.

I awoke the next morning to find myself alone in the bed. There was evidence Holmes had slept next to me, but he was not there now.

I got up to find my clothes were not where they had been left the evening before. There was a dressing gown draped over the back of a chair in the room. I put that on and went into the sitting room. Holmes was seated at the table reading the paper with what was left of his breakfast in front of him. I was at a bit of loose ends as to what I should do when an elderly, compact lady entered with a covered dish.

"Ah, Dr. Watson, you're awake. Sit down and tuck in," she said, placing the plate across the table from Holmes. I did as she instructed.

"Thank you, Mrs. Hudson. That will be all," said Sherlock without looking up from the article he was reading.

She curtsied and left the room, closing the door behind her.

I just finished breakfast when the front doorbell rang. I heard Mrs. Hudson open the door and the mumbling of some conversation. Shortly after the door closed, we heard Mrs. Hudson coming up the stairs.

"Watson, could you get the door? She is carrying a rather large package from the sound of her footsteps."

I opened the door and found Mrs. Hudson was carrying, as Holmes had said, a rather large package.

"It's addressed to you, Dr. Watson," she said putting it down on the sideboard.

Who knows I am here?

"Thank you, Mrs. Hudson. You are a treasure," said Holmes, finally looking up from his paper.

She gathered up the dishes and took the remains of our breakfast out of the room.

He put down the paper and sprang to his feet clapping his hands together. "Now let's see who sent you this package."

He examined the package carefully. There was no visible marking on the paper that wrapped the box nor did the string seem out of the ordinary.

"May I?" He asked, turning to me.

I nodded. He removed the string and paper and put it to the side. There was a cardboard box under the paper. He took a close look at the box. He opened the top of the box and then stopped.

"Watson, I think this may be a personal matter."

He stepped back and went to his bedroom leaving me with the mysterious box.

I looked inside to found a letter addressed to me and a leather box I knew all too well. I thought it had been lost in Afghanistan.

I opened the letter first and read.

Dear John,

I hope this finds you well.

I want you to know I hold no ill will towards you for what happened to Wilson. I know you did your best to keep him safe while he was in that filthy country. I heard from others all that you did for him, and for that I will always be grateful to you.

I knew about my husband's proclivities before we were even engaged. Wilson and I had agreed that we would have relations for procreation, but that others would take care of his more deviant needs. It was a marriage of convenience for us both, however we did love each other after a fashion.

But the love of his life was you, and we both know it. I will admit to a certain jealousy to the relationship you had with each other. I think if it was allowed he would have married you.

I do regret I did not have the courage to tell you to your face about your fate, but I cannot have you around the house anymore. Too many painful memories.

I wish never to see you again. I hope you understand my reasoning in this. Gregory was told you died with his father so there would be fewer questions down the road.

I have enclosed my husband's bequest to you from his will. There is also an annual income, which I have arranged for my solicitor to have paid to your house, but Wilson stressed in his will that the money was to be yours and not part of your fee. I expect you will want to make whatever arrangements you wish with your house.

I wish you well, John, with whatever you choose to do with your life now. I do pray you might now try for a normal life and leave your deviant ways in the grave with my husband.

Sincerely,

Violet Barton

I pulled the leather box out with reverence. His coat of arms was embossed on the top leather. I stroked the crest, running the outlines under my fingers. I placed the box on the table and undid the clasp. I lifted the lid and looked.

Inside the box carefully packed in the velvet lining were my leather collar and cuffs with Lord Barton's crest on each. There was also a well-used leather flail to either side of the box.

I was crying before I knew I was crying. I crumpled to the floor. *Why did this hurt so much?* It felt as though he had taken a piece of my soul with him to the great beyond.

Sherlock entered the room. I tried to pull myself together. This was unmanly behavior.

"You will forgive me, but I must know what has put you in such a state." He picked up the letter I had left on the table and read it. "Idiot woman," he muttered. "John, I want you to go to the bedroom. Strip, then go to the end of the bed and grab the rail. I will be with you shortly."

I did as he commanded. The act of obeying was calming to me.

Sherlock entered the room and tossed a rattan cane onto the bed. He removed his dressing gown, waistcoat and shirt and placed them on the chair where I had placed the dressing gown I had been wearing.

He picked up the cane and whipped it through the air. I could feel the air movement on my backside.

"Let's start with ten and see how it goes. I expect you to keep count and thank me for each. Do we understand each other?"

I nodded.

He pulled the cane back, and I felt the lash and the burn across my buttocks.

"One, Sir. Thank you."

"Good."

He then methodically processed to lash my buttocks and upper thighs. I counted and thanked him for each.

With each hit my mind seem to clear. As he progressed, the pleasant buzz of the beating ran through my bones and to my cock.

"Do you think you have another ten in you?"

"Sir, yes, Sir."

I lost count somewhere along the way. The world went away, and there was only the beating and the pounding of my heart.

I heard Sherlock say, "That's enough, I think." But it sounded as though he was under water. He helped me let go of the bedrail and then down, onto the floor on my belly. He left me in the room with my thoughts and my pain.

I don't know how long I lay there. I think I might have fallen asleep at one point. About the time I was going to try to get up I heard the door open and saw Mrs. Hudson enter the room with a basin in her arms. She ignored my murmured protestations.

"Shush, dear. Just lie still."

I did as instructed. She pulled a couple of items from the basin and put them on the bed. She took the water pitcher and filled the basin.

"Can you stand up?"

With her help I managed to get to my feet and onto the bed face down. I was past the point of caring I was naked.

She took care of the stripes on my body, washing away the blood where the skin had split. She used a cooling ointment on the welts that made everything feel a little better. She seemed awfully well versed in wound care.

She must have seen the look on my face because she said, "Yes, dear, I do know about this sort of thing. I am like you. My contract is with the Holmes family and has been since the beginning. Mr. Holmes is an impetuous and severe Master, but he is a good owner. Now if you are feeling up for it, Mr. Holmes has requested that you join him in the sitting room."

She helped me to get up and held the dressing gown for me.

I walked carefully into the room and delicately sat in the chair across from Sherlock.

He looked at me carefully. "Clear head?"

I nodded.

"Watson, I must say that you impress me. People say that they are this or that but by the time the last dog dies, they really aren't. You, however, are both exactly and quite different from what you claim to be."

I really didn't know how to respond.

"You left me rather uncomfortable, and I want you to do something about it."

I glanced at his crotch and could see his cock straining in his trousers. Here was something I could do and do well.

I carefully knelt down between his legs, hissing a bit in pain. I unbuttoned his trousers and pulled his member and balls out. It was long and thin like its owner with a slight curve. He watched me through lidded eyes as I rubbed my hand over it. I knelt up and took his cock in my mouth, just a bit beyond the tip, allowing me to use my tongue on the slit under the foreskin. I sucked and pulled the foreskin back exposing more of the glans. With one hand to fondle his balls and the other around his shaft putting pressure on it, I then proceeded to take his cock down my throat until my nose was against his pubis.

This move elicited a groan from Holmes that went straight to my groin. I proceeded to move my mouth up and down his shaft, paying special attention to the glans on the way up.

It didn't take long for me to feel his balls tighten, and he released in my mouth. I carefully swallowed his seed and used my tongue to finishing cleaning his cock. I put him back in his trousers and leaned back waiting for my next order.

He looked at me and gestured with his hand to draw closer. I leaned in and put my head against his leg. He stroked my hair. I felt safe and used for the first time since I had returned to England.

We stayed in that position for a while.

Holmes tapped me on the shoulder and said, "Let me see your backside."

I stood up and removed my robe. I turned around and let him see what he had done. He pushed and probed the marks on my rear. I kept my hands by my side and tried not to flinch. He patted my butt and gave me a little shove forward. I stepped where he directed me.

"Get dressed. We are going out today."

"How shall I dress?"

"Second-best suit I think. Something you can get in and out of quickly."

I went upstairs and dressed. I walked back into the room to see Sherlock examining my collar. A feeling of anger ran through me. *How dare he! That was mine.*

He turned as I entered.

"I apologize, Watson. I didn't mean to cross a line." He put the collar back with such reverence I felt my body relaxing a bit. I hadn't realized my hands were clenched into fists.

"Do you want to put this up in your room before we go?"

"Thank you, Sir," I said as I latched the box and took it up to my room. I placed it in my trunk and returned downstairs to join him.

"I want you to take your cane with you in case you need it."

I took it, and we left the flat.

"How do you feel about walking?"

I was surprised at his concern. "Walking is a little easier than sitting right now."

"Well then, let's get some air."

We walked through the streets of London with Holmes pointing out things I had never seen. He made observations of the people who passed us that just amazed me. I began to suspect that here was a great intellect, perhaps one of the greatest I had ever met.

So entranced and distracted was I, I barely realized where we'd stopped before he was pulling a bell.

"Come along, Watson."

The door opened, and I didn't recognize the young man at the door. He looked at me and said, "Doctor Watson! You came home!" I then realized the last time I had seen the lad he was probably six years old.

"Franklin, it is good to see you too."

"Majordomo put me in charge of the door," he said with great pride.

"And he is doing an acceptable job of it." A voice came from within the house.

We entered and were ushered into a sitting room. There I found my two trainers and the majordomo seated with a chair for Sherlock. I sank to my knees next to Sherlock and put my hands palms up on my legs. I could feel the slight pull and burn from my earlier beating. It gave me strength.

"Master, Mistress, Majordomo." I gave a slight bow to each.

"Still has his manners doesn't he, Laurel?" said my former trainer with a laugh.

"Oh, he does indeed, Sidney. But manners was never a problem with him, were they?"

"So, Mr. Holmes, your brother is currently holding John's contract?" asked my Mistress.

"That is correct. And if the week works out, I would like an open-ended contract with the good doctor."

I apparently didn't hide the look of shock on my face.

"Oh come now, Watson. You fulfill my desires and the bothersome needs of my brother."

"Well! An open-ended contract *is* rather rare, Mr. Holmes," said my former training Master.

"But not unheard of," Holmes replied. "As I understand it, however, Lord Barton had one with John."

"Five years, recurring," said the Majordomo. I realized I'd never heard his Christian name the whole time I had resided here.

"Correct," agreed Master Sidney "But that was a special situation. Lord Barton and Watson were very much in love. Can you say the same after only a day?"

"No, I cannot. I cannot replace Lord Barton in Watson's heart nor shall I try. But he seems exceptionally well suited to me," replied Sherlock.

"There is the other matter... "

Sherlock held up his hand. "Not here. Do you have any questions for John? If Lord Farrell would care to come with me, we can discuss the other matter and you can talk to John."

All parties nodded, and I found myself with two of the three people I trusted most in the world.

"John, sit on the chair, please. We don't need to stand on formality," said Lady Farrell.

I almost laughed. This house was nothing but formality. I stood up carefully and started to sit down just as carefully.

"Stop"—came her order—"show me."

My fingers were faster than my mind, and I dropped my trousers and pants, exposing my bum to them both. I heard someone stand up, and I felt the hand of my trainer tracing the lines on my backside.

15

"Well, these are lovely. Such a nice grouping. Did you enjoy it?"

"Yes, I did. It was cathartic."

"So what do you think of Mr. Sherlock Holmes?"

"He is firm but not unkind. I believe I could serve him."

"You have been with him less than a day and you know this in your heart?"

"Mistress, I knew when I met Lord Barton I would follow him anywhere and do anything for him."

"Pull yourself back together and sit down."

I knew she meant both physically and emotionally. She was right. This was the honeymoon part. How would I feel about Mr. Holmes down the road?

"He does seem to know what you need. Honestly, you have always needed a heaver hand than anyone here could give you."

I bowed my head in acknowledgement of this truth.

We discussed other matters and had tea waiting for Holmes and Lord Farrell to rejoin us, which they did after a time.

Pleasantries were exchanged, and we left. I had a lot to think about. In 24 hours I went from being discarded as worthless to being offered the one thing I always wanted.

As we walked back towards Baker Street, Holmes also seemed lost in thought. Out of the blue, he asked, "Do you like Turkish baths?"

I assented enthusiastically.

He hailed us cab, and we spent the afternoon going from room to room at the baths. I used a large towel to keep the marks on my backside from being exhibited to the other patrons. I had forgotten how much I loved a good massage.

We conversed upon a wide range of subjects, getting to know each other better as men rather than owner and slave. I found him fascinating to listen to. I learned he was a consulting detective, a profession involving investigations into all manner of sordid crimes and mysteries, and possessed a veritable treasure house of esoteric souvenirs.

We came home to a simple supper laid out in our rooms. I noticed an extra cushion on my chair. Since Holmes did not comment, I did not either, but I found his attentiveness comforting. We ate and continued our conversations. I knew I would never be bored in his company.

16

We settled in for an evening nightcap, and I could see Holmes had something on his mind. He seemed to be arguing with himself, then came to a decision.

"You are probably wondering what your trainer and I were discussing. I inquired with your house as to the amount of the bequest in the will. You can live on it along with your pension and do fairly well. Apparently Lord Barton made provision with another bank to pay out the rest of your contract without the knowledge of Lady Barton. None of us knew this until today. You are debt-free, Watson. But we know your debt is not what kept you in servitude."

"To be sure, Sir, it has always been something more."

"I know you loved Lord Barton, and it is evident he returned your affections. I know I am not a replacement for what you had with each other, but I would like a chance to be your owner. I believe we may be very compatible. I did enjoy what we have done together as much if not more than you did. You are interesting."

I honestly didn't know what to say.

"I would ask that you sleep on it, and we shall continue this discussion in the morning."

I nodded. He stood up and came over to me. He drew me to him and stroked my hair and upper back. Again I just enjoyed the act of being touched. I followed him to the bedroom. I found one of my nightshirts waiting for me in the room. Without another word, Holmes turned on his heel and left the way he came. I fell asleep quickly and more soundly than I had in a long time.

The next day I woke in the bed alone. I put on the dressing gown left out for me and found Holmes reading the paper. I sat down and removed the cover from the dish at my place across the table from him and ate.

I looked at Holmes and continued to think about my options. I now had my freedom. But I also I knew what I was and how I felt.

I knew I could never be happy without an *owner*.

But was the man in front of me the man I wanted to own me? I had once before willingly handed my personal freedom to another. I had been lucky with Lord Barton. Could lightning strike twice?

Certainly, I would never be bored with Holmes in my life. It seemed he would use me well. He had already proven he knew what he was doing, with his dab hand at caning.

I felt comfortable and... *safe*. In truth, that was all I could honestly expect from a relationship in this mode. Love didn't really come into it, although I had come to know it in the past. Perhaps that might happen again.

I said out loud, "Yes."

He did not even glance up from his paper. "Good. I'll have the paperwork drawn up today."

And that was how I became the property of Sherlock Holmes.

Olivia
By Erzabet Bishop

"That was she. The one who brought the tea." Alexandra sat, cold tea swirling in her cup and observed one of her oldest friends as he struggled to sit up. Gerald Revine was one of the most prominent men in the Marketplace network of spotters and had helped her to find acquisitions of property for years. She and Grendel counted on him to find quality candidates. To see him in decline was tearing her up inside.

"She doesn't know, Alexandra." Gerald's voice was crisp and firm, his eyes darting from the woman in front of him to the monitors positioned near his chair. His cultured appearance reflected his station in life, as did that of the woman with whom he was conversing. His brow wrinkled in thought, he barely noticed the warm afternoon sunlight shining through the sheer curtains that covered the drawing room windows.

Neatly dressed in a button-down collared blue shirt with a silver tie and a pair of dark grey slacks, his polished and dominant nature was expressed in the way he held himself together, even at a time like this. His grey hair was combed back, leaving his prominent brow and painfully thin cheekbones in full glare of the afternoon sun.

"Then you'd better tell her, hadn't you?" Alexandra tisked. "I don't like acquiring property this way, Gerald, and you know it." Her gaze narrowed. Her well-manicured nails drummed a beat on the arm of the chair in which she was reclining. She set the cold tea down with a clatter and turned her attention to the man in front of her. "And what of the others in your service? The majordomo?"

"Topher has been through all the necessary training, and I made arrangements for him. The servants will be placed through an agency. It will be done as soon as I've passed."

"Very well." Good. Bringing one stray would be bad enough, but two would've been a bit much.

Why hadn't she brought Grendel or Chris with her? They could've at least helped her to talk Gerald out of this madness. The Marketplace didn't accept a slave sight unseen. There was a process, and he damn well knew it.

Gerald paused and met Alexandra's eyes. "I haven't much of a choice, I'm afraid. These arrangements have been necessary. My health is failing, and the scope of time is withering quickly. I would appreciate knowing Olivia is safe and cared for."

"You can't be certain of that." Alexandra protested, her elegant features drawing into a frown. "The staff is capable of alerting us if your health takes a downturn. There's no need to send her away. She's done so well for you since you acquired her three years ago. Her pouring was flawless."

Alexandra turned her head to the one thing in the tasteful drawing room that didn't make sense. The row of television monitors and gadgetry.

"Why the monitors?"

"The video cameras help to monitor her progress even when I can't be there. So much of my time is spent in bed."

Alexandra nodded her agreement. "She is a lovely thing."

"Indeed. Which is why I'm entrusting her to you. To the Marketplace. I want to ensure she has a future."

"But I haven't even evaluated her yet." Alexandra protested, standing up from the chair and walking over to the monitors. There she observed a young shapely blond woman polishing furniture. She worked in a room with a large old-fashioned poster bed and matching cherry wood furniture. Masculine in nature, the room was both warm and austere, the same as the man sitting in front of her.

"Is that your bed chamber?"

"It is. Olivia takes great precautions to make certain I am well-tended."

"I can see that." Alex sighed. She fidgeted in her chair, wishing she were able talk to the girl now so she could ascertain what kind of person she was.

"Was she brought in as a slave? I remember you mentioning her off and on over the years, but I can't recall."

Gerald shook his head. "She was hired as my maid and became the slave you see before you. The girl has worked hard to find her place. I don't want any chances taken with her."

"You have a will? A capable lawyer?"

"I do."

"Good."

"She will be well taken care of financially. What I worry about is her psyche. She is a fragile flower, cultivated over time. She knows nothing of service beyond the role of slave and Master in the most basic sense."

"How basic?"

Gerald met Alexandra's gaze. "She has never had the occasion to be used in any manner sexually. I have seen to it her training did not include such things."

Alexandra blinked.

"Is she a virgin?"

Gerald sighed and turned his face away. "I don't want to speculate. She is, was, a girl in great pain who needed someone to guide her back to her true self. I was given the opportunity to help her focus on service and not on the engendered pain of what happened to drive her to my door."

"So she was a victim of some kind of abuse?" Alex sighed. There were so many ways that could go. She might embrace complete service or crumble in a millisecond the moment a man so much as twitched an erection in her direction.

"I believe so. The difference between the waif who answered my ad for a domestic and the lovely woman you see in the monitors is a vast one. Day by day, she has mastered her fear and grown stronger. But... it is time for another journey for her. A true healing. Not at the hands of one of the men, you understand. But you, Alex. It must be you."

"We can't do that, Gerald. A slave in training is a slave who learns humility, service, and the ability to engage in sex with any Master or Mistress who demands their submission. To do anything else would be to compromise the integrity of the program."

"There. On the table. The disks in front of you?"

Alex turned her head and found several CD cases stacked up. "Yes."

"Those are several training scenarios I've put Olivia through. Things she would've encountered with you at the basic level of training to ascertain her skill level. I would ask you to take and review them. Then decide."

Gerald reclined against the chair, obviously exhausted from the visit.

Alex's eyes flickered over the girl in the monitor, and she scooped the disks off the table.

"All right, Gerald. Let me take these and talk to the boys."

Gerald opened his tired eyes and his thin lips turned up in a smile. "I can ask for no more, but please. Do hurry. I won't have the strength to go on much longer." He pressed a button on a device near his hand, and mysteriously Topher, his majordomo, appeared at the door.

"Topher, would you please escort our guest to her car?"

"As you wish, Sir." The man's warm brown eyes caressed his Master and promptly snapped toward Alex. Dressed in denim and a large cream sweater and boat shoes, he looked more the part of a vacationing college student than a man who organized a large household such as Gerald's estate.

"Madame, if you will?" He bowed slightly, the shock of brown hair fluttering lightly across his forehead.

Clutching the disks to her chest, Alex nodded and went back the way she'd come. She would watch the footage and talk it over with the men in her life. That would be enough.

* * *

The silence in the house was deafening. Olivia saw the strange woman who came to visit, and something inside of her quaked with trepidation. Master seemed overly pensive of late, and she'd been afraid. Perhaps she'd displeased Him somehow? In the years she'd been under His roof, never had a day gone by that He'd not greeted her in the morning and kissed her on the forehead, sending her off to her day's chores. Until today.

Something was wrong.

Her lip quivered, and she took a deep breath. It was not about her. It was about what Master wanted. She needed to remember that.

She'd poured their tea and struggled not to look at the woman too hard. She was lovely. It was so rare Master had guests, let alone a beautiful woman like that.

Olivia put the finishing touches on Master's fresh sheets and bedding when she saw the majordomo out of the corner of her eye.

"Master Gerald wishes to speak with you." Topher acknowledged her with a firm smile, resting his weight in the doorway. In his well-muscled arms, he carried a clipboard and a stack of papers, which he laid on the dresser. He turned to go, giving her a dismissive nod. "Don't make him wait, girl."

"Yes, Sir."

He had always frightened her in a very basic way, this man who held her Master's deepest affection. She had never spoken out of turn to him and hesitated to do so now. His chocolate eyes held secrets of the household, and his hands could meet out punishments that left her backside sore for days. In the earliest time of her training, Topher and Cook had each taken turns spanking her until she learned the correct posture and behaviors of a slave. It had been a difficult lesson, but one she was happy to have finally perfected. At least most days.

When she'd applied for the job as a maid, she'd had not a cent to her name. Frank, her abusive boyfriend, was searching for her, and the bruises on her face and body reminded her why she ran. It would happen again if she stayed. It always did. It was run or end it all. She simply couldn't endure any more violence at his hands.

Olivia wasn't a quitter. She came across an ad for a maid in a large manor across town and took the plunge. She helped her mother clean houses as a child and knew her way around a kitchen and a mop bucket. It was the perfect solution. To find herself becoming a slave at first made her balk, but as she understood more of what her Master was asking of her, she gave her submission and life over to Him freely. It was a weight lifted from her shoulders. But now, with the strange woman visiting, some of her old doubts began to resurface.

Olivia sucked in a deep breath, glad she had finished making the bed. The room was done.

"Topher? Sir?"

The majordomo paused regarding her with piercing eyes.

"Is He angry with me?"

A sad smile played on the corners of his lips. Topher averted his eyes and swallowed. "Just go and talk with him, pet." He didn't meet her gaze again, and as he stepped out into the hallway, Olivia couldn't be certain, but it sounded like the man had begun to weep.

* * *

It didn't take Alex long to make a decision. Chris and Grendel had viewed the disks first and given their blessing on the unique arrangement without a fight. She scrutinized the girl doing most of the things that constituted a week of training before acceptance into the Marketplace program and grudgingly admitted Gerald had been right on target. The girl could perform a manner of housework tasks including outdoor work in the garden and stables. She presented herself in a submissive position when settling down at her Master's feet and was eloquent in bearing and conversation.

All that remained was the sexual aspect of the training. Gerald realized what he was asking, and it made Alex cringe. There were formalities and rules for a reason, but as she examined the blond girl on the disks, she began to understand why Gerald cared for her. There was an innocence about her that called out to the trainer in Alex. On the early footage, the yellow residue of faded bruising around the eyes, her face and along her arms hardened Alex's lips into a firm line. She was beaten. Most likely by an ex-boyfriend.

As the training progressed, the shy coltish behavior blossomed into that of an elegant young woman with a flair for subservience like Alex had never seen. Her voice held the proper cadence, her mannerisms fluid and artful, and finally on the last disk, she noticed a distinct wetness between her own thighs at the thought of this girl being under her tutelage. The tender breasts as they pushed against the thin fabric of her loose flowing tunic and the hint of coarse hair at the delta between her thighs.

Alex sighed. It would be different, but she would do it. The girl needed a place, and after so many years of working with Gerald, she felt she owed it to him. Her fingers caressed the cell phone as she watched a few more moments of the disks and then dialed the number.

"Gerald. It's Alex. Have her ready to be picked up this afternoon. I'm coming."

* * *

"Look at me, Olivia." Master Gerald's voice was velvet steel. "You have to understand this is for the best."

Olivia sat as still as a stone and willed herself not to react. Her Master liked her in a particular pose, kneeling at the side of His chair so He could reach down and pat her head whenever He chose. She understood the rules. The last three years had been spent becoming the perfect attendant. Her name was now Olivia. No first name. No last. Just the name given her upon entrance to this house. No possessions. No life beyond the freedom of a slave. She was the property of her Master and was happiest when she gave all of herself to Him. It was only right. She owed Him everything.

"I'll teach you the world if you'll only walk through my door."

Trust. Security. And now it was all unraveling in an instant. After years of training not to meet His eyes, it was a struggle to make herself do just that. Master asked her a question and demanded her obedience.

Olivia winced at the sharp tone. "Master?"

"You have served me well. However, it is time that you embrace a new element to your training." His kind but firm gray eyes observed her, and she felt a lump in her throat threaten to form into hysterical tears. "To do that, you must leave here."

Olivia felt the blood drain from her face, and she struggled to maintain the submissive stance she worked so hard to achieve. *No.* She wasn't ready for this. Not now. She lived to serve Him and had hoped, at the end of their time together, He would keep her. That maybe, just maybe He would come to understand she adored Him. She was well aware He possessed feelings for Topher, but perhaps there was room in His heart for her as well.

"As you wish, Master." Tears pooled in her eyes and she looked away so He would not see.

His hand reached down and tenderly cupped her chin, forcing her to meet His gaze.

"I don't wish it. More's the pity, but some things can't be helped."

Hot tears spilled from Olivia's eyes and ran down her cheek. "I don't understand. Have I displeased you?"

25

"You are more than worthy, my dear. I have been a blessed man to have been able to help you achieve your goals of becoming a slave." He tenderly wiped the tears from her cheek, and as she looked up, she could have sworn she saw moisture glittering in His eyes as well.

Master Gerald had been a better father figure in her life than her own, and it saddened her that she would be leaving the safest place she'd ever lived. Not once was she touched in a sexual way, and He'd been there to guide her when she thought her world was at an end.

"You wish to ask me a question. Make certain it is the right one before you ask, my dear."

"Master, why are you sending me away?" Olivia closed her eyes and tried to imagine a life away from the gentle instruction and guidance of Master Gerald. His townhouse quickly became a haven from the world, and she found a rhythm in her new life that gave her purpose and contentment. The thought of losing it made her want to be physically sick.

Focus. Breathe. Let the Master's will be done.

"I have to protect you, and this is the best way I know how."

"Protect me, Sir?"

"Yes, my pet." Master Gerald patted His leg, and she rested her arms on His aging knees.

"What will happen to me?" Olivia's voice wobbled as she tried not to sob.

"The woman you served at tea yesterday will come this evening to pick you up. She will take you to your new home." He patted her hands and brushed another tear from her face.

"I love you, Master." Olivia knelt down at His feet and wept, the shuddering sobs soaking the carpet beneath her. Master rubbed her back and pulled her into an embrace.

"Oh, little bird. How I wish you could stay with me." Master's voice grew raspy with emotion. "Go to bed now. I will always love you. Never doubt it." He kissed her forehead and tapped her nose, making her smile through the tears.

Her heart in her throat, Olivia made her way to her pallet and tried not to think of the night ahead of her.

* * *

She was awakened by Topher knocking quietly on the doorframe. "It's time, Olivia."

Olivia blinked in the evening twilight, her eyes still swollen from her earlier bout of crying. Her small suitcase rested on the floor next to the majordomo's booted feet.

She stood and made her way to the small washroom to relieve herself and wash her face. The cool water restored Olivia, and she combed her hair, plaiting it into a braid. The tunic she wore was slightly rumpled from sleep. Turning toward the room where her pallet rested, she found Topher contemplating her with a frown.

"Are you glad I'm going then, Sir?"

The moment the words left her lips, Olivia gasped. On any other day, the impertinence would have earned her a spanking of the highest order.

Topher's lips hardened into a firm line. "No, little slave. I am not. Now come. Your new Mistress is here to claim you. At least for now."

Olivia lowered her face away and followed behind Topher as he led her down the hallway and down the stairs to the main foyer. Waiting for her was the same woman she had served tea to the previous day. Graceful and cultured, the woman stepped forward. Olivia's eyes lifted to the drawing room, but to her disappointment found her Master already retired for the evening. It was just as well. She would not wish to shame Him by crying. Not again.

"Hello, Olivia. I'm Alexandra."

Olivia nodded. "Good evening, Ma'am."

"Your Master has given you high marks for your service. I'm here to bring you to the next level of your training."

"Yes, Ma'am. At least I think so." Olivia's voice quavered, and she thrust her shoulders back and swallowed. A curious warmth was building low in her stomach with every word the woman spoke. A Mistress. Now that would be an exciting prospect. She didn't know much about this woman and what she expected from her, but she would learn.

Alexandra smiled and opened the door. "Well then. Let's go then. To the future. To the Marketplace."

"The Marketplace, Ma'am?"

"Yes, my girl. And I think you will do just fine." Alexandra smiled and led Olivia out into the vast and infinite night.

Rain Dog
By LN Bey

"I'm like goddamn Napoleon on motherfucking Elba," she said, certain of it and certain he would be impressed. "I'm fucking exiled." She waited for his answer.

"First of all, my dear, you are not Napoleon on Elba. Napoleon returned from Elba, gathered an army and briefly returned to power. He was then defeated in a climactic battle at Waterloo. You've had your Waterloo. You are more akin to Napoleon on St. Helena, where they sent him afterward. Isolated, defeated, never to return."

Sharon stared out the window of the diner. The place reeked of stale cigarettes and grease, and she didn't understand why he'd said to meet her here in such a dingy place. It was getting dark, and the rain wasn't stopping, all she would be able to see pretty soon was the taillights on the Jersey Turnpike, people heading home. She knew the rain was going to do worse things to her hair than it already had.

"And second, you are not even Napoleon on St. Helena. You bring new meaning to the term *Napoleon complex*. You're nothing but a rain dog, wishing she could get home."

"A what?"

"Never heard of it? A dog who's wandered too far from home, and the rain has washed away the scent trail he'd left so he can't find his way back. You, my dear, are just a rain dog."

Sharon did not like the term but held her tongue. This was too important.

"So will you help me or not?" she said. She watched him sniff his coffee and set the cup down untouched.

"You realize," he said, "that would be taking a huge chance, on my part. You're *out*. Get that through your head. Shunned. Banned. *Persona non grata*. You cheated your way in, in the first place, but

28

Alexandra and Grendel took a huge chance on you anyway, because yes, you are fucking gorgeous. You barely—and I mean *barely*—passed, from what I hear. Then you got your lifelong ambition to be sold, and you ruined it. You utterly failed."

"They didn't—"

"They didn't want you for sex. Yes. I've asked around, Sharon. I still have a few connections. No one really wants to talk about it. They didn't worship you; you were a housekeeper in Texas." He stared hard at her until she looked away. "It's all about *you*, isn't it, Sharon." This was not a question. She did not answer it. She was learning, damn it. She would show him.

He leaned back and raised his arm across the back of the booth's seat. "I'm surprised you know anything about Napoleon at all," he said. "Even if you did misuse the reference."

Sharon perked up. "I've gone back to school," she said. "I'm taking European History, Music Appreciation and Literature."

"Literature! Back with the same teacher?" Damn, this guy *did* know everything. He must not have fallen as far out of favor as she'd heard.

"No, Sir," she said and bit her lip to stay quiet.

"It wasn't your lack of knowledge that got you kicked out, Sharon. It was your refusal to *learn*—anything."

The old Sharon would have given him a piece of her mind. Couldn't he see that?

"You are the ultimate example of *topping from below*." Sharon bowed her head to prove him wrong.

"Why those classes?" he asked.

"They all thought I should know about opera and classical music and ballet and shit. Fancy shit. So my owner could take me to some opera house in Europe or somewhere." She looked out the window again. "Like that was going to happen with the crowd that bought me."

Mr. Davis stared at her. "Not all of us are interested in European history or culture," he said.

"Yeah, I know, Mr. Davis," she said. "I saw all those kimonos and swords and shit."

Mr. Davis reached across the table and slapped her cheek before she even knew it. She raised her hand to ease the sting but thought better of it and put her hands in her lap.

29

"Never disrespect me," he said. "Kimonos 'n' swords 'n' shit? Do you know how that sounds? Like you're making fun of me. It's my passion."

Sharon passed through stages of hurt, anger and shame in the space of a few seconds. Mr. Davis had trained with some old Japanese guy, hardcore, Noguchi or something. He was way into that shit.

"I'm sorry, Mr. Davis," she said. "I didn't mean any disrespect, I promise you."

Mr. Davis stared at her a long time, and she met his gaze until she couldn't take it any longer and lowered her eyes to the sticky Formica tabletop.

"I shouldn't even be seen with you," he said. So that was why they were here, in this disgusting café.

He sighed and started playing with a packet of artificial sweetener. "The *only* option I can even see possibly working is to try to somehow sneak you in on the other side of the planet," he said. "Some of my Japanese or Southeast Asian contacts who are also sort of on the fringes. But as soon as you're in the computer system... "

Sharon waited as he thought.

"Even if we give you another name, a new identity, someone will recognize you, and then it's my ass that's in trouble. For good, this time."

He was shaking his head as he went through options. "Please, Mr. Davis," she said. "I'll do anything."

He looked up. "That was the problem. You won't."

"I will now. I've learned. Please. Train me. Teach me, use your connections. I will be the most grateful goddamn girl the world, you know?"

"It's a *lot* of risk, Sharon. What's in it for me?"

She shrugged seductively, glancing down at her cleavage visible over the low cut of her top. She wasn't wearing a bra. "This. Me."

"I've had that," he said.

Sharon had met Mr. Davis at a party he had thrown at his house, a big place upstate that sprawled horizontally, in little Chinese--or Japanese--looking modules, instead of trying to impress people with height and Great Rooms and shit. There were Japanese things all over—kimonos behind glass, scrolls of art, swords and old armor.

She had gone there with a Dom she'd met in the City who said there would be a few people from the Marketplace there, though he wasn't sure how they would react to her. Maybe no one would know her, she'd thought.

But Mr. Davis knew who she was. Her Dom had offered her to him and he'd accepted. He told her to strip in front of everyone—not that she was alone in that, it was quite a party—and had her perch delicately on an ottoman while he fucked her mouth and someone else mercilessly whipped her behind, which he constantly told her to raise higher. Her tears mixed with his semen when he shot it onto her face, and she was sure he'd fuck her, or someone would, but he told her to stand by the wall, come still dripping off her face like it was some kind of territorial thing. She stood there all evening, alone but for a few admirers appraising her like the suits of samurai armor she stood between. Mr. Davis gave her Dom an alternate girl to use.

Sharon's pussy remained wet and unsatisfied as she'd watched the party go on without her, gathering occasional derisive looks as the crawling slaves were chased and herded by tuxedoed guests in cruel games, made to perform, fucked.

"Be at my house at *precisely* eight in the morning, Miss Brosa," he said. "*One* minute late, and you will go home and never speak to me again."

"I'll be there, Mr. Davis," Sharon said. "You won't regret it."

* * *

"How do you solve a problem like... "

"*My Fair Lady!*" she shouted. She was naked, as she had been since she walked in the door a few hours ago. But whereas once she would have stood proud, allowing her Master the privilege of viewing her spectacular body, she now stood humbled, attentive.

What Mr. Davis did not know was she had spent the night on his front porch, under the wide canopy, wrapped in her raincoat. She'd checked the train schedules while still seated in the greasy spoon, and when she realized she'd never be able to catch the connecting trains and find a taxi to take her so far into the hills so early, she simply started that night with only the clothes on her back.

She knew she'd seen this before, in some movie or show—the determined student waiting at the door to be accepted into the training

31

inside—but she couldn't place it, and at precisely 8:59 she had pushed the button of his doorbell.

The whip struck across her backside with more severity than she'd expected, and she cried out. "Not even close," Mr. Davis said. "What did they teach you in that Music Appreciation class?"

She kept her hands at her sides. "Mostly opera and shit," she said. Another stroke on her ass, and this time she merely flinched despite it hurting even more.

"Opera... and... shit," he said. "Listen to yourself. However, you bring up an interesting point. What was *My Fair Lady* about?"

Sharon searched her memory. She didn't give a shit about these boring old musicals, didn't know much about them. But her grandmother had watched them, when she was a kid.

"Some professor takes a poor flower girl and turns her into a lady."

No whip. "Good! An educated man takes an uncouth little guttersnipe off the streets and molds her into a refined lady. Sound familiar, Sharon?"

Now the whip. It wasn't even noon on her first day yet. And she didn't know how long she'd be here.

"Yes, Mr. Davis," she said.

"You will address me as Sir."

"Yes, Sir!" Good. She liked the formality, the distance it created. Mr. Davis was something of an outlier in the Marketplace, someone with a bit of a shady reputation, but was known as a trainer of unfixables. That's why she'd sought him out. "Please, mold me into a lady, Sir," she said.

"Then why, my dear Sharon, would you say, 'opera and shit?' Do you think I want to hear such crude language when discussing the most refined examples of Western culture?"

"No, Sir," she said.

"I know you don't care about opera," he said. "I don't care that you don't care. But you'd damn well better learn to *appear* to care. *That's* what you couldn't get through your thick little head before."

That Sharon kept her thoughts to herself was a sign of progress, and she wished he could see it.

"Now... how *do* we solve a problem like... "

Sharon wracked her memory. She had no idea what he was

referring to, besides her. Her eyes wandered around the huge living room in which she stood, the same room where she'd been used and displayed months ago, where he'd taken over her and seemed to claim her for his own.

All this Japanese shit. Ah, wait—one of her grandmother's favorites!

"*The Mikado!*" she shouted. She cried as the whip struck across her lower back.

"Not even close."

"But it's all Japanese and... " She refrained from saying it.

"And what?"

"And... I thought it might please you."

"That was what two British guys *thought* Japanese culture was like. But I admire your thinking, Sharon. Pleasing me is paramount." No whip. "But becoming more knowledgeable is still one of goals now, isn't it?"

"Yes, Sir."

"So, then, since you now know about 'opera and shit': please summarize for me the plot of *La Traviata*."

* * *

"How do you feel about being sold to an Asian man, Sharon? Or woman."

Sharon was suspended by her wrists, her toes just barely able to touch the floor of Mr. Davis' big playroom. She was standing spread-eagled, the cables holding her up widening to pulleys in the ceiling, a spreader bar keeping her feet apart. Her body was glistening with sweat from the exertion—he'd left it up to her whether to struggle to stay up on her toes, relieving the pull on her wrists, or relax her feet and hang.

She thought of all the Japanese bondage movies she'd seen—hell, she was buying bootleg videos since before she was legal—and they often portrayed cruel, unforgiving men tormenting women without their consent, often in positions exactly like the one she was in now. It would be fine with her, she thought, rumors of small penises and mental images of meek businessmen cramming themselves into subways aside.

But today was her final exam for Basic Culture and Etiquette, her first round of study. Her sweaty torso was already streaked with welts and red marks from the single-tail he held, punishments for her many wrong answers. Her entire body was stinging, singing.

She knew the right answer.

"It doesn't matter how I feel about it, Sir," she said. "I will go where I am sold."

"Very good, Sharon," he said. "But do you *mean* it? You didn't do so well, last time."

Damn it. They'd auctioned her off to the most boring people on the planet, who had almost no intention of using her for sex. Grendel had told her he had no control over who bought anyone at auction, but she always suspected he'd encouraged it—a little poetic justice for the loud-mouthed girl who always wanted to be used but adored, punished but not really—anything but *bored.*

"No, Sir, I did not do so well. I have changed, Sir. I really have."

"Hm. You've done all right, so far, but we're only a month into this, Sharon."

Mr. Davis took a few steps back, appraising her as she flexed her muscles to stay elevated and then collapsed her calf muscles in exhaustion. She hated predicament games. At least he was appreciative of her body. Once she'd been accepted into training by Grendel and Alexandra, they'd shown no interest whatsoever, had refused to use her, even though they used everyone else she'd trained with. It was insulting.

Not that Mr. Davis had *really* used her—just one blowjob every day; that was it. Just enough to give her hope, just as keeping her naked did instead of dressing her like a peasant or some goddamn Amish woman.

"My methods are very different from Alex and Grendel's," Mr. Davis said. How did he always seem to be reading her mind? "We have to admit, their attempts failed."

Sharon waited, paying as much attention as she could in her discomfort.

"They told you to go study and left you alone, and you're probably the least self-motivated person I know. You left there the same foul-mouthed vagrant you were when you went in. I will not be leaving you alone. Not for one moment." So far, this had been true—

she'd been under surveillance even in the bathroom, a camera in her cage. Her one attempt at masturbation was punished with a week of sleeping tied spread-eagled. It was different, here—she was constantly on the edge, but never satisfied, no time to get bored. Alex and Grendel had tried to deny her body, show how bland service could be. But Mr. Davis was *all* about the body—her every nerve was on edge all day, and she tried even harder to please, to struggle through the stimulation to come up with the right answers.

"This is why they call me *Shuriko-sensei*—The Repairman. The teacher. Mr. Fix-it." He paused, deep in thought.

"We've covered Western Culture enough, I think. Since, in all likelihood, I'll be trying to sneak you back into the world through Asia, we'll start covering Japanese customs tomorrow. And you'll start calling me 'Sensei,' Master, instead of 'Sir.' Got that?"

Sharon nodded her agreement but mentally shook her head in resignation. All this Japanese shit—all those kimonos and swords. Mr. Davis wasn't even Japanese, but he was all over that crap like it mattered.

"Yes, Sensei," she said.

It dawned on her—the waiting at the door, approaching a Master, her exile. Her face brightened, and she was compelled to speak out of turn: "It's like that old kung fu show!" she said. "He has to wait outside the temple forever to be let in, then he's all trained to kick ass, then he's falsely accused of murder and kicked out and has to wander around! I'm just like that. Except backwards—I was kicked out, and *then* I had to wait at the Master's door." She was sure he'd be thrilled.

But he calmly walked to the wall, and hanged the coiled whip on its hook. She shouldn't have talked out of turn at all—he was likely going to go for one of the crops to punish her. But instead he went to the wall switch that controlled the pulleys above her head.

She let herself be lowered to her knees, just enough to keep her arms stretched taught above her. Blowjob time—her only contact for the day.

She opened her mouth as Mr. Davis unzipped and entered her. He always wanted his cock sucked first, her head bobbing up and down in a certain rhythm, before he would take control and fuck her mouth as she held still for him. She'd learned exactly how to move to please him. It was her specialty.

"Well, first of all, that was Chinese, not Japanese," he said as she sucked. "And second, you weren't kicked out for unjust reasons. You were kicked out for *failing*, miserably. You cost people money, Sharon."

She moved her head faster now, pumping his cock, keeping her lips wrapped around him as tight as possible. She tasted his maleness. *God*, what she wouldn't give for a good fuck. Always just enough to want more, with this man.

"You know what you are, Sharon?" he said, revelation on his face. She looked up at him, mouth full of his dick, and shook her head no.

Then she released it just long enough to say, "Rain dog, Sensei," before taking him in again.

"No. Well, yes. You're a *ronin*, Sharon—ever heard of that?" She shook her head no, making sure to make eye contact.

"A master-less samurai. Meant to wander forever, with no one taking them in. It was considered very shameful. Degrading." He placed his hand on the back of her head, and she knew to hold perfectly still. "Usually their master was either killed, or they were released because of dishonorable behavior. No one wanted them."

He was thrusting his cock into her mouth more forcefully, probing into her throat. She tried to relax, inhaled though her nose.

"That's you in a nutshell, darling." He came, shooting his warm fluids into her mouth and deeper into her throat, moving more slowly after a few thrusts. She massaged his cock with her tongue, cleaning it as he held it there.

Her lips smacked as he pulled out, and she could finally swallow his bitter load. At least he hadn't come on her face like he had that night she'd met him, here, at that party. She couldn't quite forget that night, the way he'd taken over her. Her Dom had left her shortly after that. At the time, she thought it was jealousy. But something was making her wonder.

"Tomorrow we start your new courses," he said, unfastening her cuffs. "Now get cleaned up and go to bed."

* * *

The old restlessness was coming back, and who could blame her? A full week learning how to wear a fucking kimono, and three weeks—*three weeks*—in this tiny little house, learning how to make goddamn tea. Tea. *In* the kimono.

36

It was hot as hell, the middle of summer now, and she was sweating all day, every day, in this tiny little tea house built for midgets or kids or whatever the fuck, scrunched down and learning every... goddamn... move, the precise little ritual after ritual after ritual, just to serve your guests a little cup of tea. And nasty, thick green tea at that, full of chunks and tea leaves all ground up. Couldn't they just put a kettle on? Sharon would be fine with her Master telling her to put a kettle on for someone. Who wouldn't like that?

But she kept trying, and Mr. Davis showed her, over and over again, how every little move worked, had to be done in the right order, had a fucking *name*, and on top of all that had to be graceful.

Like she wasn't already fucking graceful? Had he not looked at her, lately? She was a goddess and she knew it and he did too. He secretly worshipped her beautiful body, she could tell by looking in his eyes. Even when binding and whipping her lessons into her. Especially when binding and whipping her lessons into her! It had all worked, damn it; she had learned, wanting to impress him.

But this shit, all this *mizusashi* and *chawan* and *natsume*. And she was supposed to be something called a *Teishu*, and on and on and on... It was getting to her. It was fucking *boring*, and that was the one thing Sharon could not stand. She had tried so hard. She'd spent three days learning how to open the damn door, with just the right gestures. Mr. Davis had told her it usually took ten years to master the ceremony. Why would anyone devote that much time to making fucking tea?

Mr. Davis took careful notes during her lessons, and while he was a gentle instructor, he would beat her mercilessly and not even let her suck his cock if she built up too many demerits during the day. And sucking his dick was all the human contact she *had*. She was starting to cry herself to sleep now, rather than trying to sneak a touch.

They were in the stupid little house, the stupid little teahouse, the *Chashitsu*, which she secretly pronounced "cha-shit-su." She knew she looked resplendent in her red kimono even though she was sweating—it was the middle of summer, for chrissakes. It had little gold clouds all stitched into it and white silk around the edges, the collar and cuffs or whatever you called them, she just couldn't remember all this and couldn't care.

She was tired of listening to him talk about all the Zen bullshit. It was thundering outside, and it smelled like rain. Couldn't they just go outside and sit for a while? She'd gladly suck his cock. Just get out of this heat and this stupid, tiny little room and—

"Pay attention, Sharon. You're really slipping. This is just the first, you know."

Sharon looked up at him as she held the clay bowl she had to bring around her body in a certain way to present to the guest, looking graceful and demure the whole time.

"First what, Sensei?"

"First ceremony. This is the *Yuzari-no-chaji*, the early evening tea for summer months. We still have to learn the morning tea for summer, and then the fall ceremonies, and then the winter ones. Each one has its own rules, and the equipment differs—namely the heating method. In fact—"

No. No fucking way. This was as bad as cleaning stables back in the day. No way was she going to submit to a life of this, making goddamn tea for some Japanese guy, and who even knew if she was going to a Japanese guy, she could be sold to a Chinese, a Korean, who the fuck knew.

"No," she said.

"What?"

"No. I can't do it. I can't take this anymore, Sensei. Sir."

Mr. Davis leaned back and took a long look at her. She was still holding the bowl, perfectly in fact, and shaking her head.

"I thought as much. I knew you wouldn't be able to devote yourself to anything, to really *serve* someone else, put their wishes above yours. You have confirmed my suspicions, as well as the Marketplace's, kicking you out for good."

Sharon held the bowl, her eyes now filling with tears. Angry tears, self-hating tears.

She started to speak but stopped.

"What are you?" Mr. Davis asked.

"A fucking rain dog," Sharon said.

"In ancient Japan, you'd be told to commit *seppuku*," he said. "Declared worthless and untrustworthy—you'd commit suicide, disemboweling yourself. You'd—"

"Stop it!" she cried. "Just stop it! I just can't take this anymore. All this... this—" She turned the bowl over and smashed it against the lovely hand-sanded hardwood floor. She expected Mr. Davis to strike her—he'd hit her in the diner for just *insulting* his toys—but he just stared.

"Wait here," he said, a coldness to his voice. And he crawled out the tiny doorway.

Part of Sharon wanted to run, just squirm out and leave his property, run to the road, catch a ride back to the City, kimono and all.

She heard raindrops starting to fall on the roof of the teahouse. She heard thunder. She heard footsteps on the stone garden path. She heard Mr. Davis's voice just outside the miniature door. "Sharon," he said. "Come out here."

* * *

Sharon climbed out the little door. It was beginning to rain for real, now, not just sprinkle. He was wearing a raincoat and fedora.

"Take off the kimono, put it in the *Chashitsu*." It took her a few minutes to peel the layers of the silk garment off—first the wide outer belt, then the outer kimono. Then the belt underneath that held the inner robe on, then that robe as well. A layer of soft cotton. Finally she was free and naked, every layer neatly folded and pushed back into the dry teahouse. She kicked off her little slippers.

The rain felt cool and clean on her sweaty skin. The drops softly fell on her shoulders and breasts; she wiped the gathering water off her forehead. It felt wonderful to be out of those hot robes.

Mr. Davis had a satchel with him. He pulled out a blindfold and ball gag, two leather cuffs and a leash. She was about to be punished.

Then Sharon looked in the bag. Her clothes were in there, the clothes she last wore nearly two months ago and had never seen since. She was being sent home.

Goddamn it. She had failed again.

Did she care?

Yes, she thought, as Mr. Davis placed the blindfold over her head and sealed off her vision, she did care.

She opened her mouth when she felt the rounded gag against her lips, and he fastened its buckle behind her head.

She could smell the wet earth in Mr. Davis's garden, the water in the little flowing creek that was spanned by a miniature bridge that led to the teahouse. She heard the trickling waterfall, another of his Zen gadgets.

She held her wrists out for him as he buckled her cuffs and then hooked them together in front of her. She could smell the grass nearby, the pines overhead. She felt the click of the leash as he attached it to her cuffs.

He pulled the leash and her arms were pulled too, out in front of her body. She followed. What about her clothes?

This was incredibly unsettling—she was being pulled, guided, through a place she had never really paid attention to all summer. She tried to step gingerly, but he was moving her along fairly fast—or at least it felt fast, which didn't take much when you couldn't see.

She felt the wet grass under her feet, smooth and soft and manicured. The rain was falling a little harder, still refreshing, but distracting her from trying to keep her footing. She was glad her hands were bound in *front* of her.

She smelled fruit, felt soft, wet little things under her feet that became slimy when she stepped hard onto them. Ugh. Fallen cherries. He was always talking about cherry-blossom viewing in the spring. What could be more boring? She could hear the rain hitting his hat. She could hear it rolling *off* his hat.

The gag made her breathe through her nose, and she noticed things she'd never even thought about before. She was a city girl. These smells were not hers. She thought she heard a car in the distance—could they see her? Was he taking her to the road, where someone would pick her up and take her back to the city where she belonged? He wouldn't just leave her there bound and gagged; it wasn't a private road. Or would he?

She was aware that the rain was now falling on her back, not her front. They were turning around. Mr. Davis slowed, and she slowed too. She was now walking on stone, flat stone, another path. They were back at his house.

Then he pulled her leash, and the rain hit her left side. More soft grass under her feet, smell of flowers. She could tell by the sound of his footsteps, somehow, that there were trees around—this *wasn't* his house. She fought his pull, afraid of what he was driving her into. But he gave her a good yank, and she nearly fell. She submitted and let him guide her.

"Easy now," he said. "Walk straight." Echoing sound of water. Jesus, what was this all about?

Smell of water, smell of pine. Soft grass under her feet after some harder dirt, her feet getting coated in mud. This was all *so* foreign. She knew the sidewalk sounds of traffic, neighbors arguing. Smells of bus exhaust and the reek of the subway. She longed for somebody's dungeon.

He stopped. She bit down on her gag as he raised her arms, felt the leash that held them being fastened to something above her head. A tree, most likely. She held still for him, let him do what he willed. She sensed him stand back.

The rain was really coming down, now. And it had cooled, her nipples tightening to stiff little buds, her hair soaked against her head. She *hated* wet hair. She felt the rain run off her body, flow down her chest and stomach and legs. She felt goosebumps and waited for him to say something. She expected the whip but hadn't seen one, earlier. All she could do was stand there naked, arms stretched up, unable to move.

"It'll be very easy to release you," he said. She felt his warm hand run down her body, feel her breast, slide down her belly and across the slit of her pussy. But he didn't go any further. It was hard to hear in the rain, but she thought she heard him walk away.

She spoke into her gag, trying to say "Sir? Sensei?" but he didn't answer. She waited some more. She was getting cold, and nothing was happening. Was this her punishment?

What did he mean, it would be easy to release her? She was a bad slave, she knew. It was all she'd ever wanted, but she couldn't pull it off. Maybe she just didn't have it in her. He was sending her home.

Or just leaving her out here, in the country, in the rain getting colder by the minute—leaving her out here to die?

She called out again, a muffled cry that didn't sound like anything.

It'll be easy to release you, she thought. She gave the leash a pull. She was fixed in place. But there was some give to what must have been the tree branch. She put her weight into it, bent her knees and dropped her body in addition to pulling with her arms.

And she was free. She slipped on the wet grass, fell to the ground.

41

She lifted her blindfold and saw he wasn't there. She was alone in a small clearing, a low branch of one of the trees above her head. She couldn't unhook her cuffs, but she reached behind her head and unbuckled the gag.

"Hello?" she yelled. She didn't like this at all—he *had* left her alone in the woods to die. Naked and cold. And lonelier than she'd ever felt. She was *not* an outdoor girl.

She looked around. She had absolutely no idea which way to go. She looked around for signs of his movement, searched the ground for footprints. There were none in the wet grass.

She crouched down into a tiny ball and hugged her legs. She wanted to panic. How the hell did she, sex goddess, get into this mess?

What the hell should she do? Scream for help and run around in circles? What would panic feel like? She tried to calm herself. This was upstate New York, not the Old West or something. Someone had to live nearby. She remembered hearing a car go by.

And then it hit her: *find your way home, rain dog.* But which home did he mean?

She wanted to cry. She was soaking wet and cold, and she wanted to cry.

But she wasn't going to. Crying made her angry.

She closed her eyes and thought. She stood and faced the direction she remembered being in when she pulled off her blindfold, where he'd left her. She closed her eyes again, and remembered the rain hitting her left shoulder before he'd stopped her and hung her by the wrists.

So—turn around, let the rain come at her from the right. Okay. She walked.

Through the trees she had sensed earlier, at least she thought— who the hell knew, she was no goddamn pioneer.

She walked to the edge of a hill, overlooking some river below. She saw a narrow pathway, inches from the cliff—"walk straight," he'd said. Smell of pines. She knew what a fucking pine tree looked like.

A stone path. She nearly ran along the path until she felt completely lost again and almost slipped on the wet stone.

She tried to *remember.* She'd never concentrated so hard in her life. She recalled the rain on her back before the stone path, but how far along the stone path? But there—there was the smell of flowers. She saw them, irises, blooming blue and white. She turned into the rain and walked.

And there was the satchel with her clothes, on a low stone wall. She was at his front gate, by the road. Her clothes would be dry, and she could put them on and catch a ride downstate.

There's your way home, rain dog. Back to the city, back to starting over. Back to trying to find just one more trainer or recruiter who could give her that *one* more chance to get back in. Because that was all she'd ever wanted in life. To be a slave. An obedient slave, willing to do whatever obscene thing her Master wanted.

Suck cock, eat pussy. Stand at attention, crawl. Take a beating and beg for more. Learning the fucking tea ceremony. What was it called? Oh yes. The *Yuzari-no-chaji.* What was the winter one called? She had no idea.

Her tears mixed with the rain flowing down her face. She was cold and wet and pissed off. At Mr. Davis, at Grendel, at those creeps who'd bought her in Texas, at herself. She was not the least bit horny, for the first time in weeks. Years. She wanted more than anything to be warm. She opened the satchel, took a look at her clothes. Her apartment in New Jersey never seemed so welcoming, so warm.

She thought she smelled cherries, perhaps just starting to rot.

She zipped up the satchel and left it there on the fence.

* * *

"Grendel-san, so nice to see you again," the auburn-haired geisha said as she opened the door for him.

"Hello, Sharon," Grendel said as he looked her up and down. His face was a mix of disdain and confusion. "That's a beautiful kimono you're wearing."

"Thank you, Grendel-san," she said. "Sensei had it imported from Japan last week, brand new, but based on a 13 century design— are you familiar with medieval Japan?"

"No, Sharon. But I know how fascinated your Master is by it."

"Yes! His collection of katana—samurai sword blades—is unmatched in upstate New York."

"I'm sure it is. Is he home? We have paperwork to sign."

43

Sharon bowed demurely, making sure to keep her head lower than his when he returned the bow.

"He is in his office. Would you like some tea, later? I could prepare the *Nagori-no-chaji*; it's the Autumn Tea Season, you know. Sensei has—"

"No. Thank you though, Sharon, I can't stay long."

"All right, Grendel-san." She started to say something, to apologize for all the trouble she had once caused him.

"I have to say, I'm surprised," he said, before she could speak.

"Pleasantly so, I hope."

"Definitely. I never thought—I never thought."

Sharon smiled, demurely.

She led him to Sensei's office, and he closed the door behind him. She kneeled by the door and waited until she was to be called in.

She heard laughter, talking, more laughter.

She was finally going to be sold back into the Marketplace.

The door opened, and Sensei was holding a sheaf of papers. Sharon looked up.

"Come on in," he said. She stood and entered, took tiny steps.

"Sign here," Grendel said, sliding a page toward her on the desk. "And here."

"Congratulations, Sharon," Grendel said. She never thought this man would ever speak to her again, let alone welcome her back. Never.

Sensei had *done* it. He had not even had to sneak her in some back door, literally, some back alley in Tokyo or Shanghai. He had trained her so well he was able to approach Grendel and propose up front that she be allowed back in. She was a rain dog no longer; she was a *ronin* no more.

"Thank you, Grendel-san," she said. "I am thrilled." Her accent was delicate, almost effete, like a refined geisha. Only her gorgeous auburn hair, worn up to show off her wonderfully feminine neck, set her apart from the traditional image. She didn't even mind the bulky kimono hid her shapely form.

She prostrated herself in the traditional manner and kissed Grendel's boot, then Sensei's.

It seemed a tremendous waste of time, in a way—undergoing all this specific training to please some Japanese executive, somewhere, who'd be willing to take her in and fudge the books on her existence within the Marketplace. It all wasn't even necessary, now. She'd endured it for nothing.

"May I speak?" she asked.

Sensei nodded.

"When will I be auctioned again?" Please, she thought, anywhere but Texas. But she would go wherever they wanted.

"No, Sharon," Grendel said. "Mr. Davis has bought your contract direct, with the finder's fee he earned for re-entering you."

Still kneeling, Sharon turned and looked up at Sensei. He nodded.

"He now owns your contract outright. He can sell you anytime, of course," Grendel said.

Sharon was speechless. She didn't know it could work like this. She thought every slave was put up for auction after training. But then, she was a special case, she knew.

She wondered why she'd had to sign two papers, just now. She probably should have read them more closely—or read them at all.

"Be advised, Sharon. If you displease your Master, there *are* still families in Texas looking for manicurists and housekeeping slaves." He grinned, a look on his face that wasn't very friendly at all.

"No, Sir! Grendel-san. I've changed. Ask Sensei, if you don't believe me." She thought a moment. "If it pleases you to ask him, of course." She bowed her head.

The two men stood. "Sure you can't stay?" Sensei asked. Sharon was torn between wanting to show Grendel her new ways and just wanting him gone.

"No. This was business. Goodbye, Sharon."

"Goodbye, Grendel-san."

"You and this Japanese fetish," Grendel said and patted Sensei on the shoulder. They turned to walk out, and Sharon ran ahead of them with tiny steps to hold open the door.

She closed it behind the two men and watched them walk to Grendel's car.

But she didn't click the door shut. She *was* still Sharon, after all, not some superhuman who could completely change her personality. She put her ear against the tiny open crack in the door.

She overheard more laughing.

"Thank you again," she heard Sensei, her new Master, say.

"No, thank *you*," Grendel—Grendel-san—said.

Some words she couldn't make out, then, most definitely, she heard Grendel-san say "for keeping her out of our hair."

Sharon's eyebrows, her perfect, auburn eyebrows, furrowed in thought. She remembered sneaking into the Marketplace with false paperwork in the first place, all those years ago. But it couldn't be...

All this training—all this Japanalia. So specific. The papers she'd just signed didn't look anything like the Marketplace contract she'd signed the first time, so long ago. Of course, they could have changed them, since then.

Or not. She had no idea what she'd just signed. Was she even back *in* the Marketplace? Oh, that would be hilarious for Grendel, wouldn't it? And for her Master...

She really should have taken a better look at those contracts. One of them was still on Sensei's desk. She glanced back out the door. They were still talking. She still had time.

She took a deep breath. For the first time in her life, Sharon decided to not sneak, not to look. Not to sniff around.

This rain dog had found her way home.

Pickett Ridge: Mission Market
by Flynn Anthony

Pickett Ridge, 1992

The sunset spilling from the bay window behind him painted the file folder on the table red and gold. Colonel Beauregard Riordan, USMC Retired, put his head in his hands, massaging his temples. His halfway house had taken in countless young soldiers over the years, helping them to transition from military to civilian life, but this boy had him stumped. Beau felt certain he'd lost count of the number of the times he'd confined the young marine to his room, with orders to think things through and journal about it, not to mention the number of notations of corporal punishment present in the file. The next action was clearly to take a strap upstairs with him, before he ordered early lights out, but Beau was reluctant to do so. The boy would be predictably well-mannered, orderly and put his best foot forward for some days after a strapping—and if he followed the pattern Beau had noted, they'd be right back in this position within a week.

Unacceptable. Every time he tried to loosen the household regime, or encourage the boy to form independent habits, they wound up with a disaster on their hands. Colin's Marine Corps service was impeccable, with several commendations, and he'd come to Beau with excellent recommendations, even after three months of determined alcoholism and a handful of drunk and disorderly arrests. Pickett Ridge was the foremost halfway house on the West Coast, and he'd only once failed a boy. He would not fail this one.

No matter what he'd tried, he couldn't bring out the sense of discipline in the boy, the way he usually did, and Colin seemed more interested in abject servitude.

A memory echoed through his mind, his grandfather shouting at him, on his 16th birthday. *"What the hell are you thinking, boy? This family has been in service for generations! From the time we came over here from Ireland, boyo, do you hear me? Indentured servitude isn't a joke, Beauregard! It's a fecking serious matter, and you will attend to your family obligations! Every person in this goddamn family has taken a bonded apprenticeship since the law took that service from us—this is arranged, boy! What are you thinking, telling me you just want to go and be an errand boy at that bar? That's not how this family works! You'll sign those papers tomorrow, come hell or high water, and you'll be a bricklayer, by God and Christ. Now get to bed, boy, don't let me see you."*

Beau had snuck out that night, everything he owned in rucksack. He'd walked miles, then hitched a ride into DC, and was waiting at the USMC recruiting station at dawn the next day. He'd serve, all right, but he'd damn well serve his country, and not some bullshit idea of family obligation.

Servitude. The word echoed in his head. Servitude. He wasn't the only one to break the family mold. The twins, who were just two when he left, had taken the family dedication to service a step or maybe more than that, Beau reflected, further than the family trade. For one thing, they were both as gay as he was, and when the family had put them on the street after catching them in bed with one another, they'd made their way on the streets, stumbling into a surprisingly protective world of motorcycles and leather.

He'd received the letter in mail call in Nam. The twins had gone into what amounted to a slavery contract, for two years, in something called The Marketplace. They weren't certain how often they'd be able to write. But what Nik and Dan had written... it had been something else. He'd replied quickly, asking that they keep in touch. He fought with the revulsion the concept brought to him every time he received a letter, but by the end of it, he was nodding his head and thinking they'd done right by themselves.

He'd had to deal with enforced medical leave in '75 after he'd returned stateside, thanks to the little nurse who'd saved his life. The twins had answered his letter, and he'd traveled to New York, finding them more peaceful than he'd ever seen a pair of people before, kneeling to either side of a beautiful, dark-haired woman they'd only addressed as Anderson. The woman who had *trained* them, apparently.

He'd stayed as a guest for a few days, after a heartfelt request from Nik, echoed faintly by Dan, in the same way he remembered them asking for things they'd needed when they were two, before he'd left. And he appreciated the grace, the peace, the quiet explanations they'd given him, about The Marketplace and their service, and what they needed.

And now he needed to make a call.

* * *

"I beg your pardon," Beau asked. He'd come to an abrupt decision after the boy's last temper tantrum, fraught with tears and argument.

"I don't understand, sir."

"Then we'll go over it again." Beau was careful to keep his tone pleasant, but direct. "You are holding a list of house rules, a list of personal goals, and a list of your assignments for the last three months."

"But it's not time for evaluations."

Beau's hand slammed down on the table. "*Now.*"

"I don't understand what you want me to do."

"Assess those three sheets of responsibilities. Highlight any failures. Put in explanatory notes if you need to."

"Yes, sir."

Beau repressed his impatience while the young perfectionist contemplated each item. Beau wondered for a few moments, watching the systematic movements, but he was holding the results of the psych eval. Whatever barrier was between the boy and self-control wasn't a learning disability or any other definable psychiatric disorder.

The boy finished, his whole demeanor transforming to reflect pride, rather than the post-traumatic mousiness Beau usually dealt with.

"Now, you will sit quietly and sip at that water slowly, while I review these documents."

Beau caught a puzzled glance from the boy, but he also saw the kid relax, which was unusual. The slim hand wrapped around the water bottle, and the boy took a measured sip, not like his usual gulp while he was studying or doing chores and not thinking about things.

Even more telling. A direct, plain order got obedience, every time. Reduce the structure, and the boy started to fall to pieces.

He rummaged in the Punishment Box, where each punishment assignment was detailed on a file card, worn and tattered, with bull's eyes of pinholes in the corners. He used these cards daily on the bulletin board to inform halfway house residents of their punishment assignments. He was careful in his choosing this time, deliberately identifying twice as many as he normally might. All part of his plot. Once he had them gathered, he pulled forward a box of the Post-it notes his daughter had sent, picking up a package of the smallest size offering the greatest variety of colors.

"Now. You will take these," he said, sliding over the office supplies and the cards. "And the punishments I have selected. You will choose one punishment out of this stack, one for each line highlighted. Use the materials to coordinate failure to punishment," Beau instructed, trying not to wince at his own words. Colin reached out a smooth, innocent hand for the stack of cards and the flags. Failure was not a word he used to his boys. But this boy... .

Colin wasn't an innocent, as much as he behaved like one at times. Beau knew the things the boy would be unlikely to tell any other person on the planet: the pain of the technician who guided a missile to create countless deaths, the agony of failing to extract a team correctly from a route littered with antipersonnel mines, the bottomless guilt of—

Beau adjusted himself mentally, shedding the pain, shedding the *what if*, to focus entirely on the wounded spirit before him. A wounded spirit, he had to admit, who might not ever heal or feel peace with the terrors of war in his mind. This boy, who apparently found peace in one place only, if Beau was right.

And Beau knew what it meant, to walk out of the armed forces on an honorable discharge. Knew what it meant to suffer for service. Knew what it meant to suffer—

"Yes, sir," the boy murmured. At that point, Beau began to watch, even though he had a sheaf of papers before him on the table, which he periodically shifted. The boy was always more comfortable doing homework from his community college classes when someone else was at the table working alongside of him, and he expected this would be no different.

Better than an hour had passed, before the boy cleared his throat and made a soft inquiry. Beau had ignored a hell of a lot of fidgeting, moaning and sighing. He'd opted to ignore those things in the past months, trying to work on more critical issues—and if he saw what he expected in the papers the boy was handing him, there would be a crackdown. Eight weeks to the end of the semester—he wouldn't transition a boy in the midst of classes.

"Now, get yourself in the shower and into bed. You're grounded. Get me copies of this week's performance review and current progress reports in your classes by the end of the day tomorrow. I need to consider those as well."

"Yes, sir." Beau watched his hand twitch as he repressed a salute, something the boy would probably never lose.

"Colin. Boy, you have a new assignment. I see that hand there," Beau said. "New orders. Any time you're out of uniform, and you're wanting to salute, you stand up straight and put your hands flat on your thighs, unless there's an honest-to-God superior officer present. Understood?"

"Yes, sir."

"Good. Get a move on."

He watched the boy go and drew the papers toward himself. His young partner slipped into his view before he'd turned the first page, standing hesitantly at his side.

"I woke up when he came upstairs. I didn't want to listen to him try to settle down, Beau, I—"

"Shush." Beau pulled Jackson down on his lap, continuing to read and assess. Jackson didn't interrupt, just laid his head back on Beau's shoulder, closing his eyes. His boy was still tired, Beau noted. The nightmares had been bad the last couple of days, and he needed to tread carefully. It was clear from the dreams; Jackson was as worried about Colin as Beau was.

"Did he do okay?"

"Yes, he did. As I expected, Jackson. Never you mind the details, just know I have it in hand."

"You didn't want to give up," Jackson mumbled into his neck.

"No, baby. But I do have limits. I'm sorry you worried," he told his lover with feeling.

"I can't help it." This time the words were a pitiful whine.

51

"Oh yes, you can, my boy. I'll teach you that sooner than later. Go get me a wooden spoon out of the drawer. You know better than to take that tone of voice with me."

To his credit, Jackson moved on Beau's word. It had been quite a few days since his boy had been spanked. He nodded to himself, did away with pants and shorts, and had Jackson over his knee, smiling fondly at the sight of his boy trying not to squirm.

"Mind your manners, boy. That's the fourth reminder this month, and I get a free-for-all here," he said, beginning to bring the spoon down sharply and quickly. Jackson was yelping within a minute, and Beau let him up after a while, and put the red-faced boy back in his lap, patting at the sore buttocks.

It took some time, but Beau finished reviewing the papers with a sigh and patted his boy's thigh. "Why don't you get supper together, Jackson? Something simple. I need to put the board up, and we'll see how this goes."

* * *

And it went, he reflected two months later, looking at his logs and records on the boy who had settled more in two months than he had in the prior 18. Thrived, even, on service. Simple, exacting service. Beau had taken his care with the boy, working him while Jackson was off at evening classes. Jackson had just shelved the last of the books he'd had out for an assignment, and Beau smiled.

"Jackie-boy—"

"Master," Jackson lilted, turning with a grin.

Beau winced, instead of his usual answering smile, but he reached out to his lover, bringing Jackson closer into the circle of his arms. He wished he could protect the boy from the knowledge.

"I didn't think," Jackson told him quietly. "I know what you're about to do, you know."

"Do you now, boy?"

"You've been training him for a slave. I'm not that... um, uneducated."

"Good choice of word," Beau told him, rubbing his jawline along Jackson's cheek.

"I do try. I don't understand it. But I can see how happy he is.

And I'd like to have everything I'm uncomfortable with out from underfoot. Except... "

"Ah. Well. I'll assure you, then. No interest, on my part. You know what I like, my boy. I'll not have hidden anything from you—I've only eyes for you."

Jackson seemed reassured by this, but clearly wasn't finished with the discussion. "But you knew what to teach him?"

"Knowledge is power, Jackson."

"Does Tess know?"

Beau blinked. That was the last question he expected, as to whether his daughter knew. "Yes," Beau said quietly. There was a long silence, while Beau debated. Jackson was asking for information he wasn't really ready to give. "I'll need to go to New York, with the boy."

"I know. I want to go with you."

"Honey—"

"I want to see James and Stephen," Jackson said, surprising him, mentioning the two boys who had come through Midway and gone on to apprenticeships in New York City, about the time Colin had arrived. "And I want Tess to go."

"You what?" Beau felt more than a little baffled. "Did you—"

Jackson rolled his eyes and sidestepped the swat Beau attempted. "I want Tess to go. I want to talk to her," Jackson said stubbornly. "And I just can't talk to her on the phone very well, except the last time we did she said she misses them, and she sounded sad, and—*No!* Ow! Beau! I'm not trying to manipulate!"

Beau fixed him with a stare that had lesser officers turning tail and running. "You'd best not be, boy. See to your responsibilities. I'll be in my study."

Jackson took a few moments to breathe, Beau noted. His study wasn't officially such, it was just a huge desk set into a half circle bay window—an area meant to be a sitting room in the tiny Victorian-wannabe he'd bought reluctantly, figuring he'd add on to it or add outbuildings later. And he had the benefit of being able to see the entire front yard, most of the living room, and the rest of the first floor, if not directly then in his peripheral vision.

Once Jackson was properly engaged, Beau picked up his private line, dialing his daughter.

"Tessa."

"Beau!" She sounded delighted, which was a good start. "I'm so glad I came home, then. I wasn't quite keen on a fourth double in a week."

"I'm not keen on the idea either—you know how I feel about that, girl. Now, how's your leave schedule?"

Tess paused, and he heard the rustle as she reached for her day planner, never far from her. And then her sigh. "Needing to be used, as usual."

Beau had to put the thoughts of the fiancé his daughter still mourned from his mind. Overworking was her favorite way to compensate.

"Well, then. Jackson has requested your presence with us in New York."

"Oh!" He could hear the pleased tone in her voice. "I would love that. Do you think we might see the boys?"

"Absolutely," he told her warmly. "I've a boy here I need to take on an interview out there, to see how things go, otherwise, we can have a pleasure trip. What do you think, sweetheart?"

"Absolutely—when?"

* * *

The tears, this time, were different. Colin was given to dramatics, but this time the boy sat in silence upright on his bunk, hugging his knees, with tears running down his face. He was desperately trying to control his breathing and wiping the tears away as fast as he could.

"Boy, you are wrong." Beau's normally gruff voice was gentled, low and reassuring. "I believe there is a place for you."

Those shockingly blue eyes looked up at him, made wild by the reddening of tears and rubbing.

"You've never said that before."

If there was one thing he'd trained the boy to, in 18 months, it was to honesty.

"Tell me why I didn't, Colin."

"You never say anything unless you're d—unless you're really sure of it. It has to be a truth," the boy said, focusing intensely on Beau.

"That's right, boy. It was quite a search." The trip to New York was scheduled in just a few days, and he had a bit more work to do with the boy.

"Sir." The boy tried, interrupting.

"Zip it. You're worth it. It's not a traditional answer, it's not a common answer, it's not even a new age answer. Don't think I didn't see you with that floozy and her crystals on campus."

The boy turned a brilliant shade of red, but he kept quiet, listened, and in the end confirmed what Beau had known for months. The boy wanted to serve.

* * *

Beau yanked the bedroom door open and pointed at a spot in front of his feet. The boy... flowed... out from under the tangled covers, managing to straighten them as he did so. And the movement to kneel was flawless. Beau was struck by the grace of it.

"Very good," he praised, after long minutes of silence and stillness in the room. "Be down in my office in a half hour—and I want you there without clothing," Beau said, fighting back the difficulty he had saying that to someone other than Jackson.

"Yes, sir," Colin murmured, eyes demurely fixed on the floor. The expression he wore was the most peaceful Beau had seen in, aside from the hours the boy spent sleeping.

Beau turned on his heel and stalked downstairs, trying not to swear out loud. He knew. He knew damn well what the boy needed. He'd known for months, while he put in the preliminary training. He'd seen it before, on family visits to the twins. He'd seen it before, in the leather community. He hadn't ever wanted to encounter it personally, and yet here Colin was, pushing every fucking button Beau had. Subservience. Grace. Desire. Willingness. The boy had it all—everything he'd ever heard his brothers' chatter happily about, everything he'd ever heard one of his leather-brothers say quietly long ago, in a small room of people.

Colin had what it would take.

Beau wasn't sure what he disliked more, watching Colin discover the understanding and make peace with what the boy had been feeling for years, or watching Colin respond to his own commands with perfection and facility—something the majority of the soldiers under his command had never demonstrated, except for the rare occasion. Balls-out bravery and heart—none of the boys he'd commanded had ever lacked that or the power to seize leadership and race for victory. But this deeply personal level of deference and attentiveness was something he'd never seen in a soldier. Not until Colin.

At least, he thought, double-checking Jackson's schedule, it wasn't interfering in with his and Jackson's relationship. Jackson's plentiful flaws seemed almost endearing to Beau at times now—and the sex was damn good. Jackson demonstrated unusually high need, feeling insecurity about what Beau was training Colin to do—and Beau was feeling particularly driven to embrace *his* boy, his boy who was less than perfect, his boy whose feelings ran so deep, his boy who never could quite obey an order completely or quietly.

Beau shook his head. Enough.

Colin was silent on his feet. Beau picked up the movement visually, just barely in the dim evening light. There was the slightest hesitation as the boy crossed over the visual boundary of his so-called office in the big bay window, where plain hardwood gave way to parquet floors. The big plantation house his grandfather had once shown him had parquet floors—the house where Beau's family originally served.

The boy flowed down to his knees, and Beau saw the hesitation that meant Colin was trying not to look up at him expectantly.

"Think of it this way, boy. You're on your knees—you've just asked me for instruction without words—and you must trust me to provide orders. Wordlessly, without motion. Do you understand?"

"Yes, sir." The modulation of his voice was such a contrast to what Beau was used to—they'd had 18 months of whining and bitching and timidity and tears, but now... Beau liked what he heard. Colin was quiet without being mousy, and spoke clearly.

Beau hesitated, then came around to the front of the desk, turning a visitor's chair around to face the boy, butting the back of it against his desk so he might keep as much distance as possible. He didn't need the boy—or anyone else—getting the wrong idea. He'd kept Jackson informed, but so far, his boy had kept himself away during appointed lesson hours.

"We are going to discuss something I cannot teach you. You may speak and ask questions, but you must maintain your physical position. You must remain calm and keep your voice even. I'll accept politely phrased questions. Do you understand?"

"Yes, sir."

"Sex." Beau was blunt. "Slavery, in most households, involves sex. I want you to take a moment to consider serving another person—male *or* female—sexually. Do not speak. Think."

He folded his hands over his knee and watched. There was a distinct and nearly violent blush—but the boy clearly turned his attention inward, rather than give way to one of his old outbursts. Beau contemplated the change, as he waited, setting aside the initial appreciation of the transformation, bringing himself to be ready to be firm.

The boy shied away from him a little, and Beau frowned at the new reaction.

"Colin. I'll give you this one, that's a big subject. You must hold your position, boy."

"I—I need—"

"Go on, boy. You have permission to speak and ask questions. That's one, by the way, for forgetting an order."

The boy's shoulders relaxed. Those shocking blue eyes came up to meet his and then dropped down at Beau's slight frown.

"I understand what you're saying, sir. I'll be a slave, if they want me. I won't have choices. I could be... used, sexually."

"That's correct. Go on."

"I can't... " The boy swallowed painfully, and Beau could see the first response he trained into all his boys, slave material or not, asserting itself. Always truthful. And the boy repeated that now. "*Semper veritatem*. I have read about being used that way, sir, and I find it... arousing."

He could see the evidence of this on the boy, and that, if slightly distasteful for Beau himself, was extremely encouraging.

"You recognize that your master, male or female, may use you sexually in any manner that pleases them, so long as it does not cause permanent physical harm to your body."

"Yes, sir, I recognize that I will be used," Colin said, dropping his eyes in a way that Beau found endearing, naked body or not.

"You must also recognize that your master may loan you to other males or females, for sexual use."

Another reaction of shock—and a little of those starry eyes he had grown accustomed to seeing lately. A good sign, then. He pushed his own distaste for the subject further back.

"You must be clear, beyond a shadow of a doubt, boy. I will not use you sexually. No one under this roof or any other under my control will use you thus. Do you understand?"

"Sir, yes sir," Colin said, nodding. "You and Jackson are monogamous, I understand. It's nice."

"I did not ask for your opinion," Beau said. "I asked for your comprehension. That's a second error. I suggest not making a third."

"Sir, yes sir. You're monogamous, you're not going to ask me to do anything sexual, is that right?" The boy quivered with what looked like a great deal like relief.

"Correct, boy. The same will not be true of an owner. And, boy—you will show me what you've read or been reading. I can't speak to the sexual practices that go on among masters. Likely what I've seen doesn't even scratch the surface—but I can direct you to further reading, if necessary."

"I—" The boy faltered and blushed. "You really want to see?"

"I insist on seeing," Beau said, trying not to do it gently but really finding himself incapable of invading someone's intimate privacy in that way. "Colin."

"I... " Colin flushed. "They're all packed into my kit, sir. I—I know they're contraband, you didn't see them, but—"

"Fetch it."

"I'm sorry?"

This time on the third error Beau rose, yanking the boy to his feet. Six heavy-handed swats brought Colin's naked ass into a brilliant flush, and Beau held him at arm's length. "Fetch. It."

"Yessir," Colin managed and waited for Beau's grip to loosen before he fled entirely.

Fortunately for the boy, he was back quickly and knelt with the box in precisely the same spot Beau had placed him in at the beginning of this little exercise. He yanked Colin up, bent him over one of the hardback chairs, and paddled him briskly and efficiently. The boy recovered, wincing, but managed not to react audibly when

Beau sat him down on it, appreciating the flinch of a boy who had to sit on a hard surface with a well-paddled ass.

It was the typical literature, Beau reflected, looking over the ammo box which the boy had emptied of his personal odds and ends to fill it with the books. *The Beauty Trilogy. The Story of O, Screw the Roses.* The boy had the bottoming book but not the topping book, Beau observed, repressing a snort. And then there was a substantial stack of what he knew were fanzines, which Jackson had blushingly and embarrassedly introduced him to a few years ago, leading to some spectacular sexual escapades in their own bed—

He smacked a hand on the end of the crate and saw the boy jump, as if his own butt had been once more smacked.

"This is forbidden, as you well know. I'll need to think over whether there'll be discipline for this or not, boy. It is contraband in this house—but too, I know up until a few weeks ago, you weren't getting what you needed—"

"It helped," the boy mumbled. "Sir. Grantian at the club gave most of that to me. Said to pass it on when I got the chance."

"Grantian, eh?"

The bartender. The one person he'd talked to about Colin's situation six months ago, feeling down and frustrated. Grantian had a large network of contacts but hadn't at the time been able to come up with any concrete solution, though Beau remembered a distant look about the man's eyes.

"Yes, sir," the boy said, cringing. "I mean, you said as it was okay to borrow books from the library and such, and... "

"Lord love a liar." Beau grew grim. "That's enough. Back to the conversation. Let's get down and dirty, boy. I don't much know what to tell you, beyond what I have. Now I want to know if you have questions."

"I... you said if you're right, there's someone who could... who could train me to do what I... what I've been dreaming about."

"Fantasizing about. Unless you've been lying about your dreams at night," Beau asked, a brow rising like a stretchy caterpillar.

"No, sir! Fan... fantasizing. Yes. There's someone?"

"Yes. We'll go at the weekend. Tessa will travel with us, but she won't be present for the interview. So I've got a challenge for you, then. You don't touch yourself, you don't bring yourself off, between now and then—until the door closes on that interview. Understood?"

"Understood," the boy said, flushing and glancing down at the definite erection. "I don't really have any questions, either. I—I mean, I don't mean to be rude, but you—I don't know if you could answer them, and I don't want to make you uncomfortable, sir, please?"

"I appreciate the consideration, boy. Now. I've got a task for you. You'll note the blinds are all closed, we need a sense of propriety in this neighborhood. You're behind on your household chores, boy. And so is Jackson. So tonight, I'm going to leave in a half hour here, and you've got until Jackson's curfew to do your chores and his, without leaving the house—and without clothing. Understood?"

It took the boy a moment to whisper his answer. "Understood, sir."

"Excellent. Now, get your sorry hide upstairs, and lay out my best pair of black pants, a white T-shirt, and my black leather vest. Try to think like a valet. I'm going to answer some correspondence here, and then go up to shave and change, before I go."

The boy nearly saluted but caught himself and went to his knees again, just as gracefully, bowing his head and waiting, no sign of hesitation or impatience.

Beau managed by some miracle not to startle, when he'd stripped down to an undershirt and boxers, and went to shave. There was the boy in the bathroom, on his knees, holding the tray of Beau's shaving articles, at a precise four inches higher than the counter—and exactly at the height that would make it truly comfortable for Beau to handle the contents of the tray, rather than leaning slightly down to the counter.

He steeled himself and shaved without comment, exiting the room without a word, listening to the sigh, which sounded remarkably like a sigh of relief. His clothing wasn't laid out perfectly—but it was so damn close, he had to let it pass. He needed the hell out of the house.

* * *

"Beau," the boy whispered, as they went up the walk. The brownstone row loomed above them, and Beau tried not to smile.

"Do as you're told, Colin. That's all you need to do. You'll be just fine, boy. And remember, this is an evaluation, not a guarantee. She's agreed to consider, not accept."

"Yes, sir."

He appreciated the care and deference as the boy's attention turned to supporting him up the steep steps of the old brownstone. Beau's gait on stairs was still unsteady when he was stiff, and the flight had been murderous. Shaking his head, Beau hit the doorbell once, and it opened a moment later to reveal a familiar face.

"Parker," he said, pleased. "It's good to see you."

Chris' dark head inclined. "Colonel Riordan. Thank you, please, come inside. Anderson's had to take a call, I'm happy to show you to the parlor in the meantime."

"Thank you. Parker, this is Colin Fyveson. Colin, you're to obey Parker as you would obey me."

"Yes, sir," the boy murmured, glancing up at Chris and nodding, but not saying more.

"You'll find the chair by the fire the most comfortable, Colonel," Parker said, and Beau could see Colin subtly watching Parker. Not that it would get him anywhere, and Beau was certain it wouldn't pass Parker's notice.

Beau nodded as he accepted the seat, watching to see if Parker would relax at all or continue to stand nearly at attention—civilian attention, he thought fondly. Parker was beautifully attentive and oriented, but there was something lacking, he mused, taking a seat. Whatever it was, it was elusive. Colin sank with extreme grace to his knees next to Beau, and the Colonel had to work to repress the pervasive feeling of negative rejection that brought to him. The boy needed this, whether Beau liked the need or not.

Parker smiled faintly at Beau, and the older man just shook his head. "Parker. Not where I expected to see you. Understand you're training, these days."

It wasn't quite a blink, but Beau felt satisfied by the involuntary motion, slight as it was.

"That's true, sir. Secondary to Anderson, of course."

Beau chuckled, an evil edge to it that brought out goose bumps on Colin's exposed arms. "Well, it increases my confidence that Colin here will get what he needs."

Colin didn't move, though Beau detected a slight tilt of the boy's head, which meant he was listening with every fiber of his being. Beau himself didn't like the submissiveness, but that little quirk he'd always appreciated. Parker's expression changed, ever so fractionally.

"I should have expected you would do some spotting on occasion, Colonel. The twins attended The Academy a few months back, it was a pleasure to interview them."

Beau shook his head, though he chuckled. "I never could figure what they wanted with this," he said with a wave of his hand.

"Clearly, a sense of stability and a place of belonging," came the sultry female voice from the doorway. Beau observed Colin didn't move, though his attention clearly shifted.

"To each their own, Anderson. To each their own," Beau commented as he rose from his chair. The boy rose with him, eyes downcast.

"Is this the boy?"

"Yes—"

"No, no introductions, I had Parker start a file. Frankly I think you've got a little boy who needs to be spanked six ways to Sunday, Beau, but I'll give you the benefit of the doubt. Are you leaving him with me?"

"That is my intention, if it suits. Colin, you're to obey Trainer Anderson as you would myself." It was hard to ignore the request that denied the formal introductions he was used to, but he managed.

"Yes, sir. Yes, ma'am," the boy offered.

Anderson snapped her fingers. "Come here, boy. Present!"

The boy went down to his knees again, grace in submission, and directed his clear blue eyes up to Anderson's face. Beau felt an odd wash of relief at that and checked Parker's expression. The younger trainer's demeanor barely changed, though it grew more intense as they waited, the boy at attention.

"Well, well, Colonel Riordan," Anderson said. "Strip, boy," she commanded next. Beau sighed, but the boy's hands went to his button-down shirt and then his pants, stripping off underwear and socks, having left his shoes at the door. Beau had been provided with leather house slippers, but the boy had nothing.

The Trainer strolled around him, trailing a finger along the boy's shoulders. She seemed impressed he hadn't flinched. Beau hadn't expected him to. Colin had never had the sort of 1,000-yard stare a traumatized youth might have, either. The set of strap marks on his behind from the hotel were vivid, still colored to a nice shade of red.

"Does his cock work," Anderson inquired, and Beau grimaced at her, at the vulgarity of it. She seemed amused by his discomfort.

"Yes. Anderson—"

She held up a hand, still strolling around the would-be slave, considering. "Parker. Take him out and test him. I might consider keeping him, if he can maintain an erection and manage not to lose control under such duress."

"Yes, Trainer Anderson." Chris bowed. "Colonel Riordan," he said with another bow. Then he snapped his fingers. "Follow." The boy hesitated, with a glance at Anderson, but obeyed.

Anderson chuckled, when the door closed behind them. "Beauregard."

"Imala."

She softened, momentarily. "I believe you. What I'm having trouble believing is that you managed the preliminary training."

Beau shrugged, grimacing. "I know enough about it, Imala. And after two years... it's clear what that boy needs. Whether he needs the proper environment or an excellent fantasy environment—that I need to leave up to you."

"I understand." Her voice carried some compassion, in this. "This can't have been easy."

"No. Parker's likely to find him lacking—the boy's only got the literature for bedroom references. I'm not willing to go there, Imala, and I refuse to invite someone into such a private situation as the halfway house to give him the training."

"I'm not criticizing, Beau. Parker knows how to evaluate a slave, inexperienced or highly skilled. Your boy's pretty enough and graceful enough to work. I'd take him on that alone, given I know you don't train. I'm experiencing something akin to shock, actually. You've given me some lovely spotting tips before, after the twins demonstrated their need and success for you. But you've never, ever trained someone to *that* level, Beauregard. Explain."

"Imala. It was just... it was plain. I've never coached a boy for this long, never. Eighteen months that boy went with me, with the discipline becoming increasingly severe. It was pushing boundaries I don't care to cross, as a mentor. I remembered my own family and thought of the twins... So I began to test him. I spent months testing him, to be damn sure it was what he needed, and then more time with the training—for God's sake don't expect him to have all the basics. I did what I could."

"Beau, it is all right. Parker will return—we will train your boy, help him find his place. You know this."

His shoulders sagged, just for a moment. "Even from that brief glimpse."

"Even from that brief glimpse—that, the phone call, and the correspondence. I appreciate the file—it's not a standard Marketplace file—"

"I didn't mean it to be. That's an official copy of his Pickett Ridge file, with the additional notes from the last two months, after we closed the halfway file."

A young woman ghosted into the room with a tea tray, placing the silver and teak on the table between Imala and Beau. He watched with amusement as she poured two cups, adding a single sugar and a dash of cream, just as he preferred, and handing the cup to him.

"Thank you," he acknowledged. She inclined her head prettily, with a faint blush, and then turned to pour a second cup, which she handed to Imala. Anderson tisedd. "Parker is with a client, girl. Report yourself to him afterward."

"Yes, ma'am," the young woman said and hurried out of the room.

"Imala—"

"No. My household, my rules. She's training, Beauregard. And that's a behavior we don't want to see, not in this case. Perhaps if you'd dandled her on your knee and gotten her wet—"

"Enough." Beau sighed. "Please."

"Only for you."

They sat for a long while together, sipping at tea, until her attention turned to the doorway, even before it was filled with Beau's young charge and Parker. "Present."

Parker followed Colin inside. The young marine sank to his knees no less gracefully than before, though there were tear marks streaking his face. Beau tried not to sigh, thinking of what had likely put them there. But Colin knelt and looked up to her, just as she'd ordered. He was sporting another set of strap marks—and Beau turned slightly away, realizing the boy's cock was rock hard.

"Parker, join us," Imala invited, and a moment later, the girl was back, pouring and handing Parker a cup. Beau could see the minute hesitation, but she was quick. Parker's eyes went to Imala afterward.

She nodded, and Parker sighed, shaking his head.

"Beauregard, I thought your partner had traveled with you?" Imala's inquiry was a welcome distraction from the boy.

"Yes. He's with my daughter, visiting two of my boys who live locally."

"Really? Now who are they?"

"James Riordan and Stephen Allan."

"Parker?"

Beau repressed a twitch, realizing she was still baiting him, and refusing to give in to her eloquent pressures.

Parker coughed. "I've been introduced to them, ma'am. With intent," the young trainer suggested, and finally Beau felt his worry lift as he laughed aloud.

"I know what that means, Parker, and the two of them aren't Marketplace material."

Chris grinned. "I could see that, sir. They're well-respected in the community, I only have good things to tell you."

"As it should be." However, that was not the deterrent Beau had hoped for, in the face of Imala's keen eyes.

"Beauregard Riordan. Your *daughter* is here?"

"Yes, my daughter is here." He kept his voice even. "She's close with the boys."

"Your daughter, of whom you never speak."

"Imala."

"So not estranged, but protective. I wonder why that is," she said playfully. Beau saw Parker glance between the two of them and tense.

"Her involvement in the lifestyle is not up for discussion," Beau said, and Imala blinked.

"In the lifestyle. Beauregard. I wasn't aware of that."

Around the corner came a young man, bearing three glasses of amber liquid and a decanter on a tray, and conversation stilled. Beau tossed what he was handed back, only to have the young man pour a second, larger drink for him and vanish.

His hand tightened into a fist, where it rested on the chair. "Imala."

She just smiled, and Beau saw Parker cast his eyes down.

It was that which decided him. "Yes," he said. "Against my wishes, against my advice. And no, I don't love her any less for it. I learned to support it. She's skilled in her own right, Imala. She's... she's nothing to do with all of this." He waved a hand at the room, including Parker and the Master Trainer in the gesture.

"Beau—" Imala leaned slightly forward, lifting one hand, but Beau wasn't going to stop for that.

"She's still mourning her—dammit. Her fiancé. Should have been her husband. Killed in action in Grenada. Together eight years. They played together. Taught some... "

"Beauregard."

"You wanted to know," Beau said, staring at her. Imala winced, looking away. Parker could have been ornamentation for the room, as still as he was.

"I did," she said finally. "Is she aware of the Marketplace?"

"She is. In confidence."

"Beauregard—"

"She's a Major in the goddamn United States Army. Knows the twins." Another look of shock crossed Imala's face, and Beau saw her pale a little.

"Beauregard Riordan. You'll bring her by, at the end of the week, for supper. And your partner. Consider it one of the conditions of the evaluation for your boy." She smiled slowly, recovering her color along with her command of the situation. "After all, if you're going to train quality merchandise for me, I need to know you better. Parker, take the boy upstairs to his room, and explain the house rules but nothing more. Beau will look in on him before he leaves."

"Yes, ma'am," Parker replied with a bow. A second short bow was addressed to Beau as well. Then he gripped the boy's arm, who gave no flinch, only an attentive look. "With me," he commanded, and Colin rose and trailed him out of the room.

* * *

The door was answered by the same obsequious slave who had poured the scotch, earlier in the week.

"Colonel Riordan, Anderson is waiting for you in the parlor."

His daughter watched as the slave spirited away their coats. "Very nice," she murmured to Beau. He nodded and checked Jackson, who simply looked interested. Good. They'd had a long conversation about this, and after months of worrying, he finally felt Jackson had some understanding of the situation where slaves and the Marketplace were concerned.

Anderson and Parker both rose when they entered the room. Their greetings were warm, and he thought perhaps he needn't have worried. It would be fine. There was no sign of Colin.

"May I present my daughter, Major Theresa Riordan," he said, hearing her murmur she preferred Tess. "And my partner, Jackson Ross."

"A Navy man," Parker commented, and a smile bloomed atop Jackson's solemn expression.

He nodded to Parker. "Yes. Ten years," he offered.

"Jackson was wounded in the Gulf," Beau said quietly, glancing at his boy, and noticing the Navy pin on the lapel of Jackson's suit jacket, in the same place he wore his own USMC pin.

"Well. I thank you for your service," Anderson said, inclining her head. "All of you."

Jackson shifted, clearly a little nervous. "Did you serve, Mr. Parker?"

"Not in the military," Chris said with a little smile. "My older brother did, however."

Jackson gave the man a nod and seated himself when Chris gestured. Anderson neatly turned the conversation away from the military, complimenting Tess on the stunning dress she wore. It shimmered as she moved, midnight silk clinging to the curves of her body and flaring out into a fuller skirt than was popular.

Tess smiled. "Thank you. It's such a pleasure to be here. I was very appreciative of Father's suggestion that I join him."

Port was served all round, though Jackson quietly refused the server. Beau watched subtly as Parker refused as well, with no seeming reluctance, though he'd never seen Parker turn down alcohol before. Interesting. As he expected, Jackson relaxed enough to actually chatter a little with Parker, who was at his most charming.

* * *

It was Parker who led Tess and Jackson back to the parlor after supper. "I'm sorry to separate you from Beau, but Anderson needs to speak with Beau privately, regarding Colin."

"I don't suppose you might say whether he's been accepted or not?" Tess asked.

Chris nodded. "I obtained permission from Anderson. Yes, we'll take him on."

Tess glanced at Jackson, who shifted in his chair. "Mr. Parker—"

"Chris, please."

"Chris. Both Jackson and I have met the twins, of course—Beau is closest to those two of all his siblings. We're aware of the Marketplace. But perhaps, if you would be so kind, explain a bit more for us?"

Chris looked thoughtful for several moments and then finally nodded. "Of course. What would you like to know?"

"If we might focus on Colin, I suspect it might allay many of Jackson's concerns, as well as mine."

"The answer is yes," Chris said. He watched the dark-haired woman, returning the intensity of her gaze as he observed her.

"And?" Tess arched an eyebrow, expressing no amusement at Chris's obvious discomfort. She had seemed no more than your usual wary military personnel, observant and calm, throughout supper. But this, this was something more. This was a hint of what Beau had mentioned.

Jackson coughed, and Chris had to suppress a grin. For Tess didn't flinch, didn't turn her gaze away.

"The Colonel was right to bring him here," Chris said. "He has a lot of work to do, but he is demonstrating his willingness to do so and has shown no fear."

"He was really nervous," Jackson interjected. "I'd really like to see him?"

"You will," Chris reassured. "Anderson is discussing the finer points with Beau right now, and then they'll call Colin in. Anderson will tell him he needs to choose, whether he stays or goes. Once he's made his decision, your father, the Trainer and the boy will come in here. If he isn't with them, I will let Anderson know you wish to see him. If he is with them, he'll be obeying Anderson's commands alone, though he is required to show no less respect to the Colonel— or either of you."

68

Tess took a moment before she spoke. "I would like further details." Chris drew a breath to carefully phrase a denial. "I am perfectly aware you are unable to give them—at this time," the woman said, standing and striding over to the fire, staring into it for a moment before she turned, and her attention returned to Chris. "Father will provide me with details about Colin. I personally want more information about the Marketplace, and how, aside from yourself and Anderson, I might contact a representative of the Marketplace, particularly on the West coast."

"*Tess*," Jackson burst out. "Beau said he didn't want you to have anything—" His words cut off abruptly. Tess had done nothing more than snap her fingers once, her attention still focused on Parker. "My apologies, ma'am, sir."

"Thank you. I am aware of my father's opinions—and I happen to agree with them. I am not interested in becoming a part of the Marketplace in any capacity."

Parker stared at her, clearly out of his comfort zone. He sipped his port and recovered, inquiring, "Might I know your purpose in desiring this information, ma'am?" Beau was one of Anderson's oldest friends. A whistleblower would ruin that comfortable friendship, and—

"I'm a nurse in the Army our United States so kindly deigns to put forth in any battlefield. I see a great many young men and young women. They're often baffled and confused—my father has a fantastic system for straightening that out. I don't refer all of them to my father," Tess said. "And I would like a contact."

"I will find you one personally, ma'am," he told her, his face clearing. "I understand."

"You don't," Tess retorted. "But you might after you've seen a few of what I'd like to send that way."

"Of course—"

* * *

"Colonel," Jackson said as he rose, though Tess and Chris were a hair late for managing the same gesture.

Colin was not with them.

Any respect Jackson had demonstrated faded as he turned to

69

Beau. "I thought you said," he began, sounding hostile and accusing. The Colonel landed two strong swats on Jackson's backside, the sound ringing in the room. Parker was watching Tess, though, which Beau found amusing. His daughter hadn't blinked, of course, and Parker was obviously intrigued.

"Mind your manners," Beau told him. "Now sit down. Thirty-second moratorium on any thoughts going through that head of yours. Tessa?" His question finally broke the intense eye contact between Tess and Chris.

"How is Colin, sir?"

Anderson laughed aloud. "Beauregard, your daughter is a delight, and shame on you for not introducing her ages ago."

Tess flinched slightly but shifted her attention to Anderson, who inclined her head after a moment, with a nod.

"Colin is content. He'll be along in a few moments, he needed time to compose himself."

Parker's lips twitched with what might have been a smile as Tess and Jackson both rolled their eyes in perfect synchronicity.

Which was of course, the moment Colin darkened the doorway, going straight across the room to Anderson and dropping heavily to his knees.

"A correction," she said, brushing the end of his nose. "You're more graceful than that. Do it properly."

The boy rose again, and this time knelt smoothly. Jackson had looked aside, though after a moment he squinted at Colin, who was now wearing a locked collar.

The obsequious blond boy who had served the meal and attended to drinks ghosted into the room, handing Imala a folded paper. She raised an eyebrow but glanced at it.

"If you will excuse me? This is something in the nature of an emergency—"

"Of course, Imala," Beau rumbled.

"Parker, stay here. Colin, you may take this time under Parker's supervision to say your farewells. Parker will tell me how well you've done."

"Thank you, ma'am," Colin responded, eyes shining. He remained kneeling until Imala left the room, and then he glanced up, clearly a little doubting and confused, at Parker.

"Go ahead," Parker said, almost gently. He glanced up at the others. "If you will forgive me, and if Colin will forgive the break in protocol, this is a training opportunity I wish to take advantage of." At the landslide of nods, he turned back to Colin. "You will make each person comfortable with your presence. Show me how you would do that, as you thank them. You need not adhere to formal words or actions at this time."

"Yes, sir. Thank you, sir," Colin responded and rose, turning to the rest of the room. He perched on the edge of a chair next to Jackson. "You've been just that patient with me—"

"The fuck I have!"

Beau twitched strongly in Jackson's direction, but the man didn't say a word, just redirected his attention to Parker, asking a question.

"You have," Colin said to Jackson. "I know you and I are different people, with different needs, and I really want you to know this is truly like coming home, to comfort food and a soft bed."

"You won't get either of those."

"I know, and I value that."

"I just don't understand—and I want—I want you to be safe." Jackson choked.

"I am safe," Colin said, trying not to reach for Jackson's hand.

"You want it," Jackson asked, holding his own hand out.

"I do," Colin said, taking it and cradling it with extreme gentleness. "You held my hand the first nights I slept in Pickett Ridge, when I was so afraid I wouldn't make it through."

Beau twitched again—he had not been aware of that fact until now.

"I did. And I want to keep doing it—but I can't, with you here, and the things—"

"You can't, while I'm here," Colin repeated. "But," the boy said. "I have every small thing you have ever given me, to remind me of you. Because of you, I know when you think you can't possibly try any harder or push any further, it is still possible to do so. And this isn't exile. A slave still has a life, beyond service—that's not a good way of putting it," he said, responding to a sharp motion from Parker. "I will be allowed to send and receive correspondence through the mail. I would like it, if you're willing."

"I can," Jackson said. "But my handwriting sucks."

71

"I don't need someone who's perfect," Colin reminded. "I need someone—"

"Who's practical and can see through you like an awkward pane of glass," Jackson finished. "I promise."

"Thank you," Colin said, squeezing the hand he held before let go. His attention turned then to Tess.

"Ma'am," he said, inclining his head. "I want to thank you for your counsel and your patience."

Tess raised an eyebrow and made eye contact with Beau, who nodded. "Parker," Beau rumbled.

No one quite had time to blink before Colin was bent under Parker's arm, receiving a series of painful corrections with the shiny leather strap Parker carried.

"Sir! This—"

"No," Parker said. "You have an order to obey, now obey it."

Colin sank down on his knees at Tess' side. He shuddered a little. "I am afraid of you, yet I trust you. I would serve you in any way you asked, to honor the Colonel." His eyes were buttoned closed, clearly not wanting to look at Tess.

"Well," Tess replied, in a pitch that carried through the whole room. "That's extremely satisfying. You have a nice hand, Parker," Tess said. "Colin, I'll expect you to keep up your correspondence as well. Now go on, speak to Beau."

"Yes ma'am—and thank you," he said, flushing a little, before he turned to Beau, his eyes pleading, which Beau ignored. He hovered for a moment next to the Colonel and then reached his hands out. Beau raised an eyebrow but took them as the boy settled himself on Beau's lap. The older man chuckled and pulled Colin in.

"Well. Here we are, boy."

He leaned back on Beau's shoulder. "Thank you," he whispered. "You're the only person who knows me."

"For now," Beau told him, surprisingly gentle. "There will be others," he said with a glance at Parker. "Now, little boy, you go on. This is what you need, and my daughter put it very well when she suggested you keep up on your correspondence. I'll expect that."

"Thank you," Colin whispered. He kissed the old man's cheek, rising ,then kneeling before Parker.

"Go upstairs, and unpack the suitcase onto your blanket. I will go through everything and determine what you are allowed to keep while training, and anything forbidden will go into storage."

"Yes, Chris," the boy said and bowed just slightly, exiting the room.

Jackson shifted in discomfort.

"It's a hunger, Mr. Ross," Chris said, leaning heavily on the words, and the intensity of his gaze would not let Jackson look away, to Beau's amusement and, apparently, to his daughter's as well. "It's something needed from within. People grow ill when their deepest needs are denied. In the last months, has Colin been steadier, more settled, perhaps happier, if you will?"

Jackson's intense gaze dropped to the floor. "Yes, sir."

Parker snorted. "Not to you, I'm not. Colonel Riordan, he's reminded me I wished to offer you access to some training materials."

"Parker, I'm not that interested in training—or even spotting."

"I understand," Parker said. "But I believe there is need."

The Colonel raised an eyebrow, and Parker looked down, taking a small step backward. Imala laughed from the doorway. "You certainly have the touch, Beauregard. And Mistress Tess as well."

Tess's head came up, and she gave Imala a slow smile. Beau looked at both women sharply, but let it pass.

"Well. I'm very pleased," Imala said. "How often does one acquire a quality slave trainee, and a pair of spotters, and who knows what else in one day?" The smile on her face rivaled a cat's in a creamery, and Beau threw back his head and laughed, knowing his boy was finally home.

73

Blind Emotions
by Kimiko Alexandre

Jessica glided through the hotel's circulating door with the ease and grace of a high-class attorney. The cool air of the lobby hit her face, a transition from the world outside. The deep-blue, three-inch heels, which matched the color of the pseudo-kimono with its gold lame dragons, clicked with surety, echoing slightly on the marble entryway. The lithe curves of her calves were bare, all the way up to an inch above her knees where the dress ended and a slit betrayed the beginning of her left thigh.

Her soft waves of dark brown hair were up in a stylish bun, wisps artfully arranged around her bare neck and equally bare ears. Her make-up was understated. She'd given a touch of black eye-liner to rim blue eyes made more vibrant thanks to her choice of fabric, a touch of peach to accentuate already slightly flushed cheeks, and red matte lipstick that helped form a bow under a button nose.

The clutch matched the outfit and was held lightly in her hand. She gave it the gentlest of squeezes to remind herself of the key card that had been delivered to her modest apartment earlier. The lightness of it and her keys made her think of the phone that still sat next to her bed, reinforcing she had only a few minutes to commit to an opportunity no one else knew about. This wasn't a casting call that could leave her, at its least, horrified at a sexual outcome and at its most, dead on a hotel room floor. No, this rare chance probably included everything but death. A chance that could lead, if she was very, very lucky, to be put up for sale, as human property. Some would think she was crazy for being here like this, everyone but a few... who got it.

Her clicking heels came to a stop in front of the gold-trimmed elevator doors and she pressed the button to go up. The hum of people was a constant in her head she tried to tune out. She needed to get herself together if she expected the evening to go well. Jessica absent-mindedly reached up to touch a gold-linked chain, her fingers curling an inch away from her skin when she remembered that it wasn't there anymore. It had been a plaything, really. A toy. But a toy that gave her cause to seek out the real thing. She swallowed almost painfully in memory and used it as an excuse to lift her head a tad higher. Toy or not, it had meant something.

As she waited, a woman sitting at the lobby bar gave a high-pitched, false laugh. Jessica could tell it masked a budding anger. "He thinks I'm a hooker!" She heard the woman's thoughts in her mind. A look at the pair and Jessica knew. The man was drunk and the woman was there hoping to catch a millionaire. What most people would catch through body language, Jessica got through her ability to sense emotions and thoughts.

The ding of the elevator's arrival cut through the thoughts the woman had caused to swirl in Jessica's head. The doors opened to the mirrored car, giving her a last chance to make sure she was dressed appropriately.

Pressing the button for the 11th floor, she stepped back and allowed herself a steadying sigh that flared her nostrils. She was happy to be in the tiny box, alone with her thoughts for the brief ride up, and she took that moment to close her eyes and allow her doubts a final shudder down her body. When the car stopped, she raised her head, opened her eyes and stepped forth confidently when the doors opened. The walk down the hallway, however, was less pleasant.

Wisps of emotion floated through the doors she passed, like one hideous mixture of perfume. She'd gotten good at tuning out the voices that followed the emotions, but when her nerves were this ratcheted and the stakes so high, others' emotions came on stronger. It was just a tad harder to stay out of people's heads. It was something that might make or break her.

Even more than her desire to do this, to be property, her psychic talent was a closely guarded secret. If most people could not understand her desire to submit, fewer could understand how she could *hear* others all the time.

Focus. Snapping open the clutch, she took out the flimsy credit card-like key. She didn't even allow herself a stop for composure as she slid it into the correct door and walked in. She'd felt the spotter's feelings steps from the door and knew it wouldn't be wise to hesitate.

Agitation. Boredom. Amusement. Lust. Dominance.

She took it in like wine, swirling the mixture in her head to a moderate level. The butterflies in her stomach gave her something to focus on, to help block out the surrounding sensations. As she entered and closed the door, it swished behind her with an audible click. She saw him in the hotel's mirror. The practiced smile that came to her lips wasn't entirely false. He was handsome, and she didn't need to read his emotions to feel the dominance he exuded, even in that one brief look. She repressed a shudder of excitement.

Jessica walked further into the room and came to a stop, stood still, and her hands instinctively went to her back as she had been trained. She took in the small suite he'd rented while he kept her there waiting. The room allowed for more then the usual narrow alleyways that typical hotel room furniture required. This one had a desk and an entertainment center that played part-dresser.

The man sitting in the plush chair across the room, the king-sized bed a barrier between them, looked her over as she expected. Her position gave him a full view of her. He set a piece of paper down on a side table. Having not looked him in the eye, she had a chance to see that it was her headshot.

Approval. Lust. Curiosity.

"Jessica." He stood up, walking around the bed toward her.

"Sir." She was proud that the word came without a warble. She stayed out of his mind out of respect. That faux pas had been beaten into her long ago.

"I don't like wasting time, so let's be blunt." His voice was deep and touchable. She imagined feeling the purr of it from his lips as he whispered into her ear. That was a heady fantasy. He walked around her, taking his time. The lust from him flared, and she had to still her face to keep from showing she knew. "This isn't going to be a test of 'what I had for breakfast' or 'what my favorite color is.' Your application states you have a proficiency in empathy and clairaudience. Useful, but I'm curious how far reaching those abilities can go." He came to a stop in front of her, his polished dress shoes, crisp forest green pants, and black belt the only things in her view.

He reached out a hand and, with the lightness of holding a bird, lifted her chin, then let it float back down. She kept her head where he had placed it but kept her eyes cast downward—again as she had been trained. His hand was warm and sent tingles through Jessica's chest. "You can look."

She lifted her gaze and met green eyes that matched his pants. Jessica didn't need her gifts to see the desire in them. He was her height, with the added inches of the heels, 5'7". He had a well-muscled but not overdone frame. His hair was just this side of holding curls, a chocolate brown. He'd rolled up the sleeves of his white dress shirt, and the tie kept with the monochrome theme.

"Put your clutch down." His voice was as delicious as a thick pile rug. It was commanding without having to be loud. Jessica reached out and set it down on the dresser near them. Her hands went back in place. The urge to fidget ran through her under his microscopic gaze.

She felt his curiosity deepen, "Turn around and place your hands in front of you." With a tip of her head, Jessica acknowledged his order and then did as he bid. Goosebumps raised the hairs on her arms when he drew a light line along the flesh of her exposed neck. She managed to stay still, without gasping, but knew her shoulders betrayed her, rising of their own accord. It was a sweet spot. Jessica allowed her eyes to close for just a moment at the wondrous sensation.

"Feelings," came his crisp voice. She knew he was asking about his. They were beginning the test, and Jessica pulled on all the resources she'd taught herself at the hands of the men and women at clubs she had frequented. In truth, the tests had started as soon as Jessica entered the room.

She answered with a level voice, "Intrigue. Curiosity. Amusement. Dominance"—then grinned knowing it traveled in her voice—"Lust, Sir."

As he spoke, his finger inched down the spine of the cloth stopping at the golden sash. Her tongue darted out to lick her lips, and she swallowed. "Call me *Sir* at appropriate intervals," he ordered, curtly. Then the questions came in rapid succession, as she dipped her head, again to acknowledge him.

"Yours or mine?"

"Yours."

"You said intrigue and curiosity. That's the same thing."

"Not in this case, Sir."

"Why not?"

"I believe the intrigue refers to your interest in me as a person. The curiosity would probably count as to my answers to your questions and actions."

"Believe or know?"

"Believe."

"Why don't you know?" She felt him tug on the golden bow that held her dress together.

"It's impolite to delve into someone's thoughts without permission," She let her arms fall to her side as the dress gaped open and the sash slid from her waist.

Approval. Impatience. Lust.

Jessica smiled before a sliver of fear sliced through her brain feeling the impatience. *Calm down, you know there are different reasons for feelings. You're letting your emotions get in the way.*

His warm fingers slid into the collar, and the material slipped from her shoulders to land at her feet.

"What if your owner told you to monitor other's thoughts?"

"His orders would override anyone else's permission." She shivered but not from the chill in the air.

The back of his nails slid down her skin. She was naked except for the black thong and blue heels. She knew he was trying to distract her. "It must be nice to know when you are pleasing your dominant," he mused. It hadn't been a question, so she didn't answer.

His nails raked back up to her hairline, thin slices of pain. This time a gasp came unbidden.

Amusement. Aggression. Pleasure. Lust.

"Are you a masochist, Jessica?"

"At times, Sir."

"And what times would those be?" amusement slid through his voice.

"Sometimes, I just feel pleasure from it. I don't know why that is. Sometimes, I can feed off the top's emotions." The sting was starting to fade from the lines he'd made.

He chuckled, "Ah, so you're a psychic vampire." He walked around to face her.

She looked him in the eye. "If that is what you'd like to call it, Sir." Her voice lowered. She tried hard to school her mouth from twisting in disgust. She was pretty sure she'd managed it.

Triumph. Amusement. Lust.

He smirked at her, "So, you don't like being called a leech."

Jessica dropped her eyes immediately. She hadn't felt disapproval from him, but she knew she'd shown an undesirable trait. She didn't have the luxury of showing bad anything. This had to go perfectly. The hoops she'd gone through just to get an appearance with the exclusive club's spotter had taken her months of preparation and another month to get noticed. And that was with a referral. She worked to not chew her lip in worry.

He laughed at her. "If you were perfect, I'd be shocked." He seemed to be as good at reading body language as she was at emotion. Of course, he'd have to be, wouldn't he? The acceptance of her action did nothing to calm her nerves, though. She stood stock still, eyes on the carpet and the tips of his shoes, waiting.

He checked his watch, then hummed, a low rumble in his chest. "I think I've satisfied my interest with how you perform this close. Turn, bend over and put your hands on the bed."

She did so, thankful she was allowed the scrap of black lace that provided a tiny barrier to her complete exposure. Her body lay across the cool, airy bedspread, her back lightly arched, her legs making a long line from her still-shod feet up to her now upturned ass. She hoped her profile was pleasing, and she sucked in her belly, just to make sure.

Arousal. Approval. Mischief. Interest. Curiosity.

Things were going well for her, but another small fear welled in the back of her brain. She didn't have casual sex, but she supposed she'd have to get used to it, if she was accepted. She knew he wasn't going to ask for her permission. She'd given that when she walked through the door, as well. Even knowing that, though, it was still not easy for her to consider being taken in such a fashion.

Past lovers and play partners had been extremely correct. If she'd given just the hint disinterest or reluctance, a new path had been chosen. Did she really want to enter a world where it did not matter in any sense of the word what she wanted or didn't? Yes, yes she did.

"You are to stay out of my mind. Emotions you are welcome to. Can you even turn those off?"

"With effort, Sir." Trying not to fidget, she studied the lines of thread that ran through the plush bedspread.

"Hmmm. Well, it will be interesting to see if you can differentiate mine from the others, anyway."

Before she could even do more than startle at the mention of *others* and what that might mean, an immense amount of enjoyment and lust hit her senses at the same time as the belt cracked expertly on her ass. She struggled to hear what he was saying as her fingers dug into the bed to keep from moving or making a sound.

"Directly across the hall. Tell me what's going on." All the humor had left his voice.

The pain lanced like fire, racing down her knees. She had to speak. It had to be even. She closed her eyes against the pain and concentrated. "A couple. Two men. One in service. The dominant man is smoking a cigar. He is bored. The servant is straining from standing so long but trying not to show it. The dominant man is amused by this." Jessica wondered exactly how he knew if she was telling the truth or not, but it was an afterthought as the pain started to spread out into her body, easing away.

The man behind her laughed, a velvet sound to her ears, and it helped take a measure of pain away. She was correct. She knew it from his emotions.

"That sounds like Bradly. We've kept him waiting for 20 minutes."

Had it already been that long? It seemed as if she'd just stepped into the room minutes ago. Jessica realized the spotter had staged the room across the hall.

"What is he thinking?"

It came to her like she'd just heard it. "He wonders if you've fucked me yet, Sir." The man's hand ran over her ass, squeezing. It felt good, though still had a mixture of pain tossed in.

"And?"

"And if I'm as good as Paul claims I am."

"In bed?" The delicious sensation of his hand ran from one cheek to the other. His finger slid into the thin strap of the thong and moved further to delve between her wet lips. She startled but arched just a bit more to allow him more access.

Desire coated Jessica's voice when she answered, "My abilities, though he wonders about my sexual skills as well."

80

He played along her opening. "Are you sure? He's gay." He was trying to trip her up with his actions and his words. She felt the dishonesty, or perhaps he simply didn't know Bradly as much as he thought he did.

"I'm sure, Sir. He would fuck me if given a chance."

"Perhaps I'll let him," he mused. She couldn't help but wiggle as he played with her. She was embarrassed by how wet she was. It had always been a flaw. If he were the one who could read people, she wondered if he'd comfort her or use it. So far he seemed like a gentle and fair man. Not at all what she was expecting from this interview.

His finger slammed into her cunt, and her eyes went wide, her mouth forming a silent O. "Next door. What is the woman thinking?"

Jessica felt two women, and she wasn't sure which one he meant. She hesitated a second, not knowing if she should ask for clarification or simply supply both thoughts. "Are your powers fading so quickly with just a simple finger in you? You'd be useless if it was a cock," he snarled.

Pleasure. Complete Attention. Lust. Amusement.

He had been right. It was nice to know the emotions of the person she was dealing with. He was trying to trick her again. She wanted to dig into his mind. Wanted to see if he wanted her to move into his hand, but she obeyed him despite the temptation.

"There are two women in the room, Sir. Do you have a preference for which woman?" she panted, fingers kneading into the bed. She was straining to keep her legs straight as his finger moved like magic inside of her.

He snorted. "All right. The brunette." His curiosity hit deep into her mind. He probably wondered how she would be able to tell. Her gifts didn't include the ability to see things, only feel and hear. She took a few seconds to sort through both of their brains, looking for clues to which was which. *There. She's envious of the woman's hair.* From there, it was a simple matter of reading the other one. Jessica almost laughed, despite his hand in her and the belt running along her leg. "A horse walks into a bar. The bartender asks, 'Why the long face?' Why do blondes wear big hoop earrings? To... "

"Enough." He laughed, and Jessica knew it was a sound she would give just about anything to keep hearing. Her reward was two slow strokes inside of her. She moaned low, dipping her head.

81

Licking her lips, she brought her head back up, and she couldn't stop her muscles from clenching around his finger. Jessica was curious if it was another set up, and if so, how long the woman had been sitting there repeating jokes to herself.

He pulled his finger out of her and reached around, his chest almost lying against her back. The warmth of him seeped inside of her, making her desire flare. He held his finger out to her. She took it into her mouth and slowly sucked it clean, allowing her tongue to lick around it before he pulled it out.

"Good girl," he intoned. Jessica flushed with pleasure. He pulled away from her, standing and stalking back and forth behind her, his belt tapping against his leg. It was hard not to count the seconds until it would come slamming against her ass again, a question sure to be close on its heels.

"You've done well so far, Jessica. But what I really want to know, more then what your abilities can do, is why you want to be sold, bought, and owned?"

She was surprised at the question. It tipped her off guard, and she checked his emotions. They all read the same.

"It's a feeling that is simply hard to explain. I... " She searched for the words. "It feels wrong not to be owned. Lonely. Adrift. Unsure." She realized she was naming emotions like she read them.

"Unsure of what?" She heard him stop behind her.

"Unsure if my actions are correct. If I'm behaving as I should. If I'm being everything I can be or just lazily going through the motions."

"This isn't a fix-me show, Jessica."

Boredom. Concern. Fear.

Jessica longed to be inside his head. To answer the questions he wanted answers to. She furrowed her eyebrows, her lips turning down in a slight frown. How had she gone from approval to boredom? And what was he afraid of?

They stood there in silence for what seemed like minutes. Her worry swirled in her stomach like bad lunch, and his emotions weren't telling her what she needed to know. Had she damaged her chances? Did he believe her? Was it the wrong answer? What was the right one? She was so concerned with the *whats and whys*, she failed to pay attention to where he was.

So, when the man took two firm strides toward her, slid his fingers into her hair in a tight grip, and pulled her upright in one swift motion, she made a squeak of surprise as reality flooded back. Her hands instinctively came up to grasp at his hand as a serrated knife was suddenly and acutely pressed into her throat. Jessica's legs almost buckled, the gasp coming from her loud in the quiet of the hotel room. Her excitement dripped down her legs.

His voice was rough, demanding, in her ear, "Down the hall, two doors, on the right. What is the girl feeling?"

Jessica's eyes darted back and forth. She gave the answer as fast as he'd grabbed her. "Intense fear."

"Isn't that yours?"

"Perhaps a bit, Sir." She swallowed, feeling the knife's edge bite along her skin.

"Why is she afraid?"

The water, it's almost too high. If he doesn't turn it off, I'll go under! The words were loud in her head.

"She's afraid of drowning, Sir," her voice came out as light and breathless. She worried for the girl.

The man's hand came out of her hair, he took away the knife, then turned her around to face him. Her legs wobbled but held, even in the heels. Searching her face, he gave a soft smile. "Don't be scared for her, Jessica. She is enjoying herself as much as you just did."

She sighed in relief, both from the fact that she was okay and that she had pleased the man. She also flushed and glanced down in embarrassment at her own enjoyment being pointed out to her. He trailed the tip of the knife down her front, between her breasts to her belly button. The sensation gave her goose bumps. "Thank you, Sir."

"You're welcome." He slid the knife into a sheath that must have been at his back in the belt.

"My... job," he said, slowly letting his eyes drift down her then back up to meet her gaze, "allows me freedoms I sadly don't have time to test on you. But I can say, the taste I did get, was extremely pleasant." The corner of his mouth lifted in a wry grin. "But you know that." Jessica felt a hint of disappointment at his words. It came from both of them. She still didn't give it up freely, but she would to this man.

He took a step back from her. "I'll be recommending that you are given further examination. Your gift is extraordinary and would be an amazing asset in the right hands."

Disappointment. Desire. Amazement. Intrigue.

"And now, I need to go get our *test bunnies* and let them know they can go about their business. Good job, Jessica." He winked at her, then turned and headed for the door. As it opened, before he stepped out, he said. "You're allowed." The door shut.

She was still standing in the middle of the room, in her blue heels and her black thong now a little worse for wear. Hair mussed, bun falling as the door shut behind him. Her eyes holding desire, longing, as they stared at the closed door.

She heard/felt from the hallway, *Perhaps, I'll show up at the auction.* A smile spread slowly across her face... she had done it!

Jessica waited five full heartbeats until she felt him down by the *near-drowning* girl's door, then squealed, grabbed up her fallen dress, and plopped herself back onto the bed behind her. She sat there, crumpled blue material in her hands, and grinned from ear to ear, her emotions of elation and triumph overriding all the others in that moment.

The Brill Boy at Kaleigh
By Scott Harris

It was stiff to the touch, muted in color. Trey drew his fingers lightly against the embroidered material, the Kaleigh patch's edges tightly hand-affixed to the light grey wool coat by stitches unseen. The threads shimmered in a shaft of particle-laden light from the blazing lantern above him. It made his eyes water a bit, having made it this far. He felt so much pride it hurt, a stabbing in his chest, he felt... like a damned fresh squire touching a knight's armor for the very first time. With hitch in his throat, as his gaze waivered and then snapped up, he looked around abruptly at all the other boys scrambling to get themselves presentable and quick before guests rose for their day. Everyone would soon be busy with morning meal preparations. Trey still couldn't help himself. He looked around, wanting some moments to last. This, damn it, was one of them, was it not?

The cold sunrise was barely smudging against the thick oily glass of the dormitory windows, the bunk rooms below were cramped for space, but every inch of it was highly polished, well-cared for old dark woods and scuffed up cubbies of useable space, shelves with pressed crisp uniforms, spit-shined leather shoes, belts, and small iron hooks like the one before him that held his greatest prize: the Kaleigh waistcoat with the Kaleigh crest upon the breast.

They were not allowed any small possessions to clutter their spaces, like watches or rings or even photographs. They brought nothing into the castle with them. It was clothing on your back, and that was currently stored in a chest somewhere in the castle he hadn't even seen yet. Once he'd finished showering last night, he was given clothing to wear to bed. At his bunk each boy had his uniform already laid out for the morning.

The castle of Kaleigh loomed over the cottages in the area; it had been mysterious and dark when he had arrived late last night with two other boys. Some might call it looming and ominous, but Trey saw only the warm glow of lantern lights from rooms. The Castle only excited him more as they had drawn nearer. After all, it was 1957, things were going to be great for him. He'd left his home and traveled for days by ship and by train to reach Kaleigh, but his journey here had been much longer, and that secret little thought made him smile.

Danny, one of the Irish blokes, a funny sort from Cork who had traveled with him aboard ship and arrived with him late last night, slapped him on the back excitedly as he passed him. Trey broke into a good-natured wide smile in return to the friendly freckled redhead, who had eyes as bright blue as his own and was half-dressed in his livery clothing, Trey had been gifted something much more; he would be working the actual floors of Kaleigh herself.

"This is really it... " he marveled under his breath as he hurried then to change into the Kaleigh uniform. It was deemed such a great honor to train here. Guests from all over Europe with places in highest society, and many of the most elite of the Marketplace too, often walked these halls. It was a great place to be seen, to work on skills, refine skills. *I am part of it all, part of the Marketplace.* That thought alone gave him a bit of a surge. It felt rather good but made carefully lacing up his trousers difficult.

The majordomo in charge of the dormitory was a tall man in his 30s with elegantly cropped blond hair edging out in a silver grey and a broad set of shoulders. One could imagine under those fine clothes he was very muscled and lean man. He stood at the wide deeply set door, looking every bit like a pressed statue of cloth and skin. The only thing separating him from a complete soldier's look was the long onyx cane grasped in his left hand. It made a series of taps on the floor.

Three taps, not good, he was almost out of time. Regal, damned regal, that was the word that came to Trey the first time he'd seen the infamous Major Chatham late last night when he and Danny had arrived much past dark with another boy they had met on the train. The walk from the train had been brutal really; it was a chilly night with a thin layer of snow set upon everything the eye could see; but they had managed to keep a good brisk jogging pace and kept their spirits up only to show up to see the dark pillar the very tall Major

Chatham waiting silently for them outside the main gates, holding out that already dreaded pocket watch, cane shimmered under the moonlight.

Still it hadn't been such a bad welcome to Kaleigh, three lads bent over a tackle box in the servant's entry with the loud cracks of a series of hard blows of that same cane across his still sore skin, three very neat lines wedged across his upper thighs and three across his bottom. It would have been a fonder memory if the stiff bunk sheets they slept in didn't remind him of it all night. Hell, he had planned it all in his head to do nothing but the best of work here to please his Master and his Trainer. He mulled on it as he laced up his shoes, he would have admired them more if he wasn't pressed and trying to dodge taking on more punishment for being late.

The man seemed frozen in his position taken up in the door of the dormitory silently holding out that dreaded pocket watch, but Trey seemed to hear those moments passing, clicking off in his head like a dull beat of a drum as he looked himself over carefully. He felt like he was actually stealing moments from that watch and yet knew deep inside that was just impossibility. So he put on a burst of speed, reaching up and grasped the pressed coat while he tucked his undervest and felt the razor sharp shirt collar scrape lightly across the back of his neck, leaving a small red welt that itched uncomfortably. A snap of suspenders into place and then he froze. He had only worked one button when he saw it, and his world came crashing down.

A stain...

Tiny but there, dark ink perched just above his belt line with tiny frays from a rather poor attempt at scrubbing it off. His eyes stabbed at it in abject terror and disbelief, shock faded to the edges of anger as willing it away simply did not work. It was still there and too damned obvious. Its very presence slowly dunked him in a cold immersing thought: someone switched his new shirt with this damaged one. Eyes reeling, his visions of doing everything right at Kaleigh were slipping away and fast. His Trainer was going to be damned disappointed with him, but no excuses, right? Isn't that what he said. There was a loud crashing in his ears. Oh damn, the last few taps of the cane, time was up.

He was doomed.

His gaze turned brittle and intense at such an offensive gesture on his first day, and his gaze swung, hunting from handsome face to handsome face. Most were about the same age as he, 19, and there was one slightly older man, maybe in his late 20s. In the sea of freshly scrubbed youthful faces, he noticed only one took the time and stared him down with more than a mild curiosity. In fact, he was staring at him. Vince, that was his name, wasn't it? One of the head service boys, who worked in the finery of the dining room. Trey cut a dark stormy gaze back at him, suspicious. Vince was beautiful; no doubt, he was so relaxed because he was taking a damned spa bath in Trey's nerves. Still, he wished it wasn't Vince. That natural beauty, not rugged, more a finely sculptured bronzed boy of about 22 with green eyes, leaning rather arrogantly across the bunk rows with his pals. Trey felt his heart skip then sink deeper as the twitching edges of those beautiful perfectly shaped lips suddenly vaulted and cranked into a rather ugly and cruel smirk.

Man, it was he. It had to be.

Trey gaze afforded some violent reprimand, but the taller blond laughed it off and whispered to his mates. They all were chuckling as, one after the other, each presented himself for inspection to the majordomo then left with that brisk walk all Kaleigh boys learned fast. The tall blond winked, losing the smirk so completely he actually looked handsome again. Then he sauntered past Trey like a prince.

Trey felt the heat of anger and embarrassment climb over his neck. It made his skin ruddy against the dark curls at his neckline. There just wasn't any time to address it, and he bloody knew it. He tried to hide the stain, but the starch in the shirt was so thick it sprang from his waistline with every step he took toward the door. He prayed silently to make it past the tall Major's hardened look of scrutiny he gave to all the boys. A detailed inspection really, which seemed to take hours when in fact it was mere moments. Trey stepped up to the door last. Why did he have to be last? His gaze dropped just below the Major as he moved to proceed past him like the others did. Then he heard wood cracking wood, hard. The sound was like a gunshot; it made Trey jolt and step back.

It was the dark glossy cane that tapped the wood door casing in front of Trey. It snapped broadside taut against Trey's chest, not allowing him to pass from the room. Trey swept himself into a presentable attention before Major Chatham. The whispers from other boys haunted his ears, though they were long gone, already running top speed to their duties.

The Major was something of an institution within the walls of Kaleigh. Even Trey knew of the warnings from the underboys: mind the Major or else. Trey could feel his heart thrashing a bit.

First damned night... in trouble. Second day... more trouble.

He closed his eyes, briefly imagining his disappointed Trainer getting these reports, and felt crushed. Trey was doing more things horribly wrong; at this moment he wanted the world to stop so he could take a longer break and start it all over. But it wasn't going to start over, ever. It just did not work that way.

"Eyes front, lad."

The cane braced in Major Chatham's fists rose. The cane caught him gently on the chin, lifting Trey's gaze against his will. *God no, please, don't make me look into his eyes!* Trey trembled and buried his eyes in tracing the lines of those strong, well-veined hands. They looked like artwork sketches his brother Tomas used to draw, when they were just boys working in the stables of the great estate he grew up on, where his father and mother were under contract. His father was the head gamekeeper there, his mother was one of the cooks, and the positions afforded the family a great deal of comfort and happiness while in service. They had a tiny cottage on the property and full lives.

Such happiness, in service, and here he was betraying them all.

* * *

The moment swept him back, to sunlit hay of his youth, the rolling green grounds of the great and old estate. The smell of horses, the scent of leather and tack oils; it had been the happiest of childhoods romping among it all. Trey had been 15 when his father sat him down and explained to him about the Marketplace, about his contractual service, and how his own father and grandfather had served that family before him. It had been a quiet night, in his father's tiny study, a small pool of lantern light between them and a real talk between them as men. Trey remembered at first everything made sense. But then came curiosity and questions. His father was patient and explained Trey and his brother would make their own choices about their futures, and it was time for Trey to understand and think on his own possibilities.

Trey did think on it, for almost a year while still working under his father and learning more about the Estates. Trey simply could not imagine a life so different than that of living under the helm of his father's dedication to the Estates. Everything else seemed foreign, selfish. As years passed, Trey grew into a sturdy young man, at 18 he found, more and more, he wanted to give back, to stay working for the grand family who had been nothing short of kind to them all, for generations working hand in hand to produce an estate worthy of sustaining them all. Trey, always eager to watch and learn, worked for two years inside the walls of the great house, learning how to be a footman. He cared well for the Master's carriage and luggage and woodwork, and in his spare time he helped his father with game upkeep. It was something Trey loved, being outside, walking in the groves, swimming in the ponds and fishing the streams.

Trey thought his life was grand.

One morning he was dismissed from his usual duties in the house, and he felt lost for well over an hour until he was summoned to the Master's office. There was a man there, named Dalton. Trey was properly introduced to him as a Marketplace Trainer and told to relax though he'd never felt more under the gun. Dalton's gaze seemed to seize every movement he made, monitored every word he said.

Trey actually felt like he was taking a series of tests. The Master of the Estates, an elegant friendly older man, excused himself after the first portion of questions. Trey was left for the afternoon to answer all Dalton's questions, to perform some minor tasks and a few major ones Trey had never tried before.

He liked Dalton, a lot.

He felt himself blushing a bit at some of the rather straightforward questions he was asked. Personal questions. Trey had never been so open with anyone before, but with Dalton, it just seemed, natural. When Dalton left the Estates, no one asked him about the meeting. He found over the next few months, he actually mourned his time with Dalton and reflected on it quite often, reshaping those answers he gave to him, wishing he had a second chance to redo those tasks.

"Sometimes we have but once to show others who we are Trey, we have to secure the moments we have," Dalton had said to him when he was asked to remix the polish to get it right. Trey began to feel heavy-hearted, like he had somehow let them all down, failed some test. He continued to work his duties about the house, but they had dropped him back to lower footman. He didn't often ask why these things happened; it was more to give others a chance he rationalized to himself, a way to keep staff fresh.

That was his theory anyway.

It was during the very busy month of October when Dalton's carriage returned to the Estates and Trey was suddenly thrust into the underbutler position and sent to serve Dalton. Dalton seemed to continue questioning Trey at length as Trey did routine tasks, poured him a strong drink or laid out pressed clothing for him. Near the end of Dalton's stay, Trey still heard nothing from anyone. It was driving him slowly into madness, all this normality in their work, but was he never to be accepted into the Marketplace like his family? Trey had actually panicked, and the butler himself found him in tears in the root cellar. He demanded Trey clean himself up and present himself to the Master's study immediately.

Trey's heart floundered. *Was this a yes, or no? My God, did I pass muster? What will I do if I'm turned away, I would have to leave everything I know, everything I want to keep in my life.* Trey cleaned himself up in a hurry but managed to look impeccable taking care of his Master's clothing he had afforded Trey to wear.

He rapped his knuckles twice on the door. Had he been family, he would have rapped just once, but he was staff and there were rules. "Enter, Mr. Brill." Holy Christ, he had never heard the Master call him by his last name! It sent a small shard of warning and excitement coursing through him at the same time. He entered the elegant study crowded with well-dusted and -cared-for volumes, a large globe swung idly under Dalton's fingertips as the Master once again excused himself from their presence. Trey approached Dalton ducking neatly out of the way and stood frozen as the Master passed by him.

"Where did you learn that, Trey?"

Dalton's voice had broken the long silence after the Master left. Trey had decided to stay in his current position until Dalton said or did something to release him from it. Trey's gaze came up when Dalton motioned to a chair near him, and Trey moved to take a seat with him nervously.

"I don't really know, Sir, I guess watching staff maybe." Though he couldn't really think of anyone who did it just like him and felt it was a lie of sorts and so quickly added.

"It... just felt right, Sir?"

Dalton smiled then, and Trey felt his own lips work into a nervous smile. Trey then realized there was a beautiful set of papers beside him, he recognized his name emblazoned upon them, and Dalton's signature and the Master's signatures were perched just above a blank spot. Trey's heart soared a moment then dared no longer flight then that.

"Am I accepted then, Sir? Am I to be Master's property like my parents?"

He couldn't keep the excitement from his tone. Dalton seemed entertained by Trey anyway. Soon Trey wasn't speaking at all, he was listening, devoutly so. It did not take Dalton long to go over all the details of his contract in the Marketplace. He explained to Trey about his contract and asked Trey no less than twice if Trey was solid in his decision to move forward in the life his parents chose. Dalton tried to stress what a life contract meant for Trey. Trey could barely hear Dalton, his pulse was ebbing in his ears. Yet each word landed so clearly it struck him like a chord on an instrument. Trey's fingers shook as he finally inked in his name under the two signatures. His was rather shaky and not as finely written as the others.

Dalton then described the castle of Kaleigh. Trey, who had never been anywhere else in his whole life, found the journey there was going to be a daunting one but exciting just the same. His Master wanted him trained there. Dalton rose and put Trey through a few paces, Trey was shown a few new positions, positions that made his clothing feel too tight in certain places.

When Dalton concluded and rose to go, Trey stayed on his knees by the abandoned chair, it just felt... right.

"I think you will make us proud, Trey." Dalton, his new Trainer, had paused to watch him before speaking. He stated his orders quietly as he left the room. He left Trey to recover himself for exactly an hour, when the chime struck on the Grandfather clock, then he was promptly to go pack his things. It felt like days, every tick of the clock as everything he had been told sunk in. It was delicious to Trey.

"I'm property in the Marketplace now." A little voice inside him whispered. "You always were." Trey smiled to himself and felt tears of happiness burn in the back of his throat.

* * *

There was a clearing of his throat. No, he listened more carefully. Not his throat, someone else's.

Major Chatham smelled like leather, he smelled damn good. Trey's nostrils flared, breathing it in as he pinned his gaze steadily upon Major Chatham's neck and jawline. He was such a handsome man, like Dalton but more rugged, more physical. Trey had heard many of the stories of the Major's career in the British Armed Forces on the ship here. Danny seemed to know everything about the man, and it was a nightly ritual for them to tell each other stories while on the ship's passage. Trey knew Major Chatham had fought in two wars, was heavily decorated for battles. He had been wounded, it was why he had a noticeable limp. The man was a complete and utter charming hero, saving his men valiantly and spending months recuperating at Kaleigh herself. Word was, rumor alone since really nothing was ever said in front of him by any of the boys, he just never left after that and became part of Kaleigh.

Trey fought with his typical urges of wanting to prove himself to the Major, of all people, to Mr. Blake, to his Trainer, Dalton, to them all. He fought the natural war of standing still and the dire urge that over whelmed him to sink to his knees so fast he'd crack them.

He held his breath a moment.

"You're one of Dalton's boys, I expected great things from you." Trey's heart broke a bit hearing him. A flood of useless needs washed through him. *Tell him about the switch,* screamed a voice inside his head. *Tell him it wasn't your fault! Tell him it was possibly the prince-like Vince!* His teeth hooked into his lip to keep from saying any of those things. It did not serve the situation or the need for a clean and tidy shirt and now he was making them both late for their duties.

"Eyes to me, boy." The Major's tone was crisp, no-nonsense and layered with that deep rumble from inside his chest, which made Trey nervous, but it was one of those moments before you went over the waterfall kind of moments. Trey's gaze drew up and landed helplessly in the Major's. Major Chatham's eyes seem to pierce his, hunt him down, and he felt circled, trapped, really frozen there.

"Well?" Trey fought again against the swell in his own heart and simply shook his head. "Of course I have no excuse, Sir, and forgive me for my error." Trey thought for a moment he saw a hint of amusement in the man's eyes, but the fierceness there seemed to flare as he searched deeper.

The cane shifted and abruptly came down and hooked the hard wood and hitched under his balls. The wool certainly didn't help his level of comfort. It itched and the cane was jostling him. Trey gasped from the suddenness of the movement, and a ruddy blush instantly colored his pale features.

"Three strikes of the cane for making us both late for duties. Three for the ink stain. In the future, Trey, I expect you to harness your abilities and prove yourself more fit to conduct yourself to reflect upon our traditions here at Kaleigh. Is that clear, boy?" His voice seemed to boom.

Trey nodded quickly. "Yes, Sir, Major Chatham."

"Then take your position, son."

Trey's brain finally seized in a moment, and his balls slithered off the Major's cane. He turned, unlacing wool trousers that sank down the muscled indented curve of his ass. His cock was already at half-mast and paying careful attention to the very presence of the Major. He bent and reached out and grasped the rather indented dark wood of nearest lower bunk and waited as he breathed in deeply.

"Count well."

The Major's cane connected with fresh skin, and he hissed under his breath. No one was ever ready for the first strike. He again grasped the bunk wood and noted just how worn this wood was, years of boys like him grabbing it for a punishment or two.

"One, Major Chatham, thank you, Sir... "

Each strike was a painful and delicious stab of pain followed by a rush of pleasure and warmth. By the last strike, his cock was so hard it was almost impossible to fumble the thick wool and lacing back over himself. Trey's well-veined cock was pulsing and making certain thoughts wash over the moments of clarity incised by the canes blows. He finally got himself back in order. The corners of his eyes were wet, but he was a strong boy. He stood again at attention before the Major, though he wanted to sink to the man's feet.

"Good lad, find a fresh shirt and report to the kitchens; it's the bottom up with you." Trey caught himself after a moment, correcting his position and attempting to disguise his heartbreak, while mingling feelings of excitement lingered from the cane strikes and the Major's presence.

"Trey."

The Major paused in midstep, slithering the cane back to the floor with a thump. Trey gazed up and delved into the Major's eyes silently with no animosity at all, just a hint of sweeping pride. "I know the bloody shirt was switched. Vince will get his due."

Trey's breathing hitched.

"Welcome to Kaleigh, Trey Brill of Southerby Estates." Then the Major actually cut a wink to him with a glimmer in his eye, and his lips parted to a rather casual and cheeky grin. Then he was gone from the doorway. Trey gasped, reeling a bit. Shocked, appalled and amused. *The Major knew! The Major winked!* Trey found himself wearing that crooked grin, exploding on his own face. He chuckled and moved to find another shirt.

As Trey pulled the shirt on, wincing a bit in pain, his fingers slid down and raked over the fresh welts on his ass. He smiled more fully than before. He was happy to be here at Kaleigh.

After all, he was a Southerby Boy.

Isis of 10,000 Names
By Steve Dee

The cold slate of the chapel floor was a great aid for focusing—at least that's what he told himself. For James the minutes felt like hours as he became increasingly aware of the discomfort his vigil would entail. A thick fog of incense stung his eyes, and his body ached with the effort of holding himself in stillness.

This vigil was the pinnacle of his training and the doorway into the life he longed for. Few understood the path he had chosen, and of those who did understand, even fewer embraced the challenge. As he fought to bring his attention back to his breathing and body, his mind drifted to the journey that had brought him both to New Orleans and Isis of 10,000 Names.

His late teens had been a time fraught with confusion. Escape from village life in the South West of England had come in form of a punk band and the minor success that gigging in Bristol had brought him and his bandmates. He fulfilled most of the bass player stereotypes as the quiet one at the back who watched on in wonder at the adventures, both straight and Queer, the others pursued. They laughed at his bookish distance and called him *the Monk* whenever he tried to talk about the texts he'd been trying to read. While they were his friends, their surge out into the world seemed far from what he was looking for.

In struggling to make sense of why *normal* desire felt absent, he had lurked at the edges of the online asexual noticeboards. Reading the stories of others, he was struck by the sense of relief they had in realizing there were other ways to be, other ways to live. Being an outsider this had made so much sense to him, and yet he couldn't escape that desire still remained. His just needed to take a different course.

It was Riot Girl 23 who had spotted what he struggled to see in himself. In a thread discussing how asexuals might be involved in BDSM without it having to entail sexual desire, she had been the one who had gently questioned his longing for "some kind of service." As they swapped private messages, he heard more of her life in North Carolina, and he was struck by the sense of purpose she possessed. James was set alight by her story of how a straight-edged feminist ended up serving a Butch Dyke she called her Daddy.

The paths to the Marketplace were many, and it was Riot Girl who suggested the Isis Temple as a place that seemed to offer what James was seeking. While superficially it appeared to be some form of pagan-inflected ministerial training, it was clear from the available online material, it served as preparation for something far more focused; not many spirituality courses had *Venus in Furs* on the essential reading material! Rumi, the Gospels, and the mystics all pointed to a life shaped by service and self-emptying. While many groups sought to promote these goals, the temple had evolved a unique approach to attaining them.

That was two years ago, but it could have been a lifetime. Following an immersive week-long retreat in the noise and close heat of New Orleans, James had returned home, sold his bass and amp, and cashed in the little he had saved for his vague plans for university. Both of his hippy parents understood the spiritual yearnings that were driving their son, but he decided to spare them some of the temple's more *tantric* dimensions. His first visit to the temple had been a homecoming, and he knew he must return. Yes, it had a library to die for, and it had an awe-inspiring Goddess temple, but it also held the promise of so much more.

While many spiritual paths saw progress in terms of a move away from the passionate and visceral, the temple viewed the offering of service to the Goddess in human form as the highest of goals. During his time at the temple's small seminary, James had not only absorbed considerable chunks of mythology, but he was also initiated into the psychological richness of D/s relationships. While inspired by classical mythology, the temple made no claims to ancient lineages; rather it placed its beginnings at the heady convergence of the postwar neo-pagan revival and birth of Leather sexuality. This connection to a tribe of serious players had eventually drawn the attention of some of the Marketplace spotters. The sense of *fit* between the Isis Temple and Marketplace seemed to lie largely in the deep sense of vocation and service both groups viewed as essential.

Like many temples, large parts of the day were spent in maintaining rigorous standards of cleanliness and in attending to the practical needs of visiting retreatants. For James the sense of purpose and structure this created felt dizzying. At the beginning of each day, the novices were required to attend the temple's main altar space. While the center of the altar contained a statue of the primal Mother as the Venus of Willendorf, she was flanked either side by both Severity and Mercy. While the left side contained images of Kwan Yin, Green Tara and Guadeloupe, the right contained the Goddess as sadistic top: Sekhmet, Kali and Cerridwen. For the novice to be deemed ready for the vigil it was vital they must understand and embrace both of these aspects.

His time was not only shaped by his studies and his service in the temple, he was also required to act as the personal attendant to his mentor, the Reverend Christina. Under Christina's tutelage, James strove hard to master skills of both a practical and sensual nature. Christina seemed to place the same value on a correct dinner setting as she would an intense session of body worship. While he had struggled to locate desire when expected to be in the driver's seat, when he was responding to the passion of others, he found his own was awakened.

In her own 20 years of service, Christina had served mainly as a chaplain at a small private hospital run by the woman doctor who had owned her. The spiritual direction she provided helped him appreciate the unique role played by the temple's servants:

"Often we get called on to minister to the needs of other slaves within the Marketplace. Offering service 24/7 is bound to kick-up conflicts for those who take the collar! Sure, good spotters and training should help us identify those who will have too many issues, but we can't forget that we are all humans and we all come with baggage. Even those who have been longtime players may have spiritual crises as their service forces them to look at who they thought they were."

"What if those slaves have no connection to Goddess worship?" asked James. "What if they come from say, a Jewish or Buddhist background?"

"Of course it's not our job to hold expertise about everything. Often we may refer on to a rabbi or priest who we know is Kink-friendly, but most of the time the feelings and issues people struggle with are similar. Being owned doesn't make us immune to anger, resentment, or confusion. It's part of our job to sit with people as they work this stuff through."

For most slaves seeking an owner, going to the block was an experience that held equal parts longing and terror. Within the life of the temple, the final vigil was a similar ordeal. The ability to undertake long periods of silent meditation was an important focus within the Temple's training, but it was only during the final vigil that their potential owners observed their practice. In the cool confines of the Goddess sanctuary, James and the two other candidates were all too aware the congregation held not only their tutors and chosen friends, but also those who had read their files and viewed the footage of their interviews. These people would know of their hopes and aspirations, their experience (or lack of it) sexually, and their performance during the practice placements they had undertaken. The vigil provided an ideal opportunity for those qualities to be both tested and evaluated.

The closing liturgy of the service caused James to snap back to the present:

"Listen to the words of the Great Mother,
All acts of love and pleasure are my rituals.
Let there be beauty and strength,
Power and compassion,
Honor and humility.
Know the Mystery,
That which you seek is within you!"

The first he knew of her presence was a hint of Chanel No. 5 and the gentle pressure of her hand upon his shoulder. Fixing his eyes on her black patent pumps, he felt the grey hood of his robe being pulled back and the cool steel of a collar being draped about his neck. He felt her hand beneath his chin, and as he gazed up into her grey-blue eyes, she simply said, "Hello, James, my name is Cybele."

Once his new owner had paid his stipend to the Temple and James had said some rushed farewells, he found himself on a flight headed to Seattle. Since the vigil, James had grown accustomed to the striking appearance of his new owner—at 5'9" she was only slightly shorter than he was, and the severity of her slicked back short blonde hair was further accentuated by a dark business suit. While in the air, Cybele had gently probed him with a steady stream of questions. Keen to create a good impression, James provided details about both his musical interests and his training placement that offered outreach to sex workers in New Orleans.

"It was a real eye-opener," said James. "Before my placement I hadn't met many trans or genderqueer folks, but while helping run the street kitchen that all changed. Being able to offer support to those people was great. Some of them became good friends." James looked away as he blushed slightly. One of these friends had become a playmate, and while the Reverend Christina had known, he was unsure what had gone into the reports Cybele had read. As if reading his mind she said, "Christina told me about Mike. Given that you believe you have a rather low libido, tell me what drew you to him."

"Ah... Mike was great." James hesitated. "He was a real top-man. Always busy with his regulars. He was visiting the Kitchen with friends when we started chatting. He's a Radical Faery and was keen to hear about why I was involved with the temple. When I visited his play-space I was blown away by the array of impact toys he owned. When I told him about wanting to live in-service, he had some really interesting views."

"Mike believed many owners actually wanted to receive sensation rather than give it. He felt a slave should be able to be a good service-top and meet their owners' masochistic needs. We became friends, and he trained me in the use of the whip. It was great; I got to learn from both sides of the lash! He understood I had to move on, and I hope we'll stay in touch"

When she told him something about herself, the fact Cybele was transgendered, while initially a surprise to James, was not a problem. Unlike some pagan groups that got caught up in some sort of dead-end belief about what it meant to be *a real woman*, the temple recognized the Goddess could be made manifest in anyone, whatever their biological sex at birth. Cybele herself explained to James her choice of name was in honor of the Great Mother who was often served by a trans priesthood.

They took a taxi from airport into the heart of the downtown area where Cybele owned a well-appointed apartment. James's head had swum as she pointed out an array for favorite eateries as well as the nearby art museum. Although the flat wasn't huge, its clean lines and minimal clutter seemed a world away from his past life in a Somerset village. She had great views of the waterfront, and he could imagine the sunsets over the Puget Sound would be as beautiful as she had described them.

While she had no obvious play-space he could see, he was quick to note the sturdiness of her black, iron-framed bed. Above it was a large black and white print that showed a woman whipping the naked back of a person whose face was out of frame. "It's by Aubrey Beardsley," she told him as a smile played across her lips. "Those skills you learned from Mike are going to be a crucial part of your service to me."

Life in Seattle soon found a regular shape. Cybele continued to work at the accountancy practice she had founded a decade previously, as well as being on the board of two nonprofits. One of these provided support for homeless Queer youth in the city, and in that setting James quickly found an outlet for his ministry.

Given his limited sexual experience, James was worried he would fail to meet Cybele's expectations. While he could see the sense of *fit* in relation to her other interests, he was unsure how he would measure up to meeting her other needs. Cybele was quick to address his fears and to reassure him.

"James, I spend almost all my working life giving out to others. Whether my clients, my colleagues, or my charitable work. The last thing I want in my bedroom is a slave with fixed ideas or yet another needy bottom whose demands I have to meet!" She smiled at James and continued, "The point of a three-year contract is it gives you time to learn what I want. Like with your music, this is about the subtleties of how you read my cues and changes in tempo. I don't expect you to get it right first time, but I do expect you to learn. I also expect your devotion."

During his time at the temple, via both Yoga practice and an elective in massage training, James had acquired a far deeper appreciation of the body. During the first weeks of his contract, he was pleased to put these skills and knowledge to work for benefit of his owner.

After a particularly draining day of difficult clients and an annoying computer issue, a careworn Cybele collapsed onto the pale leather sofa and closed her eyes. James quietly entered the room and placed a chilled glass of Pinot Grigio on the table in front of her. As he kneeled before her, she kicked off her shoes and placed her feet on his lap. She moaned softly as he worked his thumbs into the arch of her left foot. His fingers gently traced the smoothness of her ankles, her shins, and her calves.

Cybele stood briefly to unzip her skirt and unbutton her blouse and let them both fall to the floor. Kneeling astride her James poured a small vial of oil into his hands to warm it. Slowly he let it drip onto her now naked shoulders, and he began to work it into her back. As Cybele gave herself to the floor, he let his weight push into her as his musician's fingers worked their magic. In response to her sighs he used his nails to leave trail marks on her back. Slowly he let his hands work downward. He knew she loved it when he massaged her bottom, the steady pressure pulling at her sex as he used his hands to bring her pleasure.

The slowing of her breathing revealed the extent of her relaxation, and he gently placed a light blanket over her sleeping form. In offering her service he had become all too conscious of the erection straining in his boxers. From the outset of his contract, Cybele had been clear his climax was hers to demand or withhold. While her current state of repose sadly prevented his asking, luckily for James the temple placed great value on the Yoga of forced chastity during their training. While he would have welcomed the release, he simply grinned as he shifted into the half-lotus position and pushed his heel against his perineum. For now, the dull ache in his balls and his owner being rested would have to suffice.

While Cybele slept, he padded out to the kitchen where he started to prepare their food. For James, being able to support his Mistress in leading the life she wanted, gave him a deep sense of contentment. At times the holy grail of anticipatory service seemed within his grasp, but he realized his journey, as both an initiate of the temple and as a slave in the Marketplace, was only just beginning. He had found his place, and he was in no hurry. As one of the gurus had advised: patience

Something More
by Dani Hermit & Nevi Star

"Eugene." The office manager poked his head into the accountant's office. "Finish up with the last round of daily numbers and close up shop."

The man sitting behind the desk sighed and nodded. When he had put himself up for auction the second time, Eugene had hoped for a different kind of owner. One who might put him to better use than his first had. Well, what was he expecting? His trainer had warned him over and over that being sold as a slave might not be like his fantasies.

Eugene gave a start as all the phones around him went off at once. It was the end of the day, and every department of the large corporate office wanted to leave. None of them was allowed to go anywhere until they made sure they had reported in to accounting. Reaching out, Eugene held each of the phones aloft, spoke into them using the standard greeting and promised to get to each in turn. Beginning the process of taking down their daily inventory counts, production rates and sales, Eugene was for a moment glad he was a tentacle beast. The writhing appendages made doing his job that much easier. It also didn't hurt that he had a real head for numbers.

What wasn't so great about being a handsome young man with tentacles was having the sort of inclinations Eugene did. He'd believed when he had first come to the Marketplace his days of hearing "but you've got tentacles, don't you *want* to rape me?" were over. He'd dared to dream someone might make him submit in all the delicious ways he fantasized about. But in the three years of service, he'd learned the hard way being a tentacle beast who enjoyed being used was a thing to be ashamed of. His only way to be useful to his owners was being regulated to office work.

So at 6:00 every weekday, Eugene gave his reports to the company president and his owner, Mr. Ambrose. Once that was done, he retired to his sparse slave quarters in the upper levels of the building with the other slaves kept for office use. There he was free to devour book after book while he tried not to think about the lithe werecat twins who went home with his owner. Timothy and Bonnie weren't office workers, though they had menial positions in the company. They were bought with the sole purpose of servicing the sexual needs of Mr. Ambrose.

But that would be changing now. Today had been their last day in the office, though they had stopped serving the week before. They were heading out to find a new owner. The gossip Eugene had heard was they found Mr. Ambrose too hard to please. No doubt, though, there were new slaves ready to move in at any moment. And no doubt he'd get through another hundred pages in his book tonight.

Ah, yes. His life as a slave was so exciting.

Finished with filling in the spreadsheets, Eugene printed his reports, gathered up his papers, and prepared himself to recite the relevant parts to Mr. Ambrose as he did every night.

"Hello, Eugene," the perky blonde Cyclops who served as Mr. Ambrose's secretary greeted him.

"Hi, Marilyn." Eugene gave her a brief smile.

"You're at it a bit late tonight."

Eugene only nodded in reply. She said that every night, no matter what time it actually was when he appeared to deliver his reports. He didn't take it personally though. Marilyn wasn't being intentionally rude. While quite useful for keeping out unwanted visitors, the Cyclops—like most breeds of Ogres—weren't known for their brains. She probably had memorized a greeting for each person who regularly visited Mr. Ambrose's office. Or, more likely, they were taped to the desk calendar she was always staring at.

"Mr. Ambrose will see you momentarily."

"Thanks, Marilyn," Eugene mumbled. He shifted from one foot to the other while he waited his turn.

The door to the inner office opened, and Mr. Ambrose appeared, filling up nearly half of the doorway. He stopped when he saw Eugene standing in the outer office. Blinking his huge green eyes several times, recognition slowly dawned on his face. "Ah, Eugene.

We haven't done the numbers yet, have we?" With a sigh and an annoyed flutter of his translucent wings, he gestured to the young man to follow him back into his office. "Let's get this over with."

Mr. Ambrose returned to his desk and sank tiredly into his large seat, carefully arranging himself so as not to sit on his gossamer wings.

Momentarily transfixed, and not for the first time, Eugene opened his mouth to begin his report. He was appalled by what came out instead. "Would you like me to present, sir?" He bit his lip and fought to keep his inky violet eyes on the shimmering creature before him. Just when the hell had his overactive imagination decided to betray him? Of all the damnable things to say. He lost his battle to stay focused and began glancing anywhere but the lingeringly silent Mr. Ambrose.

Wings fluttering, Mr. Ambrose sat up a little straighter. He regarded the awkward accounting slave with an unreadable expression. "Yes, why not?" He waved his delicate fingers vaguely at Eugene. "That'll make this not so dull. Can you recite the numbers while you do so?" The tone of his voice told Eugene that he'd be sorely disappointed if he couldn't.

Eugene tried not to panic. He couldn't remember the last time he'd been asked to present. Maybe it wouldn't be a big deal. After all, his owner seemed distracted. As long as he could do a passable facsimile of presenting, would it even matter? He wondered if he should do something to capture his pretty master's attention.

What do I have that he hasn't seen before, Eugene asked himself, running fingers through his soft blonde hair. He fussed with his tie and was soon working on the buttons of his crisp dress shirt. Pausing in the rambling of the numbers, he remembered one thing he was good at. He cleared his throat and slowed down his speaking voice, giving the report in a more calculated way than he could ever hope to get undressed. If high school debate class had been any measure, his voice had a strange, mesmerizing effect on most people.

Not that it helped at all when everyone who saw his other unique feature, his glorious tentacles, immediately expected that he would be a beast that would enthrall and then plunder them.

"You're rubbish at this," Mr. Ambrose observed, a playful smile dancing across his tired pixie face. "When was the last time you took your clothes off?"

It took a moment to process that he was being spoken to. "Formally?" The young man found some words to string together. He hoped they made sense. "It was before I belonged to anyone."

Eugene was trying to slip out of his suit pants, but his foot got stuck and his lack of practice was on full display. "Perhaps it was foolish of me to offer such a service. Or perhaps the fault lies in an owner who never tested me." Eugene almost missed what it sounded like he said. Eyes wide, he stumbled over some more words to try and make it right. "Not you, sir. Of course. My... previous owner, I meant."

"I see." Mr. Ambrose steepled his fingers and watched as Eugene finished removing his clothes. The young man seemed to be fumbling for which of the traditional positions to take nearly as much as he had been fumbling with his clothes. "Assume the pose that will best expose you to my eyes," Ambrose helpfully ordered.

A chill ran down Eugene's spine. He could feel his long tentacles itching to uncoil from where they were hidden beneath his skin. *No*, he silently told them. *Absolutely not. What a way to ruin the mood! Not that this was going anywhere, but if that fairy creature lays eyes on what we both know but never speak of... Well, he's going to want things, expect things. They always want...* things.

But I can do this properly. Knees apart. Back straight. Hands laced.

He felt fully exposed. Well, nearly. Full exposure would require him to reveal the bane of his existence. He held his eyes front, focusing on the wood grain of Mr. Ambrose's desk, and remained as still as possible. He tried to keep his breath even as well, but failing that, he just prayed Mr. Ambrose wouldn't notice how nervous and out of practice he really was.

"You're very nice to look at," Mr. Ambrose observed, rising from his chair to approach Eugene. He was held aloft as he moved across the room by his delicate wings. They moved quickly, much like a hummingbird. Circling his slave, Mr. Ambrose made a soft sound of disapproval. "But I believe I requested that you fully expose yourself, Eugene."

The moan that escaped the young man was painfully telling. He brought his hands to his sides. Well, it had been nice while it lasted. They weren't separate from his being, no matter how much he wished them to be. He let the tentacles uncoil, slowly cascading from his upper arms and back. A second wave emerged from his thighs and lower back. He let them fall in a labyrinth of coils around him, a shimmering sea of blue, green, and lavender. He could feel his cock pleading as much as any of the highly sensitive tentacles waiting for attention. He couldn't deny that it felt good to be this completely naked.

He acknowledged his mistaken thinking as he waited in the tense silence. Being stuck doing office work and nothing else was Hell, but to almost get what he was so desperately craving and being met with the same old expectations was much worse. He closed his eyes. Maybe it wouldn't be so bad. Maybe he could pretend that he wanted it. To be the aggressor. To take another with no apology.

Except what he wanted wasn't something he could demand. If it wasn't such a risk, he might have cut off the damned things and been done with it. But he'd never actually be able to do it. He wasn't into the pain or supposed glamour of self-mutilation some of his slave brethren enjoyed. Tentacle removal was the equivalent of slicing off your cock with a letter opener. Over and over. There wasn't anything that could convince him to go through with it.

A few of the beasts tapped the floor impatiently, revealing Eugene's emotional turmoil. He did his best to steady them along with his heartbeat and overworking mind.

"Is it painful for you to... unleash them?" Mr. Ambrose asked. He trailed soft fingers along one tentacle. "Softer than I expected," he observed, moving on to stroking it with his full palm.

"No, sir. It's more painful to keep them coiled. Imagine clenching your fist without reprieve for hours on end. Sometimes for an entire day." Eugene held back any kind of purring noise that his master's touch was eliciting. "If you wish, I can tense the muscles beneath the skin and make them more"—he stumbled over the words, unable to sound as calm as he was trying to pretend to be—"firm to your touch."

"You have that much control over them?" Mr. Ambrose picked up another tentacle and let it slide through his grip as he considered Eugene's offer. "Good to know, but not necessary at the moment." He moved back, his rapidly flapping wings making a soft humming sound. "On your feet, Eugene."

Oh good, he's as uninterested as ever. We'll just chalk this up to

*a slightly embarrassing interchange, and I can go upstairs and get
lost in one of my books. Maybe start a new series. And we can all
pretend this never happened.*

Eugene grabbed for his shirt as he rose to his feet but dropped it
almost immediately. No matter how much he wanted to get dressed
and sprint to his room, he was better trained than that. His trainer, that
bastard, would beat him shamelessly for days for such a discretion.
He spared another moment to embrace the music in the tones of his
owner's command before he accepted the fantasy was ending.

"If that will be all, sir?" He spoke in a flat tone, hoping this
would dissolve the situation and save them both a great deal of
embarrassment.

"Are you so disinterested in serving me?" Mr. Ambrose asked.
"I'll admit I've been rather distracted by those darling kittens, Bonnie
and Timothy, these past months since purchasing you. However, I
was under the impression you were available to me for more than
your admittedly magnificent office skills."

"No. I mean, of course not, sir." Eugene kept his eyes on the
floor and the borderline irritation out of his voice. "There is nothing I
desire more than to meet your every need. I live to serve you. I was
just... " He trailed off, suddenly unsure of what to say. There was
nothing in his mental database of appropriate responses for a mistake
of this caliber.

"Hoping to avoid yet another unsatisfactory contract?" Mr.
Ambrose asked. His hands were on Eugene's tentacles again, moving
them, pulling them gently as he spoke. "Afraid of having to pretend
that my needs supersede your own? Or terrified that you'd be caught
giggling at your owner's diminutive fairy cock?"

"Never, sir! I mean, I'm certain your cock is... ample." He
squeaked out the last word, realizing how stupid he sounded. Mr.
Ambrose was four feet tall, at best, with a typical wispy fairy body.
Unless his cock was comically large, he was absolutely correct to call
it diminutive. But the touches Eugene couldn't ignore were making
his head fuzzy, and his thoughts weren't the neat orderly things he
was accustomed to. "And... and... of course your needs are of the
utmost importance. That is, of course, how my needs get met." His
nerves were causing some of the ignored tentacles to misbehave,
poking at his master for attention. Horrified, Eugene did his best to

get himself back under control and make the damned things lie still. "Forgive me, sir. There's no need for you to be displeased."

"You're also rubbish at answering my questions." Mr. Ambrose ducked under one of Eugene's tentacles, while pulling another around to the front and winding it around Eugene's legs, down to his ankles. "Your trainer would be appalled."

What was happening here? Eugene swallowed. He couldn't argue. It seemed all his training had slipped out his ear and lay pooled on the floor with his shivering tentacles. "Thank you, sir, for pointing out my awful behavior." There. That was better. Letter perfect. He was voice trained, for heaven's sake. He couldn't be this pathetic.

"I fear that just pointing it out won't correct it." Mr. Ambrose replied serenely. "Raise your arms, Eugene. That's it, up over your head. Now, clasp your hands together. Good."

A pair of tentacles were wound around Eugene's arms, the ends looped over one of the low beams that decorated Mr. Ambrose's office. "Be a good boy and tense up these ones. Like you said you could do."

The young slave's heart stopped for a beat. He hadn't been trying to get punished. Admittedly, he had thought about it. He'd just been too self-absorbed to act on it.

Oh yeah, there's a great trait for a slave. He heard his trainer's thickly accented voice in his head. *Self-absorption. One day, you're going to make someone feel like they have to break you, Eugene, if you keep that up.*

Forcing his mind back to the present, Eugene did as he was told, tensing the soft, fleshy tentacles, and felt his feet lift off the floor. The tentacles Mr. Ambrose had looped over the beam served to hold him suspended with his toes about two inches from the floor. Eugene couldn't stop the low rumble of pleasure from escaping his throat. He tried to disguise it as though he were clearing his throat before speaking. "As it pleases you, sir."

There was no way that this was going where it felt like it was. Mr. Ambrose was a pixie, and they were notoriously not the type to dominate. Okay, maybe when he called down to the accounting office, he could certainly *sound* like the type. But this was going to end badly if at least one of them didn't start to embody their proper role.

He understood, even if he didn't pity, his owner. The little fairy creature was most likely more bottom than top, and there was no shame in that. He wouldn't have purchased a tentacle beast if he wanted to dominate something. That just didn't make sense. But here he was, trying desperately to save face in front of a bitchy, self-centered slave. It was time for Eugene to act like he was supposed to. He had known this would happen again if he went to the block after his last contract. His trainer had given him time to think it over, but he'd still chosen this over going back to the clubs and degrading internet hook-up sites like Plenty-Of-Limbs.com.

It was really the best thing to do for both of their sakes.

"I asked you a question, Eugene," Mr. Ambrose's cool voice held an edge of annoyance as he drew back to examine his handiwork. "You are expected to answer me. Are you in pain? Your face says you might be."

"It's restrictive, sir, but not painful." Eugene answered quickly but clearly. He absolutely hadn't heard the question the first time. His ears were pricked up now, but it was still going to be hard to hear anything over his pounding heart and spiraling thoughts.

"Ah, then you are just having internal conflicts." Mr. Ambrose nodded sagely. "Understandable. After all, your previous owner wasn't able to take full advantage of your unique features."

He hovered his way across the room to his large, antique wardrobe. Eugene had noticed it many times before, often questioning what on Earth that monstrosity was doing in a pristine office like the one Mr. Ambrose kept. But when asked about it, the twins had only giggled, and eventually Eugene wrote it off as a decorating mistake by his owner that was none of his business. Mr. Ambrose opened the doors and considered the contents. From where he was suspended, Eugene couldn't see inside.

It wasn't just internal conflicts fighting for the young slave's attention, however. Hope and curiosity were unraveling within him as he fought to keep some of his tentacles tight around his limbs while the others remained soft, graceful decorations. He watched his master with a wonder he'd be ashamed of any other time. Heat was threading through his hands, feet, and cock. Need, desire, and the undeniable ache to answer this man's, this master's every demand were fast overwhelming every other impulse in Eugene's body. It was hard not to think about the position he was in as what felt like hours rolled by.

If I were not better trained—Eugene ignored the internal sound of his trainer laughing at the presumptiveness of that statement—*I would be mortified by this. I'm tied up with my own tentacles. Hell, I control how tight my bonds are. There'd be shame in that, too.*

Instead of letting that in, he let the unexplainable rush of submission to another, to himself, drive his every sensation. He played with the tautness of his bonds, seeing how much he could take and how loose they had to be before he lost some of the thrill. If Mr. Ambrose didn't make his mind up soon, Eugene's mere imaginings, growing bolder now that they were released, would do the job for him.

"I'm afraid I'm not familiar with the specifics of your previous training, and I *would* like to maintain racial sensitivity," his owner said with true apology in his voice. "Do you take offense to a flogger?" He produced a whip from the wardrobe. It had at least a dozen long, braided leather tails. Each supple strand ended in a knot. Mr. Ambrose held it, threading the tails through his fingers as he watched Eugene for a reaction.

Eugene's dark violet eyes followed the tails like a cat watching the little red dot. He could feel every part of himself perk up, his cock especially, and he feared what he would sound like when he spoke. "Nothing you do will offend. I trust it will be exactly what I need to remember the lesson, sir." Eugene indulged in a moment of pride. He'd managed to keep his voice rich and smooth as he answered.

Mr. Ambrose nodded. "That is my hope as well, Eugene. You see, now that the twins have moved on and our dear Marilyn is as useless as ever, you will have to assume the role of senior slave in the office. Much will be expected of you."

Ambrose laid the flogger out in plain view on his desk and retrieved something else from the wardrobe before closing the doors. He approached Eugene and took his cock in his tiny, cool hand. "Of course, since this is a punishment, I can't have you getting confused about my intentions." He laid a strip of smooth leather against the underside of Eugene's cock. Deft fingers adjusted seven thin bands around the shaft, the first at the base and the final one just below the head. The leather created delicious pressure all along his cock, but would also serve as a means to prevent Eugene from coming. "That should do the trick."

So many promises in his words. So much of a future Eugene could barely fathom. He was full of questions he was afraid to ask. He kept them to himself, instead whispering, "Yes, sir. Thank you for the reminder."

Although he was sure it would change, nothing about this felt the least bit like punishment. And Mr. Ambrose was beginning to reveal an aptitude he wasn't anywhere near prepared for. A pixie who could torment a man like this? It was almost as ridiculous as a tentacle beast bottom.

Eugene squirmed, feeling everything a bit too much. The cool leather grip around his cock. The sudden nearness of his owner. The hum of Mr. Ambrose's wings. The chilling hush of his voice. He struggled to wrap his mind around the words "senior slave." He found himself hoping that wasn't one of the positions that came with more paperwork.

All of it was causing his tentacle bonds to clench tighter. When the time came, he feared he would be well and truly punished. Jealousy had made him deaf to the myths of their master. Bonnie and Timothy had whispered about what went on in the office and back at Mr. Ambrose's home frequently. Maybe he should have listened closer.

But no. He wouldn't want one idiosyncrasy, one kink, one whispered hunger spoiled by gossip. He wanted to discover them all first hand.

"I expect that this is all quite outside your realm of experience." Mr. Ambrose picked up the flogger and just stared at it for a long while. "It was much the same for me when I was similarly seen for the first time. You would think in this day and age, and especially within our Marketplace community, that racial stereotypes would be a thing of the past."

Mr. Ambrose drifted gracefully back to Eugene. His skin gave off a soft shimmer as he moved. "I believed I would find myself the perfect owner. One who would see more than a fairy. More than a pretty thing to violate. I did not." Ambrose disappeared from Eugene's view. "I became an owner to provide an... opportunity for oddities and misfits to serve."

The flogger fell across Eugene's back. Mr. Ambrose did not use the gentle strokes of a man who feared to do damage. His lashes were firm, well-timed and relentless. As each new strike left lines across his back, Eugene's cock fought for its freedom. It was hard to separate the pain from the flogger and the hidden, aching need to be seen for *who* he was more than *what* he was. Eugene stopped trying, choosing to cry out in acceptance of it all. It had taken years and many wrong turns to find it, but here was the reason he'd so eagerly surrendered his life to the Marketplace. Here was pain he could understand and enjoy. Here was a way he could serve.

He wanted it to hurt. He wanted to take every bit of it in and hold it safe in the deepest recesses of his heart. In this punishment was something unspoken. More than a contract. Maybe a dare to touch the sublime by using each other to blur the lines of years of misery, being left wanting, unfulfilled, and hating themselves.

"Open your mouth." The lashes had stopped, and Mr. Ambrose was hovering near Eugene's ear. When he wasn't obeyed quickly enough, he took hold of Eugene's chin and forced his mouth open. With his other hand, Mr. Ambrose pushed the end of one of Eugene's tentacles into his mouth. "Suck it," he ordered.

Eugene was shocked to realize the undefinable squeak that suddenly rang in his ears was his own, made in the moments before suffering the sweet indignation of working his mouth over his own tentacle in front of the insistent audience of Mr. Ambrose. His eyes pleaded with his unpredictable master as he tried to decide if hesitation or really going for it would provide what it was Mr. Ambrose was looking for. But it was his own desperate need to get off that made him begin to shamelessly service the tentacle in his mouth.

"Very good," Mr. Ambrose spoke quietly but with the same cool tone he always used. He gently extracted the tentacle then forced it back in until Eugene was fairly gagging on it. "Make it hard for me."

The young slave was visibly shaking now. The slightest movement sent prickling barbs of fresh pain from his back. He was trying to control not only his tentacle bonds, but also trying to keep the rest in check. A few were attempting to behave like naughty little fingers and peel the bondage straps from his cock to gain release. He hesitated, taking far longer than he actually needed to bring the choking object in his mouth to its fully active, erect state. He felt the smooth flesh grow fat and rigid against his tongue, cutting off any sounds he might have wanted to make.

"Ah, that's more like it." Mr. Ambrose drew the tentacle away from Eugene's eager mouth. He pressed two dainty fingers against his asshole, applying slow pressure that made Eugene groan. "Prepare yourself."

Not letting go of the tentacle, Mr. Ambrose moved directly behind Eugene. He pulled his fingers away and replaced them with Eugene's stiff appendage. "It would be best not to resist me," he informed Eugene as he guided the tentacle slowly inside him.

Eugene's throat released a scratchy, primal moan. He fought to relax the undisturbed tentacles, while maintaining the few he'd been ordered to keep stiff. He was failing. The tentacles were writhing and pounding against the ground in their reflection of Eugene's emotions. He struggled for control, not able to guess what would happen if he disobeyed and fell. Not sure it would be better or worse for his straining cock and foolish pride, he lost himself and encouraged the playful violation as much as he was able, hanging from the ceiling as he was. It was really more of an internal surrender to the naughty act of fucking himself up the ass, and he was praying that Mr. Ambrose couldn't notice how much he was enjoying it. In all fairness, he had said "don't resist." So he was still following orders.

Ambrose released Eugene's tentacle once it was positioned just how he wanted it. He flittered around to hover at eye level with Eugene. "I want you to violate yourself as thoroughly and violently as you've ever been forced to take another. Hold nothing sacred. Deny your tentacles nothing. Come until you're completely drained. Scream until you're hoarse." Ambrose ran his cool fingers down Eugene's chest, over his belly, until they rested on the tip of his cock. Slowly, starting with the strap nearest the head, he released the bands of the cock ring.

"I'll be watching. If I am not satisfied, you will begin again." Mr. Ambrose flew back to his desk, brushing the rumples out of his perfect suit. Sitting on the edge of his desk, twirling the cock ring around one finger by the widest band, he nodded to Eugene. "Begin."

Second Opinion
By Madeline Elayne

The album had gotten to the part of the concert when you could hear Keith Jarrett singing along with his melody. The quiet, singsong "Doodily doot-doo doo-dee doot" was clearly audible alongside the main theme while he tapped his foot along with the music as he played and occasionally, Cameron could just imagine, banged his head against the frame of his piano as well. It was a very good recording, considering the year it was made, and that all his best works were live concerts. Enya be damned, the Koln Concert was the ultimate music to scene to. Just like good rope play, it was vastly improved with skill, theory and practice, with a basic framework in mind; once he got on stage, though, it was completely off-the-cuff and reactive, born of passion and breathtakingly engaging. Not even people who for some unfathomable reasons didn't care for solo piano jazz improv could deny the passionate energy he played it with, especially if they listened closely enough to hear him moaning along. And the melody was transcendent.

Cam's partner was moaning along, too, but for very different reasons. As a special treat, she'd allowed Leah a gag today, and it had muffled more than its fair share of yelps and screams. Her body was a work of art of the most entertaining kind. She was kneeling upright on a knee-high padded bench, with her thighs spread uncomfortably wide. Her arms were stretched taut behind her back, wrapped from wrist to elbow in thick coils of white rope and fastened securely to the rope binding her ankles. Her torso had been similarly bound, leaving her upper arms, thighs, and calves free and available.

There was barely a space left on the exposed parts of Leah's burnished copper skin that wasn't now striped with parallel ridges of pale skin where the welt was raised, haloed by a lovely red. Cam had taken her time with these, too, just as she had with the bindings themselves. The yelps and whimpers had long since faded to soft sighs and moans as she let Leah slip into the luxury of surrendering to the sensation. She pulled back on the end of the graphite rod and let it flick the short distance to the exposed soles of the bound woman's feet, right near the arches. It didn't take much motion at all to raise a near-instant red stripe. Laying down the next two strokes in quick succession, Cam was not at all surprised that Leah let out no sound at all in reaction. Her head lolled slightly, and Cam reached out to steady her with a rough grip on the back of the neck. That elicited a sigh behind the gag, even if it was a soft one. The younger woman tilted her head to look up at her, a lovely motion that brought its own temptation, exposing her throat.

But Leah's wide and unfocused eyes said it all. She would never ask to stop unless it was explicitly expected of her, but for now she was done. Cam slid the dripping cloth gag from Leah's mouth and tilted her chin to plant a firm kiss on her lips. Then she reached behind her to undo a couple of the most restrictive slipknots keeping her bound, and helped her slide off the bench to the carpet at Cameron's feet where she would be free to loosen and remove the rest of the rope herself when she felt capable. Leah gingerly positioned herself to be able to press a single, lingering kiss on each of Cam's fluffy orange sock-clad feet before finding a less-uncomfortable-than-others position on the floor in which to lie and recover slightly.

Cam slid the table holding both of their travel glasses of iced tea closer to where it was within reach of both of them and spent the next few minutes enjoying the rest of the recorded concert, sipping her drink with one foot perched gently on her partner's thigh while she gave the other woman a few minutes to rest up and compose herself.

"Thank you, Syr," Leah finally whispered, several minutes later. It was the first time either of them had uttered a word in hours. Cam smiled down at her.

"Welcome back to the land of the living."

Leah had gotten about half of the ropes off and neatly coiled back up when Cam's cell phone began to ring, the tone indicating an unknown number. She shot a look up to Cam to see if she would like her to take it, but Cam waved the offer away and answered herself.

116

"Cameron. It's so good to hear your voice," the woman on the other side of the phone call began.

"Is that Siobhan? Isn't it good to hear from you, likewise, eh? I haven't heard hide nor hair of you in a dog's age. How are things with you, my darling?" Cam couldn't help herself sometimes. When she got on the phone with a mainlander, the Newfoundlander in her just went into overdrive. *'Ow are t'ings wit' you, moy darlin'?* It did the trick to make her friend chuckle warmly.

"Well, to be honest, things are a bit complicated over here right now. I was hoping that I might be able to lure you out here for a peaceful semi-vacation on the lovely St. Croix River for a couple of weeks. Travel would be my treat, and the soft world house could use some part-time counseling hours, at your usual rate. Are you still courting that promising young spot you mentioned in your last letter? Maybe you could bring them around with you, I'm sure we could find a way to keep them entertained."

"I am indeed. In fact she's right here in the room with me," Cam said, shooting Leah a wink and a grin. "I'm hoping she'll be ready for me to shop out for placement interviews by next month, so I suppose it might do some good to see how a real training house works before she applies to surrender herself to one."

"That's perfect, then! Is a flight out tomorrow afternoon too early for you both?"

"You know, Shiv, my love, I do find it amusing that you're just assuming I've already agreed."

"That's one of the many things you love about me, Cameron, my dear. Which is, of course, why I knew you would say yes. There's a flight out of St. John's tomorrow at five. Will that work?"

It was Cam's turn to chuckle. "Aye, love, that'll work just fine. Tell you what, I'll text you young Leah here's number and email address. Have one of your trainees send her the details, and she can make the arrangements for us on my end. And then you can tell me all about your new complications."

Siobhan hung up after a few more short pleasantries, and Cam gave Leah a friendly nudge with her foot. "Looks like you've got some packing to do for us tonight, my puppy. Everything we'll need for two weeks stay, and there're laundry facilities on site. Pack outdoor casual for me, and I want you to dress to my preferences for you, nothing flimsy, and all vanilla appropriate. You can pack us each one Leather outfit and one for more formal occasions in case we'll need them. And swimming and fishing gear. We're headed to New Brunswick for a couple of weeks! I'm guessing you'll get an email within a half hour or so with our travel details."

* * *

It had been over an hour's drive after they landed to make it to the House, the last 15 minutes of which were along dirt roads. For a building of its size, it looked remarkably appropriate to the acres and acres of woods surrounding it. Two stories high and sprawlingly wide, the well-maintained siding was a rusty red, and the trim was simple and subtle. The appearance of comfort was even more prevalent inside, with slightly mismatched but sturdy furniture that all looked as if they were designed for comfort first and appearance second.

The overly polite young man who greeted them at the door offered bottles of water and led them to a washroom to freshen up before taking them to meet Siobhan. As usual, Cam emerged looking just about as crumpled as she went in; more than one lover had sworn the butch woman could look rumpled in a freshly pressed Donna Karan. Leah, though, was another story. She had gone out of her way to make a good impression, and it showed. She was sharply dressed in snug white jeans and a royal blue vest over a white tank. She had gotten very good at cultivating the look that so charmed Cam, and from the outside it was nearly impossible to tell what sexy bits she had hidden under the outfit. Comfortably tiny tits or a carefully tucked cock (or both or neither!) all seemed equally probable. She'd re-dyed the very tips of her short inky black hair a rich blue to match her vest the night before, and she looked good enough to eat or, possibly, to tie down and fuck hard. Cam growled in appreciation when she emerged, and the young man led them to Siobhan's office.

Shiv stood and greeted them with a smile, looking resplendent in a gauzy white sundress. Her long black hair had acquired a few more strands of silver since she and Cameron had last met, and the effect ironically took a few years off her face rather than adding to it. A simple gold chain necklace and bracelet brought out the bronzed tones in her skin. She was glorious, as always, and Cam was gratified to hear Leah gasp slightly in admiration on seeing her for the first time.

Cam crossed the distance to her old friend in three huge steps, sweeping her up in a giant bear hug that brought her up a good couple of inches off the floor. Given the half foot in height Siobhan had on her old friend, it was quite a comical sight. She let Shiv back down and draped herself over the nearest chair.

"Good to see you, my darling! I'd like to introduce you to my newest recruit. Puppy, come say hello to Ms. Connors, and don't you go embarrassing me, you hear?"

"It's a pleasure to meet you, Ma'am," Leah said, with only a hint of a quiver in her voice. Cam looked on in amusement as she struggled with the appropriate greeting. Her hand raised a tiny fraction, the handshake instinct difficult to suppress at the best of times, but she put it back down quickly only to bend slightly at the knee, as if she were about to kneel instead but thought better of it. Finally she settled on a sweet-looking dip of the shoulders, bowing her head at the same time. Siobhan seemed satisfied with the choice.

"I don't remember you ever having a polite protégé before, Cameron. Have you gotten soft on me? Leah, dear, please go ahead and kneel if that makes you more comfortable. You did well, I promise."

Leah bowed her head again and settled onto her knees at the foot of Cameron's chair. Cam reached out and toyed with a blue-tipped lock while the unassuming young man who'd met them at the door came in with tea settings and a plate of ginger snaps.

"I've got a room for you to share all prepared in the north house. Cam, feel free to set your own counseling hours, but the house is prepared to pay for up to four hours per weekday. The rest of the time is, of course, yours to do with as you please. There's been an incident I will discuss with you later that has caused some significant distress, and the ladies would greatly welcome an extra understanding set of ears to help them work through it.

"As for you, Leah... Before we chat further, may I ask you what pronouns you prefer?"

Leah blushed prettily, not a small feat given the darkness of her complexion, and stuttered a little in her response. "Thank you. I mean, I appreciate you asking. She and her are just fine, if it pleases you, Ma'am."

"Since I am not your trainer, nor are you in contract with me, it pleases me to use the pronouns with which you're most comfortable. She, it is. Thank you for the information.

"Cameron tells me that you are hoping to join the Marketplace soon, Leah. If you are finding yourself at a loss for something to do, and your patron approves, you are welcome to have free rein here at the training house. If you were officially a training applicant, you would be junior to everyone here, of course, but since you are here as a free guest, you will find the trainees and staff here will be quite friendly and accommodating. I'll ask, though, that since you are not trained in the handling of clients, that you not do too much direct interaction with the trainees, outside of conversation and general house matters, of course.

"This is a specialty house. We don't train general use clients here; we train what the Marketplace as a whole charmingly calls 'grudge slaves'." Siobhan grimaced in disgust at the word.

"The concept takes some getting used to. It can be... distasteful to outside observation when taken out of context. You may see some protocols, behaviors, or possibly even some marks and bruising that may seem shocking or even abhorrent to you. What I ask you to keep in mind, though, is that all the trainees here are carefully chosen and petition quite aggressively to be here. Not only do they consent, but they actively compete for a place, so please reserve judgment until you have taken the time to learn more about what it is we do here, the service we provide."

"I... of course, I wouldn't... I mean, yes, Ma'am. I'll try and keep that in mind. I never... expected to, to... " Cam gave a tug on the lock of hair between her fingers and shushed Leah's rambling before it got too far out of hand. "I will. Thank you, Ma'am."

There was a twinkle in Siobhan's eye as she smiled in Cameron's direction. "You *have* gotten soft!"

Cameron just grinned and rolled her eyes toward her old friend.

"Leah, if you'll excuse us, I have some confidential business I need to discuss with your patron. Lisa will give you a ride over to the north house, and there should be some supper waiting for you in the kitchen. I'm sure Cameron will have told you, but just to reiterate, the north house is both a soft world and vanilla space. Most residents are not Marketplace-aware. I'll expect you to behave accordingly."

"Yes, Ma'am. Thank you for the reminder."

Cam gave Leah a swat on the ass as she stood to head out, and delighted in the fact that the poor girl looked about ready to die from embarrassment. "That one, I'm going to be sad to see go, Shiv, I tell you."

"She seems delightful. But it's the nature of what we do that we're just a stepping stone in their path. We have to let them move on to where they're meant to be, don't we." It was phrased more as a wistful statement than a question.

Cam sighed. "Yeah. That we do, my love. That we do. Now, what is this traumatic event that required my absconding from my beloved St. John's, eh?"

It was the older woman's turn to sigh. Siobhan stepped over to her desk and drew three file folders from the drawer, laying them out side by side on the table in front of Cam.

"Here are the last three residents we took in at the north house. RCMP cracked down on a sex slave ring in the Niagara region a couple of weeks ago. I'm sure you heard about it. It was a pretty bloody bust. The man they believe responsible for abducting them and two of his compatriots were all killed during the raid. These three"—she gestured at the folders, each of which had a five-by-eight-inch photo paper-clipped to the front—"had no family or friends they could turn to, so their caseworker got them a placement with us."

Cam picked up one of the folders and frowned in surprise. "These girls... they're all white?" Much as the media liked to wax poetic about the *white slave trade* it was actually fairly uncommon for a given sample of involuntary sex trade workers from the same ring to be 100 percent Caucasian.

Siobhan nodded. "Almost all of the women rescued were. It was surprising to the investigators, too. These two are Serbian; their families came over around the same time in the 90s during the Yugoslavian conflict. Katherine's family has since moved back home. Tania's mother died a few years ago. No families nearby, cultural isolation, low education... easy targets. The third one, she claimed she was a product of our glorious foster care system."

"Claimed?"

"Yes. It turns out that she was lying about a lot of things. Whether this was one of them is anyone's guess. From what I've been able to piece together, Tina, here, wasn't actually a sex worker in the brothel. She was the pimp's girlfriend who decided to play victim so she wouldn't be arrested as an accessory. Unfortunately, we only learned this when she tried to stab Katherine to death with a kitchen knife shortly after arriving here, blaming her for having gotten her boyfriend killed."

"Sweet motherloving fucker!"

"My sentiments, exactly. On paper, that's why you're here. Everyone here is very shaken up. You can imagine, North House is meant to be a safe haven, where women who are escaping terrible situations can start to rebuild their lives. For one of those terrible situations to follow them here... "

"I understand. I'm surprised you managed to keep the situation so quiet, my love. I mean I'd read about the bust in the paper, of course, but this is the first I'm hearing about any stabbing attempt. How did you keep it out of the news?"

"It wasn't easy, I will say that much. But that's not really what I wanted to talk to you about. Honestly, I hoped you'd come for the third girl, Tania."

Cam pulled Tania's folder onto her lap and flipped it open. "Tania? What about her?"

"She stepped in between them. She was quite badly injured by taking the stabbing meant for Katherine, actually."

"Huh. That's definitely admirable, my darling. But I'm not sure it's very surprising. Things like this have a habit of bringing people closer together. Especially if they share the same background, like these women seem to."

"Have patience. I'm getting to the root of my concern, but first there are some details that you should know. One, is that these women were kept extremely isolated. Until they arrived here, they had never actually met one another, and even when they got here, they were still adjusting, keeping pretty much completely to themselves. I'm not sure that Tania was even aware Katherine was also Serbian. Two, Tania made no move to fight the other woman off. She heard the signs of a struggle and imposed herself bodily between the two until help arrived. Her injuries were far from trivial."

"This woman who attacked them. I'm right to assume she's not here any more, am I?"

"Of course. The Mounties responded fairly quickly. She's been arrested and is being held pending charges."

"Okay. Well that's good then. So obviously, Tania is one of the girls you'd like me to use my fancy social worker counseling skills on. Which is all well and good, of course. But I get the feeling you wanted me here in my spotter hat, too. I have to tell you, Shiv, right now I'm really uncomfortable with that.."

"And I would expect you to be, with only the information I've given you so far. Hell, I have all the information I want to give you, and *I'm* really uncomfortable with it. Maybe, though, once you learn why she says she did what she did, and a bit about her actions and conversations since then, you might wonder too if maybe she requires your services. I'm certainly too invested and far too underqualified to determine that myself."

Cam took a sip of her now quite lukewarm tea and patiently waited for her friend to continue.

"Cameron, you know, in as long as I've had my own house, I've never had a single crossover between my soft world house and my training house. I would never compromise any of my girls from North House. They've all been through so much, I would never let anyone take advantage of them, let alone do it myself. But this woman, Cam. She baffles me. It's like she has a soul meant for service. Even after she was hurt, and was supposed to be on bed rest, I would find her actively struggling to improve the quality of life for someone else in the house in some way or another. It's like she needs to be useful. She needs to *serve*. She may not have chosen her lot in life previously, but I think even then she saw the service in it, and now that she is in a position where she cannot and should not be of service sexually, she's branched out into doing everything else.

"I'll give you an example. One of the ladies here has a pretty bad case of celiac disease. She's quite self-sufficient, doesn't ever make a big deal about it, and prepares her own meals separately, but she had a reaction last week to the peanut butter because the last one to use it had left toast crumbs in the tub. When we got up the next morning, Tania had created a gluten free cupboard, complete with a very user-friendly guide to gluten intolerance taped to the cupboard door. She'd also made three types of rice flour and corn muffins to keep in the deep freeze for easy reheating. Cam, she is doing these things constantly. Never a thought to herself, but if there is anything, anything at all that can make my life or the life of one of the other girls' just a bit better, she jumps on it. I've never seen anyone so desperately eager to help, to serve with no thought to reward or recompense. She seems to thrive on it.

"I'm worried that I've met a natural. Not just a natural Marketplace client—because of course I've met those—but an honest-to-goodness natural, dedicated and thriving slave. And we've stolen her out of her slavery. I wonder how long it will be before she goes to look for it again. I'll be damned if I let another asshole like the one who kept her caged in that awful place be the one to own such sublime devotion. I want her to be happy and fulfilled.

"Can you see if you think that means she should be with us somewhere? Obviously, this house wouldn't be where she should train, but I need to know if you think she should be somewhere. With us. So that she can be protected and cherished for her service."

Cam slowly nodded, getting to her feet. "If you feel that strongly about it, my darling, of course I'll talk to her. And I promise I'll do it wearing my counselor hat and my spotter hat both. I can't promise you I'll see what you do in her, though. Knowing nothing else but what she's been through, I'd be willing to bet she's just too damaged to be able to know what she really wants right now. But I'll do my best to keep an open mind."

The evening was just starting to cool off and there was a light breeze, so Cameron decided it would be nice to head up to North House on foot. She wasn't in any rush; she wouldn't even start looking at scheduling counseling appointments until the next day.

Leah was out on the front porch when she got back, and was vibrating with excitement as she showed her up to their shared room. Someone had left a plateful of cookies for them there, as well. Cam eyed the treats lustfully and groaned. This visit was going to prove to be sugar city.

Cam sat down on the closer of the two twin beds, both of which were already turned down for the night. Leah knelt at her feet to help her off with her boots. Cam gave a contented sigh when she started to rub and knead the day's tension from her feet.

"Okay, Pup. Out with it. You look fit to explode if you don't get to talk about something soon. You have my permission to speak freely. But mind your volume, since we're in a soft world space, eh?"

"Oh wow, Syr. Just wow. Are all trainers so... "

"Dreamy?"

"So amazing?"

Cam chuckled and tousled Leah's hair. "How would you know, ya silly goose? You only met her for a half an hour!"

"That was enough, though! She's just so, so in control. And elegant! And not at all what I expected! I mean, the way you were talking about her, I kind of pictured a slightly older version of that princess from *Brave*. But she is so much more. She's gorgeous and powerful. And I've never met anyone from her generation who's asked me my pronouns before! Is she... "

"Is she what, love? Indigenous? Would that be a problem, even with a name like Siobhan Connors?" Leah flushed, looking abashed, and started to stammer, but Cam couldn't keep the stern look on her face for more than a second. Leah's excitement and good humor were just too contagious.

"It's okay, my love. I'm only teasing. You're wondering if she's trans, like you, I'm guessing?"

Leah nodded, mutely.

"Yes. She is. Shiv comes from an old family of *very* well-to-do Marketplace owners, going back to the establishment of the Hudson's Bay Company. So you can imagine her family's reaction when she moved to San Francisco in her 20s to do the drag circuit. That was decades ago, now, though. One day, she got tired of pretending to be a boy in between shows, and so she came back home to Canada, as Siobhan. She tells me her mum didn't speak a word to her since that day, but after she passed, her dad came around. Even wrote her back in to the will. Now she's got hordes of nieces and nephews, and great-nieces and great-nephews who think Auntie Shiv is the best thing since champagne met chocolate."

Cam made a gesture, and Leah climbed up on to the bed behind her to start working out the kinks in her neck, next.

"She *is* the best thing since champagne and chocolate! I want to know everything about her!"

"Well you'll have two whole weeks to ask her anything you want to yourself, you know."

"I know, Syr. And I want to be patient. But she's just so... wow!"

125

"Okay, tell you what. I'll tell you what I know for as long as it takes for you to get my poor tired muscles into some semblance of relaxation. But after that, anything you want to know about your newest crush you will have to ask her yourself, understand?"

"Yes, Syr! Thank you!"

That statement was followed by a moment of resounding silence, which Cam filled with an amused chuckle. "You have to ask a question to get an answer, you know, pup."

"Sorry, Syr. I'm just trying to figure out what to ask first. I guess I most want to know the big questions. Like, what exactly is a grudge slave, and why did she choose to train them, specifically? And what about this place? North House? How do voluntary, contracted and trained grudge slaves fit in with a shelter for former sex workers? How did she get into all this?"

"You weren't kidding when you said you wanted to know everything! Okay, I'll start with your first question, which has the simplest answer. A grudge is a very specialized type of Marketplace slave whose sole purpose it to bear the brunt of abuses, degradations and punishments that would be against the contract of most other Marketplace clients, for the benefit, the gratification or the pleasure of their owners. It's a very, very rare type of client who is suited to this role, and they're trained extensively in self-care techniques, and they have a support network and safety net proportional to the risk of their chosen niche. Not to ruin your fairy tale view of the Marketplace, but some of the worst people you could ever know are grudge slave owners, and among other things, it's Shiv's job to train them, provide them with slaves, and make sure they follow the rules."

"Oh, my god. But she's so amazing, and caring! Why would she choose that specialty?"

"Because, my love, it's far better than the alternative." Cam popped open the top button of her shirt, and Leah took over without missing a beat, unfastening the top and sliding it down off her spotter's shoulders. She continued her rubdown against bare skin, pausing only long enough to splash a bit of rose oil onto her palms.

"Okay, let me see if I can give you a little bit of background, and maybe it'll help you understand. You'll remember, there, when Shiv first came back to Canada, she was pretty much on the outs with her whole family. Truth is, she didn't want to have anything to do with any of 'em. So she did what any rich kid with a conscience and without any real demands on their time winds up doing at one point or another. She became an activist.

"Have you heard of that Amnesty International movement, No More Stolen Sisters? Well, back when Shiv first came back to Canada, no one had. Not to say that it wasn't a huge problem, it was, but no one was talking about it. Hundreds of indigenous women and girls were going missing or being killed, and it was like the whole country was just sweeping it under the rug. I think the number's at something horrible like 1200 now. That's where North House came from, originally. If so many First Nations women and girls were being tortured, abused and killed at the hands of their fathers, their brothers, their husbands and boyfriends, then Shiv was damn sure she was going to give them somewhere that they could disappear *to* that wasn't a shallow grave somewhere out of the nation's sight and mind.

"It was working with these women that she learned how many of the disappeared women were absorbed, mostly against their will, into the sex trade. Way, way too many. So she started making contacts with law enforcement and with social workers like me. If we shut down a sex trafficking ring, and someone we pulled out had nowhere to go, we would send them to Shiv, and she'd make sure that they had everything they needed, including counseling and vocational training. She was a lifesaver. And that's how I met her. Before I even became a spotter. It's also where she crossed paths with the type of person who would ruin a woman's life for their own pleasure. And those people weren't limited to any single social class or ethnic group. The only thing they had in common was the willingness and desire to hurt people who wouldn't fight back against them.

"Like I told you, though, when her mum died a dozen or so years ago, Siobhan's dad wanted her back in the family. And part of being in the family meant owning slaves. Even at his age, her dad was very active in the Marketplace community. He often had other visiting owners and trainers staying with him, sometimes for extended periods of time. One of those times, it's gotta be about ten years ago now, she was visiting her dad at the same time as three owners and their personal slaves. One of those slaves, she learned, was a grudge slave.

"Now, one thing you have to know about grudge slaves is that part of their specialized contracts includes provisions for a huge amount of downtime and recovery time, both emotional and physical. So Siobhan had plenty of time to sit and talk with him, and you better believe she took advantage. I think she had it in her head to rescue him and whisk him away to her shelter where no one would ever be able to find him. But instead, she found out that he was exactly where he needed to be.

"I swear, puppy, Shiv and I spent a whole night not sleeping once, talking about the stuff that they discussed during that visit. It was just mind-blowing stuff to me. I can't imagine how much more revelatory it must've been to her."

Cam stretched out on her stomach on the bed, and lifted her hips enough for Leah to slide her shorts off. Now fully naked, she near purred at her young padawan's continued ministrations. This was the life.

"I've told you how rare a natural slave is, even in Marketplace circles, right? Well to hear Shiv tell it, and I believe her, a grudge is a member of a tiny subset of those. These are people who not only thrive on being able to suffer for the pleasure, satisfaction and/or emotional health of others, but they're capable of shouldering that suffering with little to no ill effect. That takes a phenomenal amount of emotional fortitude. And of course, they have to be in incredible physical condition too. The demands of their role just don't compare to anyone else in the Marketplace I've ever known. But here's the thing. These remarkable people are actually happier, and *better off*, inside this role than without it. As hokey as it sounds, it's like they've found their purpose.

"And that meeting, that one meeting, was all it took. Shiv had, to put it glibly, found her own purpose. You see, what she and I understood perfectly was that the type of person she was used to dealing with, the type of person who are, in great numbers, amongst those who purchase grudge slaves, are the type of person who will always, *always* cause that kind of pain and harm to *someone*. These aren't the only kind of grudge slave owner, you understand, but just like you'll find more psychopaths in a maximum security prison environment than in any other, you'll find more of this particular brand of evil amongst the grudge owners than anywhere else. Except, maybe, among patrons of sex slave rings.

"It came down to the vastly lesser of two evils. On the one hand, you had patrons of people who voluntarily submitted themselves to this treatment, who had people there to ensure that their rules were being followed, to care for them during and afterward, and to whisk them away at the first sign of trouble. Or you had the missing and the murdered, many of whom were innocent children when they were first harmed.

"So Shiv asked me to take over her House for long enough for her to undergo training as a Trainer, and she's been working to perfect and improve the methods of training and caring for her treasured grudges ever since. And they love her for it. Almost as much as you do, eh, puppy?"

Leah giggled and set three fluttery kisses on the back of Cam's neck.

"Don't worry, I still love you too, Syr!"

"Ha. You'd better remember that! Now get your cute little arse to bed and dream of sexy trainers putting you through all kinds of exacting paces. I need my sleep. Don't wake me 'til seven with coffee and something sweet, eh? We're on vacation, after all."

* * *

Cam's two-week working vacation went by far too quickly. With Leah's help, she had her counseling schedule completed and filled on their first day there. On her off time, she taught Leah how to catch, clean and cook smallmouth bass. Leah, to her surprise and delight, taught Cam how to ride bareback. At night, the two of them fucked frequently, and in the pleasant afterglow, Leah regaled her with stories of her adventures with Siobhan and her trainees. She learned everything from a crash course in formal manners—including (in Leah's own words) the most gorgeous fucking apology you'll ever see—to how to bake a perfect batch of traditional New Brunswick scotch cakes. It was a beautifully relaxing time.

Most of Cameron's energy and attention, though, was expended in spending as much time as she possibly could with Siobhan's young enigma. And that was, by far, the best part of her trip. The more she talked with the young woman, the more convinced she became that here was a talented, brilliant, devoted and strikingly selfless individual who anyone would be better off for having known. And also, that her beloved friend and confidante Siobhan was without a doubt the stupidest smart person she'd ever known.

The afternoon before they were scheduled to leave, she and Siobhan each packed a snack and a beach chair on their backs and took the scenic route back through the trails on the eastern border of the property until they hit the river. They sat and watched the water together, until the sun set, and stayed a good while longer to watch the stars, too.

They had another one of those mind-expanding nights like the one they had a decade ago, but this time, it was Cam doing all the talking.

"I need you to see what it is that I do, my darling, from my point of view. You know, as well as I do, that this business we're in, it's all about love. I mean, look at me and tell how I feel about Leah."

"You love her, absolutely. It's clear as day."

"You bet I do. But it's not just her, you see. It's anyone I've ever spotted, for my seven years on the job. If they've made it far enough that I tell them about the Marketplace, then I've loved them. It's that simple, even the ones who were giant pains in my arse.

"There is no question at all in my mind that you've loved every single client you've ever had train through here, too. You've probably loved most if not all the girls in North House, too. It's the business we're in. It attracts people who are quick to love. They love us, too, of course. It's why they're willing and able to give us all we demand of them. And we demand so very, very much. You, more than any of us.

"But I think there's a piece of the puzzle that you're missing, there, my darling, because you've never been in my position. You see, love is a necessary, but it's not a sufficient condition for someone to be meant to move on to training with someone like you. Yes, they will love me. But they have to love the service itself more. Otherwise, they will love me, and they will love their trainer, but there is no telling whether they will come to love their owner or even, at the very least, their service to him or her or them. And if they don't love that, then they won't stay. They will never get past their first contract, if they even get that far. This world of ours isn't built on single contracts. I don't have to tell you that. It's built on lifetimes.

"So, my love, what you're missing, is the context of your Tania's behavior. Yes, absolutely she loves to be of service. But it's not the service that's the final object of her love, you goose. It's you. If you want my advice, you'll keep her as long as you're damn well able. With a bit of training up, she could be running North House for you, better than you ever could. And she would make one fucking hell of a lover. But she's not a slave. Not any more, not now that she has a choice. She is just a dazzlingly talented woman, with very, very good taste."

Prospect
By Moxie Marcus

"If you follow me, he's right this way, Margaret."

Her steps were even, measured. He kept his eyes downcast. She moved quietly with a precision that made him wonder what kind of demands she would make on him. He couldn't let any of those thoughts show on his face.

When she came into view—or rather when her feet came into view—he was surprised to notice she was wearing canvas high-top tennis shoes. They were plum-colored, with ivory toe-boxes and ivory laces. Most of the other prospective buyers wore boots or expensive leather shoes. This one was wearing dark-washed jeans that were cuffed at the bottom.

He was standing with his hands clasped behind his neck. His hair had been combed so it hung in a shining dark fall to his waist. The tattoo that wrapped around his forearm was displayed nicely, the colors making stark contrast to his fair skin.

"He's fresh to the Marketplace?" the woman asked, quietly.

"Yes, but he's been thoroughly trained. His skin shows marks beautifully."

"I'd like a demonstration then, please."

"Of course," Gwen snapped her fingers twice. He walked briskly enough to be efficient but not so quickly that he wasn't still graceful.

He was six and a half feet tall and lean. If he didn't maintain his regular exercise routine, his body tended towards naturally sinewy, a state that wasn't always appealing to a Master. Part of his training had included conditioning himself so his muscles would add some contour to his body without adding too much bulk. If he was dressed in a suit, he looked elegant and statuesque. Of course, his mode of dress would be selected by his Master.

131

He draped himself over the arm of the couch. The curve allowed him to brace his stomach and get his feet directly underneath him so his ass would be presented in a perfect position. Whenever Gwen talked about marks, it meant she would bring one of the canes. She was especially fond of a thicker one that landed against his skin with thudding smacks. The welts it left started to turn purple within seconds. He still had a couple of them the color of raisins from the last pre-auction showing.

"How would you like him Margaret, strong and silent or wailing for mercy?"

"This one wails?"

"Exquisitely."

"Yes, I think I'd like a noise demonstration as well, then. I have to make sure he won't make my neighbors complain. The Housing Association can get so uptight about things if the police get called."

He bit back a sigh. They all wanted noise, which meant Gwen was going to give it her all when she hit him. He let his head fall forward so his neck made an arch and took a deep breath. The cane landed full across his butt with a resounding smack. He grunted. Warmth rose in the skin. His cock immediately rose to attention.

That first taste of pain flooded through him. Adrenaline spiked into his system. He fought his natural inclination to pant and tilt his hips back to meet the next strike. He was fully trained, after all, not a slavering animal, unless that was what his Master demanded of him. Another deep breath expanded his lungs.

Gwen and Margaret cheerfully talked about some remodeling Margaret was doing on her house. She talked about paint colors she wanted to select and how much difficulty she'd had finding carpet she liked. He breathed through the respite with the understanding it would be brief. His legs and arms tremored slightly as he steeled himself for the next blow. The tension in his limbs would be visible, but the shaking would be imperceptible, unless Gwen or Margaret touched him.

With lightning precision, Gwen lashed out with the cane, making two diagonal welts across the horizontal ones already there. With each blow, he let out a sharp, distinct cry of "Ah!" She had laid out a perfect hashtag across his ass. He felt hot, a flush rose from the new marks decorating his skin up his back to his cheeks.

"Would you like to try?" Gwen asked Margaret.

He had realized almost immediately Margaret was not a tall woman, but he had also learned during his training never to make assumptions about the pain a Master would inflict based upon their appearance. The most intense session he had ever had came at the hands of a tiny blonde woman with ringlet curls dressed in a lace-frothed Victorian gown. He had thought her underskirts and the sleeves would get in her way. They had made no difference. He bit down on his lip as his cock stirred at the memory.

Margaret stepped closer and tapped lightly at his hip. Then, he felt the cane brush against his inner thighs. It was a light caress, followed by the feel of cool, impeccably lacquered wood nudging ever so slightly at the underside of his scrotum. He clenched his teeth and swallowed, his throat clicking around the movement. He had never been so keenly aware of his own genitals in his life. He had never minded a few light slaps now and again, but the idea of being stuck more harshly terrified him. No one had ever done that to him, though he supposed it was a distinct possibility.

But, no, Margaret had no intentions of doing any such thing. She was tormenting him, making him aware of what could happen. He felt tears prickle his eyes in gratitude for her kindness. She pressed the cane against his inner thighs again, a clear indication she wanted him to widen his stance. Obediently he did as she asked, allowing his solar plexus to rest against the arm of the couch.

Her first hit caught him just at the crease at the tops of his thighs. The skin there was still alarmingly delicate. Because restraint had not been requested, he let an inarticulate noise tear from his mouth. It was a ragged whine.

Then she landed a mark across his back. He could feel the line of exquisite fire from his left shoulder to his right hip. He gasped and arched his back upwards. His panting moved the muscles of his shoulders and upper back. He already felt the distinctive pull of rising bruises tightening the skin.

Her soft, padding footsteps made him aware she was changing position. When the cane impacted the other shoulder, he cried out again, his voice filling the room. He didn't beg, he didn't plead. She wanted noise, and it was entirely her choice as to whether she would deign to show him mercy. His body was punctuated with the marks of her pleasure, and it was so enthralling that he responded with pleasure of his own.

Margaret wound his hair around her fist and pulled his head steadily back. He fought to breathe through his mouth as he looked into her eyes. He wasn't sure if it was the position he was in or the caning he'd just received or if it was hope, but the tears that had threatened earlier spilled over, leaking from the corners of his eyes.

Margaret had dark hair pulled back in a ponytail. Rather than the sleek, polished look so many of the buyers displayed, she had a few loose tendrils of hair escaping her hair tie. The hand resting on the couch was wide, with short-trimmed nails. She didn't even wear any makeup. She wore a T-shirt with some kind of logo on it. Somewhere, his mind dredged up the information that it was a superhero. She looked nothing like any of the potential owners he'd seen.

"Have you pegged before?"

"Yes, ma'am," he answered.

Her expression stayed neutral. He had no idea if she had enjoyed what she had seen or not.

"Stand up," she said.

She had not ordered him to resume his former stance so he straightened awkwardly. His managed to retain his balance. The air in the room felt cool on the unmarked portions of his body. His nipples tightened at the variation in temperature. Automatically, he clenched his hands behind his neck.

He had not climaxed. Margaret studied him. She quirked an eyebrow as she saw he was still erect, despite the tears.

"Gwen, do you have any clothes for him? I'd like to see him dressed."

"Of course, Margaret. I have something I'm sure you'll find suitable."

Gwen snapped her fingers three times, and he followed her to a closet adjacent to the playroom. She opened it and pulled a few things out of the drawers. He took the stockings and waist cincher without a sound. Other slaves may have needed reminded that they wore their clothing at their owner's pleasure, but he had never required that to be explained.

"You will dress here," Margaret said.

He nodded, avoiding eye contact once more. He leaned back against the painted wall behind him. The paint was almost shockingly cold against the welts on his ass. He rolled the dark silk painstakingly up his leg. The fabric was incredibly soft as it slid against his skin. He settled the top of the first stocking against his thigh with a quick snap. The process was repeated with the other leg, paced so Margaret could watch without becoming frustrated.

He wrapped the cincher, which was black satin patterned with intricate green vines, around his middle. The boning pressed against the marks on his back, making them throb in time with his pulse. He checked the tightness and removed it to tug the laces. He adjusted each side and then wrapped it back around him. He could still breathe easily, but not deeply. The room was silent enough that he could hear each of the hooks snapping closed as he fastened them.

As soon as he was dressed, he put his hands back behind his neck. She scrutinized him. He felt desperate to look at her face just so he could try to figure out what she was thinking. He started to feel uncomfortable. The cincher was compressing him. He knew that the marks on his ass were framed by the stockings and the half-corset. Air seemed to be in short supply. It was anxiety, he knew that. He wanted to please Margaret and Gwen, but they weren't telling him what they wanted, and he didn't know Margaret well enough to anticipate her desires.

Then, Margaret nodded at Gwen, and they left the room. Just as they reached the doorway, Gwen said over her shoulder, "Take those things off. Wash the stockings and hang them to dry. When they're dry, put them away."

"Yes, ma'am," he answered.

The next day was the auction. He was washed and impeccably groomed, then stood on a platform in the great room of the house. Buyers came in to view him in a steady trickle of individuals and small clusters of two or three. Some of them were familiar; they had visited Gwen prior to the sale and had private sessions with him. Many of them had applied canes or floggers to him to gauge his reaction and his responsiveness.

He had experience doing mechanic work and could serve as a driver, as well as doing the routine maintenance on any vehicle. He enjoyed reading and drawing. Gwen had gotten him some formal lessons in the proper handling of art supplies, qualifying him as an artist's assistant as well.

He had been taught how to do laundry properly, including the washing of intimate apparel. Gwen had seemed to take special delight in making him clean all the gear in the house. He knew the correct method to handle and clean silicone, rubber, leather and any other materials that would be found in a playroom or workshop, depending on the owner's favorite terminology.

He spoke Italian well and French passably. Gwen had been pleased to discover he had a bachelor's degree in literature. He had read the bulk of the novels on most of the great books list. She had spent several evenings with him curled on the floor at her feet discussing the finer points of Tolstoy or Marquez.

The weak points were his height. He would not fit average-sized pallets, nor would he comfortably fit in an average-sized vehicle. Handcuffs and ankle restraints were no difficulty, but any time an owner might want to tie him to a frame, it would either have to be custom-built or improvised. Then, of course, there was the matter of his knee.

He had injured it in a motorcycle accident when he was in his early 20s. The knee had required surgery, and years later, it gave him trouble in cold weather. If he knelt too long or stood unsupported for an extended length of time, the knee would start to ache and swell. If he pushed himself too hard physically, his knee would lock up, and he would have to elevate it and ice it for at least a full day.

Gwen had experienced the most difficulty with his training making him realize he had limitations. No Marketplace owner was going to accept his willingness to go far beyond his endurance as an asset. He was dedicated to giving his best performance in all aspects of his life. It had taken her weeks to make him understand a slave who worked himself into a sick day at least once a week wasn't the kind of slave anyone would want to own. She had to get him to understand it was not weakness to tell his owner honestly when his knee was reaching its limits. It was good practice that would ensure he and his owner would be able to enjoy their partnership for as long as it lasted.

There were a few of the buyers who looked very closely at his knee. He had known Gwen would disclose the flaw in his folder. He was asked several times to demonstrate his language skills. He answered fluently and quickly, missing not a single word from his statements.

He kept waiting to see one particular buyer come through the room. With each new person who walked past him, he felt his heart sink. She had not appeared. His stomach clenched, and his ears rang as he considered the possibility he had not pleased her. He found himself reviewing every detail of the encounter the day before, trying to understand where he had gone wrong. If she were outbid, he could accept going to one of the others, but if she simply did not show up to make an offer that indicated he had failed. When Gwen had brought her to see him, she gave every indication Margaret would at least like what she saw. Her face had been impassive enough when he had glimpsed it that he couldn't be sure if she had even been interested.

He kept his face schooled in a neutral expression. It would not be proper to let any of the buyers see his disappointment. That would reflect so poorly on Gwen, and she had taken such care in his training. No matter what happened, he would be sold today, and he had Gwen and her excellent training to thank for that.

It was only a few minutes until the bidding and viewing process was scheduled to end. Margaret strode in purposefully. She was dressed in jeans and a T-shirt with another superhero emblem across the chest and those same canvas high-top tennis shoes. She didn't so much as glance at him as she marched into the bidding room.

The pounding of his heart was matched by the beating of his pulse in the welts the cane had raised yesterday. She had come. She would bid. If nothing else, he had the joy of knowing, yes, Margaret would make at least a token effort to own him. He had not failed.

A hush fell over the bidding room as she walked in. The others knew her, then. He couldn't strain to listen for any hint why they had gone silent. It would have been unseemly, especially since they were bidding on him.

A gong rang, signifying the end of the bidding. Gwen announced they would take final offers from the preferred bidders in the room. He heard nothing else from any of them. A few of the house servants who had been circulating with hors d'oeuvres and champagne walked past him with empty trays. Gwen was, as always, an impeccable hostess.

Then, Gwen led the group back to where he was displayed. She smiled at all of them.

"I'm pleased to announce that the winner of today's sale is Ms. Margaret Moira."

The crowd clapped politely, and Margaret stepped forward to snap her lock into his collar. It was that moment when he realized who Margaret was. She was a painter famous for her beautiful compositions and her eye for detail. Her favorite subjects were people who had been bound. He had seen several of her pieces on the walls of the Marketplace members he had visited with Gwen during his training. She signed them with *Moira* in the bottom right hand corner.

Margaret gave Gwen a brief hug, then announced, "I'm sorry, I have to leave immediately. I've got a gallery showing starting tomorrow afternoon, and I have a few things I still have to get ready."

A few of the others made some quiet sounds of disappointment. Margaret offered them some polite platitudes. Then she turned to him.

"Follow me."

Margaret didn't lead him out of the house, as he'd half expected. Instead, she took him to one of the side rooms. A set of folded clothes was sitting on top of the dresser. He unfolded the shirt on top. It was a dark green long-sleeved Henley. When he pulled it over his head, he discovered it fit him perfectly, grazing close to his body without clinging. There were some charcoal gray boxer briefs and dark washed jeans. As he dressed, he glanced down and saw a pair of heavy black engineer's boots he was certain would be his size.

"We'll be driving to the hotel, which is right across from the gallery."

"Yes, ma'am."

After his boots were on, he followed her outside. She walked as purposefully as she had when she'd come to bid. He couldn't quite keep his surprise in check when Margaret wrapped her hands around the handlebars of a low-slung black Harley-Davidson. She knocked the kickstand with her heel popping it up neatly. Then, she settled into the saddle and looked at him.

"Your helmet and your jacket are in the saddlebags."

He opened them, his hands caressing the hardened black leather. The jacket was a racer-style, tabbed-collar one devoid of studs or ornamentation. As plain as it was, however, the jacket was very well made. Margaret had already tightened the strap of her skid lid helmet around her chin.

She nodded once he was dressed and then, finally, asked, "What's your name?"

"Connor, ma'am, Connor Cane."

"Well, then, Connor, get on the back and hang on tight. We're in for one hell of a ride."

650.13

By Caraway Carter

"650.13" is the Dewey decimal classification for "Personal Improvement and Success in Business Relationships," under "Management and Auxiliary Services."

There are many kinds of service in the Marketplace, but a Marketplace slave can't always serve the way he wants to or the way she most enjoys. When you enter the Marketplace as a slave, it is no longer about what you want.

I'll be honest. I entered the Marketplace to please one man, and one man only. Jamie. He found me, he made me realize what I was, and then he made me need it. We had an understanding: I would enter the Marketplace to train as a slave. I would finish the training, and then I would be his.

Then, at my six-month visit with him, he told me *he* wasn't ready for a slave of his own. He needed some time, and he needed me to be able to manage other slaves in his household. Without that, I was useless to him. So I entered Imala Anderson's training program to become a trainer, instead of a slave.

Some time became lots of time. Weeks became months, months became years. Jamie paid for my training. He assured me he'd call on me when he was ready.

When I was nearly done with the seven-year program, a drunk driver took him from me.

Ma'am—Ms. Anderson—broke the news to me and held me as I fell into her arms, stunned silent. I was nearing the end of five years of training with her, but without Jamie, I saw no point in finishing the trainer program. I was a slave, and I only saw servitude in my future.

She removed me from the trainer program and placed me back

139

into slave training. We agreed finishing out my managing duties would be beneficial for us both, and she promptly suggested I read all the manuals and white papers she had available on service, to broaden what I could offer a buyer.

As my training came to a close, I knew I would be a good service slave. But I never put two and two together about the rest of my training. I knew slaves had no voice, but I thought she would treat me differently. But the day I re-entered slave training, she had Greta remove my things from the room upstairs and place them in the slave quarters.

Gone was my soft bed, my closet, my private bathroom. All of it was replaced with shared everything, a firm mattress on a pallet and assigned bathroom times. I could wear simple clothes most of the time, but at a moment's notice I could be ordered to remove my clothes, to kneel, to service a trainer sexually. I could be ordered to pull my pants down and bend over a table to be spanked. I could be told to hold a tray for hours as a ribbon was tied around my cock.

I knew all slaves were trained in all kinds of service, but I shielded myself with the idea that, at the end of it, I would only be in charge of *her* library. I couldn't imagine she'd suggest anything else. Certainly, I was not intended for the block.

But the training continued as if she thought I was. My body, never especially attractive, became a focus for her. She was determined I'd lose 30 pounds. I was sent away to a personal trainer for a month here and a month there, exercised like a champion racehorse—or perhaps a workhorse, considering how much weight I had to carry. There was a month at a fat camp, where I learned how to eat poorly and exercise hard. I worked harder than I thought possible, but nothing was working to change how I felt about my body.

I looked in the mirror every morning and still saw an average-looking, late-30s, slightly chubby librarian. That was all I could ever be. So I couldn't understand why Ma'am was investing so much time in this particular aspect of my training.

* * *

The room was just as it always was. That's what made it so calming to the clients who came looking for new slaves.

140

"We're looking for someone who can organize our new house, starting with its library," Sonja said, as she sat back in the chair before the woman.

Anderson flipped through her book, nodding. After a few moments, with several pages caught between her fingers, she pulled four dossiers from her filing cabinet and sat down with the Travises again. "Is that all you need them for? A two-year contract to organize the house?"

Drew Travis leaned forward. "Well, we would like them to be our majordomo, eventually."

Anderson set down the dossiers on the table between them. "Where's the new house?"

Drew sighed. "It's Uncle Mert's big property in Marin. It's a mess, but we thought we'd open it up as a resort for the Marketplace, and it's a huge undertaking."

Anderson nodded. "We were so sorry to hear of his passing last month. We assume he left Mira and Howard to you in the will?"

Drew nodded, sipping his coffee. "Yes. Thank you for suggesting Mira to him, by the way. She was invaluable to us in his last days. And yes, Mert left them to us in the will. I'm pretty sure it's so she can stay on and care for Howard."

Anderson nodded thoughtfully. "So it's a big project. Does it matter whether the new slave is male or female?"

The couple unanimously chimed, "Male." Then they grinned, looking at each other.

"Do you want him to be more than your majordomo?" Anderson raised an eyebrow.

Drew put his coffee to one side. "What we want is someone who can do double-duty. Yes, we want an organizer. But for this project— Sonja and I want every slave in this resort to be skilled in several forms of service, and every one of them must be skilled at sex."

He looked to his wife, and she continued, "You see, Imala, we want to let owners who visit use our resort's slaves, if they wish, so we need to make sure all slaves at the resort can handle any kind of service."

"Well, then. That narrows my suggestions down to two. Vincenzo comes highly recommended. He has... talents." She handed a folder to Drew. "The second candidate is one of my own. He'll finish his formal training in a month or so, then it's on to the block, unless you decide on him." She handed a second folder to Sonja.

They flipped through the files, occasionally looking up at each other and pointing out a choice tidbit with raised eyebrows or a frown. Eventually they traded folders and repeated the whole process with different tidbits. Finally, they looked back to Anderson.

"Vincenzo's pretty, but I'm not sure that accountant experience is going to help with the mess we have. It's a *35-room house*, Imala. It's not like our place down in Bel Air." Drew set the first folder aside regretfully. "We need a bigger skill set than he's got."

Sonja nodded. "Uncle Mert's house... Imala, it's going to take a *manager*. It needs clearing out, it needs organization, it needs carpenters and plumbers and painters and interior designers... " She trailed off.

"Mert was a hoarder, wasn't he?" Anderson nodded in understanding as she took back Vincenzo's folder.

"It's more that the people he bought the place from were hoarders, but you know what Uncle Mert was like. If he saw something pretty, he just *had* to have it. Totally impractical, that man." Drew rolled his eyes as he reached for his coffee again.

Anderson laughed, remembering Merton Travis' countless orders for slaves that were physically pretty, even if they had no brains. "I quite understand. Well, then, what about Tobias? He's got the skill set you're looking for."

"There is that... but he's older and chubbier than I would expect for a slave from you," Drew said.

"Is his weight really that important?" Anderson tilted her head. "I assure you, Tobias is everything you're looking for."

Drew cast a sidewise glance at his wife. "He's not that pretty, though."

Anderson nodded. "He isn't, but he more than makes up for that in skills. So let me try to sell you on the strong points. Tobias is a manager. He has a master's degree in library science, and he specializes in curation. We'd originally trained him as a trainer, so he can manage a household of slaves, no problem. But the man he was training to serve passed away suddenly during his training, so I retrained him for the block. Your situation seems tailor-made for him, Drew—Sonja," she added, looking from husband to wife. "You have a mess, and he's perfect for *that* job."

As the resistance faded from their faces, and they leaned forward to take a closer look at his file, Imala Anderson sat back and thought, *And this will fix that last little problem he's been having. If serving these two people does not convince him, nothing will.*

* * *

Two months isn't a long time, when you think about going on the block in the Marketplace.

And it was nowhere near long enough to correct what Ma'am called my *last little problem*. It wasn't the weight, although nothing I tried to lose weight worked. It was that I was having a hard time convincing myself I could be a pleasure slave to anyone. The thought made my entire body tingle; my face would go red and my hands would shake. Ma'am's houseguests were allowed to use me however they wanted, and apparently my performances were always exemplary. But at the end of it, all I could do was look at myself in the mirror and shake my head.

After catching me looking in the mirror, Ma'am called me into her office and ordered me to strip.

"Toby... you, my boy, need to own your talents."

When I heard her use the nickname I tensed up. I tried not to, but I did, and the crop sliced through the air and stung me seconds later. I held firmly to my place, didn't wince, and took it.

"I didn't hear you, boy."

"Yes, Ma'am. I need to own my talents."

"You are a lovely man, Toby. You are intelligent. You are skilled, on your knees and off them. I've seen you manage a household of slaves, leaving them with orders for work and knowing it will get done. You are able to serve in every way you've been trained, but you don't believe that. You just... you disappoint me sometimes, Toby."

She said the nickname, because she knew I hated it. She tortured me more often with words than with beatings. And mostly it happened when she was disappointed in me.

* * *

143

Two weeks before my training ended, Ma'am had a dinner party.

She locked me in a metal cock cage an hour before her guests arrived. I was allowed to wear nothing else, except a little black collar with a leather bow tie on it locked around my neck.

I was forbidden to look in the mirror anymore, but my belly felt huge to me.

Ma'am brought me to the dining room and had me kneel in one corner, presenting with my face to the room. Humiliating, but it was part of my training, so I did it. Her guests were already chatting in the living room when she came in with a long, pink grosgrain ribbon and tied it to one of the bars of my cock cage. I looked up for a split second, and received a slap for my disobedience. "Own your talents, boy."

When I had calmed my face, the slap stinging under my cheekbone, she continued. "It's a party for a friend's birthday tonight. Everyone has been gifted with a length of ribbon. They've been instructed to tie one on you whenever they feel like it. *You* are the lucky gift I'll present to the birthday guest. They don't know this yet; it's just for fun. Both of you should be happy at the end of the night."

I kept my eyes lowered and took a deep breath. "Thank you, Ma'am."

And her guests came in.

By the end of the soup course, I had three ribbons tied on my cock cage and one around my upper arm, like a weird tattooed armband of black silk. By the end of the main course, I had gained five more. One of the men reminded me of Jamie, and when he tied a purple ribbon to my left thumb, I had a hard time keeping my composure. By the time the other slaves were clearing away the dessert bowls, my cock cage was festooned with ribbons, and I had a few others tied in my hair, around my wrists, and—ludicrously— around my big toe. I knelt and waited for the humiliation game to be over.

Then I noticed Ma'am was looking at me and crooking her finger for my presence at her side. I rose a little stiffly and went to her. "Yes, Ma'am?"

"Turn this way, Tobias. Back up a bit so we can all see you." I obeyed as she turned to the man who looked like Jamie and the blonde woman sitting next to him. "Well, Drew, Sonja? You've seen him serve. What do you think?"

The dark-haired man—Drew?—nodded thoughtfully and turned to his flaxen-haired wife. "Hmm. Better than I expected. Sonja, what do you think?"

"I think we should unwrap your birthday gift, and we'll decide in the morning." Sonja looked at Ma'am, who smiled indulgently. "But I have to say, I'm leaning towards a 'yes.'"

"You'll need this to unwrap him completely," Ma'am said and tossed a key to the blonde woman, who picked it deftly out of the air. She and Drew rose and beckoned me to follow them.

I began to walk, and Drew stopped and looked at me sharply. "On your hands and knees, boy," he ordered.

I looked at Ma'am for a stricken second, but she nodded and motioned me to follow. "Go on, boy. And don't let me down," she added as I dropped to my hands and knees, dragging ribbons on the parquet floor, and crawled after the birthday couple to a chorus of "Happy Birthday" from everyone else at the table.

* * *

Anderson looked over the contract and nodded, satisfied. The Travises had found Tobias more than satisfactory. The two-year contract price was negotiated, and the terms of the contract set out before the Travises returned to Marin the next morning on the early flight.

She pressed her intercom. "Greta, send Tobias in here, please."

A few minutes later, Tobias entered the room and knelt by her desk as she turned from her other paperwork. "You wished to see me, Ma'am?"

"Yes, Tobias. I've found a buyer for your contract, and you've been sold for the next two years."

At Tobias' shocked look, she passed him a small cardboard box and a thick business-sized envelope. "Your instructions. Your plane ticket is in the envelope. You leave tomorrow afternoon. Congratulations, Tobias." She looked to the contract. "The terms are that you will be librarian, organizer, manager and pleasure slave for their house in Marin. Apparently you performed better than you thought for the birthday boy the other night. They were both quite pleased with you." She handed him a pen and a copy of the contract.

145

"Read this, and sign it. And be glad I did it this way—you never had to go to the block."

Dazed, he signed it without reading it, picked up the envelope and box and, at her hand-waved dismissal, left the room without looking back.

* * *

For a Marketplace slave, I was an anomaly. I didn't ever set foot in an auction. Master and Mistress had bought me outright the morning after Ma'am's dinner, so I don't know why I was so nervous. After all, they knew what they were getting, and apparently, they wanted a 35 year-old slightly chubby guy who knew how to catalogue.

Still, my nerves were getting the upper hand as I walked into JFK, schedule firmly held before me and messenger bag over my shoulder. The box Master and Mistress had sent to Ma'am was tucked inside it with my contract and the envelope of instructions for the trip.

JFK was packed with people getting away for the weekend. I drew the envelope out as soon as I reached my gate, to take a closer look at my instructions. My fingers trembled slightly as I pulled out a folded piece of heavy, cream paper. The first line directed me to the men's room before reading another word, and my face flushed as I hurried to the closest one, three gates down.

The directions were explicit and immediate: enter a stall, open the box, and put on the silicone cock cage I found within. The letter reminded me, as stipulated in line 12 of my contract, I was not allowed to orgasm unless my owners decided to permit it.

A small bottle of liquid lube to help me get it on and two plastic locks with serial numbers and zip-tie shanks were also in the box; I was ordered in the letter to put on the lock with serial number 008521. The device would stay on until they met me in San Francisco.

I went into one of the large stalls at the end of the room and set the box down on the sink against its tiled wall, hurrying through the instructions. The cage pinched; it was lined with small silicone thorns that would poke me if I started to get hard.

A thin black man with short dreadlocks, who had been behind

me in line as we went through security, was entering the stall next to mine as I came out. As I walked past him, he looked at me appraisingly, and I looked away uncomfortably. Even if I had wanted anything with him, my body was no longer mine to control. I made my way back to my seat, with my messenger bag covering my crotch. I didn't know if the curved plastic stood out in my tight black jeans.

Master and Mistress had a great sense of humor: I had a seat in business class. It made sense, though; I *was* a business transaction. Sitting in the second cabin, I stored my overnight bag above me. It contained clothes I hoped to wear once or twice during the duration of the contract. In my lap, I held my messenger bag.

I wore my favorite outfit, comfortable for the trip, though presentable: tight black jeans, oxford shirt, argyle sweater and penny loafers. I looked like a librarian, just as I had seven years before, but here I was, heading into a two-year slavery contract where I would no longer have a say in my future.

Well, at least I'd still be a librarian sometimes. I hoped.

The man who'd bumped into me in the restroom was in the first row in coach. Every time I got up to use the restroom, he waved—just a little wiggle of his fingertips, with a sly smile on his lips. The first time I saw myself in the bathroom mirror, I wondered what he thought, since I was basically crotch level to him when I walked down that aisle. After that, though, I was busy dealing with the cock cage and the new positions it demanded for simple things like taking a leak without making a mess.

The flight took forever. We were delayed at the airport, and I wished I hadn't put the messenger bag under the seat in front of me when the flight attendant said to. Bending down to pick it up was an interesting experience; I bit back a yelp as the cock cage pinched and stabbed me in new and painful ways.

As I finally got off the plane, the man from coach caught up to me in the jetway. He slipped me a piece of paper as he stepped out into the terminal before me. Opening the note, I read: *I'm Markus. If you want to fool around sometime, call me.* A number was below his offer. I shoved the note in my front pocket, smiled, and walked through the bustling crowd.

At the top of the escalator, I looked down. Waiting at the bottom was a middle-aged man who was built like a refrigerator. He was dressed head to toe in black, a white tie standing out against his black-and-white striped shirt, holding a card with *Toby B.* written on it in large block letters. I sighed.

Markus, a few yards ahead of me, stopped to talk to the man holding my sign. They laughed, he nodded, and he turned to me and waved. "See you soon, Toby."

"Toby Blanchard?" The livery-clad refrigerator winked, grinned, and didn't wait for my answer. I followed at a quick pace. He led me to a limousine parked in the sunlit lot across from the terminal, taking my luggage and placing it in the trunk. But he didn't open the door for me. Instead, he went to the driver's side door and got in.

The back window rolled down and Mistress's face appeared, looking even more gorgeous than that night at the party. "Toby, you can enter the middle door." I cringed at the nickname, but did as I was told.

Opening the door revealed Master and Mistress sitting in the front seat of the space, with the tinted privacy window closing off the driver from the back seat behind them. As soon as I closed the door, Master spoke into a phone.

"Carl, you can drive to the house in three minutes." He hung up the phone and looked at me kneeling there. I hadn't meant to kneel, at least not yet, but it was the only way I could get in and shut the door.

Master smiled. "It's great to see you, Toby. You look even better than the last time we saw you." I cringed again and lowered my head. It was a nickname. If Ma'am hadn't told them I hated that name, then I couldn't either, until they let me speak.

"Toby, strip and kneel in front of us. You have three minutes before it gets really rough for you. I'd advise not waiting." Mistress grinned. They both waited, watching me, and I started to undress.

"Did you have a nice flight? Meet anyone? Or just sleep?" Master sipped his coffee. His smile was getting colder, less friendly, more appraising.

I nodded, trying to get my clothes off without shifting the cage too much.

"You can speak, Toby." Mistress said. She noticed my cringe. "What's wrong?"

Nude, I knelt before them, and tried not to think about my belly as I answered their questions.

"It was a wonderful flight. Thank you for business class. A man slipped me his phone number, but I was too nervous and excited and—nervous, with this on me." I pointed to my caged penis. "Besides, I'm your property, so I didn't have the right to pursue it. Then I found—Carl? And he brought me to your car."

"Something's wrong, though." Mistress leaned forward. "Why do you keep wincing, Toby?"

I controlled my cringe with an effort. "Mistress, I beg you not to call me Toby. My mother used that name to hurt me as a child. It makes me feel less than a slave, as though I had no owner who cared for my well-being."

In the silence, I felt as though I had said too much and worried they would continue saying it anyway.

"Thank you for telling us that... Tobias. We will only use it for punishment." She flipped open the folder on the seat next to her, and circled something. "Imala told us of your history with that name, but we wanted to hear it from you."

Master took another sip of his coffee as he set down his phone, a text message glowing on the screen. "Markus says you controlled yourself. He's one of our spotters and works in our Los Angeles house. He's up here to check out our new home."

The car pulled away from the curb. I held my place, kneeling in the presenting pose Ma'am had trained me to: splayed knees, head bowed, hands resting at my sides but ready to grab the floor for balance. It was a pose that worked well in moving vehicles.

Mistress lifted my chin with a slim finger and tapped the cock cage with her other hand. "I do hope wearing this wasn't a problem. Oh, and in here, you may speak at will."

"No, Mistress. Aside from the difficulty of bending down, nothing has been a problem."

Master leaned forward and slid his hand under the weight of the silicone to inspect the lock. "I see you haven't changed locks. Good to know. This will be your travel cage. We have several others we're interested in seeing on you. I figure a different one each week." He smiled and his hand remained, cupping the warmth of my trapped cock.

My eyes fluttered shut. My Master was touching me. I kept my composure, as my cock swelled slightly, getting stabbed by those damned silicone thorns inside the cage.

"We live in a little community in Marin County called Tiburon. It's where we plan to open a Marketplace resort, where owners can use our slaves for weekends or longer. The grounds are huge, the house is huge and the library in the main house is packed full of... well, we aren't exactly sure."

"The *main* house, Mistress?"

"There are two on the lot. We currently live in the guesthouse, which runs alongside the main house. It's... well, you'll see."

The city grew around us. As we swerved around hills, I planted my body down, hands once or twice gripping the carpet beneath me to stay upright.

"I'm impressed, Tobias. I couldn't last that long, kneeling."

"Thank you, Master. May I ask a few questions?"

"Certainly."

"Which library would you like me to conquer first? May I wear clothes when working in the library? Will you allow me access to some supplies for the libraries?"

Mistress nodded. "The guest house library should be first. It's to be our office when you're through."

Master continued, "We'll see on the clothes. I am thinking shoes, but I want to be able to see my property, so you may find yourself cataloging in nothing but a pair of sneakers, a collar and a cock cage, boy."

"We can discuss your other questions later. Tonight, we will have you attend us in our bedroom, after you take a look at the study," Mistress said. Her hand clasped my right shoulder as Master's hand closed over my left, steadying me as the limo went around sharp curves in the down-sloping road.

"And then, *we'll* study *you*." Master's voice held a smile, but I couldn't have said what the smile looked like.

As the limo cleared the foliage, a mansion came into view, and I caught my breath.

"Welcome to World's End," they both said as the car stopped at the front steps of the mansion.

Carl opened the door for Mistress and then went to Master's door. They both waited for me to exit while I glanced between the open door and the pile of clothing on the seat behind me. "Tobias, don't make the first words out of my mouth a punishment," Mistress warned.

I exited, still nude. There was nothing but trees in all directions, save the two homes. It was truly a secluded location. I held my body straight, very little belly showing, and my head high.

Within an hour, I'd had a quick, if naked, tour of the grounds. I was given back my shoes, but no other covering except the cage, which covered nothing.

The property was immense. We walked around the outside of the main house as Master pointed out endless features: fireplaces, bathrooms, kitchens, bedrooms, a ballroom and even an elevator stack that must have been added later. Exploring and organizing the as-yet-unexplored basement and attic would eventually be part of my duties, but Master had other plans for the remainder of my day. He walked me to the foot of the long outdoor stairway that led to the entrance of the guesthouse.

"Walk up those stairs and stand waiting at that door for us," Mistress ordered. I obeyed, walking up the wide, sweeping risers I could easily imagine being forced to crawl up as punishment. My owners stood at the foot of the stairs watching my ascent, before following at a leisurely pace.

The door at the head of the stairs concealed someone—or several someones. As I stood and waited for Master and Mistress to join me, I heard hushed giggles and a piercing "Shhhh!!" behind the door.

Master reached the head of the stairs and slid past me to open it, revealing a row of three mismatched people, all dressed, and all collared. Carl was one of them, out of his livery jacket now.

Master looked them over and spoke sternly. "Slaves, this is Tobias. Do not lay a finger on him for any reason beyond safety. He is off-limits to you. He is our first pleasure slave and eventually will be our majordomo in this house. If he requires help with his duties organizing this disaster area, make sure he receives it."

Over my shoulder, Mistress followed up, equally stern. "Any improprieties and you will be punished severely. Do not test us on this." Three heads bobbed in assent as if they were marionettes with strings attached.

Mistress quickly introduced me to the elderly man on Carl's left—Howard, who had originally belonged to Great-Uncle Mert and was still "the best chef this side of the Golden Gate," and to the younger Latina woman, Mira, who had been Mert's nurse and was now Howard's. None of the other slaves looked as though they had been pleasure slaves. Great-Uncle Mert had apparently purchased a very expensive—if pretty—chef, nurse and chauffeur-slash-errand boy from the Marketplace. I wondered why he hadn't just hired local help instead.

All three of them welcomed me at Master's firm order and then scattered to whatever duties they had at Mistress' sharp one. I was led through the double doors into a large, square room, full of built-in bookshelves full of dusty books, papers, files, and knickknacks. Two tables or desks piled with books, papers, and other random things were on either side of the room, and a large trestle table in the center of the room filled the rest of the space. The floor was crowded with piles of books, files, three-ring binders, boxes of tapes and CDs, and stacks of manila envelopes. Shelves around the shaded, dirty windows were equally full and overflowing.

A room like this was a hoard of pirate treasure.

Moving without being told, I entered the room almost reverently, gently moving papers to see what was beneath them, picking up books and looking at the spines. *SM 101. The Art of Closing Any Deal. Architect and Engineer, Volume 11.* The desks were piled with ledgers and bills, statements and letters, envelopes everywhere. One row of shelves held random trade paperbacks that had no relationship to each other except their size; another held hardbacks that were losing their covers and paperbacks that had no covers at all. The papers on the tables had scribbles of notes, and so did the margins of several books. This made me cringe, as though the books were calling me Toby. A few large, beautiful paintings leaned against walls that had never had space for them; I resolved to ask if we could establish another room as an art gallery and display them properly.

Oddly enough, the two wastebaskets in the room were empty.

"Uncle Mert was a bit of a hoarder, as you can see," Master said.

Mistress added, "We know it's a lot to take in, so we are going to leave you here, to see what you can do with it." She moved through the only clear path on the floor to a set of double doors in the far wall. "We expect you to enter these doors at exactly 6:30 this evening." She went through the doors and out of my sight.

Master followed her, giving me a farewell pat on my bare ass. "Oh, and make sure you're ready for some fun, Tobias."

I stood there, my mind racing to see where I'd explore first. Because make no mistake, this was a job of exploration. After a moment's consideration, I began to excavate the things on the center table, intending to stack books there to ready them for their eventual return to the shelves. After moving piles of dusty papers, maps, and books from the table to the floor, making piles of correspondence, files, and other paperwork, I had to stop for a moment to marvel at the first real treasure I'd found beneath them.

The piles had weighed down a map of the original property, as big as the table. Coffee rings and notes in several different hands marred its edges, but I could easily see it restored and displayed in the front hall of the main house someday. Carefully, I rolled it up and used my shoelaces to keep it that way, setting it with the large paintings in one corner.

With the map now stored to one side and the table uncovered, I threw myself into the work: uncovering, discovering, setting aside, putting together. First editions and rare books went on the center of the cleared trestle table, mass-market paperbacks here, genre fiction there. I couldn't stomach the idea of throwing them out, but perhaps they could be sold, or donated to a worthy cause.

A bulletin board behind one of the desks, tacked to a plank of wood, revealed a dirty window looking down on the garden to the side of the house.

By the time I stopped to look at my work, the table was filled with more than 300 books in organized groups. One of the desks had been cleared of its surface mess as well, and filled with stacks of correspondence, files I hadn't looked through yet, and photographs. Finally, I had emptied an entire wall of shelves on the left-hand side of the room.

With the shelves empty, I started organizing the hardback books I'd found. For now, it would have to be enough to group them by subject. Later on, when the mess was cleared, I'd go back and start using an actual library system—Dewey or Library of Congress, whatever my owners wanted—but for now this would have to be enough.

I was sweating and covered with dust when a wolf whistle sounded from the door. Startled, I looked across to see Markus leaning against the doorjamb of the open double doors with a sly grin on his face. "You've done a hell of a lot of work, boy, but don't you have an appointment?" I followed his grinning gaze to the digital clock on the far wall, which read 6:12.

And I was covered in sweat, dust and dirt. I must have looked a sight. Panicked, I looked to Markus with wide eyes. I cleared my throat, but no words came. In desperation, I picked up a piece of paper and wrote out in block letters: *Can you show me to the shower?*

"Oh, not a talker either?" He laughed. "I'll show you where to go, but you'd better get a move on. They won't like it if you're late."

I followed him out into the hall, down a little flight of steps into what must have been the living room, into the dining room, and up another little flight of stairs to another hallway and a bathroom. "You and Carl share the bedroom to the right, but this weekend I'm sleeping in the bed you'll use. You'll have other sleeping arrangements while I'm here." The room had two small beds and a closet in one wall, very utilitarian. The bathroom was next door to it, small but serviceable.

I pointed to my wrist and raised my eyebrows. "It's 6:15. Better get moving, boy." He turned and left as I hurried into the bathroom, turned on the shower, stepped out of my shoes into icy cold water, and washed myself anyway. Just as the water was warming up, I finished, grabbed one of the towels on the rack, dried off in a rush that left my skin pink from the friction, and combed my fingers through my hair to make it look less disheveled. The clock on the wall read 6:27..

Leaving my shoes behind, I hurried back through the house to the library and the doors on its far side. As the digital clock over the doorway clicked from 6:29 to 6:30, I fell to my knees, my head bowed.

The door opened before me and a pair of boots, which could only be Master's, appeared. "Enter, boy, and well done." Relief swept through me as I crawled after the boots into the room, and the door closed behind me.

* * *

The room I entered was as different from the library as it could have been: tasteful décor with chocolate brown walls, pictures, luxurious linens, black lacquered floors under white throw rugs. I presented on my knees with my hands behind my head in the center of the room, waiting for whatever they wanted me to do now.

They sat in two easy chairs, Master with his coffee and Mistress with a goblet of red wine, observing me for several minutes while I knelt. Finally, they set their drinks on the table between their chairs and approached me, Master with a pair of scissors in one hand.

I had to trust them. I was their property. They had signed a contract that required them to return me unharmed at the end of it. Even so, I had my doubts as Master lowered the scissors between my legs.

I shouldn't have worried; Master held my balls with one hand, and with the other slid the scissors into the zip-tied plastic lock to cut it from my cage. He removed the cage and set it aside, stroking my cock in brisk, firm strokes, while Mistress' gentle hands caressed my shoulders, neck and ass, one finger circling my exposed hole.

I felt myself relaxing, no longer resisting at all, as Master's hands hardened my cock and Mistress' finger pressed deeper into my ass. Then, once I was gasping and filled with needs I hadn't let myself acknowledge in a long time, they lifted me from my knees and led me to a handsome black leather kneeling bench. Master tied red rope around my wrists, binding me in place. Mistress lifted my feet into holders and tied rope around them as well.

Soon, I was kneeling and bound before them, Master's cock in my mouth, pressing back until I nearly choked, his hand laced through the hair on the back of my head, never letting up for a second. Mistress stroked my chest, twisted my nipples, caressed my cock and balls and massaged lube into my ass. As Master began to fuck my face in earnest, Mistress eased a long, thick Lucite rod into my ass, fucking me with it as well. I was caught between them, with Mistress sliding into me as Master pulled out, back and forth, over and over. I felt sure at some point they'd press into me together and meet somewhere around my chest, and then I didn't think anything else for a while.

At some point in that hazy scene, they switched places. My exploration of Mistress' pleasure was just as thorough as my exploration of her library had been; I reveled in her gasps even as Master pressed harder into my ass than I knew I could take. I was no longer "Tobias Blanchard, MLIS." I was no longer a person at all. I was a slave, being used for what a slave was good for—pleasure—and for the first time I was not second-guessing or trying to plan. I was simply giving in, letting go, being directed, being used.

No self-consciousness any more. No worrying or anxiety or second thoughts. Just me, in my slavery, and them, in their ownership, as it should have been with Jamie and never was.

I had never known I could be called to this kind of service too.

An unknown time later, they withdrew from me. My face was covered in their scents and their stickiness, but I didn't care. My hair matted to my forehead with the sweat of my exertions, but I didn't care. My cock stood away from my body, rigid and throbbing, but I didn't care. I had pleased them; I could see that.

That was all that mattered.

I sagged against the ropes as Master and Mistress attended to their own cleaning-up. I didn't mind. I was content to be here, used, serving my purpose as a decoration if that's what they wanted.

Apparently it was. They returned to their chairs, now clad in thick terrycloth bathrobes, and talked below my hearing while they finished their coffee and wine. The ropes were tied well; my hands and feet were still warm, and the kneeling bench was comfortable under my legs. I drifted, floating in a golden haze of accomplishment—of having overcome my *last little problem*.

It was almost a disappointment when they approached me again and began to untie me.

"You've done well, boy," Master said, as he worked at one of the knots on my wrists. "Better than we expected, even after that night at Imala's party. You've improved."

Mistress did not approach the knots but simply smoothed my damp hair back from my forehead and wiped my face with a cool washcloth. She wiped down my body, too, even attending to my ass, where lube still leaked from me. Her gentle touch was almost too much for me to take.

And then it *was* too much. As the last rope fell away from me and Master helped me to my feet, I found myself inexplicably sobbing—first just a trickle of tears, then a sudden torrent, like rain in the desert.

I thought of Jamie and training and being taught how to train and then how to service and serve. I thought of my fears and my anxieties about being not enough and how this had washed those away. I thought about Ma'am saying I needed to own my talents and my humiliation at the party the night Master and Mistress purchased me.

It all came together in a flood of relief and joy and excitement and love and pain. As Master helped me sit cross-legged on a round, white rug at the end of their bed and let go of my arms, I wept into my hands, rocking back and forth, unable to stop the storm ripping through me.

"Tobias? What's wrong?" Mistress knelt beside me, and then Master did too—she on both knees, he on just the one. I scrubbed tears from my eyes with the heels of my hands, but could not stop weeping. "I'm sorry... I'm really sorry, I'm happy, I am. I just... " I bowed my head, wishing the tears would stop. Somewhere inside me, a dam had broken.

"What is it, Tobias? Just say it." Master had placed a hand on my shoulder.

"I don't look like a pleasure slave. Why would you want me for that?" I managed to choke out. "I want to serve you—both of you—in any way you want, but I don't understand why you want me. *I* wouldn't want me."

"Why not?" Mistress actually sounded offended as her hand reached out to stop my rocking. "Why would you think such a thing?"

I gestured at my body. "This. A pleasure slave should be better than this. I'm older, and I'm not in shape the way I want to be, and I'm not... not pretty enough for you to show off to other owners."

There was a beat of silence as I finally managed to stop sobbing. Tears still tracked down my cheeks, but they were slower now.

Finally Mistress spoke. "Oh, Tobias. You are exactly what we want. You are everything we ever needed. I'll be honest with you. We, too, thought we needed someone different at first. But you, my precious slave, are exactly what we need. You served us in every way we had hoped for, including this." She put a finger under my chin and made me look her in the eyes. "Do you understand, Tobias? We did not just purchase a pretty slave. We purchased *you*—for all your talents."

I could see she meant it. Master, next to her, nodded gravely and squeezed my shoulder in affirmation.

"Mert purchased Howard when he was in his 30s and we were not yet born. He has served well and continues to serve, even if this is no longer how he serves. Time will change how you look and how you can perform, but we didn't buy you for your looks. We bought you for your talents, and your good heart, and *this*—your calling."

Master nodded. "You taught *us* something between Imala's party and now, boy. You are not what you look like. You are who you are."

"And what you are, Tobias, is perfect for what we need," Mistress said firmly. "So no more of this, slave. Wipe those tears— Drew, can you hand me that box of tissues?—and get to bed. Here, at the foot of our bed." She pointed to the pallet, blanket and pillow laid out at the foot of the enormous mahogany bedstead, and handed me the tissues so I could wipe my face.

I was stunned into silence. I wiped my face and put the tissue box to one side. I crawled from the rug to the pallet, turned, and knelt up, presenting myself to them.

Master locked a metal cage around my deflated cock and balls, with a metal lock this time, smiling. I smiled back at him as the lock snapped shut.

They both kissed me, and then they went to their bed. After a moment, I curled up on the pallet, pulled the thin blanket over me, and went to sleep smiling.

* * *

That was the night I found out what my slavery really means. I knew some of it from that moment of peace when I was alone in the aisle, kneeling before the altar of books in front of me. There were times when I had my list of books, my trolley to gather the tomes, and found myself overwhelmed with wonder as I did it. It wasn't because I knelt 100 times that day on the cold tiles of the library floor or because I carried a thousand books from one side of the aisle to the other or even that I chafed my fingers raw from pulling the books from their home, where they were crammed tightly on the shelf. It was because this was my service and what I sometimes got praised for doing.

But now, finally, I knew the other kind of service as well. Pleasure was my birthright, as much as books were my birthright. It was in my blood, as much as the turning of pages and the scent of old leather bindings.

They owned me, but I owned all my talents now.

The Thorny Issue
By Wade McLeod

The gaudily decorated cedar house on the 1953 International truck lumbered up next to the curb in the industrial section of Third Street, a little wind chime on the back porch tinkling. This neighborhood was not a neighborhood, one of very few places in The City where a vehicle this size could park for free, even overnight sometimes. The wooden house on wheels seemed to sigh and settle for a long-awaited rest.

The little house and truck looked like a vision stolen from the Travelers of Europe. The windows sported cheerful curtains decorated with girls wearing cowboy boots and cut-offs or high heels and pin-up-era lingerie with marabou trim. The tiny wooden porch was railed, and now a little stair extended from it. The back door opened, and a woman emerged who belonged on the same movie set as the wagon.

She was a luscious combination of the themes already called to mind. She was ivory-skinned and wore her dark hair loosely curled, layers of skirts in red, purple, blue, and orange, and a peasant blouse surging from a tightly corseted waist. Her shoes were modern platforms of calfskin in purple and red. She wore a black leather vest covered with pins of various sizes and shapes; most were silver, black, and blue. Many had little red hearts on them.

As the door closed behind her, she paused and looked all around. Then she moved toward the stairs and descended. When she reached the ground, the front doors of the truck opened. From the driver's side side-stepped a long-haired, middle-aged man. He was wearing black jeans, a black tuxedo-styled shirt, and—by now it was no surprise—a top hat.

A third person now exited on the passenger side. A young black woman with fine waist-length dreadlocks, vest with pins matching the first woman's, and leather jeans, well broken-in and well-cared-for. As were her engineer boots. She slid from the truck seat to the ground carrying a messenger-style shoulder bag of oiled leather.

The man handed the femme down the tiny steps, and they all turned as one and walked toward the Third Street Fish Market. Inside they went directly upstairs, nodding at a waitress, on through and out the back to sit on the deck facing the Bay Bridge.

"You wish for your usual, Ma'am?" asked the young woman with the dreads, opening a menu. The older woman nodded, and the young woman looked at the man. He nodded too, and the young woman went to the counter to order.

"I think she may be the best one you've found yet, Ma'am," said the man.

"Except for you, of course," she replied. He smiled and bowed his head for a moment.

"Thank you, Mistress Leonora. I do my best." She arched an eyebrow at him in response to his formal reply. She and Felix had long dispensed with most formal owner/slave protocols. Neither had any doubt about their roles or expectations. One thing had never, would never, change. The collar he wore was not his to move. It was hers to put on or take off. Everyone in their daily lives knew this.

"I hope you are not trying to make some pointed remark, Felix. I find myself obtuse today." He said nothing, just followed Yolanda, the young woman, with his eyes. She was his responsibility. So far she had done well, but he kept watch. She was the first slave who would go to the Marketplace having been trained primarily by him.

An hour and a half later, the patio was packed and loud. There was a dozen more dressed as gypsies, and even more modern leatherfolk, as well as a widely varied mob wearing widely varying styles of dress. All were hugging and clapping one another on the back and shouting cheerfully. These were old friends who had some catching up to do. The young woman stared around her.

Eventually, everyone had eaten, drank and shouted enough at one another for the moment. A man stepped onto a picnic table in the center of the patio. Hugely muscular, wearing only a vest for a shirt, with leather cuffs on each upper arm and a dozen visible piercings, he looked like Mr. Clean's dirty-minded evil twin. He reached for a glass and spoon to call the meeting to order, but the crowd was already quieting. He leaped back off the table to stand in a circle that had opened on the deck.

"Welcome, my friends and my family! We are here again!" Loud cheers rang around the patio for a moment. "We open for business in two days! We have work to do!" He spoke only in exclamations. "Who has goods to offer?" The room fell silent.

Leonora stood. "I have a new trainee I would like to offer for auction." She snapped her fingers at Yolanda, who stood promptly, stepped forward to the spot Leonora pointed to, and bowed her head.

"As do I," said a dark woman in leathers. She also pointed to the center of the room, and a pale, slim young man in leather shorts scampered to join Yolanda. He stopped and stood, staring about him. His Mistress glared at him until he noticed and abruptly ducked his head.

Mr. Not-so-Clean looked around. "Anyone else?" Some shuffling, but no one spoke. "Okay. We have—what is your name, little one?" He bent his shiny head close to her mouth. "Yolanda!" He beckoned the young man and whispered in his ear for a moment. The lad blushed and whispered back. "And we have Gavin—with an I! Give us a turn there, kiddies." He waved them in a circle.

He smiled at the buzz of conversation. "While you think about it and check your wallets, let me remind you of some details." He read from a card. "The subjects you are offered are still trainees and as such, are expected to behave with all possible deference and obedience but not required to be skilled at anything in particular. If you lease one for the stated time-period, you have all typical rights and privileges of ownership except! You may not use them sexually or damage them in any way. Any marks must disappear within two weeks. Any punishable failures shall pertain to the owner, who should be informed and shall choose punishment, to be administered by the owner or whomever the owner decides, which may be the leaseholder."

He paused. Almost everyone here already knew each detail, but the attention was all he might have hoped for. "If you receive exceptional service, you may reward the slave according to the owner's permissions. If you add exceptional value, the owner is expected to reward you according to their gratitude. The service period starts tomorrow at midnight. Remember, the Open House tomorrow night ends at ten." He bowed slightly and backed out to the perimeter of the circle that had formed.

"Any questions?" He looked around the circle slowly, twice, and then nodded. "Let the bidding begin!" He beckoned the boy, who blushed again and scrambled to follow his pointing finger.

"What am I offered for this healthy young lad?" He scanned a sheet of paper handed him by Sonia, who had brought the boy. "He is a good housekeeper, a chef, everything back of the house. He speaks English, French and Creole, is an athlete accomplished in several sports, and certified to teach yoga—" Titters ran around the back of the crowd where the younger attendees, most too broke to bid today, gathered in small groups. This earned them a scowl from the auctioneer. Abrupt silence.

"He is an excellent all-around household helper, and a quick and willing learner... What am I bid?"

"One hundred!" called a middle-aged woman.

"Two!"

"Two-fifty!"

So it went until he sold for a respectable amount to a woman who went immediately to Sonia to settle the deal.

"Ladies, we have one more for the block today!" He patted one pocket then the other for the bit of paper with Yolanda's information. Finally, he said, "Mistress Leonora, would you tell us about her yourself, please?" He bowed his head with the request.

Leonora moved gracefully into the center of attention, timing her arrival to coincide with the last of the shuffling and chattering. "This young woman has been training with me for a year; I found her at a convention with a woman who had trained her for two years already. Some of you may know Lilith." She paused for appreciative murmurs. "This is Yolanda. Lilith herself called Yolanda a diamond. She is strong and willing, capable of much physical work in a day, and an expert with several musical instruments, including her voice. I leave the rest to be discovered by the lucky bidder who wins her for these two weeks. That said, I do hope we will all get to hear her play in the evenings."

By the time the bidding was over, she had fetched a stunning amount for a two-week lease. Leonora's offerings always brought top dollar. Her reputation assured they would be well trained and useful.

The auctioneer then effectively ended the evening by admonishing those present. "It has been a long road for some of us. Rest up tonight, folks. Tomorrow night we celebrate!" He found his Owner and knelt at her feet. She stroked his shoulder once.

The crowd broke up and small groups made their way to the street, now crowded with at least a dozen recreational vehicles sporting fringe and Christmas lights. These were RVs only in licensing terms. Most were charming little wooden houses with peaked roofs like the first one. After much consultation, the collection of vehicles organized itself into a caravan and rolled away toward the southern edge of The City. It arrived shortly at a large disused parking lot of an abandoned big box store where several trucks and trailers were already parked. Here, the vehicles quickly made a small town in an efficient style. The new little town settled into the night. Within a half hour, all the exterior lights were out, and the town seemed to disappear.

* * *

A block away, Ryan Deckford watched from his personal car, 12 years older and more normal for this side of town than anything the force owned. When the last lights went out in the colorful new encampment, he dumped his cold coffee out the window and drove home.

They were back. This time, he would catch them before another young person disappeared.

He had first come across the Thorny Issue Traveling Circus of Human Foibles back in his rock 'n' roll days. He had started his career as security for rock bands back when the duties included securing drugs and girls for the stars and keeping most of them away from the band until after the show. Oh, and the occasional odd request, usually very much on the QT. He had learned a lot about the black and gray markets of urban America.

It was very hip for rockers to be into S/M in those days. They kept it quiet though, leaking just enough references into their fashions and lyrics to tip the cognoscenti but lose no customers. The Titchuff group, as they styled themselves, were performance artists and S/M players who were often part of the entourage of world-famous rock bands. Their specialty was infusing a touch of S and M into everything they did.

When they turned up as part of this missing persons case, Ryan was surprised to find they still existed.

They had morphed over time into a traveling band who offered everything from S/M sessions to massages to tarot readings to dance classes to theme weddings. They maintained a huge network of alliances in various strata of society while staying off the general public's radar.

First thing next morning, he pulled—again—all the unsolved Missing Persons files for those times when Titchuff came to town. Seven for sure, and maybe as many as a dozen more over 20 years or so.

When most of the guys had dropped this from active investigation, he kept it. He took this case personally. Several of these people had gone missing from his world. One was last seen at a party he himself had attended. These were his people.

Some of the missing were excellent citizens. Most were clean-livers, no trouble with the law, other than three who had been bordering on homelessness. He was not sure those belonged in this file. The others were all exceptional: one expensive hand model, two software coders with serious skills, a nanny to a CEO's kids, a lawyer, and so on. The ones who were barely making their way in the world were not the same caliber, but even they were special. One had been the live-in lover of an Eastern city's famous symphony conductor. He had an advanced degree in philosophy (There is one direct route to living under a bridge, thought Ryan) and was kicked out by the conductor after a tiff. Said conductor was frantic to get him back or at least be sure he was okay.

As other officers arrived, he came in for a good bit of ribbing over the file he was reviewing.

"Deckford's white whale is back!"

"So you feeling a lack of frustration in your life these days, Deckford? Got a girlfriend again?"

He joshed back with them and kept reading. Rereading. The pages he had read dozens of times. Every spring when the troupe came to town.

There was the hand model with an odd British name: Toppy. She was, as they had put it, quite posh. She would not have been up to *that sort of thing*. Yet he himself had seen her at an underground play party two weeks before she had gone missing. Everyone there had seen her; she stood out like neon in a swamp. But he said nothing. He did not share his extracurriculars with those on the force. He had added some notes to the file from an *unnamed source*.

If they knew he went to play parties of that sort, he would be in for endless torment and not the fun kind. If they knew he bottomed! He always stopped his thoughts right there. He just could not imagine the police allowing him to continue in this job he loved if they knew he liked to wear the cuffs himself. When he had been young and romantic about the force, he had thought how similar it was to the S/M world, with its hierarchies, loyalties, its code of honor. He loved the motto *To Protect and To Serve*. He had been an idealist.

So he had been there—masked as usual—when the lovely British hand model had received a flogging he doubted he himself could handle. Afterward, she had knelt and thanked her top by crying and kissing his boots repeatedly. The top had been a man he recognized, a movie producer quite famous for his quality pornography.

Two weeks later, she had gone missing. The movie producer, of course, claimed he knew nothing about it. There were no leads, nothing to follow. Even Ryan, who knew the S/M connection, could find nothing more. She had vanished. No body had been found. Her parents had come over from England to *move it along*, as their friend had told him. For all their fussing, her parents had gone home with nothing.

No bodies had ever been found. As many as 20 persons missing, no bodies. At least two of the victims had visited the Thorny Issue within a month before disappearing. One was the posh model. The other was also a player at S/M parties, an organizer in fact, the best presenter of play parties in town by some accounts. That fellow had been known as a heavy bottom. Only the two, but this was a case curiously devoid of clues. The Thorny Issue was his best lead. He had put himself on their mailing list under two different names ages ago.

Ryan and his new intern Fred looked at the photos. "So, this is a cold case?"

"Sort of. It might not be a case at all. People can drop out of their lives legally," said Ryan.

"Ah." Fred flipped through the pages. "This is why the white whale stuff. So why do you keep looking?"

"Most people don't just drop out of their lives. All these individuals have loved ones who think there was a crime." Ryan looked at Fred. He was 20 years younger and wore a collar that was once a sure signal of a person in the Scene. It no longer meant anything. It had even passed the stage of being hipster jewelry. "These families are heartbroken every time they wonder what happened. They have to be supposing their loved one is in trouble, in pain, dead. Someone has to keep looking."

"Okay. What do you want me to do?"

"Mostly just do the nuts and bolts of our other cases while this Thorny Issue is in town. Free me up to take a little time on this." It was good to have a partner to work with.

Of the dozen or so whose files sat on his desk, none had owed debts, and only one had even been expected back at a job. None had told the loved ones in their lives they were leaving, although a few of those loved ones reported the sort of heavy conversations that seemed, in retrospect, to be goodbyes. This was the sort of thing people imagined to console themselves, Ryan thought. Hardly reliable.

Still, two of them had paid off their credit cards in lump sums right before they vanished. This was the part that always sent his mind wandering. What if. What if they had moved on to a new life? What if that life... Again he stopped his thoughts right there. Fairy tales do not come true.

No, there was someone evil traveling with the Thorny Issue. Someone no one else was looking for.

He pulled a business card from the file. Dialed. "Hello. I would like to make an appointment."

* * *

Inhabitants of the strange new community were moving around before dawn, hanging brightly colored curtains on frames to create walkways and setting up large pieces of stage scenery. By noon, the little town looked like a medieval fair crossed with a princess fantasy. The routes from stage set to dining area to session tent were a maze of curtains, multicolored or painted with floral designs with a medieval flavor. Everywhere, there were tall faceted-glass lanterns and tents, lots of tents.

Many of the tents had sandwich-board signs in front. Decorated with calligraphy and gold foil, they advertised Ancient Oriental Healing, The Torture Palace, Indulgences, and the like.

By dawn, there was an entryway to the entire area created by wooden fencing and curtains. A sign hung over it with Old English lettering: The Thorny Issue. It was bordered by roses and foliage, as well as curlicues that looked like bullwhips.

Through this entryway, around noon, walked an elegant woman. She wore a business suit of the latest style made of doe-skin the exact color of her brown eyes. She walked into the center of the encampment and looked around at the wagons. Then she strode directly to Leonora's.

Tugging the bell pull hanging from the roof of the little porch, she said loudly, "Leonora, good morning. It is Janette."

A muffled bit of conversation came from inside as Janette seated herself at a table that now stood in front of the little house on wheels. Janette looked around at the neighborhood. Each wagon or RV had its own little seating area in front of it now, a table with two or more chairs, each distinct and decorative. There were lanterns by each little homey spot.

Yolanda exited the wagon, holding a tray with four mimosas in champagne flutes. Janette watched as she navigated the tiny metal stairs, not gracefully, but well enough. She spilled nothing, caused no anxious moments. Well done, thought Janette.

The young woman put three glasses on the table, then the last one and the tray on a mat on the ground nearby. She settled herself on the mat in a waiting pose. Janette looked her over, not disguising her scan. Yolanda looked down at her knees. They both sat quietly.

Five minutes later, the door opened again, and Felix came out, who offered his hand to Leonora to help her descend the stairs gracefully. She was entirely in shades of purple today, including a saucy hat made, it appeared, entirely of feathers. They joined Janette at the tiny table and lifted glasses together in a toast.

"You too, Yolanda," said Leonora. "This is a toast to your future." Yolanda raised her glass. They all sipped. "Our new protégée, Janette. Is she not delicious?"

"Of course she is. You never fail to amaze. I understand Sonia has one this time too."

"That one is not ready. But you may see him if you wish. Felix, go visit Sonia. Tell her our visitor would like to see her and her new boy." Felix headed off immediately. Janette's eyes followed as he went around the corner. Leonora waited until Janette's attention returned.

"He is still not available, my Felix. But it proves you have a good eye if still you want him after all these years."

"I recognize quality, that is all," Janette said dryly.

"Yes, the very soul of appreciation, you are. How go things in the Marketplace? Is everyone rich and well-fed as ever?"

"Yes, we are all well. I'm sorry. I do not have much time this morning. Did you want something else from me?"

"Always business with you. I want to know what is the new thing in the Marketplace. The news, the gossip. If you hate so to come here, send someone fun."

"Nothing new to report."

"Well then, what do you think of my new toy? Will this bonbon be a hot ticket?" They looked at Yolanda.

"So she is ready? Does she speak only English? In an American accent?"

"Also Spanish and a bit of French. She is good at accents and languages; she will learn whichever are required. She is a very talented musician." She chuckled. "If you dare return tomorrow evening, we have our Open House; you may see for yourself." They both knew this would not happen.

"A black American slave in the States... challenging. We have extra screening, but... you know."

"I am fond of Yolanda, but I know it is a long shot to ever see any of my protégés again after the sale. If you sell her in Europe, it would be very good for her."

"Yolanda, child, stand and show yourself." Yolanda did the standard display poses. Half an hour later, having seen the boy as well, Janette left, promising to be in touch.

* * *

Mistress Alexandra led Ryan through a labyrinth of curtains. It seemed the routes were color-coded and labeled with different flowers. This route was hung with blue curtains decorated with irises. One crossing it, in yellow with jonquils. Another, red with roses. Mistress Alexandra led him to a circus tent, with seats and flimsy waist-high barriers around a central performance area. There was a square of four St. Andrew's crosses in the center, a small table with a sound system inside the space made between them.

"You have come quite early this season, chéri. We do not open until tomorrow." She spoke like a movie siren. "What are you hoping for today, my handsome man?"

He looked at her, wishing she could just read his mind. Blushing a little, he said, "I want to be whipped."

"How hard? Have you done this before? Do you worry for marks?" She went on, running down the usual list of questions to create a safe situation. He went through the process patiently, wanting to just get on with it. He really wished one time for a woman to just fling him on the cross and whip him until he broke down.

Good fantasy material, buddy. And anyway, I need to focus on clues.

"It feels so exposed, does it not?" She gestured around the seats, watched his face closely, then added, "We can do this a little more... intimately." She pulled a hanging tassel slowly, and curtains surrounded them and the four crosses. She turned on the small stereo, and odd yet compelling music joined them.

He ignored the tiny voice that asked how he was to find clues while he was tied up... intimately. She turned up the music.

An hour later, he was groaning and sagging from the cross. Such a relief. When he first cried out, she pressed herself against his back and turned his face gently toward her, peering intently into his eyes. She said nothing and went back to flogging him.

Each time he reached a new level—when he first sagged in the cuffs, when he first shook his muscles loose after a blow, when he stomped the floor—she came close, not touching, and again turned his face and looked into his eyes. Each time she went back and continued to strike him. He started to cry. It had been way too long.

She stepped quietly up and asked softly in his ear, "Shall I continue?"

"Oh, yes, please," he said. "Please." He kept sobbing as she continued striking him in rhythm with the music for another half hour.

"We must stop now," she whispered in his ear. She wiped his back gently with a damp cloth, followed by a soft dry one. "You will have mementoes for a while."

As he followed her back through the fabric labyrinth and the yard, he floated. He noticed details of the life they lived here, saw a community going about its odd workaday world. As he got in his car, he wondered if he had seen anything that would help the case at all.

He drove three blocks into a warehouse neighborhood, parked his car behind a factory, and called a cab. He did not want to come down just yet. His car was a junker. He could leave it there until later.

He chuckled as he unlatched and disarmed the layers of his home alarm system. He had nothing to protect beyond his own precious self, and he had just paid to get that very self bloodied and bruised.

He felt more relaxed than he had in ages. Note to self, he thought, eat and drink plenty of water before crashing. Okay, maybe just the water. He face-planted on his couch in the front room.

* * *

The next day was the official opening of the visit of the Thorny Issue to the City. Ryan arrived 45 minutes after the start of the Open House. The atmosphere was festive. Lanterns shimmered and glowed in the twilight. Metallic threads in the curtains sparkled with each bit of breeze. Mistress Alexandra joined him just inside the front gate.

"How are you feeling, chéri?" She stroked his back softly, sending sensations up and down. He felt his dick warm and fill. Having its most urgent need fulfilled yesterday, his body was ready for more playful action.

"Alive! How are you?"

"I'm surprised to see you at this event. You seem more of a private player," she said. If it were possible to put a nudge in your voice, that was what it sounded like.

"I'm curious. This whole thing is such an oddity. How did this ever come to be?"

"Ah, that story is not very exciting really. It started back in the 60s or 70s, long before my time." She nodded minutely at a man just entering. "Some of the original members are still here. Would you like to meet some? I have an appointment."

Perfect. She handed him off to an older man who seemed suddenly to appear at her elbow. He was all in black except for his silver jewelry, which he wore in abundance. Among other bracelets, he wore simple cuffs on his wrists that matched a collar he wore, also mixed in with various more ordinary necklaces, amulets on chains, and whatnot. Ryan took him for an S/M servant or slave.

"Hello. Mistress Alexandra would like me to show you around, if it pleases you." The man bowed elegantly, in an old-fashioned style. "I am Felix. And you are... ?"

"Heath. I met the Mistress yesterday." His scene name came as readily to his lips as his mundane world name. They were in fact both given names. Heathcliffe was his actual first name, thanks to a romantic streak in his mother. Ryan, his middle name, was good for daily use, especially at the police force.

"Ah. You are a fortunate man."

Ryan laughed. "And you are a polite man."

"One does one's best." He nodded. "Now, what would you like to see, to learn? We have much to share."

"I remember a troupe of performers from the 70s with a name like yours... "

"Ah, the Titchuff. The Thorny Issue Traveling Circus of Human Foibles. Did you ever come see us in those days?"

"I was too busy working," he lied immediately. "But I did know a girl who performed with the troupe sometimes. Eleanor, like Rigby, she used to say."

Felix stood very still and then said, "She is still with us. Would you like to see her if she is available?"

Ryan froze in his turn. Suddenly he was a trembling young man again. "Yes, if it's possible." He felt sick. What if she were the perpetrator?

She was his first intemperate affair, maybe his only one ever. They had tried everything: drugs, sex, drugs and sex together, S and M. As for rock and roll... rock and roll was the backdrop for their lives. She was a regular backstage guest. One of the exotic tastes

171

some of the performers chose. The British rockers especially had preferred her. There was a world-famous rhythm guitarist who would not play before he had spent a private hour with her.

Ryan had discovered his cravings for pain and submission experimenting with Eleanor. Eventually, they had both moved on. He did not remember them breaking up. What had happened?

He never forgot her. Sometimes she laughed at him in his dreams, when he had not bottomed for a while. He might see her soon. His dick revived the interest it had lost since Alexandra had dumped him on Felix.

Felix led him to a café area. "I must leave you here while I check. What do you drink?" Ryan paused.

"Have you a fruit cider?"

"Ah, a temperate drinker." Felix was no dim bulb. "Yes, we have pear or apple, both light on the senses. I recommend the pear." Ryan nodded and off Felix went. Within two minutes, a young man brought him the cider. Within ten minutes, Felix was back. He beckoned, Ryan followed, and soon he was seated at another tiny little table, deeper inside the swirling maze of curtains and wagons. Felix put Ryan's glass in front of him again.

"Hello, Heath," she said from behind him. He stood, tumbling the tiny chair. "No, sit. I will join you." She entered the pool of light from the torch, but he could tell little of how she looked. She was dressed in the gypsy style skirts, vest and full hair popular in this little world.

"Eleanor!" He found he had nothing more to say. As he stared, the light fell across her face. He soaked up the vision of her.

"Please. Do sit. You will make me quite anxious." She did not seem the least bit anxious as she alit upon one of the tiny chairs. "How have you been?"

She looked great. Looking at her now, he realized how unfinished she had looked when they knew each other before. She had been a beauty, no doubt. Now she was a woman in full bloom. His dick approved. He scrabbled for the chair he had toppled and sat. Still, he had nothing available to say.

She sat and gazed at him, looking him over at leisure. "You look wonderful. Who are you after all these years?"

Who indeed.

"For one, I am a police detective."

"My, my."

"After all our talk about the Man in those days, after all our fooling around with questionable things." He shrugged. Could she be party to something so awful as kidnapping? Murder?

"Yes, we did some questionable things, didn't we? Even S and M was illegal then. Not by name, but still." She shook her head. Her every move was sultry. "But how did this happen? How did you come to be a cop?"

"Natural progression, I guess. The security teams for concerts got more serious, and then they turned into private bodyguard services, drug wholesalers, and so on. At the same time, some old friends went into legitimate police work. Remember Sam? He helped me with a couple of lucky breaks and managed to get me straight into detective work."

"You still play, yes?"

"Oh, yes. In fact, I came here yesterday. Alexandra is quite good."

"You are the early bird! I am so glad she made you happy," she chuckled. "Alas, then, I must wait a few days for a chance at your back."

He laughed. The laughter caught him and grew. She started laughing, and time became elastic. There was one thing he had learned over these years: there is illegal, and then there is immoral, unethical, inexcusable. She was never those. He doubted she had become those.

She sat looking at him as he searched her face. Yet how could people go missing from here and she not know? She seemed as transparent and as innocent as that young woman he had known, the most open person in his world.

"There is a problem," he said finally. "Missing persons."

"You're here to catch kids who run away with the circus?" She might as well have winked. He waited. "You want me to be serious. Okay, then. Tell me more."

He pulled an envelope from his pocket and showed her the photos, a dozen in all. She looked through them one by one.

"Tell me more," she said again.

"All of these have disappeared. All of them when the Thorny Issue was here in town." This was an exaggeration; some had vanished shortly afterwards.

"May I keep these a day or two? I can ask around discreetly." He nodded. She stood. "Now I must get to work. The Open House, you understand. Here is my card." He looked down. It had a single rose, complete with stem and thorns. He had seen this tattooed over her heart many years ago. He smiled as his dick awoke again. This time, she did wink.

* * *

Later that evening, she sat at the tiny table, looking again at the photos. She recognized most of them. She had spotted or trained eight of them herself. He was indeed trying to find those who had run away. To the Marketplace. She pulled out her phone and dialed Janette again.

"Janette, we have a problem. When can I visit you?" Long pause. "Okay, I'll be there at ten."

* * *

Sitting in his car listening to his earplug, Ryan swore. She was involved. It was midnight, so ten meant tomorrow morning.

Next morning, he was in his ugly car parked just off the most likely route to, well, anywhere from the campsite. At half past nine, she drove past in a maroon 1976 Chevy Monte Carlo in mint condition. Well, that would be easy to follow. She drove directly to the Financial District and dropped her car with a valet at a huge office building two blocks from the Embarcadero. He parked around the corner and put a police placard on his dashboard, hoping for the best. He watched from outside while she entered from the garage and headed to the elevators. Stuck in the process of getting past the security desk, he missed which elevator she took. It had been going too well.

He went to the directory. The only likely looking name was a talent agency on 21: JPerkins Talent. That could be it. Or it might be any other stinking office here. Why did she not make her precious Janette meet her at the Thorny Issue? There was nothing he could do here. He went home to do some Googling.

When he started looking, he realized he might have gotten lucky right out of the gate: the JPerkins Talent Agency was owned by a woman, first initial J. It described itself as an agency of distinction for specialized talent. It did not mention the entertainment industry. Or any other. It could be a very fancy call girl operation. He kept looking.

An hour later, after a phone call with his partner, he packed a bunch of gear and groceries in his car. He might be sleeping and eating in his car for a couple of days. He hoped it would not take longer. If it did, he could always figure out something to push the river.

He had been sitting in his car long enough to be screamingly bored when he got a call from Eleanor. "Hello?" He hoped he did not sound too eager. Goddess, it would be great to cut this short somehow.

"Heathcliffe. When can you come visit me?" She had only ever called him his full name in serious moments.

"Um, sure. Anytime. Right now? I could be there in an hour." Long enough to go home and shower. Leave a trail just in case, an email triggered to send if he did not cancel it within six hours.

"Good. See you then."

He entered the grounds and realized he would never find his way back to Eleanor's tent. Before he had his phone to his ear, Felix was bowing before him. He followed.

"Heath, come inside. Felix, guard." It was a command, and Felix turned and stood in a parade rest position at the back of the wagon. She led Ryan up the tiny stairs. He had to duck under the roof and into the doorway. Once inside, he stood, to discover he was inside a jewel box.

Everything was made of carved and polished wood. There was not a right angle in the place, making it otherworldly and oddly feminine. A high platform at the back was covered by a quilt in a rainbow-colored pattern. She showed him a chair and sat herself on a tiny sofa, probably also a bed. Stained glass in the window behind her showed a man on his knees.

"You wanted to know about the missing ones. How long have you been looking for them?"

"About ten years." Her eyes widened.

"Heath, can you promise me complete secrecy regarding this conversation?"

"Only if there is no crime. You know I can't if there is a crime."

"Yes, I understand. But otherwise?" She looked at him for a long moment. He nodded. "Heathcliffe, I need you to say so clearly."

"Okay," he said. "If there is no crime, I promise secrecy."

"Good." She relaxed. "Do you remember that argument we had over and over? How you were so clear about the relationship you wanted and I wasn't ready?"

"Yeah. That was it! I was trying to remember why we had broken up. So?"

"Do you remember the different kinds of S and M we tried?" He nodded. Where was this going? "You wanted to go deeper than I did."

"What has this got to do with anything? That's ancient history now." His foot itched suddenly.

"Heath, this is my life now. I live what you wanted then."

"Like, Felix is your slave, you mean?" She nodded. He waited.

"These people, Heath," she handed him back the photos. "They all wanted what you wanted. They all got it."

The silence stretched as he thought this over. "If there is no crime, I will keep your secret. Tell me more."

"There is a Marketplace. It is real. Those people have all gone into voluntary slavery, Heath." She was watching, waiting. What was she expecting from him? "This is what we talked about, all those years ago. It really exists." He said nothing. What was there to say?

"The Marketplace does not exist officially. You cannot put this in a report for the police. We can make up a story of where those people went and create proofs. We can get some of them to write to family members or visit or something to make those missing persons reports go away. What we cannot do is tell the truth about this." She looked at him. "Heath?"

"It's real? Real slavery? And these." He waved the stack of photos. "That's what happened to them?"

"Yes. That's what they chose."

"Wow." He looked into her eyes, and his own filled with tears. "How?"

"They are found, trained. There is a system."

She stood, filling the tiny space. Leaning over him, she said, "What would you give to be owned? To be used to the utmost of your abilities? To be valued property, to give service every day with pride? I know you, Heathcliffe. What would you give?"

"Anything," he whispered. "Everything."

"Sort out your life, Heath. By the time the Thorny Issue leaves town, you will have what you need to close those cases. I will prepare you for the Marketplace."

Blood, Lust
by Elizabeth Schechter

"But what are we going to do with him?"

Grendel didn't really expect an answer. Alexandra knew that. Grendel had been ranting for nearly ten minutes at that point, and she agreed with him. The *him* in question was named Daniel. He'd come to them with glowing reports from the Spotter who'd discovered him performing in one of the worst BDSM clubs in New York. Alexandra had to agree with the Spotter—Daniel was gifted. He had the need to serve, raw skills just waiting to be honed into perfection, and he had an amazing capacity for taking punishment. He wasn't the best-looking boy on the block, but looks weren't everything. His sweet nature more than made up for it.

What the Spotter hadn't mentioned was, Daniel was a cutter. Rachel had been the one to catch him, stopping him before he used a razor blade left behind by a departed guest. He'd confessed immediately and tearfully, to the sexual thrill and the release he felt when he cut himself. And he had agreed to both a longer training period and to begin working with a therapist if that meant being allowed to stay. He had worked diligently, taking the medications Doctor Kauffman prescribed and doing everything that was asked of him. Only to confess to Rachel he wasn't sleeping, and when he did, he was dreaming of blood and blades. Rachel had brought him to the trainers. Now the potential slave was sitting in the library under Rachel's supervision, waiting to learn his fate.

"He needs help," Grendel finished. "More than we can offer him. And having him collared will only hinder that."

"So what? We send him away? Tell him to come back when he stops?" Alexandra asked. "That's only going to make it worse."

"That's not our problem," Grendel pointed out, turning towards the closed door as someone knocked. "Come in."

The door opened, and Chris came into the room. He closed the door behind him and bowed slightly.

Alexandra didn't wait for Grendel to speak. "I want your opinion on Daniel," she said.

Chris nodded once, slowly. "He's good. He's very good. And he's very good at hiding the self-harm. May I ask what the latest reports said?"

"He's somehow managed to get the self-harm wrapped into his sexual identity," Grendel said. "We'll have to talk to Jackson about keeping an eye on anyone from that club. From what Daniel says, it's where the wannabe vampires hang out." He snorted. "Looks like Daniel's string of pseudo-masters all used him the same way. He says they called him a blood donor, they'd go heavy on him then drink the blood off his skin while they fucked him. And he said he's never had sex any other way until Jackson pulled him out of the soft world. Breaking him of this particular fetish is going to be hard. And I don't really think it should be our problem. We need to cut him loose."

Chris paused a moment, and a slight frown crossed his face. "If we send him away, he'll be dead in a year."

"You think he's suicidal?" Alexandra asked, alarmed. Had Emil missed something?

"Unlikely," Chris answered. "That's not typical for cutters, and Doctor Kauffman would have said. Did he mention anything?"

"No," Alexandra admitted.

Chris nodded. "Then it will be an accident. Or he'll go back to the club where Jackson found him, pick up another fake vampire." He shook his head. "He's made for the collar."

"You know there's no way we can send him to auction now," Grendel snapped. "Another waste of time."

"Unless we consider private sale," Chris said.

"Private sale?" Alexandra asked. She glanced at Grendel then turned back to Chris. "That's highly irregular, to have a private sale for an entry-level slave. Especially one with... issues. You have something in mind?"

Chris went still for a moment and bowed. "I do. Would you object to acting as an agent for Daniel?"

"An answer that isn't an answer," Grendel said. "Chris—"

"A full answer would require me to break a confidence," Chris answered smoothly. "I would need to make a few telephone calls first. Possibly long-distance."

Grendel scowled but nodded. "Go ahead."

Chris bowed and left. As the door closed, Grendel looked at Alexandra, who shook her head.

"I have no idea."

* * *

Chris let himself into the study and closed the door, mentally calculating time zones as he crossed to the desk. It would be nearly midnight in Tokyo. Not necessarily too late, given the hours he knew Sakai-san kept, but also well past the time propriety allowed for a business call. He sat down at the desk, studied the telephone for a moment, then picked up the receiver and dialed.

"Hello?" The voice that answered the phone was accented and deep.

"Good afternoon, Vicente," Chris said. "It's Chris. Is she available?"

"Mister Chris, hello! Give me a minute and I'll see." Chris heard the click-clunk of the receiver being put down on the counter, followed by distant, receding footsteps and a door opening. A few minutes later, there was another click.

"Well, well," the familiar harsh voice said with a laugh. "The prodigal returns. Should I kill the fatted calf?"

"Good afternoon, Trainer," Chris answered.

"Oh, a formal call. What can I help you with, Chris?"

Chris looked down at the desk blotter for a moment. "*Kyuketsuki.*"

There was an intake of breath on the other side. Anderson murmured, "And how did you know about that?"

"I met two, in Tokyo. Sakai-san implied there were others within the Marketplace. That there are... specialized slaves that serve them."

A long silence.

"Chris, why do you want to know this?" Anderson asked.

"Because we have a problem child." Chris quickly explained the situation with Daniel. He heard a rhythmic thumping on the other side and a jingle—the Trainer was drumming her fingers, making her

179

omnipresent bracelets ring. He could almost see her doing it and found himself smiling.

"Has Emil seen him?"

"Yes."

"Right. I'll call Tetsuo and see what he says." She added, "I'd like to meet this problem child. Tell Grendel and Alexandra you both are coming here for dinner. Bring his file and anything Emil sent to you. And expect to spend the night."

Chris coughed in surprise. "I wasn't expecting you to take such an active interest in this."

Anderson chuckled. "You've caught my attention. See you tonight. We're having fatted calf."

The line went dead. Chris looked at the receiver for a moment before hanging up. He continued to stare for a moment, then he rose and left, going back to report to Grendel and Alexandra.

* * *

Daniel clenched his hands and forced himself to look out the window at the traffic on the Southern State Parkway.

"You can relax," Chris said. "She won't bite you."

"But... she's the Trainer!" Daniel blurted then sighed and looked down. "Sorry, Chris."

"For being nervous? Don't be." Chris smiled slightly. "Just be yourself, Daniel. Remember your manners, and remember we're trying to help."

Daniel swallowed and looked back at Chris, barely hopeful. "And... do you think I'll be able to stay?"

"That remains to be seen," Chris answered. Daniel swallowed around the lump in his throat and turned back to the window, trying not to think about having to leave. He couldn't fail. Not now. Not when he was so close to having something he'd never even known he needed.

The Southern State spilled into the Belt Parkway and veered away from the airport onto the Van Wyck. As they merged onto the Jackie Robinson Parkway, Daniel closed his eyes and scraped his nails across the back of his neck, digging in hard. It helped but not much. Not enough. He opened his eyes to see Chris looking at him. It was hard to read his eyes behind his glasses. Daniel winced and tried not to hunch over in his seat.

"If you want to tell me, I'm listening," Chris said quietly.

"You've read my file," Daniel said. "And made notes in it. I saw you doing it once."

"True, but there's a world of difference between a written history and spoken one. The written one doesn't show me who you are, and it doesn't tell me everything. So if you want to talk... " His voice trailed off.

Daniel looked back down at his hands. "You know I'm gay," he said slowly. "Well... bi, I suppose. I don't mind girls. But... yeah. Bi with heavy shades of gay."

"And your family? I don't remember any relatives listed."

Daniel sniffed. "That's because I don't have a family. Mom died when I was 12, and I never had a dad. Went into the system and stayed there until I aged out. No money for college, so I... well, I did the best I could. Got a job during the day as a bike messenger, worked at night in the Blood Bank." He glanced at Chris. "That's the club where Jackson found me. I'd been there... five, maybe six years? Yeah, that's right. I started hustling drinks, moved up to tending the bar, then got up on stage as the main course."

Chris nodded. "Go on."

"That's where I met Greg. He was the first." Daniel tipped his head back against the headrest. "Before I met him, I thought all the guys with the theater teeth and the black leather and angst were doing live action role-play—"

"Live action what?"

Daniel grinned. "That's what I said. It's a new thing. There's a game all about vampires, and they play it for real instead of on paper. It's like being in a play. Anyhow, that's what they told me. Greg... we went out. Had dinner. Went back to his place, watched a couple of movies. Had a couple of drinks. Went to bed... and he bit me." Daniel snickered, grinning. "I didn't know any better. He was my first... I mean... I was a virgin. And it... well, it was a turn-on. He wanted me. Wanted all of me. First time that had ever happened."

"And then?"

"He told me he was a real vamp. Which was really kind of weird, but I was naked in bed with him, and he wanted me there. So

I'm all 'Yes, Sir! Whatever you say!'" Daniel heard Chris snort. He grinned then sobered. "I moved in with him. He was nice, when he didn't have the teeth in. Just... he wanted me to bleed for him. And I wanted to bleed for him. Because he wanted me." Daniel looked out the window; the car had gotten off the highway and was moving slowly through city streets. "We're almost there?"

"Almost."

"I'll make it quick. After Greg left, I met Colin. After Colin came Jessica. Then came Max. Max was the one who got me on stage as a bottom and as a bleeder. He was the first one who tied me up when he cut me, and he called himself my Master. And he wasn't happy when I broke up with him to start seeing Jackson." He looked at Chris. "He went after me with a scalpel while he had me tied up on stage. Is that in my file?"

"Seventy-three stitches. Yes."

Daniel nodded, absently running his nails over his forearm. "That's the whole of it. People want me because I love them enough to bleed for them."

"So why with Mister Stevens?" Chris asked. "He told us you took a whipping well, and that you were surprisingly talented in bed, more than he would have expected for a novice. Enough so he thought you should be considered for further training as a pleasure slave."

"He said that?" Daniel gasped. "He liked me?"

"He did," Chris answered, nodding. "So why cut after?"

Daniel thought back to that night, seeing the look on Rachel's face when she found him with the razor blade. "Because... as nice as he was... and as good as he was... there was something missing. It felt... it felt like I was cheating. Because I didn't give him everything I should have." He looked at Chris. "Does that make sense?"

"It does to you," Chris answered. The car slowed and pulled up to the curb. Chris unbuckled his seat belt and slid out of the car, holding the leather case Daniel assumed contained his file. Daniel checked the traffic and got out on the street side, following the driver to the back of the car. Daniel took the two small bags the driver retrieved from the trunk and looked to Chris for direction.

"Just around the block," Chris said. He turned to the driver. "I'll call when I know what time tomorrow. Thank you."

The driver nodded and went back around the car. As it pulled away, Chris started walking. Daniel fell in behind him, trying not to worry. And failing miserably.

* * *

The townhouse was nicer than Daniel was expecting, even though he'd be the first to admit he had no experience on which to base his assumptions. And the Trainer was definitely not what he was expecting. He bowed deeply to the tall, thin woman with the long hair, not letting go of the bags. If he kept his hands full, he wouldn't be able to gouge his own skin off.

"Well, you follow Mary upstairs, and she'll show you where to put those," Anderson said.

"Thank you, Ma'am," Daniel answered. "Is... is that the proper honorific?"

"Ma'am is fine. You don't get to call me Trainer unless I'm training you."

"Thank you, Ma'am. If I may... is there any service I can be to you?"

Her smile was both stern and understanding, and he wondered how she managed that. "If we keep you busy, you won't hurt yourself?" she asked.

Daniel looked down and nodded, feeling his face grow warm. "Yes, Ma'am."

"Well, at least you're honest. Mary, once the bags are put away, take him to Vicente."

"Yes, Trainer." The petite brunette dressed in a plain, gray dress bobbed a curtsy, turning to Daniel. "This way, sir."

* * *

"Tell me why Grendel hasn't just thrown him out on his ass?" Anderson asked, not looking up from Daniel's file.

"Because we can all see Daniel is worth it," Chris answered. "Untrained, he was better than a good number of novices we've seen this past year. He's got the instinct and the drive."

"And an unfortunate habit, but one we can use. In this case, it's a

183

selling point," Anderson added. She sat back and picked up her coffee cup. "So, let's stop dancing around and get to the meat of it. Tell me what you know."

Chris didn't need to ask what she was talking about. "Sakai-san provided slaves to *kyuketsuki* Owners while I was in Japan. I met two of them when they came to a private auction. I know they're part of the Marketplace in Japan. Sakai-san implied they were part of the Marketplace elsewhere, but that's not something I've heard of anywhere else."

"And you wouldn't. It's strictly on a need-to-know basis." Anderson looked at him. "Emil knows. It's usually the medical professionals who know, and who make the referral to the trainers who specialize in this kind of placement." She shook her head, sipped her coffee, and looked down at the papers. "I talked to Grendel, and he has no objections to me taking the problem child off his hands."

Chris stopped, his own coffee held in mid-air, trying to keep a straight face. "Daniel's a novice. You never take novices."

Anderson smiled. "Oh, I'm not taking him. I'm transferring him to a trainer who specializes in this kind of work. Grendel will remain trainer of record, though."

Chris finished his drink and set the cup down. He considered his words. "Trainer, how long has this been going on?"

Anderson looked thoughtful. "No idea. Since the beginning, maybe. I don't suppose I need to tell you why it isn't common knowledge."

Chris smiled. "No. I can understand why. What I don't understand is why you're telling me."

"If you hadn't come to me about it, I wouldn't be. But you know, and I don't see the point in closing the barn door when the horse has already been stolen," Anderson answered. She set her own cup down and laced her fingers, her bracelets chiming softly. "If it had gone the way it usually does, Emil would have done what I just did—recommended Grendel send Daniel to another trainer, one who specializes in slaves who need this kind of help. No, I'm not telling you who."

"I wasn't asking," Chris said. "And then... what?"

Anderson closed the folder and tucked it back into the leather case. "The contracts for a blood slave are similar to those of a grudge slave. Short-term contracts, frequent checks by the agent or trainer, much more stringent boundaries for both Owner and slave. Correspondingly higher slave fees, although slaves of this sort don't usually leave the Marketplace. The retention rate is nearly 90 percent."

Chris nodded slowly. The burn of curiosity was there. How to ask the question? "How many eventually become owners?" he finally asked.

Anderson grinned. "None. It's against their rules. There's also no such thing as a lifetime contract for a blood slave."

"So... I don't think I want to know how the rules are enforced," Chris said. He smiled slightly. "It probably involves garlic and stakes."

"Behave yourself," Anderson chided. "If you think Marketplace society can be tight-assed with rules and regulations... Well, we have nothing on them. We don't handle the rule enforcement, they do."

"They self-police?"

"And in the years I've known about this, I've known of two violations. Both Owners have never been seen again."

Chris frowned slightly. "In the Marketplace?"

"At all." Anderson rose. "Let's go check on the problem child."

* * *

Daniel rinsed off the last pot and set it on the drainboard, pulled the plug out, and the soapy water swirled out of the sink. The cook was an infectiously happy man, and Daniel felt more relaxed than he had in a long time. He used the sprayer to rinse the last of the soap out of the sink and went cold when he saw what the suds had hidden—a small paring knife.

It would be easy. So easy. An accident. He just didn't see it in the soap. Just a mistake. Not his fault. Daniel swallowed and looked down into the sink. No one could blame him for an accident.

He could. He could blame himself. He slowly picked up the knife, washed it, rinsed it, set it onto the drainboard. He swallowed again and rinsed his hands, drying them on the towel he'd thrown over his shoulder.

"Good choice."

Daniel jerked at the harsh voice, turning to see the Trainer and Chris standing in the doorway. He tucked his hands behind his back and slowly went to his knees.

"Thank you, Ma'am," he said. "I... it was tempting."

"I could see that," Anderson said. "That's why I said you made a good choice. Were you ordered not to cut yourself?"

"Yes, Ma'am," Daniel answered. "Mister Eliot said I wasn't to handle anything with a cutting edge at all. Not even a letter opener, he said."

"So why did you?" Chris asked, his voice sharp.

Daniel flinched. "Vicente said I was to wash the dishes, and I didn't know there was a knife there until I was done."

"Did you tell him you weren't to handle knives?" Chris demanded.

"He did, Mister Chris," Vicente answered, coming back into the kitchen. "I must have dropped one into the water by accident."

Anderson nodded. "Stand up, Daniel."

Daniel got to his feet, keeping his eyes on the Trainer's shoes. He waited, every noise in the kitchen sounding as if it was amplified and intensified by his nervous fears. Was he being sent away now?

"I expect you to be on your best behavior, Daniel," Anderson said. "There will be a guest for dinner, and he's here to see you."

Daniel's head jerked up, but he managed to keep his mouth shut. Here to see *him*? Why? And who? Not another doctor, he hoped. He dismissed the thought. Why bring him all the way to the Trainer of Trainers if it was just to see more doctors? He reined in his curiosity and nodded once. "Yes, Ma'am. I will. Thank you, Ma'am. Is there anything I can do to help?"

"Vicente, how soon will dinner be ready?" Anderson asked.

"Half an hour. And the guest—" A bell rang, and Vicente nodded. "The guest is here. Enough time for drinks before dinner."

Chris looked at Daniel and smiled. "You were a bartender. Guess what you're going to be doing?"

"Yes, Chris."

* * *

Daniel trailed behind Chris as they walked out to the front hallway. He kept his hands clasped behind him and tried not to worry. Or, at least, show he was worried. He heard the Trainer greet someone, heard a deep voice responding. He came around the corner into the hallway and saw the man standing inside the door. He was tall, taller than the Trainer, dressed neatly in a suit Daniel was certain cost more than his portion of the rent on the tiny apartment he had shared three other people. His hair was long and pure white, pulled back at his nape into a sleek tail. He had just set down a small attaché case and turned when Chris and Daniel came into the hallway. His eyes widened when he saw them. Then he laughed and bowed toward them.

"Parker-san, I had not expected to see you."

From what Daniel could see of Chris' face, he looked startled but only for a moment. He bowed, more deeply than the other man had, and answered, "Itami-san, I didn't know you were in New York. It's very good to see you again."

"It's good to see you as well, my friend. It's been too long, and I did not know you had come back from Japan."

"You two know each other?" Anderson said, sounding amused.

"Yes, Trainer. I told you about the auction I attended with Sakai-san? Itami-san was one of the Owners." Chris turned back to Itami. "And how is Mariko?"

"She was delightful, but she expressed a wish to marry," Itami answered. "I released her from her contract before I moved to New York. She lives in Kobe and will be married in the spring. I have not yet decided if I will attend the wedding. I will tell her you asked after her."

"And please tell her I extend my congratulations," Chris said.

"Of course." Itami smiled and looked at Daniel. "And will you introduce me to your friend?"

"Of course. I apologize for being remiss. Itami Hiro, this is Daniel, a trainee."

Daniel stepped forward, his mind racing. *Kobe. That's in Japan. That means Itami is Japanese. So Itami is his last name, and his given name is Hiro. And he's an Owner. Don't blow it, Danny.* Daniel took a breath and bowed, making it deeper than Chris's had been. "It's an honor to be presented to you, Itami-san," he said as he straightened. He kept his eyes down and his hands behind his back. He heard no movement, but all of a sudden, Itami-san was *there*, standing in front of him. Daniel caught his breath, startled. He fought the urge to step back. Instead, he slowly sank to his knees.

"Very nice," Itami purred, and the sound of his deep voice made Daniel shiver. "Of which House?"

"He's been training with Grendel Eliot and Alexandra Selador," Anderson answered. "But Chris has also had a hand in."

"I should have known," Itami said with a laugh. "There is a... ah... my English is not what it should be. But all those you have touched have this, Parker-san. My Mariko had it as well."

"I am honored you think so, Itami-san," Chris said. "I am but a humble—"

"Humble?" Anderson scoffed. "Hardly. Proudest trainer I've ever trained. Now, we have time for drinks. Daniel, on your feet and show us what you can."

Daniel saw Itami's polished shoes move away and got back to his feet. "Yes, Ma'am. Where am I going?"

"This way," Chris said. Daniel followed him into a room that turned out to be a nice sitting room. There was a bar in one corner. Daniel went straight over, ducking behind it and checking to see what he had to work with.

"You handled that nicely," Chris said softly. "Very proper. I don't recall you saying you studied Japanese culture, and it's not in your file."

"I didn't," Daniel answered, looking over the back of the bar. Ice, a bowl of lemons and limes, even a bar blender. Everything he'd need. "The public library used to show foreign films on Sundays. I like them. I think I've seen just about every Kurosawa movie made and most of Nakagawa's. What can I make for you, Chris? Your usual?"

Chris paused. "No. Not at the moment. There should be sparkling mineral water back there. Pour two, both with ice and a twist of lime."

Daniel nodded and picked up a lime, cutting it and prepping the twists, painfully aware Chris was watching him carefully as he used the knife. Once he set the knife aside, Chris looked away. Daniel set two highball glasses filled with ice on the bar, found the bottle of mineral water and opened it. He filled both glasses and added the twists of lime before passing them both to Chris. Chris carried them across to where Itami and Anderson had just entered; Anderson took one glass with a nod toward Daniel. He smiled in response and turned his attention to Itami, who was coming closer.

"What may I pour for you, Sir?" Daniel asked.

"Make a suggestion," Itami purred, his eyes half-lidded and sleepy.

Daniel licked his top lip and stepped back, surveying the bottles. "Do you have any preferences, Sir?"

Itami just smiled. "Surprise me."

"Yes, Sir. Excuse me, Sir." Daniel crouched behind the bar, looking at the bottles racked on the lower shelf. Surprise him? Oh, boy... Usually, he liked a challenge like this. But this was an Owner. He looked up to see Itami peering over the bar. Daniel grinned, considered him for a moment. Very smooth. Very dashing. Old-fashioned, from his manners. Classic cocktail, then. What... oh, yes.

Daniel rose, quickly collected what he needed. He picked up a martini glass and set it in front of Itami, then went to work, mixing gin, lemon juice, orange juice, sugar syrup, and grenadine with ice in a Boston shaker. He closed the shaker and raised it, shaking in neat, economical motions before expertly cracking it open over the glass and pouring out the drink. He set the shaker down and slid the drink a little closer to Itami. "Sir?"

Itami looked down at the glass of amber-colored cocktail and back at Daniel. "And this is called?"

"A Gin and Sin, Sir," Daniel answered.

Itami stared at him, before bursting into laughter. "Truly? Gin and Sin?"

"Yes, Sir," Daniel said. "It's a classic cocktail from the fifties. If you don't care for it, I'll happily make something else."

Itami picked up the glass, and Daniel held his breath while the other man sipped the drink. Itami looked pleasantly surprised, and he nodded. "An excellent choice," he said. "Was this part of your training, Daniel?"

"No, Sir," Daniel answered, bowing his acceptance of the praise. "I was a bartender before I entered training."

"An exceptional skill. Thank you." Itami turned, walking back toward Anderson. Daniel closed his eyes and took a deep breath. When he opened them, he saw Chris watching him. He smiled slightly and nodded, then started to clean up the bar. There was a deep conversation going on across the room, but Daniel couldn't hear the words, only the tones. He kept an eye on Itami and Anderson, though, watching the level of their drinks.

189

"If they need more, I'll serve," Chris murmured, coming over and setting his half-empty glass on the bar. Daniel nodded and picked up the bottle of mineral water; Chris shook his head slightly. "You're doing well."

"Thank you, Chris. I'm terrified I'm going to blow it, though. Should I take things to the kitchen now or wait until they go in for dinner?"

"What do you think?"

Daniel frowned slightly. "That taking things out now might disrupt their conversation, and if they want another drink, I might not have what they need because it's in the kitchen. But if I wait... am I expected to attend at dinner?"

"You are." Chris sounded amused.

"I'll delay dinner. That's not good either." Daniel looked down and frowned. "We never covered the protocol of tending bar as a slave. Can we do that when we get back to the House? Someone might want me as a bartender." Daniel tried not to think about the chance he wouldn't get that far.

"It seems likely. You're very good at it. Yes, we'll cover that, and I'll make certain it's in your file," Chris said, and Daniel almost fainted. He *would* be sold?

"Thank you, Chris."

"And you wait until after dinner, when you're released for the evening," Chris added. "Assuming you are released for the evening. If you're not, the housekeeper or majordomo will know and will make certain that things are cleaned."

Daniel looked up as Itami came back to the bar. His glass was still mostly full. "Sir?" he asked. "Do you not like it?"

"The drink is perfection," Itami answered, putting the glass down on the bar. "I wish to see if the bartender is as well. Attend me, Daniel."

Daniel swallowed, his mouth suddenly dry. Lost for anything else he could do, he stepped back from the bar and bowed deeply. Itami smiled and turned, walking toward the door. Feeling somehow both terrified and elated, Daniel followed him.

* * *

Daniel felt as if he were trespassing as he entered a bedroom on the second floor. Itami closed the door behind him, and Daniel heard the click of a lock. He closed his eyes, took a deep breath, and let his training take over—he knelt the way he'd been taught and waited for instruction.

"You are wearing far too many clothes," Itami said, brushing his fingers over the back of Daniel's neck. "Rise and strip."

Daniel started working at the buttons on his shirt as he stood up, letting it slip from his shoulders and catching it before it fell. He folded it and set it on a chair near the door, then undid his belt.

"You have scars," Itami said suddenly, his voice sharp. He came closer, and trailed one finger over the scar that trailed across Daniel's chest, from beneath his right nipple to the collarbone on his left. He touched Daniel's bicep, tracing an older scar that was barely visible. "This one, you did to yourself. The others I can see, those you did as well. But who did this?" Itami touched the first scar again. "This is not... self... self-made."

"No, Sir," Daniel said. "I was attacked by someone I thought I could trust. An ex-lover." Itami arched a brow, clearly wanting more. Daniel slowly stripped off his pants. He folded them and set them down, letting his hands fall to his sides, trying not to fidget. He was used to being naked, so why did he feel so vulnerable? "I left him, and he tried to kill me. Tied me up, and... it's... it's all in my file."

"Ah," Itami murmured. "I will look. So as not to cause you distress."

"And... I didn't do all the cuts," Daniel added. He looked down and took a deep breath. "I... let people cut me."

He heard the intake of breath and fully expected to be ordered out of the room. He felt a hand in his hair and gasped as Itami pulled him closer, tugging his head back. He chuckled, leaning closer to Daniel, smiling broadly enough that Daniel saw his teeth for the first time. The canines seemed to be extending, growing into fangs. He whimpered, and Itami laughed.

"You are just what I thought you were," Itami whispered, his voice slurring as the canines became more prominent. "Now we shall see if you can be more. Kneel to me, my lovely slave." He let Daniel go, and Daniel dropped none-too-gracefully to his knees. Itami laughed again, stepped back and taking off his suit jacket. He laid it over a chair and tugged his tie loose.

191

"You have questions," he said as he started on his shirt buttons. "You may ask."

Daniel stared up at him then whispered, "You're really real? You're a real vampire?"

Itami smiled, baring his fangs. "I am *kyuketsuki*. Do you know what that means?"

Daniel frowned. Why was that word familiar... wait. "*Onna Kyuketsuki*. I saw that movie." Itami laughed again, letting his shirt hang open to reveal a white cotton undershirt that barely veiled his muscular chest. Daniel swallowed and tipped his head back, appreciating the view. "Are you going to bite me?"

"Nothing so gauche, no," Itami answered. "It is considered... barbaric to feed in that manner. I will, however, cut you. If you allow it."

Everything stopped. The conversation, the room, the house, everything outside the house. The world stopped spinning. The universe stopped doing... whatever it was the universe was doing. Daniel forced himself to take one long, shuddering breath. As he let it out, everything started up again. He wondered if anyone else had noticed the pause in creation. "You... you want to cut me?" he whispered.

"I will understand if you refuse. Given your history, it would not surprise me."

"I'm not refusing. I... I would like it if you cut me, Sir."

Itami looked almost relieved. "And... may I bind you as well?"

"Yes, Sir," Daniel answered, surprised his voice didn't shake.

"Rise, lovely slave."

Daniel slowly got to his feet, and Itami went to a chest of drawers in the corner and took out several coils of rope. He put all but one on the bed and came back. Without a word, he moved behind Daniel. The rope slithered and tickled over Daniel's skin. His arms were arranged so his forearms folded against his back. His wrists were tied firmly and pulled up, with the end of the rope wrapped several times around his upper arms and bound off. Coils were cinched between his arms and his body and more rope wrapped around his body, below his nipples. Once these were cinched, Daniel couldn't move his arms at all. Itami stepped back and nodded.

"This suits you, Daniel. Come to the bed." He took Daniel's arm and guided him toward the bed, steadying him until he was lying face down, facing the leather case Itami had been carrying when he arrived.

Cool hands slid down Daniel's lower back and over his ass. Daniel groaned and shifted, his erection sliding over the scratchy blanket that covered the bed. Itami laughed softly and wrapped one hand around Daniel's ankle, wrapping it in more rope before bending it double and winding the ends of the rope around Daniel's thigh. By the time Itami was done, Daniel was completely immobilized, in some of the most restrictive bondage he'd ever experienced. He squirmed, the rough blanket torture under his cock, and gasped as the ropes around his chest tightened. Itami had grabbed the ropes from behind, effortlessly lifting Daniel up to kneel on the bed. He laughed as Daniel gaped, leaning forward until his nose was just brushing Daniel's.

"I am stronger than mortal men. Faster, as well. You saw that earlier. The movies you have seen have that much correct. Does that frighten you?"

Daniel licked his lips and met Itami's dark eyes. Then he leaned forward and gently kissed Itami just over one of his protruding fangs.

"No, you don't scare me, Itami-san," Daniel murmured.

Itami drew back and ran his hands up Daniel's body, fingers trailing over skin and rope until he stopped with one hand on either side of Daniel's throat. Daniel was certain that Itami could feel his pulse, pounding like a drum. Itami smiled, reminding Daniel of a sleek white wolf.

"I cannot kiss you when I am like this. I will. Later. For now, do you wish a gag? For you will scream, my lovely one."

Daniel swallowed. "Whatever your pleasure is, Sir."

"A very good answer. No, I wish to hear you. And I imagine Parker-san wishes to assure himself of your safety." Itami glanced over his shoulder. "He is outside the door. I can smell him there."

Daniel looked toward the door and back at Itami. "I'm not worried."

Itami's smile softened, and he reached past Daniel, dragging the case toward him. He opened the catches, flipping the top up to reveal the velvet-lined interior, and the double rows of folded straight razors. Daniel shuddered, and he must have made some kind of noise, because Itami laughed.

"Ah, you like these?" he asked, picking one up and opening it to reveal the gleaming blade. "Good. Very good." He cocked his head to the side, clearly studying Daniel, then reached out and drew the blade lightly over Daniel's collarbone. The metal was cold, and for a moment, the chill was all that Daniel felt. Pain chased the chill away, and Daniel threw his head back, whimpering as he felt trails of heat running over his skin. He heard Itami groan. He was in the *kyuketsuki's* arms, Itami's mouth pressed against his collarbone, his tongue rough against Daniel's skin. Pain vanished, and Daniel moaned, straining against the ropes, wanting more. Itami's tongue trailed up over his throat, lingered briefly over the artery. Daniel tipped his head back further, offering. There was a chill of cold air as Itami's mouth moved away, followed by the chill of cool metal and a rush of pain and lust as Itami's mouth closed over the cut on Daniel's throat. He growled and tipped Daniel down onto the bed.

Helpless, Daniel writhed as Itami carved bloody calligraphy into his skin, erasing it with broad sweeps of his tongue, leaving Daniel so lost in sensation it took him a moment to realize Itami had stopped. And where the razor was currently resting. He whimpered, unwilling to move with the sharp blade against his aching cock.

"Shall I?" Itami murmured, leaning over Daniel. His long hair had come loose somehow, and it tickled against Daniel's cheek. "Shall I mark you as mine?" He moved away; Daniel felt Itami's breath, hot against his cock, warming the metal blade. The razor moved, just a touch. Just enough—Daniel shrieked as he came, feeling Itami's mouth closing over his cock and drinking him dry.

He moved away, and Daniel tipped forward to lie face down on the bed, limp and panting. Dimly, he heard Itami moving around, felt the bed tip and shake but couldn't bring himself to spend the energy to raise his head and look around. He felt hard hands on his shins, forcing his bound legs apart. Fingers coated with something cold probed at him, slipping into his ass, making him whimper.

"You did not ask my leave," Itami growled. He twisted his hand, making Daniel yelp. Then his hand moved away, and Daniel felt the bed shift again as fingers slipped underneath the ropes at his back. Without warning, he was lifted off the bed, the ropes cutting into his arms as he hung suspended from Itami's hand. Itami turned and sat down on the edge of the bed, settling Daniel onto his lap; Daniel had a heartbeat to realize what was happening before Itami's cock nearly split him in two. Daniel howled as his own weight drove Itami deeper, a howl that was muffled by a hand over his mouth. Itami's other arm encircled him, pulling Daniel tight against his chest. He growled something in Japanese into Daniel's ear, and the hand on his mouth pulled Daniel's head back. A sudden, sharp pain lanced through his throat, and the last things he saw as he blacked out were Itami's dark eyes.

* * *

Daniel woke up lying under the covers of the bed. His legs had been untied, but his arms were still bound. And he was bound by flesh as well—arms were wrapped around him from behind. He turned slightly to see Itami looking at him, smiling. There was no sign of the fangs.

"Thank you, Sir. Sir, I—" Daniel started. He stopped as Itami's embrace tightened.

"I apologize, Daniel," Itami said. "I allowed instinct to overcome reason. It will not happen again."

Daniel felt his heart sink. "It... it won't?" he stammered. "Because... if you wanted to bite me again... Please would you bite me again, Itami-san?"

Itami blinked, and his face went blank. Then he laughed and let Daniel tip onto his back. He leaned over Daniel, his hair falling like a curtain around them both.

"My name is Hiro, my Daniel. When we are alone in bed together, you will call me by my name."

Daniel's breath caught, and he met Itami's—Hiro's!—eyes. "You... want me?"

"I think that has been made obvious, Daniel," Itami answered. "You will be mine. You will leave here tonight in my collar, if that is acceptable to you. I will discuss this with Parker-san and Anderson-sama." He smiled. "I would like to kiss you now, Daniel."

"Please?"

Itami smiled and lowered his head; Daniel strained up to meet him, tasting copper and salt on his lips. Itami pushed him back down onto the bed, laughing as he got out from under the blankets. Daniel rolled onto his side to watch Itami dress.

"Sir?" he asked. "Did you really cut my cock?"

Itami burst out laughing. "No, *koibito*. I used the back of the blade. Did you think I would damage you?"

195

"I wasn't sure. Yes. I mean, others did," Daniel admitted.

"Your others were not of the Marketplace. And they were not *kyuketsuki*."

"Yes, Sir." Daniel nodded. He tugged against the ropes on his arms and tried to sit up. "Shouldn't I be helping you, Sir?"

"No," Itami answered. "After I have taken your blood, you will rest. I will ask that a tray be sent up for your dinner, which in my impatience we have missed." Itami finished buttoning his shirt and came back to the bed. He leaned down and kissed Daniel lightly on the lips, pushing him back down onto the mattress, running his hand up Daniel's chest to rest on his throat. "I will come back once my negotiations are complete. Then it will be my turn to feed you. Now rest, my lovely blood slave."

Daniel watched as Itami picked up his jacket and left the room. As the door closed, he closed his eyes and sighed, rolling onto his side. Sleep seemed like a good idea.

With any luck, his dream would still be here when he woke up.

The Counselor
By Amelia Horo

Morticia Lapenta stood at the podium, papers in a stack before her, and waited for the judges to file into the room and take their seats. The pearl grey suit was conservatively cut, and she fingered the onyx stones set in her silver cufflinks. The tie was a shade darker than the suit and matched her shoes. Her black hair barely reached the bottom of her ear lobes, which were pierced by onyx and silver stud earrings.

The chief judge nodded and said, "You may begin, counsel."

"May it please the Court. I am here to represent the Appellant in this case." She ticked off the legal points of her argument and demonstrated how the facts applied to the statute and case law. The judges interrupted her with questions, but she was well prepared and answered the questions with ease and completeness. The bell rang indicating her 15 minutes was up, and she moved away from the podium to counsel's table with her papers. Joey, her guide dog, accepted the papers into the pocket set in his vest and resumed his position at her feet. She heard the whispers from the bench, as the judges realized the attorney who had just presented the argument was blind and had spoken from memory, without notes.

Morticia sat erect with her hands in her lap, listening to the argument from the Appellee's counsel. The slight sheen of sweat on her back was the only betrayal of her nervousness. Each droplet nipped like a bird's beak at the welts her Lady had placed there last night. She would not move to ease the pinpricks of pain; it was part of her training to bear what she must at her Lady's hand and desire. When she realized opposing counsel had brought up nothing that needed a response, Morticia startled the judges a second time by giving up the right of rebuttal.

When the chief judge shook her hand before leaving the room, she told Morticia, "I have never had an attorney turn down an opportunity to speak before. I am a bit shocked."

Morticia replied, "I did not see a need to speak further, Your Honor." She then bowed slightly.

* * *

Back in the hotel room, Morticia stripped off the suit and placed it on hangers in the closet. She rubbed down Joey and gave him some water and a treat for being so good in the courtroom. Once in his crate, Joey curled up and went to sleep.

She thought back to how she had gotten to this place in her life. Two decades ago, she was a newly admitted attorney, wondering how she would succeed in the practice of law with her decreasing vision. There was also the hole in her heart where purpose should have resided. She had thought going to law school and becoming a lawyer would help, but it did not. During her childhood, her father had told her often, "Someone without a purpose is a lost soul. Find your purpose, dear daughter, and your life will be full of happiness and meaning."

Morticia had tried marriage, but it was not the commitment she was looking for; she wanted something more meaningful, more substantial. It was too easy to get a divorce these days for a marriage to be something of real value to her. So, after six months, she found herself in a divorce hearing.

After the divorce, she floated from job to job before entering law school in the vain hope of finding that elusive purpose for her life. On the weekends, she went to clubs where she heard of relationships that were strictly enforced by those involved: a Master/slave contract was signed, and the terms agreed upon. She teased out some information and entered her first gay leather bar, trying not to stick out too much or offend anyone. She was dressed in a white T-shirt, jeans, and sneakers. Her lack of pulchritude was helpful here, as well as her penchant for short hair. She stood at the end of the bar, sipping a beer and looking around in brief glances so as not to be seen staring at any one person.

A tall woman walked into the bar, smiling and greeting the men at the bar. Morticia watched her, fascinated at the ease with which this woman handled herself in the bar filled with gay men. She was a bit shocked when she realized the woman was studying her and quickly looked away and down at her beer.

Ali noticed the nervous polishing of the bar with Morticia's right thumb and the instinctive tightening of the shoulders. She approved of the slight straightening of the spine, as if Morticia were bracing herself for a confrontation. Ali strode over to Morticia and pointed at her feet. Shocking herself, Morticia kneeled at this woman's feet, gazing hopefully up. "Eyes down!" she barked. "I did not give you permission to look at my face."

Stomach quivering, Morticia immediately cast her eyes down, blushing deeply. "Good girl," Ali crooned. Ali considered the kneeling woman and sighed. Once again, her instincts proved to be spot on.

* * *

Ali studied the sleeping form at the foot of her bed, trying to decide whether she was worth handing over to a trainer for grooming as a slave in the Marketplace. Morticia had performed well for someone who had no training at all, but was the desire to serve deep enough? Tapping her lips with a manicured finger, Ali went over last night again in her mind. The girl had obeyed all commands willingly, if not expertly, and reacted well to instructions. The night's activities confirmed her observations of the last few weeks. Ali went into the next room and picked up the phone, dialing the number from memory. The conceit of a rotary dial on her landline was something she cherished.

"Deva?" she purred into the phone. "I've found someone you might find interesting. She's a new lawyer but with a lot of potential for the auction block."

"You want me to train her?" Deva Graham asked. "Why me?"

"I've heard you're a trustworthy trainer, who values merchandise rather than using slaves as mere sex toys like some in the United States. I think you could train her to be a good slave in the Marketplace. Do you want to take her in hand?"

Deva leaned back in her chair, running her hand across her cheek and thinking hard on what Ali was telling her. Did she really want to train a person who had finished law school and found out she was not happy as a lawyer? Could she train someone who might be a lot smarter intellectually than she? Did she really want to work that hard? Deva wondered if Chris Parker's hand was somewhere in the background in this situation. It seemed like something Chris would do, but a person could never be sure.

"Okay, I'll take her on for a two-month trial," Deva answered cautiously. "But if I don't see progress within two weeks, I get to return her to the streets. Agreed?"

Ali nodded approvingly into the telephone. "That's fair. Can you fly out to meet her over dinner?"

"What will you be serving?" She grinned, knowing Ali's cook was superb so the meal, at least, would be worth the trip from Chicago to New York.

"A rack of lamb, with baby potatoes and asparagus. The wine will be a blush from my cellars. Will that whet your appetite for the young morsel I'm offering you?"

"Yes, that'll do just fine!" Deva hung up, pleased with the night's plans.

* * *

Deva was greeted at the door by a naked woman dressed only in the stripes from a caning. She took Deva's jacket and hung it on the coat tree and then stood by the wall, awaiting further instructions. Deva strode into the living room, calling for Ali, who entered the room wearing a caftan and jeweled slippers, her hair neatly coifed and her make-up exquisite.

"Dear Deva! It has been too long since we saw one another!" Ali kissed her on both cheeks and looked her over. "How has life been treating you lately?"

Returning the kisses, Deva asked, "How are you, Ali? Is Chris coming over tonight?"

Ali clucked her tongue. "Please! Not everything is done at the behest of that man, you know. I'm very independent and do not need to seek permission from Chris Parker to make certain arrangements when I find a treasure. Let's eat first, and then you can see what I've found in my travels through the city."

After dinner, Deva sat in the drawing room with a brandy in her hand. "Well? What do you have to show me, Ali?"

Ali brought forward the woman who had greeted her at the door. "This is Morticia. I think she could be trained to be of service. Present yourself, girl."

Morticia dropped to her knees, legs spread wide and placed her hands behind her head. She did not look either Ali or Deva in the eyes, having learned quickly that was something one must be granted permission to do. Deva looked her over, thinking. She was not beautiful in the fashion model sense of the word and, even naked, she looked almost androgynous.

"Why are you here, girl?" Deva asked.

"I wish to serve a master," Morticia replied.

"What can you do to be of service?" Deva asked.

"Whatever is asked of me," she responded, blushing deeply. It was clear she thought Deva was asking about sexual service.

"I am not talking about sex, girl. What talents do you bring to the table? What can you do for someone?"

"I am a trained attorney. Well, actually I am just at the beginning of my career, but I learn quickly. I can speak several languages, and I can cook and bake."

Deva looked down at the kneeling woman. "Look at me." Morticia quickly raised her eyes and looked at Deva directly. Her intelligence shone through, and once more Deva wondered if she was walking into a trap. She shook off that thought and made a decision.

"Okay, Ali, I will see what can be done with her. How much does she know?"

"I haven't told her much; only that if she truly wants to be in service to someone, she needs a lot of training and must be willing to learn and do whatever is required to achieve that goal."

Frowning slightly, Deva looked at the kneeling woman, whose gaze had turned hopeful, tinged with curiosity. "Are you willing to give up your current life completely? Including cutting off ties with family and friends?"

A wave of nervousness ran across Morticia's face as she answered. "Yes, I am. If it means that I have a purpose to my life, then I can do it and I will do it." She ended her sentence with a fierce determination.

"We'll see if you have what it takes, girl," purred Ali. She smiled at Deva and handed her the folder containing Morticia's information. She looked at the contents, noting some items for future reference, and sat back, satisfied.

"Okay, we will begin your training in one week. Come to this address with all your affairs in order." Deva handed her a list of what needed to be done for Morticia to begin her training and a business card with the address of her training facility in Chicago. "Once you close the doors to that address, there's no turning back, so use this week to think very carefully what your choice means to the rest of your life."

* * *

Morticia made it through the training with Deva and had ended up on the auction block in New York. Her first owner was a wealthy couple, who had her working with their CPA to make sure their wealth increased during the difficult years of the recession. She'd performed with distinction during her two-year contract, but her heart was still empty. She had indeed found purpose, but it was limited and not all-encompassing, so she went back to the auction block, hoping for a different kind of owner.

Lucille looked at the woman on the auction block and then at the folder in her hands. While the first bloom of youth had long passed, Morticia was well-formed and not unpleasant to look at. She frowned at a notation under the *Medical* section of the profile, which indicated a gradual loss of vision in the last few years. Nothing major yet, but it would become an issue. While this could drop the price of the merchandise, it all depended on the uses one would have for the slave. Lucille considered the possibilities and consequences of such a purchase. She ran a hand along the side of Morticia's body, noting the reactions to her touch and slight warming of the skin. Lucille looked at the other offerings and did not find another one that came close to her needs. Decision made, she entered a number on the tablet and went into the next room to join the other owners.

Morticia heard the bell indicating the auction was over. Did someone purchase her or would she return to the mundane world? She trembled slightly but did not break her pose, waiting to hear from Deva if her degenerating vision had cost her a chance at finding the purpose she needed to live fully. She heard footsteps stop in front of her, and a strong, female hand pulled her chin up and locked the collar around her neck. "I am Lucille, your new owner. Meet me at the doors with your things in one hour."

"Yes, Ma'am." Morticia noted the designer clothes and professional manicure. She also noted the strong hands were not unfamiliar with hard work, being callused on the palms. What kinds of duties would Lucille have her perform? She hoped for more than just the dry aspects of the financial and tax law her prior owners had wanted from her.

Deva came into the auction room, smiling at her. "You did well. Very well, considering everything. I think you will find Lucille is a better fit for what you want."

Morticia looked at her hopefully. "I really hope this is what I've been seeking, Deva, but I'm beginning to doubt it exists. I think my father was telling me tall tales all my childhood."

Deva smacked her gently on the ass and told her to get dressed. "You have one hour to be ready for your new owner. Got everything packed and ready to go?"

"Of course I do!" Morticia giggled slightly and ran out of the room, the locked collar bouncing on her neck.

* * *

That first night in Lucille's house opened Morticia's eyes and heart to a new dimension in her life. She had been taught during her training with Deva how to please sexually both men and women, but this was so different.

Once she had put her possessions away in the room assigned to her, Morticia reported to Lucille in the drawing room of the large house in Northern Virginia. Lucille motioned for her to approach, and Morticia did so, wondering what her duties would be.

Lucille looked at Morticia, remembering what she looked like naked and noting the plain suit she was wearing now. "Where did you buy that suit?" she asked.

"At a K&G store, Ma'am. I was provided with sufficient funds to purchase three suits on sale." Morticia responded, her tone neither happy nor disapproving.

"That won't do in my house. From now on, your suits will be tailor-made, and I prefer you to wear slacks."

Startled and happy, she replied, "Yes, Ma'am!" Morticia had been uncomfortable wearing skirts but was not permitted to express such sentiments to her prior owners. It was one of the reasons she chose not to renew her contract with them.

Pursing her lips, Lucille noted, "You will also use a gentleman's cane as an accessory. At first, it will be a bit of a conceit, but in time, it may become more necessary. I'd like to keep your vision issues at a minimum for as long as possible. Do you require a large screen monitor yet for your legal duties?"

Morticia paled but spoke truthfully. "I do need some technology to accommodate my vision problems, Ma'am."

"Very well. Let the housekeeper know what you need, and I'll see that you have it. If you can't perform your duties as a lawyer, then I just spent a lot of money for nothing." She smiled gently. "I run a program for people with immigration problems, and I'll use your skills to enhance that program."

Morticia stared. "I don't know anything about that area of the law."

"Are you unwilling to learn it?"

"No, Ma'am! I'm quite willing to learn immigration law. I'm just informing you I have no experience in that area."

"Well, then, I'll have someone come over tomorrow morning to start your instruction. You'll be ready to review case files by the end of the week."

"Yes, Ma'am." Morticia knew she would have to work very hard to be ready in a week, but she was determined not to fail her new owner.

"Come here, girl." Morticia approached Lucille, who reached out and grabbed her chin, pulling her down for a deep kiss. Lucille broke the kiss and told her to follow. They went through several rooms and down a hallway to a large room with various closets built into the walls. Lucille opened the first closet, and Morticia gazed at the neat rows of floggers hanging within. The second closet held paddles and canes made of various materials. The third closet contained shelves of flechettes, scalpels, and needles of varied gauges, gleaming and glinting in the light of the lamps hanging from the walls. Lucille did not open the other closets, and Morticia wondered what they contained. In the middle of the room hung chains with shackles, and a St. Andrew's Cross stood at an angle.

Lucille pointed to the floor at her feet, and Morticia walked forward and kneeled, head bowed to show the nape of her neck. Lucille looked down at the woman trembling at her feet and smiled.

"Take off your clothes and place them by the door," she instructed.

Naked, Morticia kneeled once again at Lucille's feet and waited for the next order. "Stand at the cross."

Lucille tied her to the cross with padded cuffs on both wrists and both ankles. "Your contract says no permanent markings. Do you wish a safeword for pain thresholds?"

Morticia considered the question. "No, Ma'am. I don't believe that will be necessary."

Lucille smiled at the answer: an acknowledgement her initial instincts were correct. She turned and picked out a flogger with wide leather falls. She started warming up Morticia's skin, hitting her on the breasts, belly and upper thighs in rhythmic motions. Morticia whimpered as the strokes throbbed through her body and her mind. When the skin was a nice shade of rose, Lucille changed to a flogger with a heavier leather and thinner falls. The sound changed from a thud to a slap as the falls hit Morticia's skin, much more stingy that the first tool used on her.

When the whimpers turned to cries of pain, Lucille uncuffed her from the St. Andrew's cross and locked the cuffs from the hanging chains to her wrists. Lucille created a matrix of stripes on Morticia's back with one of the bamboo canes, pausing after each stroke to allow the flash of pain to seep deep into Morticia's body. She extended the pattern down the back to include the thighs and, eventually, the calves, delighting in the dance of Morticia's feet in reaction to the strokes.

Lucille paused to consider the weeping woman hanging from the chains in her playroom. Was she ready for more? Contemplative but concentrating deeply on the reactions, she took a tiny flechette from a drawer and pinched a bit of skin above Morticia's nipple on her right breast. With a quick jabbing motion, she inserted the flechette and watched Morticia rock backward, a screech of pain ripping out of her throat. Two small droplets of blood trickled out of the wounds and Lucille slowly licked the blood off her skin. "Mmmmm. So tasty!"

Lucille undid the shackles and Morticia sank to the floor. "On your knees and look at me!" Morticia struggled to her knees and looked upward at her mistress, eyes a little glazed from the endorphins rushing through her system. Lucille put her fingers on the flechette, and Morticia kneeled there, waiting for the next move in this dance they had begun in the auction room. Lucille slowly removed the flechette, licking the blood from the instrument once it was removed from the breast. She dropped the flechette into a basin in the closet and closed the door.

"Come with me," she ordered and strode out of the playroom, toward her bedroom. Morticia paused briefly next to the pile of her clothes and then quickly followed her mistress down the hallway. At the door to the bedroom, she waited for instructions, feeling the cane stripes on her back and the stabbing pain where the flechette had been implanted so briefly. Her breasts, belly, and upper thighs were flushed from the floggers, but it was not really pain. She thought a bit more about it and realized it was not pain she felt. Rather it was a warmth throughout her body and a longing for sexual use. Would this happen now? Or would she be sent to her room as had happened at her former owners' house?

Lucille sat on the bed, reading the thoughts flashing across Morticia's face. She was a sadist but also liked to sexually arouse her playmates. Lucille could smell the moistness between Morticia's legs and was pleased. She poured some water into a crystal glass on the stand next to the bed and motioned Morticia to enter the room.

"Drink this."

Morticia drank the water and handed the glass back to Lucille. Lucille set the glass down on the stand and cupped her hands around Morticia's face, looking for signs of rebellion. She saw none. She kissed Morticia gently on the lips and then took possession of her mouth, sucking and biting on her lips and then forcing her mouth open to accept her tongue. Lucille pulled her onto the bed and pushed her down. She stroked with both hands down Morticia's body, pinching the nipples and biting the breasts in quick little nips. Morticia tried to remain still but was forced to squirm under the sensations she was feeling.

"React fully to what I am doing, girl. I want to see everything; hide nothing from me."

Morticia squealed when Lucille's hands dipped between her legs, stroking and pinching in ways she had never felt before. Her hips bucked upward, and her legs opened wider so Lucille had full access to her. The hands scratched her upper thighs, quick cat-like scratches that inflamed the tender skin and brought more moistness out of her. Morticia neared the edge of climax, but knew she must not do so without permission. She heard herself begging for permission to climax and, horrified, heard Lucille chuckle as she denied permission. "Please!" she begged.

"Not yet, girl. You have not fully pleased me." Lucille lay back on the bed, her robe opening to reveal a lush body. Morticia, dizzy from the emotions and sensations, looked over at her mistress and brought her fragmented mind under control. She touched lightly Lucille's breast, stroking it and gently pulling on the nipple. Lucille smiled and urged her to proceed. Morticia used her mouth and tongue and hands, tasting and licking each part of Lucille's body as she stroked the velvety soft skin. The sounds Lucille made, when she felt the blood rushing to the areas Morticia was caressing, served as a goad, urging Morticia to go further and do more.

Morticia licked and nibbled her way from Lucille's breasts to her belly, stopping to worship at the navel before she opened Lucille's legs and ran her tongue along the labia. She flicked her tongue gently across the clitoris, then sucked it into her mouth. She inserted a finger into the vagina, stroking the wet skin as her mouth played. Listening to the sounds Lucille was making, Morticia knew she was pleasing her mistress and worked harder to bring her to climax. She pushed her thighs higher and found the right angle to run her tongue the length of the labia, ending with a flick to the clitoris at the end of the stroke. Morticia inserted two fingers in the vagina, twisting and searching for the G-spot she knew was in there. When Lucille bucked violently, she tapped the spot a few times and was rewarded with a gush of fluid and squeals of joy from Lucille.

"Come now!" Lucille screamed, and Morticia felt her body spasm with the climax just from those words. She writhed between Lucille's legs as wave after wave of sensation flooded over her. Morticia sat up, and when her climax was over, Lucille pointed to a pad on the floor.

"You may sleep here tonight, girl."

"Thank you, Ma'am," she murmured as she got off the bed and curled up on the pad. There was a soft blanket, and she wrapped it around her naked body. Morticia fell asleep quickly.

* * *

Morticia woke up the next day a little disoriented at finding herself at the foot of a bed, on a pad on the floor. She learned to treasure such moments; they were a gift from her mistress for work well done.

Her two-year contract was ultimately renewed, and at its end, she talked to Deva about a longer one. Deva approached Lucille, wondering if she would really want to deal with a slave whose eyesight was declining so rapidly.

"Is Morticia still a slave you wish to have in service?" she asked. "She's losing her vision, and it doesn't seem to be stabilizing."

"Her service to me doesn't require eyesight, just devotion and meticulous attention to detail. With me, I believe she's found her calling. If she's willing to enter into long-term service with me, I'll sign such a contract."

"Morticia will need a guide dog soon," Deva responded. "It'll require an absence of a month or two for training."

"I'm well aware of this, Deva. It'd be good for her to do this prior to returning to my home in service. I'll have time to make arrangements for the dog's needs in her absence."

Deva sighed in relief. It would have been difficult to find another owner for Morticia. Few saw the value of a slave with a disability, and the purchase price would have been ridiculously low.

Lucille knew well Morticia's value and the wide range of abilities she brought to the table. Her legal skills had won the group many cases involving the trafficking of bodies for illegal purposes. Lucille felt the irony of a Marketplace slave working to free those designated as illegal sex slaves. The difference was clear to both of them: Morticia chose to be in service to Lucille because of a deep need in her soul; those poor souls sold involuntarily into sexual slavery did not know that was their destiny and were duped into unwilling servitude without any rights. Their souls did not hunger to serve the masters who bought them; their souls shriveled from the mistreatment and anguish of the torture they lived every day.

Morticia received the new, long-term contract, almost not believing what she had just read and signed. In service to Lucille, Morticia used her intelligence to fight in court. The cases which Lucille's group decided were appropriate changed the lives of many. She used her body to serve Lucille at night. The few hours she had on weekends, Morticia used new technologies to offset her declining eyesight. Her father was right, of course. With service, she had found purpose and, with that purpose, a reason for being alive.

State Change
By Soulhuntre

Prelude

I idly swiped through the catalogues for the auction with the voice of a concerned business associate droning in my ear. Some of them were pretty enough, but if I saw one more dossier that seemed to think silver polishing was a critical skill, I was going to buy and smash something Victorian on general principal. I was going to have to get over that.

The noise finally stopped. My turn.

"Kyle, I understand you have probably done everything you can. So why don't you just tell me who on the board is being the most difficult and then leave everything to me."

I kicked in the transcription process as he responded, the name of the offending member, Robertson, and the description of his attending advisor flowing into my note for the day. After hanging up, I reviewed them quickly then with a gesture sent both over to Natalie's daily task list for further research.

Reminded of Natalie, my eyes flicked to the video output monitoring the workout room. She was on the rock wall and would be done in ten minutes or so. Work complete, I allowed myself to admire her form as she climbed. She was five foot four with long dark hair and large eyes, light-skinned but with mixed features that allowed her to appear Midwestern or Asian as my mood dictated. The sports bra and shorts showed her toned form to advantage, the black cloth bringing out the colors in her growing tattoo work strongly. She knew I was liable to be watching her at any time, and I felt sure that the perfect handprint in climbing chalk on her right buttock was purely for my benefit. Wiseass.

* * *

Background

I grew up around Marketplace servants. My family had them as part of the house staff, and of course my father had his toys. As I got older, I accompanied my father to auctions, visits to training houses, and so on. I was drawn to it all and not just for the obvious reasons a young man might. Within their ranks was often found a dedication and sense of discipline I rarely saw outside of the martial arts or military service.

Unfortunately, I also found much of the Marketplace to be slow to adapt and somewhat stifled by too much unnecessary tradition. It was all well and good to ensure quality and continuity, but evolution was critical.

Compounding the issue, I had no love or longing for the bygone days of the Victorian or Edwardian Eras so many of the clients and trainers use as archetypes in the US and European market. Asia was doing something more to my liking, but even then, they were in many ways not just tied to the past but mired in it.

What I wanted was something different and thoroughly modern. I grew up on Bond villains and graphic novels. As a result, my self-image ran more to Tony Stark than Sir Stephan, if you take my meaning. I was not quiet about my views, and these days my reception in those circles could best be described as *mixed*.

When the time came for me to go out and make my own way in the world, I was given a small sum to use as I wished. Traditionally, in my family this money was used to start a company by purchasing supplies, machinery, or land.

After a year of planning, I used it to buy Natalie.

Then, I used Natalie to get everything else.

After purchasing her right out of her initial training, I spent the intervening time shaping her into the anime wet dream *executive assistant* (yes, I have read the series) she was now.

The result? My girl could fight her way into a boardroom, negotiate a multimillion-dollar contract, then fuck her way through anyone who still needed convincing, before rappelling down to the sidewalk just when her ride from Uber pulled up.

211

It was simply amazing what you could accomplish with a good business plan, negotiation skills, and a devastatingly hot assistant who somehow kept enthralling the right people. More than one deal had come back from the dead with a conversation that contained some variation of: *"...of course, I understand. I'll inform Natalie she doesn't need to fly the contracts out... "*

She was also fun to play Halo with and knew exactly how much sass I found attractive while retaining the ability to lock into perfect formalism at a gesture.

By now my company was secure and very, very profitable. With the acquisition Kyle was so worried about complete—Natalie could handle Robertson easily—I would be free to turn the bulk of my attention to other areas. Tonight was an important step in that direction.

Natalie was a prototype.

This auction represented my first purely Marketplace event in several years and would double as Natalie's *coming out*. While I had friends and associates within the hierarchy, it was well known I was considering going my own way outside of it. Going rogue was always an option, but I had decided if I could operate within the demands of the Marketplace without compromising myself, I would do so. Events at the recent Academy indicated there might be more room for change than before.

The smart band on my wrist vibrated, snapping me out of my thoughts, the small display reminding me it was time to begin getting ready. Natalie slipped into the room as well, having finished while I was musing.

"Sir, it is 7:00. Do you have any specific preferences for this evening?"

With the moment upon me, my various options crystallized, and I realized that *yes*, I did have some very specific preferences. "Indeed, I do. We will take the CBRs tonight, so attire accordingly, and pack the dress steel... It would not do to be too casual."

"Hai." Her smile matched my own as she replied. The extra twitch of her hips as she turned to go indicated her enthusiasm for the evening. Had I mentioned I liked this girl?

* * *

En Route

I could tell you my favorite part of tearing through the city on an overpowered racing bike was the wind in my hair, but the truth was the opposite. I enjoyed the fact I did not feel the wind at all. My helmet had all the information I needed reflected onto the glass, and thanks to the wireless connection, I was able to hear anything from a whispered phone conversation up to full on road trip tunes. As I followed the bent over form of my servant around a turn, I had to admit the view wasn't bad either.

I used the time to once again review my preparations and decided to add a few finishing touches. I stroked the attention button on the grip with my thumb, and a small chime let me know Cortana was listening as I spoke. "Notify me if Felix is close, and keep an eye on Natalie until further notice."

The reply came after the briefest pause as my phone and systems behind it made the changes instructed. It carried the slightly mechanical cadence that even the best synthesized voices still did. "Of course, Sensei."

Don't judge me, there was nothing wrong with your phone being respectful. I spent more time talking to it than I did people.

* * *

Arrival

We turned the last corner, and even though I had been expecting it, there really was something inspiring about it all. The organizers had rented a museum for the evening, and an honest-to-god red carpet rolled down to the curb where a limousine was waiting. The signage boasted some society charity event, but the few paparazzi who might have shown up no doubt left in confusion when they recognized none of the faces. I pulled ahead and was first into the curbside as we arrived, my visor rising on its own as I killed the motor.

Swinging off the bike, I flicked the fob at the slightly disconcerted valet. They would have someone available who could handle parking them... Attention to those sorts of details was a hallmark of these events. I left my now disabled helmet on the seat just in time to sense Natalie slide up beside me.

213

We joined the other arrivals making their way up the steps and into the atrium as I made small talk with some of the other Owners. One or two gave an appreciative glance to my companion, and I theirs. Think of it as our version of sniffing each other's butts. You could tell much about a person by what they chose to own, and how they chose to make use of it.

In the atrium-proper, more servants were waiting. Nothing as crude as a coat check tonight—you simply slipped what you wanted to be free of into helpful, waiting hands and could be assured it would be right there when you were ready to leave. I let them take off the Kevlar and leather of my riding jacket, leaving me in my black shirt, armored pants, and boots. The gloves went inside the helmet, and they got that, too.

Natalie did not have a jacket to check. Her riding gear was a single discreetly armored leather affair from neck to boot tops. It had a very inviting zipper that made most of the journey as well, with the tab just low enough to set off her modest cleavage and showcase the titanium collar around her throat. She handed over the gloves and helmet and then took a moment to retrieve the architect's case slung over her back and slid out our steel. She handed the case to the attendants as well. That done, she slipped the straps of the swords over her shoulders again and took a moment to refashion her hair in a bun (fastened with lacquered bamboo, of course) before assuming the relaxed posture I preferred when she was waiting for me.

You do remember the whole anime/samurai/assassin thing I mentioned, right? Of course there must be swords! She carried two, the longer one being mine. Though at need, we could both be quite effective with the blades, they were purely affectation on a night like this. Then again, wasn't all this ceremony essentially an affectation? Taking a breath and making a small hand gesture for her to follow at heel, I led the way to the doors granting access into the main auction area.

* * *

Encounter

The auction space itself was set up in the traditional manner. A row of blocks held various clients awaiting sale with their neatly printed dossiers nearby. None had caught my eye in the catalog, and tonight was not the time to be speculating on a new acquisition in any case. Though there was something about seeing them all there that couldn't help but stir the blood for new encounters. Still, with Comic-Con only a week away, there would be no trouble finding someone signaling the appropriate fetishes via their costume choice, and I could indulge in a little slumming then.

I glanced at my wristband when it vibrated to see Natalie's heart rate had jumped, presumably upon seeing the blocks or their contents. I turned to her with knowing look. "Down, girl."

She actually blushed. Score one for me.

Another vibration could only mean Felix was near. And there he was, heading my way. I put out my hand in greeting, and he clasped it warmly.

"Well, I made it."

"Indeed, you did," he replied. "The question is, how long are you staying?"

There was more to his tone than the obvious query, and we both understood this was why I had come. Showing Natalie off had its charms, but I was doing that admirably via other means. The real reason I was here was to feel these people again. To decide if I wanted to become part of it, rather than remain outside. Felix knew I would not make a final decision on our plans until I was sure.

I took a moment and cast my eyes around the room. Did I want to embed myself in all this long term? The owners told me little, though I was friendly enough with some of them. The clients told me more. I recognized how easily I slid back into the comfort that came from having a significant number of highly skilled and attentive servants around. Most informative were the trainers and house heads. These were the people I would most need to find a home with. Not all of them liked what I intended to do... and I was never one to fade into the background. Still, I could admit there was much here to respect and so much to learn.

To establish myself as an accepted trainer I needed formal entrance to the Marketplace hierarchy and structure beyond just being an owner. Apprenticeship in the house my family had purchased from most of my life was the obvious choice. As heir to that house, my friend Felix was just about to begin the last year or so of his preparation to take over for his father. Now was the perfect time for

215

me to apprentice alongside him, as well as help Felix bring in some new ideas. I would obviously need to spend time at other houses to bolster both my knowledge and network, but that could be easily arranged.

Yes, it felt good and right to be here again.

"I'll be staying as long as I need to." The resulting fist bump drew a few disapproving stares, and I could see Natalie's eyes water a bit as she fought not to roll them.

* * *

Epilogue

Speaking of eye rolling, a young trainer apprentice approached us as if on cue. Jeremy and I had tangled a few times before. He had a penchant for the *manor house* stuff I did not find interesting, all riding leather and banisters. Frankly, I don't think he was so much attracted to it all as much as he simply lacked imagination. The pair of respectably good-looking blonds following behind were attentive, well trained, and nicely dressed. I wondered who he had borrowed them from.

"I see you couldn't stay away from us!" He emphasized the *us* with the sort of friendly voice you only really got from people who wished you had died in a traffic accident on your way to a society event. He reached out to run his hand along the handle of the swords but pulled it back when Natalie's posture shifted. Perhaps he wasn't completely stupid.

To cover for the motion, he turned it into a hand wave indicating both the swords and Natalie, "Very pretty, but can she do anything with them?"

I looked him in the eye, pretending not to see the barely restrained laughter in Natalie's eyes or the pleading in Felix's to play nice. I waited just long enough for my friend to have raised his drink to his lips before I replied.

"Well, she *can* polish them, and isn't that what's really important?"

As Felix started coughing, I decided I was going to enjoy this.

Transcendence
By Jamie Thorsen

The bondage frame allowed her no movement, and an inflatable gag and a well-padded leather hood muffled the only sounds she could make. Any effort at coherent thought was overwhelmed by the effort needed to breathe through the hood's nose holes, the fire-kissed pain of clothespins lining each thigh, the barely lubricated dick in her ass, and the vibrator strapped to her clitoris, set just below the threshold she needed for orgasm.

She felt pressure around her mouth, a panel was unsnapped and the gag removed. She gasped for air before hands grasped the side of her head, and her owner slammed his cock into her mouth. After eight years, she could identify it even like this. She tried to time her gasps for air, but he'd timed his rhythm to the person behind her. Each breath was a fight between the need for oxygen and the need to scream.

This is the last time. Then her autonomous mind took back over, fighting to breathe, giving up on processing or thinking or anything other than existing in this perfect onslaught.

* * *

Dark Eyes had never had an orgasm. She didn't really miss it. The night after the gang rape that served as her initiation into the VGC, the Versai Gangsta Crips, Z-Cash claimed her as one of his women. It was a way out of her mom's tiny house in the lower ninth ward, a place to belong, to be useful. All she wanted was to be useful.

"Run some shit over to Nickeldown fo' me, will ya, babygirl?" her man asked, dropping a baggie of white powder on the bedside table. He jammed a pistol in the waistband of his jeans and casually, groped her before throwing a shirt on. "Popo be lookin for me down there."

"Gonna gimme bus fare?" Dark Eyes replied. Z-Cash dropped a pair of twenties on the mattress. He walked out the door without a word, leaving Dark Eyes alone in the rundown apartment.

She stumbled to the bathroom to clean herself off as soon as the door closed behind him then flipped on the TV and took an hour to watch her stories. She knew better than to think she could escape this existence, but soap operas gave her a window to a world that wasn't her own.

A couple hours later, she got off the bus in Treme, ignoring the men who called after her, but she put a little extra shimmy in her walk. They knew better than to do anything but catcall; everyone in this hood knew she belonged to Z-Cash. She walked down a narrow alley, through an unmarked door, then up a flight of stairs.

"Wazup, cuz?" Nickeldown greeted her as he opened the door. He ran his fingers across her ass as she passed. Z-Cash might give her to him for a night for his loyalty, but touching one of his women without permission might start a turf war. More likely, Z would just play it off and ditch her to avoid the fight without losing face; Nickeldown made him money. She kept her mouth shut and took it.

Three men sat in the living room, passing around a blunt; she took a hit, and Nickeldown cut her a line from the baggie she handed over. She leaned back on the couch, letting the rush of the coke carry her away.

The world shattered in splintered pieces of door and screaming men in dark blue uniforms. Nickeldown pulled a gun; his chest erupted like the door, and his body fell onto Dark Eyes. She just lay there, covered in screams and blood, as uniformed men swarmed the room, as she was pressed facedown into the floor and cuffed, as one cop pulled her back up onto her knees and a second one backhanded her so hard droplets of her blood mixed with the blood of the man who died on top of her.

She never snitched, no matter what the assistant DA promised her. The VGC had given her somewhere to belong, and Dark Eyes was loyal even if she wasn't sure how to spell the word. Her loyalty amounted to nothing. Her only witness at the sentencing was a drunken public defender who was barely awake as the judge condemned her to three years at the Louisiana Correctional Institute for Women. Z-Cash never even bothered to see her.

* * *

Bonds loosened, and Marie was dragged to her feet, pulling her mind from the dust-strewn tracks of memory. Her arms were pulled up, and cuffs wrapped around her ankles and wrists. Deft fingers worked at the back of her head, unlacing the hood that kept her cocooned. As the leather pulled free, she was pushed forward into the cross, her chest resting against the leather-padded split of the X. She blinked twice; the face behind the cross came into focus. *Ken?* She thought, hazily recognizing her. When Quentin chose to have her trained to assist him as a spotter, she'd spent a month with Ken Mandarin. That was six years ago.

She felt Ken's small fingers trace her cheekbone as she felt the first line of flame erupt across her left shoulder. *I just wanted to belong*, she thought, and then the second strike of the whip kissed her right shoulder. The slight spark of awareness she'd regained since the hood came off was snuffed out as the whip wielder settled into a rhythm.

* * *

Dark Eyes began to cry, tears carving frozen paths across ebony cheekbones. Miss Eloise Devereaux, socialite, philanthropist, heiress of one of New Orleans's oldest families, moved closer to her, putting her arm around the crying prisoner. She said nothing until Dark Eye's wracked sobs calmed down, stroking her shoulder. There was no touching allowed in the visitation room of the prison, but no guard dared tell Miss Devereaux to move away.

"I got 'nother two years," Dark Eyes said. "How I get let go so early?"

"Marie, you were in the wrong place at the wrong time," Devereaux told her. "You deserve to build a life, and you can't do that here. In the years I've run the prisoner volunteer program at the Humane Society, I've never seen anyone work as hard as you. You'll be released on parole, under my supervision."

"But... thank you, Miz Devereaux, thank you," Marie said.

Miss Devereaux took a delicate, lace-trimmed handkerchief from her pocket and dabbed the tears away from Marie's face.

"It won't be easy, Marie. You're going to stay with me, and you're going to work at the animal shelter and study for your GED. You're not going back to the lower ninth, to that gang or the drugs," Devereaux said. "Do you understand?"

"Yes, Miz Devereaux. That be all I want," Marie replied.

"Dark Eyes, time's up!" a guard called.

"Another thing, Marie. This is a clean break from the past. You'll be released tomorrow, and from that moment forward you'll never use that name again. That time is past now."

"Yes, ma'am," Marie said. As the guard walked over to escort Marie back to her cell block, the click of Miss Devereaux's heels on the floor, walking away, sounded like freedom.

* * *

Her back was fire and blood, a tenuous connection between body and mind. She processed the pain without being aware of it, still floating from the sensory overload. Every time she opened her eyes, Ken was still there, and she relaxed, knowing she was safe. The whip felt like home, each crack a reminder of her past, of all she'd overcome.

The rhythm slowed then ceased. The supple whip snaked around her neck, cutting off her oxygen. Quentin wrapped the whip in one hand, tightening the makeshift noose, and Ken reached down, deft fingers stroking Marie's clit as she was pulled taut, struggling for oxygen. Marie gasped, the desperate need to breathe making her forget her bonds, her nerves, everything, before Ken's expert touch pushed her over the edge, the explosion of stimulation and pent-up need overwhelming her instinctual desperation just to breathe. She went limp, her bonds keeping her in place, and the world faded to nothing.

* * *

"It is a truth universally acknowledged, that a single man in possession of a good fortune must be in want of a wife," Marie recited. "However little known the feelings or views of such a man may be on his first entering a neighborhood, this truth is so well fixed in the minds of the surrounding families, that he is considered as the rightful property of some one or other of their daughters."

"Very good, Marie!" Miss Devereaux said, applauding. "Your enunciation was flawless that time."

"Thanks, Miz Devereaux," Marie said, her smile a sudden sunrise in the dim-lit veranda.

220

"Don't slip, even when you're excited. Remember what I said about code-switching?"

"Yes, ma'am," Marie replied.

"Good. Now I want you to get some sleep."

"I wanted to study for the GED test," Marie said. She'd gotten past her initial surprise at enjoying the nightly study sessions and now spent almost all her free time reading.

"So studious!" Miss Devereaux exclaimed, and Marie's smile returned. "You've done all you can. A good night's sleep before the test is what you need. Off to bed with you, and don't even think about that *reading by flashlight under the covers* trick tonight!"

The next day, she walked out of the testing center like a kitten after her first kill. Miss Devereaux's chauffeur was waiting at the curb, the Cadillac idling. She embraced him vigorously. "Alex, it was so easy!"

"Very good, Miss Marie!" the gray-haired man replied. Marie had given up convincing Miss Devereaux's staff to just call her by her name. "We all knew you could do it." He ushered her into the car and took a left onto Rampart, smoothly entering the flow of traffic.

"Where we goin'?" she asked. "I mean, where are we going?"

"Miss Devereaux wished to meet you for a late lunch at the club," Alex said. "She was very confident you'd have something to celebrate."

"The club?" Marie asked.

"The Southern Yacht Club, Miss Marie. The Devereaux family has been members for over a century. They serve a very fine luncheon."

Marie bit her lip. She'd heard of it, of course, the most exclusive club in New Orleans. "So that's why Miss Devereaux insisted on me dressing up nice. She told me it was to give me confidence during the test."

Alex met Marie's eyes in the rearview mirror, the dull-silver ring around his neck reflecting sunlight into her eyes. "It's my experience, Miss Marie, that Miss Devereaux always means what she says. She just may not always say everything she's thinking."

Marie nodded. "May I ask a personal question?" she asked a minute later.

"You may," Alex replied.

"I've noticed you wear that ring on yo' neck," Marie said. Alex cleared his throat. "I mean, your neck, and Marissa and Peter each wear one too. What is it?"

221

Alex paused a second, just enough time for Marie to worry she'd offended him. "I can't speak for Marissa or Peter, but Miss Devereaux gave me this years ago. It reminds me of where I belong, that I have a place in her household."

Marie smiled. "That's... sweet. Miss Devereaux is in the habit of taking in strays?" she said lightly.

"Sometimes," Alex said, smiling, and Marie gazed out the window, unsure how to frame the questions crystallizing in her mind.

The yacht club came into view; she'd seen it before, but it had always been as distant as her soap operas. The car coasted to a halt, and Alex opened the door with a flourish. She froze as the tableau became real; the impeccably dressed men at the doors seemingly guardians of a threshold she couldn't bear to cross.

"Miss Marie?" Alex asked. He stretched a hand toward her. Stunned, Marie took it and allowed him to assist her out of the car. "Miss Marie, you walk in there with your head held high and act like you own the place. Remember what Miss Devereaux says."

"Fake it 'til you make it," Marie replied. She smiled, remembering how out of place the pithy saying seemed coming from Miss Devereaux. She took a deep breath, straightened her dress, and walked in through the door, head held high.

* * *

She was blindfolded. Rough hands threw her onto a bed, and someone fastened her ankle cuffs to points overhead, forcing her legs apart. Her wrists were pulled back, cuffs locked, stretching her arms out over her head. She felt the weight of someone kneeling over her face and knew what was expected of her.

She delicately licked her way around the labia of the woman kneeling over her, but whoever this was, they weren't in the mood for anything so slow and sensual. A hand reached down to grab her hair and force her tongue deeper. Marie responded to the signal, her tongue flicking roughly into the fold around the clit, discovering a hood piercing and attacking it. She was rewarded by tiny thrusts forward and moans that sounded vaguely familiar, if she could just place them. Then she had no more time to consider it, as her mind slipped into a familiar groove, focused simply on being useful.

* * *

"Miz Devereaux, I so sorry, I just... " Marie said. "I din know why you help me, then saw you on TV talkin' about lesbian rights and thought maybe you wanted... please don't kick me out, I just wanted to be what you wanted... "

Miss Devereaux went down to one knee, eye level with the terrified girl in her bed. "Marie, don't backslide. Remember what I've taught you."

"But... but you were so mad when you came in... " Marie replied. She took a deep breath. "Miss Devereaux, I apologize for my pre... presumption."

"Apology accepted, Marie. I understand," Miss Devereaux said. She took Marie's hand in hers. "And I do find you to be a very attractive woman. You're beautiful. I was simply shocked and upset at the situation." Miss Devereaux paused, wiping tears away from Marie's cheeks. "I'm not helping you as a means to have sexual relations with you, Marie. I'm helping you because you remind me of myself, 20 years ago."

"I... I do?" Marie asked. She looked down at the crude tattoos lining her arm, each one a reminder of her past. The crude alligator she'd had done in the bathroom of her school in the lower ninth. The stenciled VGC in gothic script, her gang sign. Her name, tattooed after lights out in prison. She watched Miss Devereaux's delicate alabaster fingertips stroke the ink-pocked skin of her arm. How could she have anything in common with this woman, part of a world she never thought was real until now?

"Marie, I was born to wealth, but, like you, I spent my whole youth looking for somewhere to belong. I was trying to run away from what I grew up from, just like you. You have a steeper hill to climb than I did, but that's not your fault. I don't apologize for my privilege, but I can use it to help others, like I am with you."

Marie struggled to accept the gulf between her and the older woman could be so narrow despite its depth. She concentrated on speaking the way she had been taught. "Do you really think I can be someone like you, someday?" she asked.

"No, I don't," Miss Devereaux replied. Marie looked down, and Miss Devereaux grabbed her chin, forcing eye contact. "I think you can be someone you'll be proud of, whether that's like me or not. That's your decision, who you become."

Miss Devereaux leaned in. Marie's eyes widened as she recognized the older woman's intentions and then closed as she relaxed into the kiss. It took seconds that seemed like hours for Miss Devereaux to pull back and another minute for Marie to even realize it was over.

"Do not doubt your desirability, Marie. You're desirable for what you do, for who you are, for your capacity to serve and work with joy. You have so much of yourself to give, once you find the right venue to appreciate and value what you have to offer."

"Yes, Miss Devereaux," Marie said, still stunned.

"I'm going to bring you a robe, and then it's time for you to retire to your own bed. I believe you have a shift at the Humane Society in the morning, and after that I'd like to have a talk about your future."

Marie lay awake most of the night, thinking of every word Miss Devereaux had spoken, reliving the touch of her lips. When she finally dozed off, she awoke to her hand feverishly moving between her legs until she came explosively, calling Miss Devereaux's name.

* * *

Marie found what worked and stuck to it, licking the other woman with intensity, and within minutes, she came, both hands grasping the back of Marie's head and pulling her in. She never stopped the frantic movement of her tongue, determined to wring the last bit of pleasure out of her. The woman's screaming, shaking orgasm only made her more demanding, practically grinding her pelvis into Marie's face.

The woman came three more times before rising, Marie moaning in disappointment at her withdrawal. "I've been waiting over a decade for that," a soft, quiet voice whispered into her ear.

"Miss Devereaux?" she asked, breaking protocol and a throaty chuckle came from the woman in response, but before Marie could even begin to process her thoughts, another woman took Miss Devereaux's place.

"Sorry to interrupt, ma chéri, but I remember that enthusiasm well," Ken said, reaching behind her to flick Marie's nipples. "Focus, slave!" Obediently, Marie began to lick.

* * *

Marie slammed the door as she walked out of the shotgun house she'd been raised in. One week until she left for Virginia, to train for the Marketplace. She'd miss New Orleans, and Miss Devereaux, but she now knew what she wouldn't miss. She hadn't seen her mom since two years before she went to prison, but she thought they could at least have a nice goodbye before she left to *work overseas*, as Miss Devereaux had suggested for a cover story. Instead, she just got mockery for *talking white* and *putting on airs*.

She refused to cry, not here in her old 'hood. She took a deep breath to calm herself, the way Miss Devereaux taught her, and then began the walk to the bus stop. In a rare bout of rebellion, she'd refused to let Alex drive her. Miss Devereaux meant well, but she needed to do this on her own.

She had barely started her walk before Z-Cash stepped out of an alleyway, flanked by Dub and Spider, two of his boys. "Too good for us street folk, huh, bitch?" he said, as the others spread to block her way. Marie tried to walk between them without replying, but Dub shoved her into the wall.

"I ain't got nothin' to say to you, Zeke," Marie said. Z-Cash backhanded her, hard, and she stumbled at the impact. She looked up at him, this man who had been a god to her once, and all she felt now was anger and fear.

"I done six months lockup fo' possession," Z-Cash growled. "Fuckin' man couldn't get me on nothin' else, but they sure tried. You snitch, bitchgirl? Dat why you out early? You think you come back to these streets, no one know any better? Heard you been out a bit, maybe think we'd forget?"

"You know damn well I didn't snitch," Marie replied. "Been workin' on my GED, tryna find a job." Her eyes darted back and forth, but no one on this block was going to step in. A couple girls walked the corner across the street, glancing this way and laughing; they were probably working for Z-Cash anyway.

"GED? Gettin all fancy for a lil bitchgirl, aintcha? You had it nice, dint have you on no corner, I took care of you, and you snitched. See what happens when you go soft on a bitch, Dub?"

"I know that's right," Dub replied. Spider just laughed.

"Should dump yo body somewhere as a warnin'," Z-cash said, "but I'm feelin', what's a nice fancy word for Miss GED here, nostalgic." Dub and Spider laughed again. "We take you back to my place, do a couple lines like the old days, discuss how yo gonna pay back whatchoo owe."

Marie's eyes flicked back to the two girls on the corner. She'd seen Z-Cash do his thing; he wanted her hooked on drugs again, wanted her walking the street, making him money. She was afraid of the strength she'd gained. He didn't know he wouldn't be able to break her again, but he'd kill her rather than let her go free.

Z-Cash turned to laugh at something Dub said. She saw her opening, and she bolted. It was the last thing Z-Cash would have ever expected out of the once-pliant girl, but he didn't know who she was. He only knew who she once had been.

She heard yelling, but she didn't look back. She was only two blocks from Claiborne, a busy street with too many witnesses for her to disappear quietly. She rounded the corner onto Charbonnet, and all she could think of was a world away from these squalid streets, a world within her grasp.

A police cruiser was creeping up Charbonnet; she ran into the street, waving it down. Her pursuers rounded the corner behind her, saw the cruiser braking to a stop, and bolted in three different directions. By the time the two police officers got out of the car, they were gone.

She was only in the back of a squad car for a few minutes before dropping Miss Devereaux's name had an effect; within minutes after that, she was at the precinct, awaiting Miss Devereaux and the family attorney. She refused to press charges. She wouldn't let anything interfere with her departure.

* * *

This is the last time, she thought, but she didn't know why. She knew all these people were gathered here for her, but she couldn't remember the occasion. She just wanted to be a good slave, to show Quentin's guests a good time. She knew nothing else at this point. Her drive to be good for her owner was the only thing keeping her going.

She was on her knees, arms behind her in a strappado position, straddling someone while someone else caned her tits. She didn't even know if it was a cock or a strap-on inside her; she was too exhausted to tell the difference. It didn't matter anymore. She just kept going.

Finally, it all stopped. She collapsed as her arms were released and sighed as hands massaged the points where leather bonds had constricted her skin. She tried to kneel like she was supposed to when released from bondage, but she just didn't have the strength anymore.

Instead, she felt herself picked up and carried across the room then laid down on a soft surface. Metal clanged against metal, and the click of a padlock told her she was in the cage. Gentle hands reached through the bars and slid the latex hood from her head. The lights cut out, and she heard the door close, leaving her alone in the dungeon. She fell asleep almost instantly.

* * *

Layton Turner adjusted Marie's position, applying featherlight pressure to shift her just so. "You're going to be wonderful, Marie," Layton said. "You're ready for this. And I'll be here when you need me, for as long as you're in the Marketplace."

"Thank you, Trainer," Marie replied. She smiled nervously, inwardly debating whether it was appropriate before speaking again. "May I?" she asked, and Layton placed his foot on the pedestal. Carefully, Marie bent and lightly kissed the toe of his dress shoe. Layton muttered something about uppity slaves ruining his hard work as he fixed her position again, and Marie giggled. She knew she should feel something about being sold given her skin color, especially with the *uppity* comment, but she'd worked through her few misgivings. She would be useful. She would belong. She'd finally found a place where nothing mattered but her willingness to learn and work and serve.

As Layton buckled the ball gag in her mouth, a signal to prospective owners that her voice training was incomplete, she focused on holding her position, on making him proud. Owners walked into the room to inspect the merchandise on offer, and her eyes shone, confident her crude tattoos would only serve as evidence of how far she'd come, her very presence here meant she belonged.

227

She wasn't just another gangsta chick from the L9. She carried that girl within her, but she belonged here, and she knew that no matter who purchased her, she would serve them with pride.

It was the choice that mattered. She chose to be here. She chose to serve.

* * *

She awoke when the lights came on, sore and stretched and gloriously satiated. Her mind flickered through last night, scattered mental snapshots of a night as the focal point of the most intense BDSM orgy she'd ever experienced, her own personal Playhouse. Quentin knew her way too well. He would never admit it, but it had all been for her. This morning was the end of her slavehood.

Quentin opened the cage door and then sat down, beckoning her. She crawled out of the cage and knelt before him. "You have completed your contract and fulfilled your obligations honorably," Quentin said. "You have served well." He withdrew a key from his pocket, and she swept her hair up to give him access to her collar. A single tear emerged from the corner of her eye, lingering for a second before tracing its way down her cheek. Quentin paused for a moment.

"May I, Master?" she asked, and he nodded gravely. She bent down gracefully, every moment of her years as a slave visible in the smooth movement that brought her forehead to the floor, precisely between his feet. She thought of the first time she had spontaneously offered this tribute, before her first auction, and how sloppy she must have seemed then compared to now, although every bit as earnest. She held the pose for a long measure, trying to contain the tears.

She was ready. She knew it was time to move on to the next chapter in her service. She also knew, even though she would remain part of the Marketplace, a part of her would always long for the structure and certainty of being owned and cared for and, in a way never quite spoken of yet woven into the fabric of her time as a slave, loved.

She lifted her forehead from the floor and strove to put all her thoughts, her dreams, her love into the gentle kiss she placed on each of his shoes. She returned her forehead to its original position on the floor, then arched back up to her original kneeling position, and swept her hair aside. "Thank you, Master. I'm ready now," she whispered.

Quentin inserted his key into the lock on the titanium ring encircling her neck and gently lifted it away. The collar carried far more weight than the few ounces it removed from her shoulders; it had always kept her leveled and grounded. The wave of uncertainty that accompanied the removal of the collar was physical and palpable, but she took Quentin's outstretched hand and stood.

Quentin wrapped her in a hug, holding her as the removal of her obligation to maintain emotional control unleashed a torrent of tears and sorrow. He held her, patiently, until she was ready for him to let go.

* * *

Marie had never been happier than she had over the three months since Quentin purchased her in her third auction as a Marketplace slave. Quentin kept her busy, as both his executive assistant and his household help. He was also much more into sadistic and kinky sex than her first two owners. She learned it had been two years since Quentin had last owned a female slave, and while he was enthusiastically bisexual, he seemed to be making up for lost time with her.

She practically skipped down the long driveway to the street that morning. She'd been up late while Quentin investigated the possibilities of electrical stimulus to her labia, but she'd been allowed a rare orgasm and the privilege of sleeping at the foot of his bed. She grabbed the newspaper from the ground at the base of the driveway; Quentin would expect it when he awoke, along with his breakfast.

The headline caught her eye. "New Orleans Begins Counting Its Dead" it read, in large block letters. The picture showed houses underwater, rooftops barely visible. She easily recognized the street she grew up on, even underwater.

She sat in the driveway to read the first page and read the whole front section before making her way up the hill. When Quentin came downstairs, breakfast was unmade and the newspaper was spread out across the dining room table. The cordless phone and Quentin's laptop were both on the table, Marie had sent a frantic email to Miss Devereaux after her calls wouldn't go through and put up a frantic post on MySpace about her friends and family. She was researching Greyhound prices, impulsively considering going home to look for them without considering her collar. Quentin's arrival jolted her back to reality.

"What is this?" he asked in a low voice. Marie hadn't taken long to learn the signs of Quentin's anger, and she fell to her knees.

"I'm sorry, Sir, I should have asked first, I don't know what to do... " Marie wailed.

Quentin crossed the room, ignoring the babbling slave on the floor. He glanced over the tableau, looked thoughtfully down at Marie, and waited patiently for her to get control of herself. "You're from New Orleans, aren't you?" he asked, a minute later.

Marie took a deep breath. "Yes, Sir, I am. That's the street I grew up on, right there... " she stuttered between sobs, pointing at a picture of wreckage and water in the paper, but Quentin held up a hand and she cut herself off.

"Have you been able to reach your loved ones?" he asked, more gently.

"No, Sir. I mean, I'm not close with my family, but... "

Quentin snapped his fingers in front of Marie's face. "Marie, I will grant you considerable latitude given the situation, but you will regain your composure so I may assist you as best I am able, or I will be forced to correct your behavior. Falling apart will do no one any good."

Marie began to breathe deeply, took stock of her situation, and straightened her position. It took two minutes before was calm enough to speak as he demanded.

"Yes, Sir. I would like to apologize formally for my behavior this morning. Regardless of my personal concerns, I must comport myself properly as your slave and provide you the service you expect."

"Better. Here's what I want you to do, in this order. First, I want you to make a list of people you are concerned about so that I may make some inquiries. I want you to provide me with names, addresses, phone numbers, and any other pertinent info you may think of. Second, I want you to wake Jack up so he may serve breakfast and attend to your duties. Third, I want you to take a long, hot shower and compose yourself. Afterwards, you will report to my study."

"You're not going to the office today, Sir?" Marie asked.

"I have more important matters to attend to," Quentin replied. "Do as I said."

An hour later, Marie walked into Quentin's study and knelt just inside the doorway. "Admiral, I understand you guys are swamped, but one of my employees is beside herself. If you could just check the records when you get a second and give me a call back, I'd appreciate it." Quentin paused for a minute, listening to the other person. "Admiral Hansen, need I remind you that you owe me for smoothing out the Lockheed contract... Yes, as a matter of fact, I am calling in that favor. I'm also writing a check for a quarter mill as we speak for relief efforts, and I'll be sending work crews to assist with recovery efforts so I don't feel bad about asking for a few minutes of your time... Very well, I'll be waiting for your call. Thanks." Quentin slammed the phone down. He snapped his fingers and pointed at the ground, and Marie rose, crossed the room, and knelt at his feet.

"Marie, good news and bad news. Miss Devereaux has checked in with the Marketplace offices in New York; she flew out the day before the storm and is in St Louis right now. Her household staff is with her. Miss Albert, your former parole officer, is also confirmed alive."

"I'm working on finding your mother and sisters right now, but there's no news. It's utter chaos. They've still got thousands in the Superdome, plus tens of thousands evacuated to other cities. They're not on the confirmed dead list. There's no way of telling when or if they will turn up, but they're probably okay."

"Thank you, Sir," Marie said.

"I'm working from home today. Yardley Contracting will be sending a large force down to donate our services to the relief effort. I need you to call the office and get the GM working on pulling together crews, equipment, and supplies. I want them rolling in the morning, and given the situation, they need to bring everything they need to live as well as their equipment. You're in charge of logistics, I want RVs to sleep everyone we send, whether we have to rent them or buy them. I want two weeks' worth of food and water per person. Get with the GM over there on a preliminary crew roster and then start on the supplies and RVs. Here's my AmEx card."

"Yes, Sir," Marie began to rise, her pulse slowing. Assigning her to work on coordinating the relief effort calmed her, although she still couldn't get her mom and sisters out of her mind.

Quentin looked at her as she began to back out of the room. "Stop," he said and rose from his chair. He stepped toward her, and she looked like a deer in headlights, concerned she had missed something. He stepped up and wrapped her in a hug. "It's okay, girl, cry one last time if you need to. Then I need you to focus on your instructions."

Her tears flowed like rain as she buried her face in her owner's chest, soaking the front of his dress shirt, but he held her until she couldn't cry anymore. He dried her tears before sending her on his way and then picked up the phone to call the next number on his list.

* * *

Marie took a long, hot shower before coming downstairs to find Jack in the kitchen. "Mr. Yardley's compliments, ma'am, I'll be serving breakfast in the dining room in just a few minutes," Jack said. "He added that I am under no circumstances to let you eat in here with Gary and me."

Marie laughed. "Jack, in regards to Mr. Yardley's standing instructions to call guests *sir* or *ma'am* unless they express a preference otherwise?"

"Yes, Ma'am," Jack replied.

"You and Gary are to call me Marie," she said. "I'll be pleased to take my breakfast in the dining room. Thank you, Jack."

Fake it 'til you make it, she thought, remembering Miss Devereaux's words. She walked down the hall into the formal dining room; Quentin, Ken Mandarin, Eloise Devereaux, and Layton Turner rose from their seats as she entered. "Welcome, Marie. I hope you enjoyed Quentin's surprise," Layton said, walking around the table to embrace her. "We all needed to meet anyway, and Quentin invited us to participate in your last night as a slave."

She spent breakfast trying to adjust to interacting with these people as equals. Quentin finally forbade her from clearing the table and offered to reschedule the meeting so she could adjust to her new status. Marie declined; she trusted each person at this table completely, and aside from a Reunion she'd signed up for after her official Marketplace slave out-processing the following week, she wanted to get to work.

Hours later, paperwork strewn across the table, Miss Devereaux stood up and stretched. "I think we've got the broad strokes of this down cold. Six months of formal apprenticeship to me as my junior spotter. You really don't need it given the years you've assisted Quentin, but six months of work outside of a collar is the minimum the Regents will accept for you to work with their trainers. Another year of working together, then I can turn my files completely over to you and can retire properly, at which point you'll be an independent spotter in Ken's line. And Layton's willing to sponsor you as a Regents-certified spotter with preferred access to place your spots with trainers in Parker's line, in addition to your preferred access with Ken's affiliated trainers. I wish I'd had it this good when I was first starting out!"

Marie laughed. "Twelve years in a collar certainly counts as paying my dues, Miss Devereaux."

"I guess four years doesn't count?" Miss Devereaux asked, arching an eyebrow.

"You were a slave?" Marie replied, abashed.

"I thought you knew," Miss Devereaux replied. "I guess I never came out and say it back when I sent you off to Layton. My family had been Marketplace owners for almost a century; they were in shock. And Marie, I think it's time you start calling me Eloise."

Marie sat for a second, her eyes exploring Eloise's face, the revelation of her service so obvious now she knew, and she'd never felt so close to the woman who had saved her life. She'd grown to love spotting as Quentin's slave and assistant, embraced it as her path after leaving the collar. It was a way to serve the organization that had given her so much, to serve others like her who needed what the Marketplace could offer them. There were more Eloise Devereauxs in the mansions of Canal Street, more Marie Salazons in the ghettos of New Orleans Parish. She could imagine no greater service than helping them find their way.

"I think it's time for a cigar while Jack prepares a late lunch," Quentin announced, and they strode out to the patio. Marie accepted a cigar from Quentin; she'd given up smoking when Eloise took her in, and this, more than anything else, cemented in her head the divide she'd crossed that morning. Layton leaned over to light her cigar as Gary knelt before the group, holding an ashtray the way Marie used to. He winked at Marie.

The four spotters and trainers entered an animated discussion about the upcoming winter auctions. Marie knew they were deliberately giving her some time to process. Each of her comrades were, by necessity for their roles, far more perceptive than the norm. She smiled and watched smoke swirl up through the brilliant leaves of the oaks overarching Quentin's patio. She would miss this house.

She thought of the spots and candidates she'd worked with in Quentin's household, on the first step of their journey to the block. *I wonder where Kitten is.* She'd always obeyed Quentin's instructions to only use his Marketplace login for official business, but she would have her own login within days. She resolved to check on the girl. Hell, she'd be approaching the end of her second contract; if she didn't renew, maybe Marie could buy her.

She was getting ahead of herself. She wasn't ready to own a slave, especially one with whom she had history. She'd gotten Kitten into the Marketplace as an act of service, the way Miss Devereaux had done for her. It'd be selfish to drag her into a situation without the structure the girl needed. Maybe she'd arrange to attend a Reunion with her at some point. She couldn't afford to let the past determine her moves, when she'd never before been free.

I'm free. The thought startled her. She'd never been free before. Even Z-Cash had been her owner, although unworthy of the title. Miss Devereaux had ensured her future owners would understand the responsibility they held. Now she owned herself. How could she consider owning Kitten when she didn't even know if she was ready to own herself?

She looked at the tattoos that still covered her arm, an inkwell roadmap to the girl she once was, and she thought about the journey to where she was today. *If I've come so far from where I once was, what heights can I reach?* she thought. The world bloomed in her mind, with infinite possibility, more than that girl from the ghetto could have imagined. *I'm free,* she thought again, *and I will not be afraid.*

Unbridled Domesticity
By Elizabeth Schechter

"You want to go where?" Thomas asked, eyes wide as he stared across the breakfast table at his wife. He should have known Eugenia was planning something—they usually didn't sit down together to go over the day's business and the training schedules until after she'd broken her fast and dressed for the day. To be summoned to share her meal was an unusual privilege, one she doled out only when Thomas had done something she found particularly pleasing. Or when she had specific instructions for him.

"I said I wanted to go to New York," she repeated. She sounded amused. Amused was good. She did so delight in surprising him, trying to break his composure. "Darling, one would think you weren't listening to me." She smiled, her attention not on him, but on the apple she was peeling with a very small, very sharp, and very familiar knife.

Thomas forced his attention away from the knife and silently told himself not to fidget. Eugenia had, out of courtesy, waited until well after they were wed to reveal to her new husband and slave her skills with a blade. The sight of a knife in her hands now produced a response in him that was practically indecent. He looked at her and saw in her eyes that she knew exactly how he was feeling, that it pleased her, and that he might just have earned himself another demonstration in the very near future.

"I am listening," he said and was relieved his voice showed none of his eager anticipation. "I just don't understand, Mistress. New York? In September? That's very late in the year for a pleasure voyage, especially across the Atlantic. How long would you intend for us to stay?"

She dimpled. "Ah, you're worried about logistics. I see. We'll start in New York, and I'd like to leave as soon as we reasonably can. Have we any invitations that we've accepted?"

"There was the hunting party in Devonshire next month. Lady Mallory and her family," Thomas said. "And there's the fall slave market at the start the London Season. I thought you wanted to attend both?"

Eugenia looked thoughtful. "I had. But perhaps we'll take in the New York slave market instead. Look into that."

Thomas nodded. "If you wish. May I take notes, Mistress?"

"Of course. My lap desk is on the window seat." Eugenia turned her attention back to the apple. Thomas rose, laid on his chair the serviette that covered his naked lap, and crossed to the window seat. He gathered up the lap desk and went back to the table, standing next to his chair and waiting.

"Very good." Eugenia cut the apple in half, then quartered it, and laid it on a plate. She smiled sweetly at Thomas before setting the plate on the floor next to her chair. The silent instruction was clear, and Thomas sank to his knees. The lap desk slid easily over the carpet, and he pushed it before him as he crawled to Eugenia's side. Normally, he'd instruct a slave who'd been given no other direction to kneel in front of their owner, but if Thomas remained on his knees too long, the ankle he'd damaged in Egypt would start to ache, and he'd limp. After the last time, when the limp had lingered for days, Eugenia had forbidden him to hurt himself in such a manner again. So he arranged himself tailor-fashion on the floor, taking the lap desk onto his folded legs. He took pen, ink, and paper out of the desk, dipped the pen, and looked up at Eugenia.

"New York, you said?" he asked. "For the fall slave markets. I'll contact the Marketplace liaison and see what can be arranged. I'll be honest, Eugenia. These will be by far the most ambitious travel arrangements I've made."

"Didn't Lady Margaret travel?" Eugenia asked.

"Usually only from London to her estate in Surrey. And on occasion to Bath, to take the waters. Nothing on this scale. And for the trip to Egypt, she handled all the travel arrangements." He looked down at the paper and tapped the nip of his pen a few times. "Where else would you like to go?" he asked. "I can't see going all that way and only seeing New York."

Eugenia laughed. "You're being clever again, Thomas. Yes, I wanted to see more than just New York. The World's Columbian Exposition in Chicago is supposed to be very fine."

"So... we're doing a Grand Tour, then? In reverse, though," Thomas said, making note of the cities. "Don't Americans send their young men to Europe for a year to absorb culture?"

"Do they?" Eugenia asked. She sounded curious, interested. Good. Occasionally, his penchant for trivia annoyed her.

"So Lady Margaret told me," Thomas answered. He looked over the short list, then up at Eugenia. "Anywhere else? Or should we concentrate on the easternmost cities, and leave the west for another time?"

"We should concentrate on New York, primarily. I'll want to spend the majority of our time there."

The answer was quick, determined, and told him Eugenia was up something. He looked up to see her smiling at him.

"Ginny, are you plotting something?"

She arched an eyebrow at the familiarity, and for a moment, Thomas wondered if he'd condemned himself to a lonely bed in the servants' quarters. Then her smile broadened. "You asked me once where I learned my skills with a knife. I recently had a letter from my teacher. Lady Beatrice taught me most of what I know. She's living in New York; I'd like you to meet her."

There was a weight to her words that told Thomas she wanted him to do more than meet with this mysterious teacher, but he also knew she'd tell him nothing more. He nodded and looked down at his page. "So, I'll need to arrange to close the house. Travel arrangements—I'll need to book passage for us and for a maid and valet. Do you have one maid in particular you'd like to come with us?"

"Abigail, I think. She's coming along nicely, and this will be a good learning experience for her. And I think you should bring Ishaq."

"I was going to suggest that," Thomas answered. "Ginny... as much as I'd like to keep him on as my valet, he's ready for the block. More than ready. We could have sent him to auction last spring."

"I've been waiting for you to say the word," Eugenia said. She cocked her head to one side. "In the spring, I think. We'll have him with us for this trip. He's very fond of you."

Thomas nodded. "And I of him."

She nodded, reaching out and running her fingers through his hair. Then she looked down at the floor and the plate that Thomas had forgotten. "You haven't eaten your apple."

"I can't eat and take notes. Which would you prefer I do first?" Thomas asked.

"Notes first. Abigail and Ishaq to New York. We'll see what we can find with in the slave markets there, perhaps, for a slave to replace Ishaq as your valet. What will you need to do to make us ready?"

Thomas refrained from tapping the pen against his lip as he thought. "Well, as I said, travel arrangements. We'll have to close the house. Cancel any engagements. Your father won't be happy that I won't be at his elbow when he takes his seat in Parliament."

"He can hire a secretary or buy one at auction," Eugenia said tartly.

Thomas looked down, biting his lip to keep from laughing. His father-in-law, Baron Waterton, took blatant advantage of his daughter's collared husband, commanding his presence as secretary and assistant at any and all functions, with little-to-no warning. It was the one thing Thomas knew Eugenia and her father quarreled about— if the Baron needed a slave, he should buy his own, not forever be borrowing hers! "I'll need to see about hotels," Thomas said. "New York, Chicago. Anywhere else? Boston, perhaps, to see where they threw the tea into the harbor?"

Eugenia laughed like a little girl. "Oh, yes."

Thomas added the city to his list, looked at his notes and nodded. "Darling, I'll have to go into London to take care of all the arrangements."

"I expected so. Take Ishaq," Eugenia said. "He should learn how to make travel arrangements. Is that all the notes?"

"I believe so," Thomas answered. He cleaned the pen and capped the inkwell, putting them both back into the lap desk before setting the desk aside and getting to his knees. Crossing his wrists behind his back, he bent forward far enough that his collar bumped against his chin as he delicately bit one of the apple quarters in half. He ate slowly, staying bent over, and he sighed as Eugenia reached down and stroked his back and his neck, tugging gently on the chain that marked him as her property.

"How long will you be gone?" she asked.

Thomas swallowed the last of the apple and turned his head slightly. "A few days, I expect," he answered. "We'll go by rail, stay at the club. A day to make the travel arrangements, a day to meet with the Marketplace liaison. Three days, four at the most?"

He heard her sigh. "I'll miss you. Are you done?"

"Yes, Mistress."

"Then sit up."

Thomas hesitated then asked, "If I may, Mistress?"

She laughed. "Yes, you may."

Thomas smiled and leaned forward, pressing a gentle kiss to the toe of the periwinkle blue slipper that just barely peeked out from beneath the hem of Eugenia's dressing gown. He glanced up through his hair and then leaned even further to kiss her instep.

"Thomas... " There was a warning in her voice, but there was also laughter. Thomas drew back and sat up, keeping his wrists crossed behind his back. She shook her head and smiled, reaching out and lightly tapping his cheek.

"I spoil you outrageously, slave," she said. "Now, if you're going to London, you should leave as soon as you're able." She glanced down, and her smile broadened; she picked up her serviette and draped it over Thomas's erect cock, making him shiver. "You have my permission to deal with that before you leave. Have Ishaq take care of you."

Thomas coughed, surprised by the liberty. "Thank you, Mistress."

Her smile grew positively predatory. "And you'll wait until I get there, Thomas. I want to watch. I should see how he's coming along."

Thomas licked his lips, his mouth suddenly dry. He bit the tip of his tongue, bent his head, and bowed to his wife and Owner.

"As you wish, Mistress."

"Go on, now. I'll join you shortly."

Thomas bowed deeper, his forehead brushing the carpet. He rose slowly, backing away from the table before turning to the chaise where his folded clothing awaited him. Her voice stopped him as he reached for the pile.

"And don't bother to dress."

* * *

Having a home staffed entirely by slaves was convenient. It meant when it was the Mistress's whim that her collared husband should parade through the halls in complete and utter nudity, no one took it amiss. Or, in truth, was very much shocked, since it seemed to happen every other Thursday or thereabouts.

Thomas was certainly unperturbed by it; he stopped to correct several trainees as he made his way through the back of the house and up the stairs. The upper corridors were empty—the maids had finished their work while Thomas and Eugenia were at breakfast, and so he hurried to his own door and let himself in.

"Ishaq!" he called as he closed the door behind him.

"Yes, sir?" From the adjoining room, his valet appeared. No one had been more surprised than Thomas when, the day before they were set to return from Egypt, Eugenia had presented him with Ishaq's contract, telling him the beautiful young man was to be his first trainee as a Master-Trainer. In the months since, Thomas had overseen the young man's education, turning him into a most capable gentleman's gentleman. Now, for the first time, Thomas realized their remaining time was limited. The first slave of his House was ready to be sold, and he was surprised by how that idea hurt.

Ishaq looked at him, his eyes traveling from Thomas's face to his bare feet and back. "The Mistress is in... in a mood?" he asked. He'd proved to be a quick study with languages, and his English was improving daily. He still had a charming accent, though, and a melodious voice that would be a definite selling point.

"A bit." Thomas agreed with a smile. "And she'll be here shortly and wants you to attend. Then you'll need to pack for us, for four days. We'll be going to London later today, and you're to pay careful attention to what we do. It will count as part of your training."

Ishaq looked surprised. "London? Training? Sir?"

"We'll be making travel arrangements, Ishaq. And you'll be accompanying the Mistress and me when we go abroad. To New York," he added, before Ishaq could ask. "You'll be acting as my valet, and young Abigail will be the Mistress's maid."

"I see... " Ishaq rubbed the bridge of his nose with one finger. It was an odd gesture from someone usually so poised.

Thomas frowned. "Ishaq, is something bothering you?"

"I... have been thinking. And I would like to talk with you. And... not as my Trainer." Ishaq drew himself up and met Thomas's eyes. "Man to man, as well as slave to slave."

"We have a long road to London. We'll talk then," Thomas answered. "And I promise to try and not answer as your trainer."

"Thank you, sir." He glanced away. "She's coming."

"How do you do that?" Thomas murmured as he went to his knees and crossed his wrists behind him. Ishaq looked at him and grinned, then composed himself and knelt facing the doorway. The doors opened, and Eugenia stepped inside.

"One of these days, Ishaq, I will catch you unawares," Eugenia warned, laughing. "And I'll happily see you in stripes for it."

"With respect, Mistress, I will happily wear the stripes for you," Ishaq answered, bowing low.

Eugenia smiled, nodding. "What has Thomas told you?"

Ishaq straightened, tucking his hands behind his back. "That I am to attend now. That I am to pack for London, for four days. That I am to learn to make travel arrangements. And that we are to go to New York."

Eugenia looked at Thomas. "You didn't tell him to what he was to attend?"

"No, Mistress. I didn't know your mood or what manner you would wish for him to attend to me," Thomas answered. He heard Ishaq's quick intake of breath. So did Eugenia.

"You didn't warn him at all." She shook her head. "Thomas, I didn't think you so far gone that you'd lost all your wits. Very well, we'll deal with that. Now... Ishaq, I'll want the chair, please." Ishaq rose gracefully and went to fetch the straight-backed chair.

There was a chair like this one in every bedroom—a low-backed heavy wooden chair. It was plain enough to be called ugly, its wide seat singularly uncomfortable to sit on, and the chair served no obvious purpose save to take up space in a corner or to occasionally have a dressing gown thrown over it. It's less obvious purpose was the one with which Thomas was most familiar. At Eugenia's nod, he rose and took a seat in the chair, shifting so his arms hung over the back. He crossed his wrists, spread his legs, and waited. As Eugenia unfurled the ropes she had taken from a cabinet and slowly started to bind him, Thomas wondered if this Lady Beatrice was the one who had taught Eugenia about ropes and rigging. If so, he owed her a deep debt of gratitude—by the time Ginny was done with her task, he was bound tight enough that even side-to-side motion was difficult. Eugenia stepped back, her face flushed, her hair falling askew, and nodded, reaching out to trail her fingers up the length of Thomas's erection. He gasped, tugging futilely against the ropes.

"Very nice," Eugenia crooned. "Very nice. Ishaq, will you attend to him, please? But don't let him spend."

Thomas fought the urge to turn, to see where Ishaq had gotten to, but the other man moved forward. He bowed deeply to Eugenia and then turned to Thomas. Thomas could see the prominent tenting in the front of Ishaq's trousers. He licked his lips and swallowed, meeting Ishaq's eyes. Ishaq knew how to please a man, skills he'd learned at the hands of a harder taskmaster than Thomas ever could be—Bomani, the maniac who had kidnapped Ishaq, murdering his brothers and abusing him for months before turning his brutal attentions to his new captive, Thomas. Having briefly suffered at Bomani's hands, Thomas had been surprised Ishaq had showed any interest in any kind of bedsport at all, let alone any kind of enthusiasm. He and Eugenia had even discussed writing into Ishaq's contracts that he was not to be used in the bedroom. Then a guest at one of their hunting parties had requested Ishaq attend him and had later praised the slave's skills at great length. After the party, Eugenia had ordered Ishaq to demonstrate his skills, a night Thomas still remembered with both relish and with a touch of trepidation. If Eugenia were going to orchestrate this in her usual manner, she'd drag it out as long as she possibly could, then leave him hanging. At Ishaq's hands, that would be torturous pleasure indeed.

Ishaq gave him a wicked smile as he stopped in front of the chair, then turned, and looked over his shoulder. "I may not let him spend. Are there any other restrictions?"

"None," Eugenia answered. She moved to sit in the chair that stood by the fireplace and gestured with one hand. "Proceed."

Ishaq bowed and then moved to stand between Thomas's legs. The wool of his trousers scratched against the sensitive skin of Thomas's inner thighs, making him squirm. Ishaq smiled, stepped closer, then leaned down and kissed Thomas, lacing his fingers into

Thomas's hair. Thomas strained against the ropes, trying to lean into the kiss, wanting more. He heard a sigh, an unmistakable sound of pleasure from elsewhere in the room, and then Ishaq stepped back and gracefully went to his knees. He ran his hands up Thomas's legs and over his hips, holding on as he leaned forward and breathed softly on Thomas's cock.

Eugenia's voice was soft. "Go ahead, Ishaq. Let me see if you've learned anything new."

Ishaq murmured something, a reply Thomas missed as Ishaq ran his tongue languidly up the length of Thomas's cock. Thomas gasped and strained, trying to thrust his hips forward, feeling the ropes and Ishaq's fingers digging into his skin. He yelped as Ishaq gently bit down, a yelp that faded into a deep moan as Ishaq slowly slid his mouth down over Thomas's shaft. Thomas groaned and tipped his head back, slumping as much as the ropes would allow. His body slid forward slightly, and Ishaq adjusted his hands, sliding them under Thomas's arse. Long fingers moved against him, teasing and caressing, and Thomas felt the head of his cock briefly press against the tightness of Ishaq's throat and then force through with a pop that Thomas felt more than heard. He whimpered, panting, knowing he wasn't going to be able to stop...

"That's enough, Ishaq," Eugenia said. "Thank you. You're excused. And... you are free to find your relief, however you choose to do so. Just be back here in half an hour to pack for London."

Ishaq stopped moving, then slowly drew away, stopping only to kiss the head of Thomas's cock before he rose. He was panting, and his hands were shaking as he clasped them behind his back. He bowed, and his voice was rough as he answered, "Thank you, Mistress."

Eugenia nodded but didn't rise, staying in her seat until Ishaq had left the room. Then she stood; Thomas watched her, his breathing gradually slowing, his cock still achingly hard. She walked from the fireplace toward the bed, and let her dressing gown fall as she traveled, the blue silk pooling on the floor. She passed out of Thomas's view, and he craned his neck to try and see her.

"None of that," Eugenia chided. "You be patient, or I'll blindfold you."

"Yes, Mistress," Thomas murmured, turning forward. He took a deep breath, trying to relax. Then he heard footsteps coming closer, and warm fingers trailed over his shoulder and down his chest. He looked up, and caught his breath. "Ginny... " he breathed, taking in the glorious sight of his love, his wife, his Owner, in all her naked glory. She smiled and pressed against him, kissing him deeply as her fingers combed through his hair and ran down his neck, lingering for a moment before she drew back and brushed his hair off his forehead.

"You've pleased me," she said quietly. "You always please me, in so many ways." She ran one hand down his chest, over his stomach. "I'll miss you, while you're gone."

"I'll hurry," Thomas whispered. "I'll miss you, too. And I'll be back as soon as I can be."

"I know." Ginny kissed him again and then moved against him, climbing up to kneel on the wide seat of the chair, straddling his legs. Thomas whimpered as her fingers brushed against his cock, shifting him into position so she could lower herself onto him, gasping as he filled her. By the time she was seated fully against him, Thomas was near frantic with need, crying and gasping as he fought not to spend before she did. Eugenia rested her hands on his shoulders and laughed, the deep, full-throated laugh he only ever heard when they were alone. She started to move, grinding against him, her nails digging into his shoulders as passion overcame propriety. Then one hand slid forward, tangling in his collar and pulling the chain tight around his neck. He gasped, instinctively pulling away and only succeeding in cutting off his own air. He could feel his mouth moving, knew he was begging, but no words were coming out. He heard her broken gasping, then a single gasped word.

"Now!"

Thomas howled and shook, straining against the ropes as he climaxed, feeling Eugenia moving against him and hearing her voice rising with his own. It seemed to go on for hours, until he slumped in the ropes, his head falling back, her weight heavy on his chest. He could feel her breathing, warm and soft against his chest, and he rubbed his cheek against her tumbled curls.

"Thank you, Mistress," he croaked.

Eugenia hummed softly then moaned and shifted. "You're very welcome, Thomas," she murmured. Then she sighed and stretched. "I'll have to bathe again and have Sophie redo my hair."

"I'm sorry for the inconvenience," Thomas apologized.

"Oh, don't be. I quite enjoyed it." Eugenia smiled and leaned forward to kiss him, then slid off his lap and walked past him. When she returned, she was wearing her shift once more, holding her dressing gown. She put the gown on while he watched but let it hang loose. She held the sash between her hands and smiled slowly. Thomas knew from the look on her face what she was going to do, but there was nothing he could do to stop her from gagging him.

"There. Now you won't disturb Ishaq while he works," Eugenia said. "I'll have him release you once he's finished. He should be back... Oh, I did tell him to find his own release, didn't I? So he'll be back to let you go... eventually." She smiled and kissed Thomas's forehead. "I'll see you before you leave, darling," she murmured and then left, holding her dressing gown closed with one hand. Thomas shifted and then tipped his head back and groaned into the gag. Here he was, and here he'd stay until Ishaq returned and released him.

The Mistress was indeed in a mood.

Foster Care
By Elle Wickenden

"You're shitting me," I say. "He's Marketplace? I know he's a billionaire—but he's batshit crazy."

"Negel got him access to the auctions," Chris says.

"Oh. Well, that explains a lot."

Jack McFarlane had made a mint in software, sold it to an even bigger company, and then retired with all his money and toys to Costa Rica. Honestly, nobody thought he was that crazy when he left the States, but he seemed to pull a Captain Kurtz down there in the jungle. The stories got weirder and wilder as time went on, and then he finally pulled something even the Costa Ricans couldn't be paid or intimidated into ignoring: he shot his neighbor in the face with an assault rifle in a dispute over a noisy dog.

His neighbor was a pop singer whose career was a source of national pride, so that was pretty awkward. More awkward was the fact McFarlane went on the lam and had started issuing unhinged electronic missives from the jungle to a blogger at *Wired* magazine whose Twitter avatar, he said, was "cute, in a hot librarian sort of way."

And MacFarlane? Had bought 16 slaves through the Marketplace.

A lot of this came out in the tabloids, along with plenty of photos of the man's home arsenal, which include 81 assault rifles, a rocket launcher, and a tank, which although miniaturized to the size of a golf cart, had a fully functional howitzer. The tabloids, of course, didn't know about the Marketplace and just went on about MacFarlane's *harem* of beautiful young women. They didn't mention the house servants, or the driver, or the bodyguards, who were, of course, also Marketplace.

"I know this isn't your problem, Bette, but I thought your diplomatic skills might be useful," Chris said. "One of them doesn't have a passport, and we're having trouble getting her out of the country."

Sigh. Diplomat. Well, that's what my passport and my car plates said, but I'm no diplomat: I'm a fixer, a fixer who is retired and trying very hard to stay that way. Why, I just paid off a housing inspector to look the other way on my newly installed woodstove, a modern one from Finland with no scrolly bits and a tiny recess for a teapot.

And now I'm supposed to leave? Fuck.

"She's an American citizen, isn't she? Just have her go to the Embassy, and they'll take care of it," I said.

"They're trying to keep her in the country to testify against MacFarlane."

"Just her?"

"All the others managed to get away."

I look out the window. It had started to snow in Montreal last week, and tonight it was sheeting down between the streetlamp and the *depannéur* across the street where I picked up the paper every morning. I adjust the old windows, which are still pretty drafty, and pulled my robe tighter around me. I'd have to pack my own bag. When was the last time I had done that? I hadn't gotten on a plane or even bought a ticket since...

"Listen, you know that you can count on one hand the number of times I've overstepped like this in my life," Chris says, a cab honking in the New York background of his call. "And I know I'm overstepping now, but I'm only saying this because I really believe it. I think you need to get out of the house."

I sigh. The last time I saw Chris was at an auction, and instead of making a purchase, I ended up getting so drunk that I have no idea what happened next, although the resulting rumors and the epic hangover gave me a pretty good idea. I'd woken up in the guest room of a brownstone where Chris was working as a trainer. The next day, after I could bear opening my eyes in a fully lit room, I booked a one-way ticket to Montreal, the last place I'd been really happy, and that's where I've been for the last six months.

"Okay," I say. "Give me the information."

* * *

I don't know where the fuck I can buy a Mac power adapter in Costa Rica. Or, for that matter, a charging cable for my phone. Upon unpacking, I realize I had forgotten several other vital items: for one thing, after surveying my luggage I realized the underwear I was wearing was the only set I had with me.

Sigh. Everybody thinks I'm so capable, but half of it was Diana. I check and recheck my pockets—passports, wallet, notebook, pen, dollars, pesos. I have no idea how many times I do this a day now that she's gone, but it's enough to make me tired and sick of myself. It used to be her job, and for the past decade I never had to worry about it. Now I worry about it a dozen times a day: fuck! Where's my wallet? Oh, it's in that pocket now. I've changed from James Bond to Columbo, grumpy, disheveled—oh, stop thinking about it, I tell myself as I walk into the tiled and palm-shaded courtyard of the hotel. I buy a hat and a pair of sunglasses and let myself into the Jeep that's been arranged for me.

The sun and the wind feel good, and Costa Rican radio ain't half bad. By the time I arrive at MacFarlane's finca, 45 minutes from the city center in a tony ridgetop area called Las Palomas, I'm in a pretty good mood. I stop well short of the gate and take in the scene. There are a couple of guards, but they don't look like military or police—private security.

This is one of those cases where being female is a big advantage. Large armed men don't see me as threatening, so I can generally walk right up to them without them pulling a gun on me or having them call for reinforcements. At least the first time they meet me, anyway.

They talk about me in Spanish as I approach. They think I have a nice ass, and if they're saying that, they think I have a nice ass and don't speak Spanish. That's fine, I don't want them to know I do.

"Is Kelly still here? I used to see her at the club, and I heard she's still here. Isn't it horrible what's happened? I heard everyone was gone except for her, and I feel so bad for her." I let my voice slip up into a higher register and channel the *Real Housewives of Orange County*—a rich piece of trophy-wife fluff.

"No, she not here."

"Oh, did she go back to the States? Is she okay?" I know she's still in the country, of course.

"She went to hospital," the big one says.

"Oh, no! She didn't get shot too, did she? Oh, I'll have to send flowers! Is she awake? Oh, this is terrible!" I say, as I lay my fingertips on the big one's forearm and even stroke them back and forth a bit. I am really camping it up now. In my mind, I had one of those dogs that fit in a purse and some excellent cosmetic work. "You don't think they brought her to the city, do you? Why, I don't even know *where* to send the flowers. This is so terrible!"

"No. Not the city hospital. Santa Marta."

"Oh, thank you so much."

I even swish my ass a bit in the finest trophy-wife fashion as I walk back to the Jeep.

Kelly is in a hospital, which is not good. It's a private hospital, which is good. The guards at the door to her room, however, are not private security but actual police, which is very, very not good.

The hardware police in other countries carry runs the gamut. If you're from the US, you're probably not used to the paramilitary look of the police in many countries—the last time you got stopped for speeding, the cop probably had some standard issue combat Tupperware on her hip, but she wasn't carrying a submachine gun. This fella, however, has something in a nice extended clip sitting in his lap while he catches up on the doings of Brangelina in an English-language edition of *People* magazine.

I sit on a bench in the hallway and sift through the issues of *People*, some of which are recent and some of a vintage that can only be ascertained through carbon dating. The officer's phone trills, and he fishes it out and snaps it open. His face assumes that familiar expression of Heterosexual Man Being Harassed by Wife.

I arrange my face to indicate studious attention to the celebrity deeds and misdeeds reported by the magazine in my hands.

Ah, his mother-in-law wants to move in. He does not want this. The wife does not want this either but does not feel able to say no.

And? There's no money for a little nearby apartment for the mother-in-law.

Bingo.

* * *

249

Bribery is so much easier than they make it look in the movies. You don't really need an envelope or a dark location or any of that bullshit. You just need money. I stroll down to *un cambio* and cash in about two grand in American dollars, and on my way back I pick up the local version of a Sno-Cone, made with chunks of pineapple and syrup. It beats the shit out of 7-11, I can tell you that much.

I love bribing people. My work makes me happy.

So? I bribe Mr. I-don't-want-my-mother-in-law-in-my-house to look the other way for a little bit when I come back after dinner. He even helpfully tells me when the shift change is and offers to give me a handcuff key. I tell him, "Keep the key. I've got one already."

Like I don't have a handcuff key. Pfft. Who do they think I am?

* * *

Dinner's quite nice, a light white fish in a sauce of freshly diced tomatoes and mild peppers, followed by ubiquitous flan. I stick to soda water with lime and stroll back to the hospital, where, as promised, there's nothing but a copy of *People* on the chair next to the door.

* * *

I wish I could get used to this shit, even if that would make me like my utterly efficient and completely dead inside colleagues in the large and growing industry of fixing shit when everything goes pear-shaped. But I haven't and at this point that means I probably never will.

MacFarlane didn't shoot her, but she might have been better off if he had. There's a cast; tape around the ribs, another cast. I can't tell what color her eyes are—I'm not sure she can open them. Her arms and back look like she's been dragged behind a tractor through a quarter mile of thorn bushes. I flip open the disposable phone and call Chris.

"I'm gonna need a doctor at the other end," I say.

* * *

250

It's more complicated since she can't walk out with me, but apparently there's an epidemic of mother-in-law-moving-in syndrome, and I get to make another five people safe from its horrors—two to get a gurney, one to drive an ambulance, and another to give me a rundown of her medical condition and enough pain meds to get her through the flight. He hands me everything along with a few more bags of saline to keep her hydrated.

* * *

I know this means I'm a sick fuck, but I like sitting next to her on the plane, even though she's not conscious. I was a medic in the Army, and I like being useful. Or, really, what I like is having been useful and sitting next to someone who's not going to die in the next 15 minutes because I settled that shit.

The private jet—supplied by another Marketplace owner—has an entire mini fridge exclusively for champagne. I'd been told to make use of anything I needed.

I take out one of the bottles and open it. Kelly doesn't even flinch as the cork pushes into my hand with a loud pop—she's out cold. There are two flutes on a tray. I fill one and sip, looking at the empty flute.

That's what we used to do, coming back from a job. Champagne. We'd each drink a glass of champagne to toast another job well done.

Sigh. I think I left one of my fucking bags in Costa Rica. Fuck it. Nothing was right, and everything hurt. But I don't drink the whole bottle or dip into the copious supply of Vicodin; instead, I read Kelly's file.

* * *

MacFarlane bought Kelly three years ago at the same auction house where I'd bought Diana over a decade ago. It was a first-time contract for Kelly, who'd been trained by a reputable outfit in Chicago.

Originally from Toronto, youngest of five children, art degree, some success as an artist, spotted at a large event in New York.

251

I flip back again to the first page. Two-year contract, but the date is four years ago. I flip to the end, where the contract renewals are supposed to be. Nothing except records of repeated calls to MacFarlane with no response.

Two-year contract, but she's been there for four years, with no renegotiation and no contact.

She's not a slave, I think. She's a hostage.

* * *

At the other end, as promised, there's a doctor. There are X-rays and a CAT scan of her head.

In the flat, sallow light of the hospital room, I have a weird thought: she looks worse than Diana did when Diana was dead.

Diana died in a car accident a year ago, and except for a broken nose she just looked like she was asleep.

Kelly looked like Clint Eastwood in Act Two of one of those 70s spaghetti westerns where he always had to get the shit beat out of him before eventually prevailing over the bad guys.

I flip my phone open again. "Who do you have for foster?" I ask Chris.

"Nothing solid, but we'll have something lined up for her within 48 hours. She has to stay in the hospital anyway for longer than that probably anyway, right?"

"I wanna keep her," I say.

* * *

The fact that she's a Canadian citizen makes it easy for me to bring her home with me. Hell, I could marry her and become a Canadian citizen myself, I think.

I'm getting ahead of myself. She hasn't even woken up and said one word to me or anyone else yet, for fuck's sake.

I call home and order three twin-sized futons.

* * *

She wakes up. She passes the neurological exam. Apart from asking where she is, she doesn't talk much.

I tell her I don't have anything to do with MacFarlane, she isn't even in the same country with him anymore, she is in the United States and safe.

I ask her if she has anywhere she wants to go or anyone she wants to see, but she just closes her eyes and goes back to sleep.

* * *

Even Negel's contracts have a foster rider—if your owner dies, if your owner goes to jail, if your owner goes batshit crazy—you are entitled to foster placement: a safe place to stay until you figure out what you want to do.

Kelly doesn't seem ready to make any big decisions. She has two more operations to put pins in her wrist, and with all the pain medication even a short conversation is often something she can't stay awake for. When she is ready to be discharged, she still seems too tired and shell-shocked to decide what she wants for lunch, much less what she wants to do for the rest of her life.

She can do a lot worse than my apartment in Montreal, I think. And I like telling people what they're going to have for lunch. It's refreshing to not have to repress my native bossiness all the damn time.

* * *

I walk behind her up the stairs to the apartment. I carry my luggage, and she carries her left arm, cradling it as if it hurts.

Inside, she stands by the door, unsure of what to do. I lead her by the hand to my bedroom, where a plain narrow futon, fresh and white, lies on the floor beside my bed.

"Take your clothes off," I say. I help her with her blouse, and with the zipper of her skirt. She lies down on her side, facing away from me. I open the large black chest at the foot of my bed and pull out a white down comforter and throw it over her. By the time I close the chest and look back at her, she is already asleep, lips parted, breathing deeply.

There doesn't seem to be enough hours in the day for Kelly to spend sleeping. She's like a baby—she wakes up to eat and use the bathroom and then goes back to sleep. I have robes for her, but she seems entirely comfortable going about the apartment naked, despite the still healing cuts, scrapes, and bruises that cover so much of her body. Of course, she mainly goes from room to room where I'd placed some more small futons in places where I typically worked or read—one by my desk, one by my favorite chair where I read or watched television. Each one had a down comforter, and she'd slide under it, curl onto her side, and in a moment or two, she'd be asleep again.

* * *

Fostering in the Marketplace is a formal system—they don't just give out shell-shocked property to somebody's cousin Vinnie, and they don't forget about them once they're placed. Once a week, a Marketplace-friendly doctor visits my apartment to check on Kelly's progress.

I can never quite figure the doctor and her assistant out. Are they property? Is one of them an owner and the other a slave? It's none of my business, really, so I don't ask.

I do observe Kelly's exams, though. The physician's assistant always comes with a large case—something a bit like a folding massage table, only deeper, and with attachable stirrups.

Once the table is up the doctor examines Kelly, narrating her findings out loud, as her assistant makes notes, the notepad looking tiny in his enormous fist. As far as I can tell, he never talks.

"Felipe, please help me turn her over," the doctor says. With gloved hands, she inspects the cuts and welts on Kelly's back and, wordlessly, shoots her hand out; her assistant puts a tube of gel in it, which she spreads lightly over the wounds.

The doctor bends Kelly's leg at the knee and examines a deep cut on the bottom of her right foot that has been stitched shut. "These are ready to come out," she says. "But we'll do that after. Felipe, help me turn her again."

They turn Kelly onto her back and put her feet in the stirrups. "Note that there's no sign of sexual activity," she says. The doctor turns to me, and I just shake my head. Kelly wasn't even capable of dressing or washing herself—sex hadn't even crossed my mind.

Although now that it was crossing my mind, I made a mental note to look up portable tables with stirrups. I've always had kind of a thing for that, but it's one of those things that hasn't made it off my bucket list and into my real life yet. I shift a little in my seat. How long had it been since I'd had sex? Or even jacked off?

If I'm getting turned on by furniture, the answer is way too fucking long. Maybe I should just go for the random hookup to take the pressure off, I think.

* * *

I send Kelly back off to the futon in my bedroom while I speak to the doctor. Felipe, the wordless climbing-wall-sized assistant, goes downstairs, and in a minute, I hear the Town Car idling out front.

"She's lost a lot of weight. Is she eating?" the doctor asks

"Not a lot. She gets about halfway through a meal—but I'd say she's only eating about half of what I am, and she's a bigger person."

"But no nausea or vomiting?"

"No," I say.

"The pain medication may be suppressing her appetite, and it's almost certainly causing the drowsiness. You can cut down to four times a day. Call me if her appetite does not improve, or if you see anything else you think I should know about."

"Thanks, Doctor. See you next week."

I watch through the window as the elegant doctor approaches the Town Car. Felipe holds the door for her. He has a handsome, dark face, kind of Aztec looking. He sees me watching, and I wave.

To my surprise, he waves back.

* * *

Just as the doctor speculated, Kelly begins to perk up as soon as I reduce the amount of pain medication she takes.

She is hungrier, too; she'll finish her plate, and when I nudge mine at her and tell her to eat, she'll eat what is left there, as well.

After we work through today's breakfast, I get up from the large teak dining table, carrying the dishes to the kitchen.

I turn to the counter and begin putting away the eggs and cheese

I used to make some quick omelets. I hear water running in the sink, and I turn around: Kelly is standing at it, naked, doing the dishes.

This is one of those little miracles I'm always afraid will disappear if I interrupt it. I wordlessly hand her a white canvas apron and went back out to the living room. I sit in my favorite chair and smile at the falling snow.

* * *

Seeing Kelly walk around the house in nothing but an apron is doing wonders to thaw out my libido, which has been in the deep freeze since Diana's death. Something about just the apron turns my crank in a way that even complete nudity never has.

I know Kelly wasn't ready for that, though as her foster, I am within my rights to use her to meet my own sexual needs as long as it doesn't interfere with restoring her to health. But she's too fragile for that still.

I cannot fucking believe it, but while I I'm sitting there cruising Craigslist Montreal, fantasizing about picking up a partner just for the night, I get a call from none other than Geoff Negel.

There wasn't much unusual in Kelly's file until she met Negel—she hadn't done anything wrong to end up in the situation she was in; she just had the misfortune of running across the Marketplace's most unscrupulous trainer. He's a fraud who covers up his incompetence and greed with new-age, shallow-California justifications about how the Marketplace has to change.

But hey, that's just my opinion. TL; DR—the guy's a douchebag.

"Bette, I want to thank you for taking in Kelly after the terrible crisis in Costa Rica."

"That's funny, Geoff. She's been here with me for weeks, and I haven't heard a peep out of you until now. I'm not sure why you're thanking me when you don't actually give a fuck."

"Well, of course I care—I care about every client I train and place with an owner."

"Oh?" I say. "You trained 15 others who you placed with MacFarlane. Do you even know where the rest of them are right now?"

"Sadly, no—in the crisis, many of them fled, and no one knows where they are. Of course, Kelly ended up with you as a foster caretaker, so her whereabouts are known, thank goodness."

"Geoff, why are you calling me?"

"Well, as you know, fostering has a one-year limit, and during that time, a slave's original owner can reassert their rights of ownership."

"Are you fucking kidding me? You place 16 slaves with a defective, dangerous owner, and now you want to give them back!"

"Oh, no, no, no, Bette. Of course, we can't do that, but I still have to fill out the paperwork."

I sit there. I really genuinely want to beat the guy with a stick. He's sitting here talking so calmly about 16 people—16 human beings!—he handed off to an unhinged gun-nut and then forgot about for a month. How can he even be calling me?

A calmer part of myself says, in the back of my mind: *why* is he calling you, Bette?

"Geoff," I say, "now isn't a good time. I'm afraid I have to go."

And I buy myself some time: I hang up on Negel. *What the fuck is that little shitweasel up to?*

I don't remember standing up from the chair, but now I'm back and forth in front of the bank of windows, the snow whipping against them, my boot heels striking the wood floor loudly with each stride. I turn around, and there's Kelly, standing there in her apron looking frightened.

I'm kinda slow on the uptake sometimes. It takes me until that moment to realize that it isn't just the principle of the thing. It isn't just that I oppose Geoff's ways of using people up and discarding them with every fiber of my being, although I do.

My heart is pounding and my mouth is dry and my hands are shaking because I want to keep Kelly. I want to keep Kelly, and the thought of someone taking her away has shoved a cold block of fear and anger into my chest too big for me to hold.

I want to run across the room and grab her and hold her, but up until this moment I haven't even touched her except to change her bandages or cover her with a blanket.

"It's okay," I say. "You're safe. Nobody's taking you anywhere."

She still looks scared. Of me, I realize. Negel filing an appeal for her return might be scary, but Negel isn't in the room—I am.

257

I look at her chalky, frightened face and deliberately lower my shoulders, open my hands.

"You're safe from me too," I say. "Come here." She crosses the room, coming within four paces of me.

"Closer."

Still wearing nothing but the apron, hands clasped behind her back, she stands close enough to me that I can see the shift as her pupils dilate.

"Come sit here next to me," I say, indicating a small meditation cushion next to my favorite chair. She folds herself smoothly on it, and I sit back in the broad leather armchair. It's quiet enough that we can both hear the snow tapping against the windows. Slowly, I rest my forearm on the broad wooden arm of the chair and allow my hand to dangle over the edge.

I am just barely touching her hair, and I find this utterly thrilling.

With my other hand, I pick up the remote and put the game on—Canadiens vs. the Bruins, playing only a few blocks away at Bell Centre.

"We're a Habs household, just so you know. Rooting for teams other than the Canadiens will not be tolerated."

* * *

Maybe it is the hockey, but Kelly seems to improve dramatically over the next few days, enough so that I begin to train her to do some simple errands. This morning we go across the street to the *depannéur*, where I show her which daily paper I take, what brand of coffee and juice I like.

Watching her buying the items at the counter, I enjoy seeing how the gruff, 60-something owner, who never gives me anything more than my change, succumb to Kelly's effortless, artless charm. It's like walking around town with my own personal Audrey Hepburn.

We move on to my drycleaner, where I act pretty much like a mime, and the clerk gives me the *You Do Not Speak French—I Cannot See You* treatment. I sigh, determined to wait him out, and fish out my phone to check my email.

"*Bonjour, j'aimerais faire nettoyer ce costume, s'il vous plait. Il y a un tache de cafe sur la manche de la veste, là, vous voyez?*"

I look up. That's Kelly! Speaking French!

"Oui je vois. J'enprends note. Voici votre ticket. Ce sera prêt vendredi après-midi."

Out on the street, I pilot her around the corner into a cobblestoned alleyway and push her face against the cool granite of the building. I swat her ass with my gloved hand.

"That's for not telling me you speak French, you little minx. If there's anything else I need to know I expect you to be forthcoming, do you understand?"

She nods, making that face people make when they're trying not to smile and failing.

* * *

If Kelly is well enough to sass me a little, then I figure she's well enough to leave the apartment on her own and maybe even for a bit more.

"I want you to go to the shops downtown and pick out some clothes for yourself," I say.

"What would you like me to wear?" Kelly asks.

"Do I look like I dispense girly fashion advice?"

While she's out, I take out my toolbox and find an extension cord for the electric drill. I drill a hole in the baseboard next to the little slave pallet where Kelly sleeps next to my bed and install a hook. I install another, shoulder high, next to the front door. And a third I drill right into the wooden upright of my favorite leather armchair. Then I flip open my pocketknife and slit the tape on a cardboard box that was delivered earlier that day. Inside is a simple dog leash—six feet of shiny chain links and a leather loop for a handle. Underneath some packing peanuts is a simple leather dog collar.

I know plenty of people who go in for elaborate, custom-made collars. But I've always liked the utilitarianism of repurposing an actual dog collar—as much as I adore giving the right girl some bling, I also want a girl who will humble herself to wear a dog collar for me if that's what I want.

I clip the collar to the end of the lead and hang the leash by the handle on the hook beside the coatrack.

259

* * *

Kelly comes back with a profusion of bags full of a fresh but simple wardrobe for herself. She also comes back with a few things I hadn't asked for, including some fresh flowers and a bottle of decent Bordeaux.

Diana taught me to encourage this kind of improvisation in a slave, mainly by being so brilliant at anticipating needs I didn't even know I had. As I watch Kelly flit around the apartment I feel a slicing pang of loss; for a minute, I miss Diana so much tears sting my eyes. I face away from Kelly as she works and take a deep breath. Diana doesn't want my tears, and Kelly doesn't need them.

I sit down in my favorite chair and flip on the TV for the pregame. It's the third night of a three-game series with the Bruins, and thus far we've watched the whole thing together, me in my big leather armchair, her sitting beside me, naked on a cushion on the floor.

She trots up behind me and hands me a glass of the Bordeaux and seats herself on the little cushion by my feet.

She's wearing a Habs hockey jersey and nothing else.

This is so much better than nakedness for me. I feel instantly, dizzyingly aroused. The tips of the laces at the throat dangle against her breasts, and I can see through the jersey that her nipples are hard.

I sip the Bordeaux through the first period, and the Habs really start to get their game on in the second.

"Do you know what a power play is?" I ask, as I slip my hand down into the open neck of her jersey.

"No," she gasps, as I take one of her nipples between my thumb and index fingers and squeeze.

"It's when one team has a player in the penalty box. The other team has a numerical advantage. A team can have as many as two players in the box," I say, slipping my other hand into her jersey and finding her other nipple to give it a vicious squeeze. "With two players in the penalty box they can't possibly fight back," I say, squeezing harder. Kelly's hips thrust forward, and her head is thrown back on my lap now, her lips parted. I ease off on the sensation, and her eyes open, still unfocused.

"My glass is empty," I say. Her lips are so close. I still haven't kissed her yet.

* * *

The next day, after breakfast, the sun is slanting in through the windows and the temperature is in the single digits, Fahrenheit, the way it is in Montreal when the sun is out. It has to warm up to snow.

She's wearing nothing but her apron, bending over the woodstove and retrieving the teakettle to put more hot water in the French press for my coffee.

Some Marketplace owners frown on having property sit at a superior's table to eat, but it's my house, and I like the company. Once Kelly finishes stirring milk and sugar into my coffee, she sits across the table from me, the morning sunlight falling on her hair. I put the Op/Ed page down and say, "I have a gift for you."

"Oh?" she says. "A gift?"

"Yes. A gift of protocol."

Kelly raises an elegant eyebrow.

"I only give out protocol to those who are ready. And only one new protocol at a time," I say.

"Yes... Sir?" she says, tilting her head quizzically.

"Boss. Follow me."

"Yes, Boss," Kelly replied, walking behind me to the entryway to the apartment.

I stand before her and tug at the strings of the simple white canvas apron she wears. Once untied, I lift it over her head and hang it on one of the hooks on the coatrack by the door. As I do that, I notice she's spotted the collar and leash, and I can see her eyes get wide with that *but she doesn't own a dog... ohhhhhh* expression.

"Kneel," I say. I'm sure she's been trained to do it in one fluid motion, but her injuries still have her off balance, and she uses her fingertips against the wall to steady herself, ending kneeling facing the door.

"No, don't face the door. I want your back to this wall, the one with the mirror and the coatrack on it." Kelly turns left, her back now to the wall.

"If I want you to greet me in the way I'm about to demonstrate, I'll text you before I come home," I say. "As soon as I text you, I want you to come to this spot, kneel down, and put the collar around your neck. The lead stays on the hook, and you are never to touch the handle of the leash. I'm the only one who takes it off the hook, do you understand?"

"Yes, Boss," Kelly says, almost whispering.

"I want you to come over here and assume the position as soon as I text and stay there for as long as it takes for me to come through the door. That might be 30 seconds or it might be 20 minutes. That's not up to you, and if I choose not to tell you how long it will be, that's my prerogative."

I reach out and take the collar in my hands, unbuckling it while I speak. "I want more than just you kneeling by the door when I arrive—I want you kneeling by the door, having spent whatever time I've allowed you thinking about your role. About your position relative to me. About the fact that when you're kneeling naked by my door, connected by a leash to a hook on the wall that isn't yours to touch or take off, that you are exactly where you're supposed to be."

I brush the hair away, bending down to secure the collar around her neck.

"This is where you belong," I say. I look down on her. Her chest rises and falls rapidly, and her face is flushed.

"You belong on your knees," I say. "You're made to serve—that's not what you do, it's who you are. You are my equal in worth but not in authority. You are not my equal, and you do not want to be my equal."

I step back, leaning against the opposite wall of the narrow entryway.

"You're not eyeballing me, and that's good," I say. "It shows me that you understand your place. You know I don't mind eye contact at other times, and I even want you to eat at table with me. But when you greet me," I say, stepping closer to her, "I want you chin up," I say, putting a fingertip under her chin until she's facing straight ahead, "eyes down. Shoulders back," I say, pushing lightly on her shoulders with my fingertips. "Hands loosely clasped behind your back."

"Spread your knees a bit. I should be able to put my boot here," I say, placing my heavy, glossy leather boot between her naked knees.

"When I come in the door, you don't speak until I speak to you, and you don't move from this spot until I move you. You never, ever take the leash off the hook, or touch the handle of the leash—that's for me, and for me only. Do you understand?"

"Yes, Boss," Kelly says.

"I expect you to make a common-sense exception to this rule when it's needed. If the house is on fire or there's a burglar coming through the door, you take it off the hook and run like hell, understand? It's not locked on here. That's because I don't use locks. I expect a slave to not need a lock. I expect you to be well trained enough to stay where I put you for as long as I want you there and sensible enough to know when an emergency merits that you stand up and do what you need to do."

"Emergencies do not include bathroom visits, annoying noises, or being chilly enough to want to change the setting on the thermostat. If it gets dark? Then it gets dark; you don't leave this spot to flip any light switches. If someone else rings the bell while you're kneeling here, you don't answer it, nobody's home. If someone's ringing the bell, it's not me. I live here and I'll let myself in."

"Being on this spot, kneeling and naked, shows me you understand your role, above all, is to be available to me, whenever, wherever, and however I want you to be," I say. "Do you understand?"

"Yes, Boss," Kelly replies.

"Any questions?"

"No, Boss."

"Good," I say. I pick up the handle of the lead and loop it around my wrist and start walking toward the living room area of the loft. Kelly, not expecting that, scrambles to her feet behind me and follows me closely. She has to; the lead is only six feet long.

"Down," I say, as we approach my favorite leather armchair. She folds herself smoothly onto the meditation cushion that's always there, at the foot of the chair and a little to my left. Her eyes get wide when she sees I've installed a hook just under the broad wooden arm of the chair. I hang the handle end of the leash on the hook.

"Come closer," I say. She leans toward me, and I unsnap the leash from her collar. A brief flicker of disappointment crosses her face. I pat her cheek. "There, there, you'll be back on the leash soon enough, my girl. Now go get me a Coke, the game's going to be on in a minute."

She returns with a can of Coke and a rocks glass with ice on a tray. I take the glass off the tray, and she sets it down on the side table. "Down," I say, indicating the cushion. "Face me," I say. She turns toward me and I clip the lead back on. I lean back in my chair, take a sip of the soda, and flip the game on.

"Perfect." I sigh.

I can see Kelly beaming out of the corner of my eye, but I pretend not to notice.

* * *

I'm not even Canadian, but I root for one Canadian team, The Montreal Canadiens, and the only team I really and truly hate is another Canadian team, The Leafs. Or, in my household, The Fucking Leafs. I think it's in the water in Quebec: you turn on the tap, hate for the Fucking Leafs pours out in a torrent along with potable water.

There are few things more enjoyable than watching your team play a team you really hate. And I'm not Canadian, so I swear a lot more.

Kelly gets to hear all of my most creative swearing, things like: "You sewer-grate-living cunt! That's illegal checking, you ice-skating assbunny!"

Kelly's shoulders shake in a desperate effort not to laugh.

"Why, Kelly—you're not laughing at me, are you?" I ask.

"No, Boss," Kelly says.

"Well, that's good. Because that could end up being a very serious infraction. The kind of infraction that ends up being very painful on your ass."

The broadcast cuts to commercial. "That reminds me," I say. "I've taught you the *kneel* position the way I like it, but there are two more."

I stand up in front of her. "Kneel up," I say. She kneels, her body upright from the knees. "No, hands at your sides for this one. And this is an attention position—I want you to look at me when I ask for it." Kelly looks me in the eye. "Good. Typically when I ask for this I'm going to give you a command. But for now, kneel down."

"There's one more position, but you can't perform it on your own until that soft cast is off your wrist," I say. I circle around behind her, and she stays facing forward obediently. I cup my hand behind her neck. "It's called *kneel back*. Normally, you would put your hands behind you on the floor to support your body," I say. "Spread your knees a bit, that's right. Now, lift your hips. You'll have to lean back onto my hand."

Kelly's body is arched back, her hips thrust out and her knees spread, kept from falling only by my hand cradling the back of her neck.

"This position exists to give me access to your body," I say. I slide my other hand down her body, stroking her torso. I slap one of her thighs. "Wider," I say. "In particular, access here," I say, slapping her pussy lightly with my hand. I can feel her body jerk slightly, and she begins to tremble with the effort of remaining open to me.

"Understand?" I say. I trail the fingertips of my free hand along her labia, parting them.

"Yes, Boss!" she gasps.

"Good," I say. "You're wet. Did kneeling by the door turn you on?"

She hesitates slightly, and I slap her lightly on the cheek. "I own what's between your ears too, Kelly, not just what's between your legs. If you think you have the privacy of your thoughts, you're wrong."

"Yes, Boss." Kelly breathes. "I was aroused by kneeling by the door for you. And by the... the leash."

I push my fingers into her cunt, and she gasps.

"So you like being at the end of a leash, hm? Trailing along behind me like my personal slut?"

"Yes, Boss!" Kelly says. I don't think she can hold the position much longer, even with my hand supporting her behind her neck. I withdraw the fingers of my other hand from her pussy. "Kneel down," I say, and she collapses onto the cushion, the shiny links of the leash trailing between her breasts and looping back up to the hook on my chair. She looks like she's just finished the first big drop on a roller coaster. I return to the chair and sit in it. I put my hand on her head.

"Breathe, Kelly. Take a deep breath and let it out. Good girl."

The Habs rout The Fucking Leafs. It is a very good day.

Once the game is over, I lead Kelly to the bedroom on the leash. She shoots a glance at the abandoned tray and glass. "Do it tomorrow morning," I say.

She can't hide a smile when she sees there's another hook installed on the baseboard beside her pallet. I hook the handle of the lead onto it as she lies down on the narrow futon beside my bed. I throw a blanket over her and lean down.

"I don't have to tell you not to jerk off, correct?" She shakes her head no, vigorously. "Good. What's between your legs doesn't belong to you. No touching," I say.

I undress, throwing my clothes in the wicker laundry basket. I've always done this with the lights off, or come to the bed in a robe or pajamas. Today I don't bother with the modesty and strip off only a foot from her slave pallet. I slip into bed and snap off the lights. Let her get a good look at me, I think. I don't hit the gym for nothing.

"Good night, Kelly."

"Good night. Boss."

* * *

Lying there in the dark, I can hear Kelly's breathing, and I can tell from it she's not asleep. It's not like I can sleep, either; the throbbing from down below is insistent.

I'd really be torturing her if I jerked off only a few feet from her when I know she can't, I think.

But I like inflicting that kind of torture.

I slide my hand down my body and between my thighs. I own plenty of sex toys, but I never use them on my own, only for partnered sex. If it's just me, I always just use my hand.

I slip my hand through my curls—I haven't had any need to trim in awhile; it's been ages since anyone saw me naked. I'm wet and ready, and I press my fingertips rhythmically against my clit the same way I've been doing it since I was a wee kinky lassie.

My eyes have adjusted to the dark now; I can see Kelly perfectly well in the dim room, and I'm sure she can see me. I make no effort to hide what I'm doing, and she makes no effort to hide that she's watching.

I'm very turned on, and the fact she's watching and can't do a thing about it turns me on even more. It's been so long it takes only a few moments for me to get close to climax; I feel it coming closer; my hips start to thrust involuntarily against my pressing fingers, my back arches, and I come with a groan.

266

Christ, that was good. I'm sweating and panting, sprawled on my back. I turn over on my belly, letting my hand trail over the side of the bed. I reach out and brush my wet fingertips across Kelly's lips. She whimpers as she sucks my juices off my fingers.

When she's done, I pull my hand back, and without a word, snuggle down under the covers and fall into a deep, dreamless sleep.

* * *

In the morning, I get the call I've been dreading from Chris Parker about the status of Kelly's contract. I've sent Kelly off to the *depannéur* to pick up my morning coffee and run some other errands and told her not to come back until I call for her. I don't want her to hear this conversation.

"Technically, MacFarlane still owns Kelly, and his other property. I don't think he's going to come back to claim them, considering the fact that if he comes out of hiding he'll almost instantly be thrown in jail to await trial for murder," Chris says.

"But she never signed a new contract."

"Nor was she released."

"I don't get it—if MacFarlane is in hiding, and can't or won't reclaim his property, why is Negel getting involved?"

"Well, Negel recruited MacFarlane to the Marketplace, and as the buyers' rep for an owner who bought 16 slaves over only two years, he made a lot of money in fees from MacFarlane. As the buyers' representative, he also has an option to place a temporary hold on a slave whose owner is, well, indisposed."

"Whatever happens, MacFarlane isn't going to be buying any more slaves, so why does Negel care about keeping MacFarlane's property from going back to the block? It's not like he has to stay on the guy's good side."

"No, but if he represents an owner, and he takes possession of a slave for that owner temporarily, he's guaranteed a bounty even if the slave is never reclaimed."

"Jesus fucking Christ," I say, putting my forehead in my hand. "How much is it?"

"It can be a lot, depending on how much the property is insured for," says Chris. "And Negel's training house and brokering operations—well, a lot of people speculate that they might have turned into a Ponzi scheme. He's in trouble with money, and he needs more of it to keep everything going."

"Great. Just great," I say.

"The thing is, if you can hang on to her for the full year of the foster term, you can exercise your option to buy Kelly's contract."

"But only if I hang on to her."

"Correct."

"Got it. Thanks, Chris. Let me know if you hear anything from Negel. Or about Negel, for that matter."

"Will do."

I hang up and immediately dial Kelly.

There's no answer.

It takes about three beats for me to hit full panic. *Shit!*

I throw my coat on and jam my feet in my boots. I run down the stairs, half falling down the last flight, and bust through the door, which I don't even bother closing behind me. I run across the street to the *depannéur*.

"Did the young woman with the curly hair come in this morning?" I demand of the old guy behind the counter.

"Mademoiselle Kelly?" he asks. "*Non.*"

She's been gone for 20 minutes. It doesn't take 20 minutes to cross the street.

I flip open my phone. I installed a locator app on it, just the way I had on Diana's phone. Looks like Kelly's still got her phone. The dot is moving, rapidly, toward the airport.

I streak back across the street at full speed and get in my car, a tiny Fiat, and blast it right over the curb into the street, nearly sideswiping a recycling bin. I go down narrow, cobblestoned St. Sulpice the wrong way and swing onto the highway.

I *have no fucking guns!* I think. *Fucking Canada!* I didn't bother to try to bring any up or buy one on the black market once I was here. *Shit!*

My phone, mounted on the dashboard, shows that whomever has Kelly got off two exits before the airport. The dot's not moving now.

I get off the highway and roll into a district of distribution centers and warehouses sandwiched between the airport and Montreal's major rail yard. Following the line on the map, I pull past a warehouse where the garage door is still open. I see two men in long coats standing in the doorway, their breath making steam in the frigid air. I pull around the block and into a narrow alleyway beside the building and cut my engine. I open the door to my car and shut it quietly, creeping along the side of the building, wishing fervently that I had a gun.

"We have to wait until she wakes up to get her through security at the airport. If we tried to take an unconscious person through security, we'd never make it."

"How long will it take? We don't have that much time before the flight."

"Listen, if we have to buy another ticket, we buy another ticket. The fee is big enough—the cost of the ticket is nothing compared to that."

I take the chance of peeking around the corner. Felipe! One of them is Felipe, the Marketplace doctor's assistant!

Fuck, why don't I have a gun? Felipe is huge—there's no way I can take him, let alone him and the other guy.

I get an idea. I run back to my car and get inside, locking the doors.

Making police siren noises? There's an app for that. I swear silently at my phone, urging it to download the app faster. It installs, and I play it—loud, but not loud enough. I take out a cable and plug it into the sound system of my car, roll down all the windows, and turn the volume up to 11.

I blast the siren sound at top volume. I hear panic inside the warehouse, and a black Town Car pulls out, trunk still open and flapping. But Kelly's dot never moves. Thank goodness, they've left her behind.

I get out of my car and run toward the open garage bay of the warehouse—and straight into Felipe.

It's like running into a brick wall. Felipe towers over me—he's got at least a foot on me and probably close to 100 pounds, too. He cuffs me across the face with his massive hand, and I fly six feet sideways, my head hitting a 55 gallon drum. I see stars, but I don't lose consciousness. I throw up my hand, pulling myself up on the edge of the barrel and I feel something on top of it.

Whatever it is, as Felipe comes toward me, I grab the handle and swing it at him as hard as I can.

It's a pipe wrench, and I think I just broke at least three of Felipe's ribs. I scramble to my feet while Felipe rolls back and forth in agony on the concrete floor, gasping for breath. I run back into the warehouse, still holding the pipe wrench. I kick open a flimsy office door, and Kelly is inside, on a cracked vinyl couch.

I'm not a big person. Kelly's a little taller and bigger than I am. But in the Army I trained to carry guys almost twice my size. I throw her over my shoulders in a fireman's carry and run for it. Felipe's on his hands and knees as I run by him, a puddle of barf between his hands. I have no time for him and not a single fuck to give about his predicament. I round the corner back to my car, piling Kelly into the front seat. I jump into the drivers' seat, throwing the pipe wrench in the back, and I floor it, leaving a plume of dirt and gravel behind me.

Once I get a few blocks away, I pull over. I put my head on the steering wheel. Snot is streaming from my nose and there's a cut on my head and blood trickling down the back of my neck. I lean Kelly back in the seat and buckle her seatbelt. I take her pulse—she's alive, and it's steady. I lift an eyelid and her pupils react, but she's still out cold from whatever they gave her. I imagine Felipe had access to plenty of things from the doctor's office, and I see a small puncture mark with a circular bruise on her neck.

They must have gotten her coming out of the apartment, I think.

I dial 911 and make a report of a man in distress at a warehouse on Pike Avenue. As I drive away, I hear sirens for real this time.

* * *

It feels ten times harder to carry Kelly up the stairs than it did to run her out of the warehouse. Now that the adrenaline has worn off, I'm shaky and exhausted.

I lay Kelly on my own bed, collapsing on a stool beside it. I put my head in my hands and wipe the sweat out of my eyes.

When I look up, Kelly's eyes are open, half-lidded. They widen when she sees my face.

"What happened to you?" Kelly tries to sit up and lists sideways, nearly rolling off the bed.

I stand up and put my hand on her chest, pushing her back down.

"Listen, you lie down. No getting up," I say.

270

I feel like getting up wasn't such a hot idea for me, either, so I do a controlled fall that lands my butt back on the stool I'd been sitting on.

"I'm fine," I say. "I'll be all right."

"Let me call the doctor," she says, struggling to sit up again.

"No," I say, using That Voice. "You need to learn that I'm still in charge, even when things are bad, do you understand? If I'm out cold you can swing into action, but if I can still walk and talk, I'm in charge. You got it?"

Kelly nods. "Yes," she says, then adding, "Boss."

"But you do need a doctor," she says meekly.

"You're right, I do, but we can't call Doctor Wallace. Do you know what happened to you?"

"No. I remember leaving the house, then... nothing."

"You were drugged and kidnapped by Felipe, the doctor's assistant, and an accomplice of his. Someone I don't recognize. You still had your phone on you, and I installed tracking software on it before I gave it to you. I followed you and got into a fight with Felipe."

"You fought... Felipe?"

"Don't look so surprised. You should see how Felipe looks," I say. "We're safe here, as long as we stay inside. Nobody can get into the apartment unless we let them in. I'm going to call Chris for help, though. It's time to call in reinforcements."

I'm bluffing about our security in the apartment, but I really don't know by how much. I wasn't looking for a safe house when I rented this place. As I dial Chris, I wonder if I should rent a hotel room and move us there until things cool down.

Chris answers the phone. "You're not gonna believe this shit. Are you sitting down?"

"No, but I can take it," Chris says.

"You know Doctor Wallace, the Marketplace-friendly doctor up here?"

"Yeah, of course."

"Well, I just hit her assistant, this human refrigerator named Felipe, with a pipe wrench."

"What?"

"I had good reason—he snatched Kelly off the street in front of my apartment. He drugged her, probably using stuff he stole from the doctor, and drove her to a warehouse near the airport."

"Holy fucking shit."

"Yeah. I know. Listen, I need help. Who can you get over here? We need a doctor, and obviously we can't call Wallace. And I need muscle."

"What condition is Kelly in? Do you need transportation to the hospital?" Chris asks.

"No, I've checked her out, and she's fine—other than feeling a little nauseous from the drug they gave her, she's all right. But I need stitches. Felipe tossed me headfirst into a 55 gallon drum, and I've got a big cut on my head, and maybe one other cut that needs stitches. I can't do them myself because I can't see the cut on the back of my head."

"You know you just said something out loud about giving yourself stitches, right?"

"Once a field medic, always a field medic. Hell, I used to practice on myself."

"Jesus, Bette, don't say that. You know how I feel about that shit."

"No needle play for you, huh, big guy? Even with all those tattoos?"

"I kept my eyes closed the whole time."

I laugh, which hurts. "Can you call me back in a few minutes and let me know what you've got?"

"Sure. Hang in there, I'm on it."

* * *

I return to the bedroom. I can tell I'm a mess by the worried look on Kelly's face.

"Listen, Chris is rounding up a doctor and some folks to do security for us. I'm going to clean up a little. You are not to get out of this bed until a doctor checks you out, understand? If you need to go to the bathroom, ask me, and I'll help you."

The water from the shower stings the cut on my scalp, and the drumming water makes my head throb in time. I feel like I might barf, but there's nothing I hate more than throwing up—I'll do practically anything to avoid it. I definitely have a concussion, but that's nothing I haven't experienced before.

I get out of the shower and gingerly towel myself off, inventorying my bruises and scrapes. As I slip on a clean robe and wrap a towel around my neck, I look at myself in the mirror. Not too bad.

I take a deep breath. Just how much was Kelly insured for—and how far were people willing to go for the money?

* * *

Fifteen minutes later my phone rings. "You've got a doc and two for security on the way. I'm sending you pictures so you can verify that they're the right people, okay?"

"Thanks, Chris. This is great. I really need the help, and I appreciate it."

"Anytime."

"Listen, I have one question: isn't all this a little over the top? I mean, kidnapping? How much is Kelly insured for, anyway?"

"Good question. Hang on and I can find out."

I hear the clicking of a keyboard.

"Holy shit," Chris says.

"What?"

"She's insured for three point two million dollars. And Negel sold MacFarlane the policy."

* * *

The news of Negel selling insurance policies on the property of owners he'd represented spread through the network like wildfire. Not only would Negel get commissions on every dollar of premiums that owners paid, if owners got in trouble, Negel would actually benefit: the insurance company would pay him to *hold* property for owners in trouble.

It got even worse than that. A forensic accountant who was the personal property of a hedge fund manager looked over Negel's dealings and found Negel was *securitizing* the insurance bonds and selling them to other owners. Owners who invested in what came to be known as slave bonds would get paid when and if the insurance policies paid off—which meant that owners who bought slave bonds were essentially investing in, and betting on, the failure of other owners and the forfeit of their human property.

It's the Marketplace's very own Enron, AIG, and Goldman Sachs 360-degree surround-sound corruption clusterfuck rolled into one.

But the hearing of the disciplinary board won't be for 21 days. Never let it be said that people called before the board of the Marketplace don't have recourse to due process.

I figure Negel—or anybody else after the money—won't try anything as stupid as making a move on Kelly again, but I'm not taking any chances. Two bodyguards, lent out by their Marketplace owners, are with us night and day, taking shifts; one sleeping in the guest room while the other is awake, alert, and out front looking menacing as hell.

Kelly bounces back sooner than I do, at least physically. The next day, she seemed fine, but I feel worse than the day before, like a cross between the world's worst hangover and going three rounds in a cage match.

Kelly brings me broth in bed, the paper, saltine crackers, and tea. I sleep on and off throughout the day, glad to know we are well protected.

* * *

About a week later, I get a call from Chris.

"There are some legal papers you probably want to see—contracts and stuff, for Kelly and for other slaves. I figured they'd be useful for review before the disciplinary hearing," Chris says. "They're at a lawyer's office up there near you. Do you want me to have them messengered over?"

"What's the address?"

Chris gives me an address on Rue St. Sulpice.

"Nah, that's only a few blocks from here. I'll pick them up myself, I could use the fresh air."

"Be careful."

"They're not after me," I say. "But I'll be careful anyway."

I hang up the phone and look across the loft into the kitchen where Kelly is making my breakfast. She is in a robe and not an apron—come to think of it, she hasn't been naked outside the bedroom since the bodyguards had moved in—but that didn't seem to matter to my libido. As I watch her walk across the kitchen, I feel that familiar stirring.

I sip my coffee and let my mind drift. I imagine bending her over the counter and taking her from behind with my strap-on, fucking her roughly with my hand fisted in her hair, pressing her cheek against the counter as she moans...

"Excuse me?" Kelly says, holding a cloth napkin in her hand. I lean back in the chair, allowing her to spread it across my lap.

"This looks great, Kelly, thank you."

Kelly sits down at the table across from me as I eat; Kelly eats only after I finish, unless I feed her from my own plate.

"I'll be out doing an errand later today—just picking up some papers. Just so you know, before I return I'll be texting you and I expect you to greet me by the door."

"But... " Kelly points in the direction of the guest room, "What about... "

"They're Marketplace, Kelly. Do you think they haven't seen a naked slave before?"

Kelly gulps audibly. I stretch my hand across the table and squeeze hers. "We can't stop living our lives because of this. We have to go on. We can't let Negel win."

Kelly nods, her eyes brimming.

"More coffee, please." I don't need more coffee, really, but I want to give Kelly a moment to calm down. There is something I want to ask her, a difficult question.

When she returns to the table and sits down, I say: "Kelly, the other slaves at MacFarlane's ran away. Why didn't you run?"

Kelly looks uncomfortable and slides back in her chair. "I couldn't," she says. "I was too hurt to run. I didn't really even understand what was happening when the police came in—I didn't know about what John had done."

"I don't understand. It wasn't because you were trying to escape? He beat you before the shooting?"

"Yes."

"Did he beat anyone else?"

"No. That's why they got away—they were able to get away between the time Jack left and the police showed up."

275

"Why did he beat you and not the others?"

Kelly looks down at her lap. "I... he beat me because I had sex."

"But... the reports about MacFarlane's house was that he had half a dozen or more pleasure slaves and he encouraged them to have sex with each other."

"That's true—but I wasn't a pleasure slave. I was his personal secretary. He caught me having sex with one of the others."

"He didn't want you having sex with a man?"

"I wasn't having sex with a man. I was having sex with one of the pleasure slaves. A woman."

She gives a hiccupping gasp. "He didn't... he didn't want anyone to touch what was his, he said. He beat me to make an example of me. And then. The others. The men, he had them... I'm property, so I'm not sure I can say they raped me... "

I get up and come around the table. I hand her my napkin to wipe her eyes and put my hand on her shoulder.

"Do you understand that none of that is ever going to happen as long as you're with me?"

Kelly nods, unable to speak for a moment.

"As long as I'm with you," she says.

* * *

It's a crisp, clear, cold day in Montreal, and they are running out of places to put the snow. It's piled in the Place des Armes and in the square in front of the Cathedral. I round one of the giant piles to get to the door of Rouen & Marsan. I pick up the papers and ask if there's someplace I can sit to review them. A secretary leads me to a conference room, and I open up the blue-backed packets of paper.

As I read them, I feel a sinking sensation. I've been throwing around words like *belong* and *ownership* when I shouldn't have. Kelly is not my property—even though I have been acting like she is, and she has been very much playing along. I do not own her, and I can still lose her. If I do, my playacting at ownership will be, in retrospect, enormously cruel.

I ask a few questions of one of the lawyers about the contract. My mouth is dry, and my heart is heavy.

I go outside and stand on the sidewalk in the sunshine. I have my phone in my hand, ready to text Kelly to have her greet me at the door, just as if she is mine to keep.

I know I shouldn't do it, but I do it anyway. Even if I only get to experience Kelly this way once—even if she is taken from me—I want to know.

I want to know what it feels like to own her.

HOME IN :15, I text.

* * *

I greet Pierre at the entrance to the building and take the stairs up to the apartment. I put the key in the lock and take a deep breath to compose myself.

I open the door and shed my coat and scarf as if she isn't there at all.

I step forward, putting one of my boots, cold and wet with melting snow, right between her thighs, but not quite touching them. I lean over her to hang my coat, her face only inches from the zipper on my pants.

I stand there, pick up the mail off the side table, flip through it, rifle through a magazine.

She's being so good. Even when one of those infernal blow-in subscription postcards falls out of the magazine and drifted to the floor, she doesn't make a move, keeps her eyes lowered, chin up, shoulders back.

Just as a challenge, I brush the fly of my slacks against her lips, but she holds her composure. I'm turned on as all hell, but my composure isn't at issue.

I step back, tossing the mail on the table, and take the leash off the hook and walk into the apartment.

The days are short in December in Montreal, and though it's only 5:30, it's already full dark. A few lamps are lit, but the interior of the loft is still dim.

I sit in my leather armchair and hang the leather loop of the leash's handle on the hook. Kelly folds herself smoothly onto the small meditation cushion beside my chair, still being silent until spoken to.

"Kneel up, please," I say. Kelly kneels with her body straight, and looks right at me. "How are you, Kelly?" I ask. Slowly. Drawing it out.

"Wonderful, Boss. Thank you."

"It's my pleasure, my dear. Now, go fetch me a drink, I want to watch the Habs pregame." I unsnap the lead from her collar to let her go to the sideboard. "I'm going to go upstairs to change. When you're done fixing my drink, come back to the cushion and snap the leash back on to your collar and kneel."

"Yes, Boss."

* * *

I don't *really* need to change.

There is something else I have in mind. Taking my keyring from my pocket, I find the small key to the wardrobe in the corner of my bedroom. I open it, and within were all the things I hadn't even looked at since Diana's death.

Cuffs. Neatly coiled rope. Floggers and paddles and canes.

And in the back, on a peg, my harness, and beside it, a few silicone cocks of varying sizes.

I choose my favorite, a black one, kind of sleek with a nice curve and a big head.

I step into the harness and adjust it without looking; even after all this time, the buttery black leather straps are utterly familiar.

I look at myself in the mirror and gave my cock a quick stroke to be sure it's seated securely in the harness. Then I pull up my underwear and pants, tucking the cock in sideways before I zip up. Looking in the mirror now, I have a large, noticeable, and notably cock-shaped bulge in my pants. "Check it out, Daddy's got a hard-on," I say, chuckling to myself.

I go back down into the dim living room, where Kelly is sitting on a cushion beside my chair. Whoever trained Pierre and Jacques have trained them to be very discreet—unless they are working out front, I barely know they're here. When they aren't working, they keep to themselves on the second floor, where they have a bedroom with an attached bath.

I sit in my chair and sip my drink. "This is very good," I say.

I relax and watch the game, taking pleasure in *mansitting*— you know, when some dude's on the subway and sits thoughtlessly with his knees so far apart he's effectively taking up the seats on either side of him? Of course, in my own home, I'm not impeding anyone's access to a place to sit. But I enjoy the masculine-feeling sensation of allowing myself to take up space, not crossing my legs or folding into myself to be smaller like so many women do.

I'm not trans—unlike my trans friends who always felt like there was something not right, I've always felt at home in my body. But that doesn't stop me from being really turned on by wearing my cock, by seeing that big bulge between my legs.

I rattle the cubes in my empty glass. "Just seltzer and lime this time, sweetheart," I say.

As she returns, I spread my knees and put my hand on my bulge, slowly stroking and squeezing it. As Kelly puts my glass on the wide wooden arm of the chair, she notices it—the big, hard cock-shaped outline in my pants. She breathes in sharply. Still bent at the waist, she lifts her eyes to meet mine.

"Down," I say, pointing at the floor between my knees. She kneels obediently between my boots.

"Suck my cock," I say.

Kelly leans forward, her naked skin brushing the denim of my jeans. She unbuckles my belt, unsnaps, unzips.

I can barely breathe as she slips her hand into my pants, brushing my pubic curls with her fingertips as she grasps my cock and pulls it out. I slide down in the chair, pushing my hips forward to the edge, and let my head fall back on the soft leather of the chair.

Just because I don't have sensation in my cock doesn't mean I don't have plenty of sensation between my ears. God, I love sinking my cock into her mouth.

I look down at her, and I can't stifle a moan at seeing her wrap her lips around my shaft.

I've had some submissives who mail it in when it comes to sucking dyke cock—they figure, "She can't feel it, so why do I have to do a good job?" But Kelly seems as turned on by this as I am, sliding her mouth down over my dick and back up, licking and sucking on the head in a way that drives me insane.

"Get up here," I growl. Kelly climbs into my lap, straddling my thighs. I reach down and hold the base of my cock as she positions herself.

Oh God. She slides down on me, and I have a sudden, urgent need to be wearing less clothing, to have more of my skin touching hers. I reach between us and rip open my snap-front shirt and unhook my bra—I don't wear anything but front-hooks.

"Ah," I gasp as I come skin-to-skin with her, pressing her to me. There's no such thing as close enough now. I reach around and grab her luscious ass, rocking her cunt back and forth on my cock. She clings to me, her arms around my neck and her hands in my hair. I slide my hands up her back and lean her back into my arms, taking one erect nipple into my mouth, sucking, kissing, one and then the other, reveling in her until she cries out. The game flickers behind her, forgotten except where it traces her beautiful outline. I bite her shoulder, her neck, anything I can reach. I want her covered in marks showing that she's mine in the morning.

Fuck, I can't take this anymore. I lean her backward, managing to stay with her and not drop her on the floor. I scramble out of my jeans and boots and sink balls deep into her cunt.

I waited so long to kiss Kelly, and now I can't get enough of her mouth. I could kiss her for a year. I fuck her, pounding her. "Please," she groans into my mouth, "please, please, please."

"Too hard?" I gasp.

"Oh, God, no," Kelly says, her back arched, head thrown back. "Please don't stop. Please, fuck me, give me your cock."

I lift one of her legs over my shoulder and fuck her hard. With one hand, I reach up to a side table drawer. In it is a bottle of lube and a small bullet vibe.

I reach down and press it against her clit as I turn it on.

"OHHHHHH," she cries.

"Are you going to come all over my cock like the little slut you are?" I say.

Kelly doesn't answer; she's arched, mouth open, coming helplessly and so powerfully she tries to turn her body away from it, to flee from it; I pin her to the carpet beneath me as she holds her breath, taking only tiny gasps until a keening wail escapes from her.

She collapses on the floor like a rag doll. I roll her on top of me and hold her tightly in my arms, her head on my chest. I feel her heave a sob and hide her face against my shoulder.

"Ohhh," I say. "Oh, baby. It's okay. Let it out. Let it all out." I rock her back and forth on my chest until she's cried out. I reach to one side for the shirt I'd ripped off and thrown to floor earlier and use it to mop her face and my chest.

"You okay?" I ask.

Kelly nods against my chest. "Yes," she says. "Very okay."

* * *

One year later

In the end, the whole drama with Negel wound down without a big climax. The disciplinary hearing I dreaded, because it brought up a chance Kelly would be remanded to Negel, never happened. Negel settled, giving up nearly everything as part of a deal that guaranteed him one thing: continued access to the Marketplace.

I would have been happy to see Negel banished from The Marketplace permanently. But without a training house or the authority to represent buyers, Negel's influence—and his ability to harm—is far smaller than it was a year ago.

I have kept Kelly; in fact, I've done more than keep her. A year to the day her foster term began, I did more than take ownership of her.

Reader, I married her.

We still live in Montreal, and Kelly is expecting our first child in September.

About the Authors

Kimiko Alexandre has been in the lifestyle for over 20 years and served as a submissive during that period to the same man. Writing paranormal fiction is her first love, dominance and submission close on its heels. Aside from being a podcast hostess where she talks about writing and urban fantasy, she is a voice actress and has been in many commercial projects. She ran a stint as a female spoken word vocalist in European Hardstyle music and now narrates and produces audiobooks to help pay the bills. Her first book, *Guardians: Awakening,* is an urban fantasy. Having gotten a taste of writing BDSM erotica, she plans to include it among titles for future novellas and books.

Flynn Anthony resides and writes in the northern chill of Michigan, where even kinky folk leave their socks on to play. Her constant companion, Sneaky Anthony, prefers to reside snugly upon the author's lap, leaving little black cat hairs behind on both laptop keyboard and screen when most inconvenient for editing. Pickett Ridge: Mission Marketplace is her first publication from a series set in Tessera's World, in which Pickett Ridge has a story of its own.

LN Bey has lived in various cities and towns throughout the West and Midwest with spouse and pets in tow, pursuing various creative endeavors and playing interesting games. LN's erotic fiction has appeared in Cleis Press's *Best Bondage Erotica* 2015, edited by Rachel Kramer Bussel.

Erzabet Bishop is the author of *Sigil Fire, Written on Skin: A Sigil Fire short, Fetish Fair, Temptation Resorts* interactive erotic romances (upcoming), *Holiday Cruise, Gingerbread Dreams, Pomegranate* (upcoming), *Red Dress, Holidays in Hell, Sweet Seductions: The*

Erzabet Bishop Collection and multiple books in the Erotic Pagan Series. She is a contributing author to *Club Rook, Taboo II, Hungry for More, Potnia, Wicked Things, Unwrap These Presents, A Christmas to Remember, Forbidden Fruit, Sci Spanks, Spank or Treat, Sweat, When the Clock Strikes Thirteen, Bossy, Cougars, Can't Get Enough, Slave Girls, Gratis III, The Big Book of Submission, Gratis II, Anything She Wants, Coming Together: Girl on Girl, Coming Together: For the Holidays* and more. She was a dual finalist for the GCLS awards in 2014. She lives in Texas with her husband, furry children and can often be found lurking in local bookstores. Follow her reviews and posts on Twitter @erzabetbishop.

Caraway Carter has worn numerous hats. He's been a furniture salesman, a dresser, a costumer, an actor/waiter, a rabble-rouser, a poet and most recently a writer. He loves words and stringing them together, he loves sex and sexy men, and he writes relationship fiction that reminds you—it's never too late for love. And he has lived his tagline. He married his husband on Halloween, at the age of 49, and they are the loving parents of an adorable cat named Molly.

S. Daithi has been writing since they could write. They have been writing fanfiction before the Internet existed and still have the mimeograph ink under their fingernails to prove it. They are known in certain corners of fandom for some very kinky porn and in others as the most vanilla writer on the planet. Some of their proudest achievements still show up on lists of fanfics that should be read. This is their first professional sale under this name. If you care to read some of their more current fannish work, they can be found on AO3 under the name Cxellover.

Steve Dee lives in Devon in the UK with his family. He works as a psychotherapist in his day job and most of his other writing tends to be about spirituality and gnostic stuff. He likes surfing, drumming cats and very loud music.

Madeline Elayne is a born and bred Atlantic Canadian genderqueer, pansexual, polyamourous switch (or just "slut" for short.) She is also a raging nerd. It makes for a terrible combination, just ask her lovers.

Ever the contrarian, she actually discovered the Marketplace series initially by stumbling onto the now-defunct online text-based roleplaying game. Intrigued by the setting, she immediately ordered all the books. As research, of course. When she wound up inadvertently re-enacting one of the more famous scenes from book two while halfway through reading book one, she was hooked. Both on the game, and on the series. *The Marketplace* remains one of her most favorite smutty playgrounds of all time.

Scott Harris: I am not to others, who I am. Not a writer, an old "role player" in AOL for many years now, I work in a jail as a guard, lover of good story and characters online because I don't fit into the skin I was born with in real life but make do. This submission call was too much to pass up, actually diving in and writing into the very fabric of the Marketplace world! Simply an honor and dream come true, you've been my inspiration for years, I pick up the Marketplace series and read them at least two times a year since being introduced to them by a friend in 2000, in a strange way it keeps me sane in a life choice of no BDSM except in books.

Dani Hermit & Nevi Star: Dani & Nevi have been together as partners in love, life, and writing for 15 years. They spend every day in a nauseating haze of lovey-dovey goo-goo eyes and dark, twisted plotlines. When not writing together they are watching TV or anime, also together. It's really disgusting how much they like each other. Nevi Star is both author and artist for Hermit & Star Books. She has done all of the cover art and interior art for the Parliament of Twilight series, as well as many fanart pieces. An art school survivor, she has been slowly evolving her art style over the past 20 years. Always willing to try out a new medium, she has worked with paint, marker, pastel, and most recently, digital art tools. Dani Hermit has been writing stories as long as she can remember. She started out with really embarrassing X-Men fanfiction and went through an untold number of fandoms until, she found herself in a relationship with another writer. They enjoyed writing fanworks together, but the original worlds they built just couldn't be denied. They began with small, hesitant forays into original fiction, but then they met the characters of the Parliament of Twilight and all was lost!

Amelia Horo is a Japanese/Puerto Rican femme bootblack who has been in service since December 31, 2008. She is very active in the gay Leather community both as a bootblack and as an attorney who deals with LGBTQI issues.

Moxie Marcus is a writer living in the Midwest. She enjoys many pursuits often classified as nerdy. When she's not reading or writing, she can usually be found staring wistfully at motorcycles.

Wade McLeod: Raised in the shadows of NASA, M. Wade knows utopias of every flavor await our attention. She cavorts through the realms of Faery and hippie nation, sacred kink and domination. A sci-fi geek grrrl in corset and heels, she sprinkles short pieces of fact and fiction, opinion and fantasy, under various noms de plume. Some of that includes the world of "The Thorny Issue." A fan is collecting those pieces with the plan to post them all under one roof at mgwade.net.

Elizabeth Schechter is a stay-at-home mom who lives in Central Florida with her husband and son. Her most recent work includes the Passionate Plume winner and Pauline Reage Award finalist *House of Sable Locks,* and the *Tales from the Arena* duology. Elizabeth can be found online at http://easchechter.wordpress.com

Soulhuntre is a long time BDSM theorist, practitioner and trainer in addition to a full schedule as a serial entrepreneur. Long ago he was a co-founder of "The Estate," a unique American training trio that still informs much of his technique today. You can hear much more about BDSM on the powerinpractice.com podcast as well as keeping up with all things soulhuntre at soulhuntre.com .

Jamie Thorsen is a figure of mystery.

Elle Wickenden lives in Boston, where she enjoys being on the handle end of the riding crop.

About the Editor

Laura Antoniou is the author of *The Killer Wore Leather* (which won the Pauline Reage Novel Award and the Rainbow Award, and was a finalist for the Lambda Literary Award) and the creator of the groundbreaking, bestselling (over 400,000 books sold) "Marketplace" series of books about an underground BDSM society. Originally published under the name Sara Adamson, the first three Marketplace books became instant classics, "must reads" for anyone discovering bondage for the first time, and various volumes have been published in Germany, Japan, Korea, and Israel. She has also edited several anthologies of erotic fiction, including *Leatherwomen* and *Some Women*. Her short stories have appeared in *Best Lesbian Erotica, SM Classics, Once Upon a Time,* and many other anthologies. She can be found on Patreon at http://patreon.com/kvetch

If You Liked This Title, You Might Also Like:

The Marketplace
By Laura Antoniou

The Slave
Book Two in The Marketplace Series
By Laura Antoniou

The Trainer
Book Three in The Marketplace Series
By Laura Antoniou

The Academy
Book Four in The Marketplace Series
By Laura Antoniou

The Reunion
Book Five in The Marketplace Series
By Laura Antoniou

The Inheritor
Book Six in The Marketplace Series
By Laura Antoniou

No Safewords
A Marketplace Fan Anthology
Edited by D.L. King

The Circlet Treasury of Erotic Wonderland
Edited by J. Blackmore

The Circlet Treasury of Erotic Steampunk
Edited by J. Blackmore & Cecilia Tan

The Circlet Treasury of Lesbian Erotic Science Fiction and Fantasy
Edited By Cecilia Tan

The Siren and the Sword:
Book One of the Magic University Series
By Cecilia Tan

The Tower and the Tears:
Book Two of the Magic University Series
By Cecilia Tan

The Incubus and the Angel:
Book Three of the Magic University Series

Spellbinding: Tales from Magic University
Edited by Cecilia Tan

The Poet and The Prophecy
Book Four of the Magic University Series
By Cecilia Tan